THE FRENCH ADMIRAL

also by Dewey Lambdin
THE KING'S COAT

THE FRENCH ADMIRAL

by
Dewey Lambdin

DIF

DONALD I. FINE, INC.
New York

Library of Congress Cataloging-in-Publication Data

Lambdin, Dewey.
    The French admiral : a novel / by Dewey Lambdin.
        p.   cm.
    ISBN 1-55611-208-4
    1. Great Britain—History, Naval—18th century—Fiction.
    2. United States—History—Revolution, 1775-1783—Fiction.
I. Title.
PS3562.A435F74   1989
813'.54—dc20   89-46042
                            CIP

Manufactured in the United States of America

10 9 8 7 6 5 4 3 2 1

DESIGNED BY IRVING PERKINS ASSOCIATES

This one's for

DEREK ROOKE

Former Lieutenant, Royal Naval Volunteer Reserve
A "Wavy Navy" fighter pilot, who first 'got my feet wet'
in '76 aboard *Seafire* off Gulfport and Biloxi. See what
you started?

And for your good lady Louise, and Chris and Charlotte
Rooke of Rooke Sails, Memphis.

> But didn't we look grand
> touched mahoghany by the sun
> with sweat salt and sea salt grit
> in that millpond quiet harbor,
> everything bagged and furled
> and the motor grumbling the pier
> with white eyes and white teeth beaming
> in the last glimmer of a scarlet sky
> as we laughed to finish fifth in class?
>
> Didn't we share a conjurement
> a God-hell knockdown wonder
>
> And weren't we so alive?

Coelum non animum qui trans mare currunt.
Those who cross the seas change climate but
not their character.

—Horace-Epistle I.xi. 27

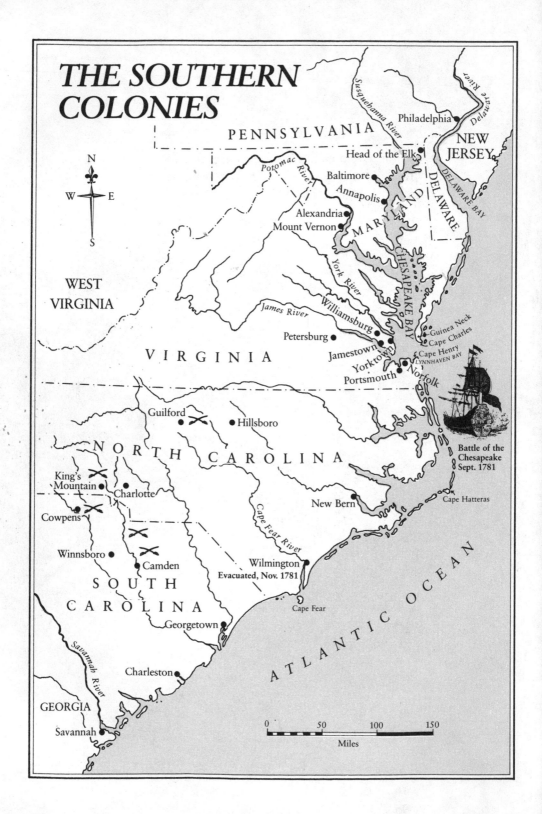

THE SOUTHERN COLONIES

PENNSYLVANIA

Susquehanna River

Philadelphia

Delaware River

NEW JERSEY

Head of the Elk

Potomac River

Baltimore

Annapolis

DELAWARE

MARYLAND

Alexandria

Mount Vernon

CHESAPEAKE BAY

N
W E
S

WEST VIRGINIA

York River

James River

Williamsburg

DELAWARE BAY

VIRGINIA

Petersburg

Jamestown

Yorktown

Guinea Neck

Cape Charles

Cape Henry

LYNNHAVEN BAY

Portsmouth

Norfolk

Guilford

Hillsboro

Battle of the Chesapeake Sept. 1781

NORTH CAROLINA

King's Mountain

Charlotte

Cowpens

New Bern

Cape Hatteras

Winnsboro

Cape Fear River

Camden

SOUTH CAROLINA

Wilmington
Evacuated, Nov. 1781

ATLANTIC OCEAN

Georgetown

Cape Fear

Savannah River

Charleston

GEORGIA

Savannah

0   50   100   150
Miles

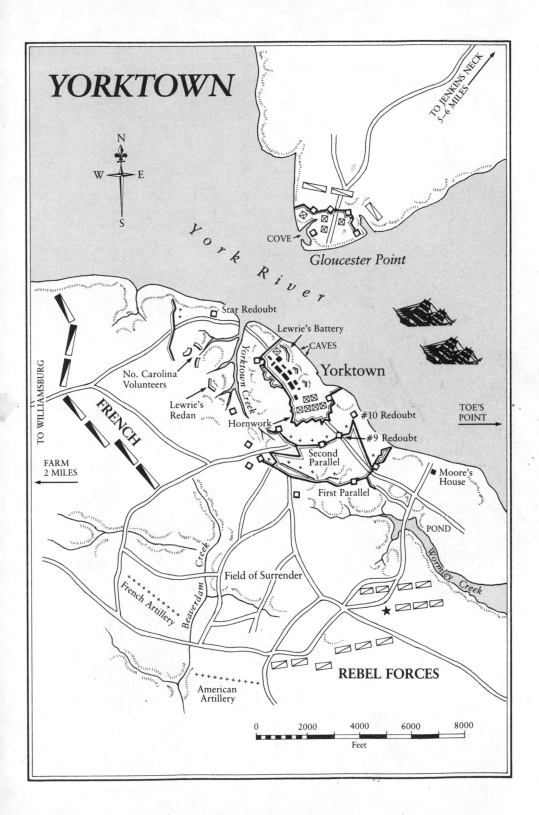

YORKTOWN

N / **W** / **E** / **S**

TO JENKIN'S NECK
5–6 MILES

York River

COVE

Gloucester Point

Star Redoubt

Lewrie's Battery

CAVES

Yorktown

No. Carolina
Volunteers

Yorktown Creek

Lewrie's
Redan

Hornwork

#10 Redoubt

#9 Redoubt

TOE'S
POINT

Second
Parallel

FRENCH

Moore's
House

TO WILLIAMSBURG

First Parallel

FARM
2 MILES

POND

Wormley Creek

Beaverdam Creek

Field of Surrender

French Artillery

REBEL FORCES

American
Artillery

0   2000   4000   6000   8000
Feet

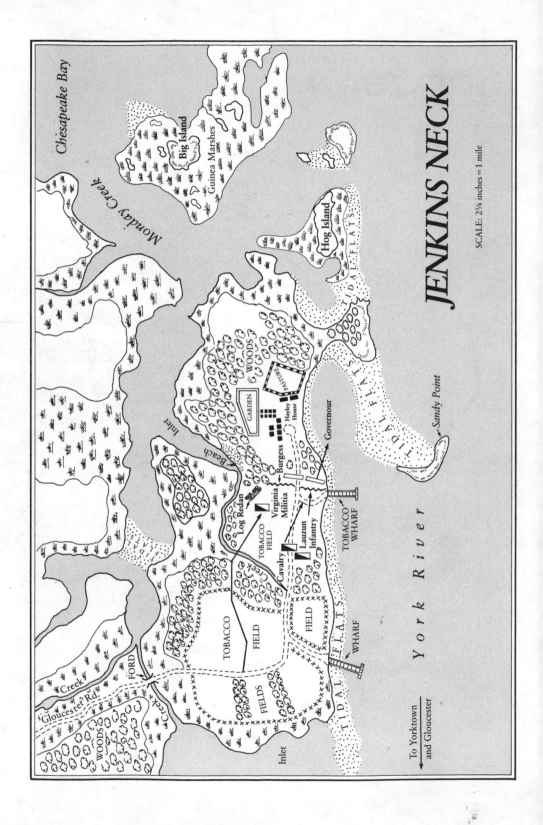

JENKINS NECK

SCALE: 2⅛ inches = 1 mile

Chesapeake Bay

Monday Creek

Big Island

Guinea Marshes

Hog Island

TIDAL FLATS

Sandy Point

G. WOODS

GARDEN

PASTURE

Hayley House

Governour

Burgess

Inlet

Beach

Virginia Militia

Lauzun Infantry

TOBACCO WHARF

Log Redan

TOBACCO FIELD

Cavalry

TIDAL FLATS

York River

WOODS

Creek

Creek

FORD

Gloucester Rd.

TOBACCO FIELD

FIELD

FIELD

FIELDS

TIDAL FLATS

WHARF

Inlet

To Yorktown
and Gloucester

THE French were out. Somewhere on the high seas, on their way to some deviltry in the Colonies, Admiral Comte de Grasse and as many as fourteen sail of the line were assembled. For the British, the Leeward Islands Squadron under Admiral Samuel Hood and the Saint Lucia group under Rear Admiral Francis Drake were already at sea in pursuit. Perhaps just over the horizon, the enemy could be found, and perhaps the British fleet was just hours away from one of those epic sea battles that would decide the fate of the Crown. Or, Midshipman Alan Lewrie thought sourly, we could fuck around out here til Doomsday.

There had been a concerted rush to get under way from Antigua, and for a while it had been exciting to see so many ships gathered together with one fell purpose, but after a few days the iron grip of naval routine had canceled out the thrill. Scouting frigates could find nothing of the enemy, and there were damned few frigates to go around.

Alan began to get the sneaking suspicion that their own fleet was ahead of the French. De Grasse had started from Martinique, south of their own bases in the Caribbean, which might have taken him longer, which was all to the good, if they were to counter any action with the French and the Rebels in combination, allowing them to get to the hinted scene of battle in the Chesapeake or Delaware bays first.

At noon sights, after almost, but not quite, finding a reasonable guess as to their position (and hurriedly fudging a more accurate fix from Avery's slate), Alan had a chance to examine the sea chart pinned to the traverse board by the wheel binnacle cabinet.

He picked up a pair of dividers and measured off a passage at slow speed inside the island chains, instead of taking the outside or windward route. There's a Frog base in Haiti, he thought, and there's the Dons with a fleet in Havana. What if this poxy French admiral stopped off for supplies or more ships? We've seen nothing in the Mona Passage or any other pass through the Bahamas. Only safe route for a fleet of fourteen sail and transports would be the old Bahama Passage, then up the coast of British Florida. Deep water for the most part, good offshore winds abeam most of the way, if not a soldier's breeze north of Savannah . . .

Alan realized with a small shock to his system that he was enjoying his speculations, which only confirmed his fears that he was beginning to fit into the Navy and gain a real interest in a career as a sea officer. God, what a horrible fate that would be! he thought. Not that being in the Navy, at sea and thousands of miles from his usual haunts was not bad enough, and none of it his idea in the first place. He had been in uniform for four months shy of two years and lately had had to work at suppressing pride in his newfound skills, and in the mostly good repute he had created for himself as a young gentleman in training.

"Wool gathering?" Commander the Honorable Tobias Treghues asked him with a lofty sniff. If Alan disliked being a seaman more than cold boiled mutton, the captain of H.M.S. *Desperate* felt the same low regard for him.

"Wondering where the French were, sir," Alan answered, straightening up and tossing the dividers down on the binnacle cabinet.

"How unlike you," Treghues said, and strolled away to the winward rail for a pace before his midday meal.

Stap me, Alan thought sadly. It was bad enough before when he just thought me a rapist and a rake-hell. Now he's been addled by that French gunner with a rammer, he's turned Evangel on us. Probably start leaping about like a Welsh miner at a Wesley meeting next.

Alan sidled off to leeward to stand next to his compatriot Midshipman David Avery, a dark-haired, merry Cornish lad of sixteen, almost seventeen. He shrugged in answer to the unspoken question framed by Avery's raised eyebrows.

"Still hates you, eh?" Avery whispered with a wry grin.

"What else is new?" Alan said.

"Who wouldn't?" Avery shrugged.

"Damned good question," Alan admitted with a soft laugh.

"Signal, sir," Midshipman the Honorable Francis Forrester, their least favorite messmate shouted from the stern rail. "Attend the flag, sir."

"Mister Railsford," Treghues bellowed. "Hands to the braces and bear up closer to the flag."

"Aye, aye, sir."

Desperate wheeled about and beat up to windward, within hailing distance of Admiral Hood's flagship *Barfleur,* rounding up alongside to leeward in a flurry of spray. No one could fault her sail tending or shiphandling, for Treghues and his officers were as smart as paint for all the gloom aboard from Treghue's new mental state.

A gig flew across from *Barfleur,* and a flag lieutenant scrambled up the manropes and battens of the starboard side with a large envelope in his coat pocket. After a brief conference with Treghues, he was back over the side and flying back to his own ship.

"Mister Monk," Treghues called for his sailing master, and that worthy made his appearance on the quarterdeck in his scruffy uniform. "Lay us on a course for Charleston, in the Carolinas. We have despatches for General Leslie."

"Aye, aye, sir," Monk replied, shambling his way to the charts. "Here now, quartermaster. Lay her due west fer right now. Hands ta the braces, smartly now. The flag's watchin'."

"Charleston," Avery said as they supervised their working parties for the mainmast braces. "We put in there once, Alan. Damned fun place, it was."

"I remember it so as well," Alan replied, almost rubbing his hands in glee. Yes, he had remembered Charleston well, too. It was full of refugees from up-country, run to the port by their rebel cousins. Cornwallis and his troops had been there, and with them had come a great flock of camp followers, traders, whores and ladies without their husbands. When he had been on the despatch schooner *Parrot* he had had a wonderful run ashore in Charleston and didn't think things had changed much in the interim. The real problem, though, was going to be getting ashore at all. Treghues might not look kindly on giving him leave.

"Be in soundin's by tamorrer forenoon, sir," Monk said, after he had paced off the distance from their noon position with dividers on his charts.

"Alan, did you realize that tomorrow shall be my birthday?" David told him. "And we are short of fresh meat. Now, if I talked nicely to the purser, he might find it in his heart to send me ashore with him, on King's business . . ."

"And if you don't take me along with you, you're a dead man, David," Alan warned him.

"Why should I do that?" David asked.

"'Cause I know where the likely widows and whores are," Alan said.

"You've missed your calling." David smiled. "You'd make a devilish grand pimp."

"You're not the first to think that," Alan heartily agreed. "And it's still early days in my career, isn't it? Now get onto Mister Cheatham before he picks somebody else. Tell him we both volunteer."

The next morning, *Desperate* stood in toward Charleston, with the spires of the churches marking the safe passage as range marks. They had been painted black by the Rebel defenders in last year's siege, but if anything, they had stood out even more prominently than when painted white, so *Desperate* had no difficulty finding the channel. Alan was turned out in his best uniform, as was Avery, while Forrester and Carey were in their usual working rigs. A copy of de Barres' *Atlantic Neptune* was in Alan's hands, the sketch book of all major towns and headlands of the American coast. It had set him back seven guineas, but it had been worth it to show the sailing master and the others a keenness at the sea trade which he did not always exemplify. He tucked the book under his arm and plied his quadrant to measure the height of St. Michael's spire, which lay just above their bows. He took the height of Charleston Light to the stern and ascertained that they were in the right path for a safe passage over the bar between the forts. With some quick calculations on a slate, he could find a rough position on the small-scale harbor chart that Mister Monk had laid out on the traverse board, and it was pleasing to see that his guess was very close to Monk's quickly pencilled X.

Cottle, Commander Treghues's coxswain, came up on deck in his best blue jacket with shiny brass buttons, his red and white striped loose slop trousers clean and his feet encased in new cotton stockings and freshly blacked shoes with silver buckles. The boat crew gathered round him and Cottle eyed them keenly so their appearance would not shame their captain or the ship when they went alongside the pier to carry Treghues to meet the port authorities with letters and documents.

"Hawse bucklers clear, sir," Toliver, one of the bosun's mates reported after coming aft from the fo'c'sle. "Best bower ready to drop, and a kedge ready in the stern."

"Let her swing nigh stern-first ta the town afore ya let go that kedge, mind," Monk said, almost as an afterthought. Charleston was a nasty harbor for all its size. On the way in, they had passed small islets and stretches of salt marsh where men were dredging for oysters only knee-deep in water, or loafing on sand spits that would be under water at high tide. "Safe across the bar now, sir," Monk told Treghues.

As if in confirmation, a hail from the leadsman in the foremast chains called out a safe depth of six fathoms. His next cast was half a fathom more, and everyone could breathe easily. *Desperate* drew slightly more than three fathoms amidships when properly loaded and provisioned.

"Are we getting ashore?" Avery asked after he had come aft from his duties with the ship's boats.

"No one had told me anything of yet," Alan said softly. "But if Treghues is going ashore, we shall be here for a while at least. Surely, we would not pass up the chance for firewood and water."

"Lord, it's hot," Avery complained, plucking at his broadcloth coat and waistcoat. "And you can smell the fever in those marshes."

"In daytime, and with a sea breeze, we have nothing to fear," Alan told him. He had suffered a serious bout of Yellow Jack aboard the *Parrot,* and had picked up enough lore about tropical miasmas for a lifetime. "Our old sawbones assured us the feverish elements only rise at night, with the mists. Just pray the biting flies don't find us. Last time I was here, the wind was off the shore, and I thought I'd be eaten alive."

"Maybe it's the flies cause fevers," Avery said.

"Don't be a superstitious ass," Alan said, but only in jest.

"Maggots are created in rotting meat, and I've not heard much good about maggots," Avery countered. "Except for eating pustulence in wounds."

"My God, but you're a cheerful creature this morning." Alan laughed.

"A little more attention to your duties there, young sirs," Treghues said in passing, glaring at both of them evilly, with a lingering glance on Alan.

"Aye, aye, sir," they answered dutifully.

"'Bout a mile off the wharf now, sir," Monk said, straightening from his latest calculation with his sextant.

"Short enough row," Treghues said, not seeing the glum expressions of his boat crew, who faced a long, hot pull ashore. "Take in tops'ls and round her up into the wind."

"Aye, aye, sir."

Desperate came about under reduced sails. The best bower dropped into the harbor and raised a circle of muddied silt on the surface as it bit into the mud of the bottom. She paid back from the light wind with a backed tops'l until snubbed by tension on her anchor cable. The stern kedge anchor was let go, and hands at the capstan took her back up toward her bower until she was held with equal grip by both anchors, bow pointed outward from the town for her eventual departure.

Even as she was making sternway to drop the kedge, Treghues's gig had been led around to the entry port, and Cottle had received his captain into her. Before the tops'l had been taken in aloft, their captain was well on his way ashore to deliver his messages and inquire about the whereabouts of the French.

"Bosun, lead the cutter round for the purser," Lieutenant Railsford, the first officer (and only commissioned lieutenant) called. "Mister Cheatham, you'll mind my own wants, I trust?"

"Indeed I shall, Mister Railsford," Cheatham said.

"And I believe you mentioned the need for two of the young gentlemen to assist you?" Railsford went on, looking at his younger charges, and noting how well turned out Avery and Lewrie were in comparison to the rat-scruffiness of little Carey or the porcine Forrester. "Can't let the image of *Desperate* down now, can we? Mister Lewrie, you shall take charge of the cutter and assist the purser ashore. And since I believe that today is your birthday, Mister Avery, you have my permission for a short spell of shore leave. Mister Lewrie may join you in your celebrations, but they had best be damned short, if you get my meaning?"

"Aye, aye, sir," they both answered. The captain's clerk was asked to write out two leave tickets for them, giving them until the end of the first dogwatch around sundown, in which to enjoy the pleasures of the town.

In a rush they scrambled down the battens and manropes to the barge to join Cheatham, and got the boat under way before anyone could change his mind about allowing them freedom from naval routine, even for a short while.

"It was good of the captain to allow me to celebrate my birthday, sir," Avery said to Cheatham, once they were away from the ship's side and the boat crew was stroking lustily at the oars.

"Captain Treghues does not strictly know of it," Cheatham said. "But we had to go ashore to replenish and cannot sail until the ebbing of the evening tide, which Mister Railsford informs me shall not turn until near midnight. Even immediate sailing orders could not rush us."

"Then we should be doubly grateful to you and Mister Railsford," Alan said with a smarmy smile of thankfulness.

"God, but you are sickening when you are in need of something," Cheatham said, but without any malice. He was not so much older than they, in his mid-twenties, and when not called by duty to be serious, could show a merry and waggish disposition. "I do not want to know what hellishness you had planned, Avery, but with Lewrie, you are in good hands for the discovering of it. Too good, in faith."

"Aye, sir," Avery replied, hiding his good humor.

"You are to return on time, properly clean and sober, or Rails-ford and I shall suffer for it," Cheatham instructed sternly. "Were you going ashore alone there would be no questions asked, but with Lewrie . . ."

"I could attend you and return without sport, sir," Alan said after a long moment of thought. Damme, I do want to get ashore devilish bad, but not if it causes ill will for Railsford or Cheatham. They're practically the only allies I have, he thought.

"No, I'll not turn a lone midshipman loose on the town," Cheatham said after mulling that offer over. "Where I suspect he's going, there are lower elements, and you're a stout enough buck to keep him safe. And sometimes show enough sense to avoid bad situations. Even if our captain . . . well." Cheatham might have said more regarding their lord and master's puritanical streak, his sudden aversion to Lewrie that no one had yet found a reason for, but that would have been open insubordination about the officer appointed by the Crown over every aspect of their lives and would also have been injurious to good discipline, especially said in front of the hands who were now working up a ruddy sweat at the oars.

"I'll not let him come to harm, sir," Alan said sincerely, "or get anyone in trouble. My word on it, sir."

"Very well," Cheatham said.

It had all, indeed, begun innocently enough, like most things that Alan Lewrie had gotten into. They had climbed to the wharf at the tip of the town's battery, and had made their way to a public house for a pint or two of cool ale. While there, they had discovered the location of the best house that could offer a good meal, had repaired to an establishment named by the publican and had eaten a magnificent dinner such as they had not seen in weeks.

They shared a middling-sized beef steak that came sizzling from the grill on a pewter platter, split a roast chicken between them, crammed themselves with piping hot local bread made of corn meal and dripping with fresh butter, and had imbibed a bottle each of sinfully good wine, which being a rarity in the Carolinas, was also sinfully expensive. To clear their heads of wine fumes for the main activities of the leave, they had finished off with fresh-made pie and coffee.

"Anythin' else, suhs?" the waiter asked them, bringing a second pot of coffee. "A pipe fer ya?"

"Not for me," Avery said, wondering what a well set up fellow of approximately their own age was doing not in King's uniform.

"Where would one find some sport at this time of day?" Alan asked, opening the face of his silver and gold damascened pocket watch.

"Ya'll want sportin' ladies, ah take it?" the waiter leered, hoping for a better tip. To their nodded assents, he went on, "This time o' day, most the good houses is closed, suhs. But they's some guhls ah know jus' down from the country that're obligin' sorts."

"Last time I was here I went to a place called Maude's," Avery said with his best man-of-the-world air, or a good attempt at one.

"Army moved onta Wilmin'ton, so did Maude's, suh," the waiter told them.

"Mother Lil's?" Alan asked, remembering his earlier adventure.

"Got ruint, suh. Parish didn't lahk 'em makin' such a row ever' naght. Patrols busted 'em up. Ain't been the same since."

"We could always fall back on your widows, Alan," David said.

"Not if we have to be back at the end of the first dog," Lewrie said. "That might do for me, but not for you. Had we several days, an introduction might do you good, but not for such a short acquaintance."

"Lady Jane's, suh," the waiter said with a knowing wink.

"I mind a Lady Jane's that used to be in Savannah," Alan said, after thinking back on the gossip he had dredged up in his last visit.

"Tha's the one, suh. Got a nahce li'l place up the Cooper bank, lotsa pretty young guhls. Two ah toldja 'bout works there. You tell 'em Mayhew said twas alright, they treat yuh special, seein' it's yer birthday an' all."

They decided on the place, paid the bill and left Mayhew a shilling for his information and directions. Once out on the bustling street, they had to stick to the shade to avoid the direct heat of the sun, which was as fierce as any latitude they had left. They found the house.

"I don't know, Alan," David said, mopping his streaming face with a handkerchief. The house was far away from the main town environs on the banks of the Cooper River, a planter's mansion gone to seed from the early days of the colony, now surrounded by ram-shackle warehouses, empty piers and scabrous cottages and shacks crammed together any old how. The yard was overgrown with weeds and once trimmed plantings gone riot in the sultry climate. The house itself needed some porch repairs and a good coat of paint.

"Well, it's not Drury Lane," Alan said, noticing how commercial the neighborhood looked, and also how quiet and abandoned in the worst heat of the day. "But then it's not Seven Dials, either. It's your birthday, David. Mayhap there's other places further back in town, but the closer we get to the port, the more the chance for the pox."

"Well, we could knock," David said, "and if we don't like what we see, we can leave."

"Amen to that," Alan said. "If nothing else, we can get some-thing cool to drink. I feel ruddy as a roasting pan."

They went up onto the porch, plied the heavy door knocker and half a minute later the door was opened by a large black house-servant.

"Lady Jane's?" Alan asked, when it was evident that Avery's tongue was stuck to the roof of his mouth at the sight of the man and his bulk.

"It is, suhs. Yo early. Come on in, why doncha?" the black servant said in a menacing deep voice. "Ah'll fetch the mis'ress."

"Well . . ." David said, hesitating still.

"Y'all kin have sumpun' cool whal ya waits, suhs," the man offered, opening the door fully and waving an arm toward the inte-rior.

That decided Alan, at any rate. He stepped through the doors into the dim coolness of the house, shut up against the searing heat of the day. It had a musty smell, as all closed houses do, overlaid with a redolence of perfume and drinks spilled in the dim past, the faint scent of bedchambers used for sport so long that the sweat and the juices had clung to the wallpaper and drapes. Smells like a bawdy house, alright, he told himself.

David followed him in, and they were steered into a receiving salon to the right, a room of more than usual seediness. The furnishings were worn and rickety, the walls stained by rain or seepage and the paint peeling in places. The threadbare velvet drapes were closed tight against the light of day, and a table candelabra burned, livening the gloom and attempting to hide the shabbiness with a romantic aura.

"Ah 'spec yo young gemmuns cayah fo some wine whal yo waits," the black man said from the doors, and disappeared into the hallway, leaving them to their own thoughts.

"What will the tariff be, do you expect?" David said, removing his cocked hat and fanning himself with it, eyeing a place to sit but not trusting the snowy whiteness of his breeches seats to the dubious condition of the upholstery.

"Nothing near a duke's ransom, I'd expect." Alan laughed. "Still, we have six candles burning in midday, and good beeswax, too, not country-made tallow dips. Must do a damned good trade here."

"But not over a crown?" David asked, fingering his purse.

"I sincerely doubt it. Here now, we split our meal, but it is your birthday after all. Let this be my treat," Alan offered.

"Done," David said quickly, which dispelled all his doubts of the establishment. "Like Tom Jones of fiction, you show a generosity of spirit."

"But get into more mischief," Alan said.

Their hostess appeared at that moment, an older woman crowned by a pale blue wig adorned with false flowers and effigies of songbirds, her face boldly painted white, as was fashionable in years past. One cheek sported a large beauty mark, and her lips glistened with red paste. She was dressed in a morning gown in contrast to the care with which she had attended her toilet.

"Young genl'men, ah swear y'all took me unawares, callin' so *early*," she gushed, sweeping into the room in grand, fluttery style. "How good o' y'all ta think o' mah humble li'l *establissement*."

"You are Lady Jane?" Alan asked, bending deep in a *congé* before taking her hand and bestowing a kiss. "A young man named Mayhew made us aware of your services as we were dining."

"Such a darlin' boy, as are y'all, o' course," she said in reply. "Do be seated now an' take yore ease. Mose shall fetch us some . . . oh, here he is as ah speak. Do have some wine with me, though 'tis early in the day for mah *usual* practice."

The servant had donned a red coat tailored from some cast-off army uniform but now sewn into civilian splendor with many brass buttons and gilt appliqués suitable for livery. He set down a tarnished silver tray on the table between them and uncorked a bottle of hock, which he poured into three glasses that at least looked reasonably clean.

"An' y'all're from the harbor garrison, mah dears?" she asked.

"Off a frigate, ma'am," David answered, a bit shy still.

"An' just in from a deprivin' spell o' sea duty." She smiled.

"Aye, ma'am," Alan said, sipping his wine. It wasn't what he'd put on his own table, a little acrid on the tongue, but still potable. Seeing that David was shy, he led off by introducing themselves, told the mistress that it was David's birthday. "So you see the reason for our visit, Lady Jane. Mother Abbess, we come for sport."

"An' how old would ya be on this August day, David Avery?" Lady Jane asked, making a jape as to the date and the month.

"Seventeen, ma'am," David said.

"La, ta be that *young* again," Lady Jane said. "Ah b'lieve ah have just the girl for you. Of a good fam'ly from up-country, *cruelly* orphaned bah Rebels. She is new ta our callin', so ya *will* be gentle with her, ah trust, young sir?"

"Oh, indeed, ma'am," David said.

"An' fer you, Mister Lewrie?" the abbess asked. "What sort o' girl excites yer humors? Or shall ah just ask mah ladies ta come down an' join us so you can make yer selection? Ah only have the five at present, but ah kin assure you they are all above average in comeliness, an' none so jaded nor lowbred as ta displease the most discernin' taste."

"Aye, fetch 'em down," Alan said, shifting on the settee.

Lady Jane tinkled a bell on the table, and minutes later, a bevy of young women entered the room in morning gowns thin enough to exhibit charms that could be theirs for a fee. David was paired with a young girl named Della, a petite blonde who indeed seemed a homeless waif—fortunately a most womanly young waif. They sat down together and Mose fetched more glasses. Alan looked over the rest of the party and settled on a brunette with a sleepily sultry expression and long slim limbs.

"Ah urge y'all ta linger over yore pleasures," Lady Jane said as the rejected girls went back to their rooms. "We usually ask a crown for our ladies, but since this is David's birthday and it is *such* a slow day for the trade, let us say only three shillin's each, plus whatever gratitude you can extend ta mah darlin's here?"

"And the wine?" Alan asked, having been caught by hidden additions to the tariff in his past experience with knocking shops in London.

"Say a bottle each, another two shillin's, mah dears."

"My treat," Alan said, laying out two crown pieces on the table.

"Take joy, mah dears," Lady Jane said, sweeping up the money and rising. "Ah shall have Mose fetch yore wines. If there is anythin' else y'all require, ya have but ta ring."

Alan was led to a small bedroom over the house's side porch that had a balcony of its own. The windows were open for a breeze and the gauzy drapes stirred in a soft river wind. Once in the room he shucked his coat and removed his neckcloth. His girl, named Bess, came to him and kissed him gently, playing the innocent at first, but warmed up quickly when he embraced her and began to fondle her firm buttocks and hips. The servant arrived with a bottle and two glasses, interrupting them. Alan almost kicked him out the door and shut it.

Bess poured them each a glass of hock, then arranged herself on the narrow bed, parting her morning gown to reveal splendid legs.

"Ya been long in the King's Navy?" she asked as he undressed.

"Too damned long," he laughed, removing his waistcoat. "You been long with this Lady Jane?"

"Too damn' long," the girl smiled back with honest amusement.

"I'm off a frigate," he told her as he kicked off his shoes and began to undo his breeches. "The *Desperate,* twenty guns, just put into port this morning." He went on, intent on his prize lolling on the sheets. Once in his birthday suit, he slipped into bed beside her and they embraced once more, and she began to moan expertly at his touches, shamming high passion at once, "Oh, mah chuck, oh, ya make me tangle all over."

"Here, how long do we have?" Alan asked.

"This ain't no hop-about place," Bess said throatily as he kissed her shoulders and neck. "No rush, ah reckon. What tahm hit be?"

"Just after one," Alan said. "We have to leave by five."

"Well, we kin have hours t'gether, then," she groaned, pawing at him as though she was trying to save herself from drowning. "Mos' men don't come hyuh til way after dark, hit bein' so hot an' all."

"Then let's not play as if we're on the clock," Alan said, undoing the last lacings to her bodice. "Let's spend our hours together trying to please each other instead of all this sham."

Bess smiled up at him, broke off her acting and gave him a hug which almost resembled fondness. She rolled over to fetch their wine.

"Ah thank ahm gonna lahk ya, Alan," she said. "Hyuh, have a drank. Le's do take ouh tahm. Hit happens sa seldom."

After that, Bess was pleasantly exuberant in bed, eschewing the normal bawd's loud performance that could not be credited. She was only seventeen, she told him as they fondled and nestled in postcoital ease, once a virgin in the Piedmont but ruined by soldiers from both sides in the partisan fighting, left behind when her last lover marched off to Wilmington. Whether true or not, Alan found it a better-than-average whore's tale.

Other than whoring, she had no trade skills, and no regard for the usual servant's or washerwoman's wages. The work was easy, the money she got to keep was good and Lady Jane took care of all her needs. She did not cry penury or guilt like most of the sorrowful stories Alan had heard from rented quim, and seemed content and blasé with the life, as long as her beauty and health lasted.

"And what will you do when you're older?" Alan asked her as he stretched naked beside her after another bout.

"Take me passage ta London an' open a house o' my own, ah reckon," she said with a smirk. "Bigges' city ah ever seed was Chawlst'n, but ah'd admire ta see London."

Alan described his former life and all the pleasures of the world's greatest city, which delighted her. In the process he touched on why he had been banished to the Navy, and under further careful coaching he bragged on what he had seen and done in the Indies.

"But whut brought ya hyuh ta the Caralinas?" she prodded.

"Going north to New York," Alan said without thinking. "There is a French fleet on the loose under an Admiral de Grasse. We took a Frog merchantman two weeks ago and found out what they're up to in the Chesapeake or the Delaware, and we're going to find them and stop them. It was me that found the letters from de Grasse to Rochambeau and Washington."

"Jus' one li'l frigate's gonna stop 'em?" she teased fetchingly.

"Whole damned Leeward Islands fleet," Alan said. "Ships up from Saint Lucia, too. Fourteen sail of the line. Would have been more, but Rodney took his treasure fleet home and took three ships with him. It's going to be one hell of a fight when we meet up with those Frogs."

"Ya thank that'll end the fightin'?" she asked. "Six month ago, ah'd've been glad ta see people stop akillin' each other. Nouh, all ya sailors'll go back ta England an' the troops, too. That'll be bad for business. Pooh, ah'll never save up enough ta get ta London."

"But with peace, Charlestown will be bustling again, and there still will be a garrison," Alan said, accepting another glass of the wine. It was beginning to taste pleasant, too pleasant, and he vowed to make it his last until the stirrup cup at the door, or they would go back aboard half foxed and Treghues would be furious. "I wager you could charge a guinea for your services and go home rich as Moll Flanders."

"Jus' as long as ah don't never have ta go back ta the Piedmont," she said, growing a little sad. She snuggled up closer beside him to throw a leg over and hug him close. "God, hit wuz horrible up there."

Here comes the sympathy plea, Alan thought sourly. Never knew a whore yet who wouldn't try to weep you out of more money.

"I've heard tales about how partisan the fighting was."

"Not jus' the fightin', Alan," she said into his shoulder. "Iver been upta the back country?"

"No."

"Hit's this rebellion," she said. "Won't leave nobody alone. Ya gotta be fer one side er t'other nouh. Neighbors turnin' agin each other, burnin' each other out fer spaht. Rebels aburnin' out Tories, Tories raidin' Rebels, the Regulators runnin' round makin' people choose the Rebels're die. An' when they fight, they don't take prisoners no more. Maybe some o' the reg'lar troops still do, but mosta the militia on both sides jus' shoot 'em all. Iver hear tell o' Tarleton's Quarter?"

"I've barely heard of this Tarleton. Cavalry, isn't he?" Alan sighed, shifting to a more comfortable position in the sticky heat.

"They wuz a fight at Waxhaws, an' Tarleton had 'em beat, an' the Rebels raised white flags fer quarter, but the Legion tore 'em apart anyways and kilt most of 'em. After that, the Rebels started doin' the same. Hit's been Tidewater people agin Piedmont, Rebel or Tory, rich agin pore, Regulators agin King's men—nobody's safe no more up thar. When Clinton took Chawlst'n last year, hit seemed the safest place. We wuz taggin' with the Legion, me an' Momma. Come hyuh where we could be safe, an' be took keer of lahk real ladies, not Piedmont hill trash. Cayn't blame me fer wantin' that, nouh kin ya, ner wantin' away from all that warrin'?"

She raised her head and looked him in the eyes. "You better kill them Frogs're the Rebels'll come back ta take Chawlst'n, er they'll be blood in the streets afore they through with the Tidewater Tories, an' all who serve 'em."

"Surely not a poor young whore with no politics?" Alan teased.

"Hey, hit's no skin offa yore ass," she heated up suddenly, angry at being belittled. "Yore out at sea, where they fight clean. You hain't seen yore neighbors laid out lahk daid hawgs jus' 'cause they give food an' shelter ta Rebels that woulda looted 'em iffen they hadn't. Er seen another fam'ly burned out the next naght when the Rebels come back ta get even with whatever people they thought wuz the closest Tories. Rich dumb-butts lahk you kin call it a war, but hit ain't nothin' but murderin'.'"

"Take it easy, now, twas not my doing," Alan said softly.

"Mah folks didn' want no part of hit," she said, now in full cry with tears beginning to streak her face. "We jus' wanted ta be left alone. But first one side an' then t'other come around atellin' us ta choose up sides er die."

"Time I was going," Alan said, rising to dress.

"Goddamn you," she cried, punching him in the chest. "Mah daddy got hung by a pack o' scum said he was fer King George, jus' 'cause he paid part o' what he owed in tax when the King's man come round with a sword ta make him pay up. Wouldn't even listen to him. An' not a month later we got burned out an' lost ever'thin' 'cause a lyin' dog Regulator got caught an' give our name ta the Tory militia. But hit don't bother the lahks o' you none, does it? Well, you jus' go on an' get yer blueblood arse kilt, an' ah only wish ta God hit wuz yore fam'ly sufferin'.''

She collapsed in tears, flinging herself back onto the bed and sobbed into a pillow to muffle her distress or to hide her lack of real tears. Alan wasn't sure which. Alan picked up his shirt from the floor and started to put it on over his head, but stopped to look down on her bare body as she wept.

Damme, I'm a foolish cully to be taken in like this, he thought, knowing that he should walk out and leave her to her tears, but moved all the same, no matter how stupid he considered himself to fall for a whore's story. He dropped the shirt and sat down on the bed to stroke her back. She hissed something unintelligible at him, but he persisted until she turned to him and took refuge in his arms, wetting his chest with real tears and snuffling and hiccuping with remembered terror and sadness.

"There, there," he said, rocking her gently like a child. God what if she is telling the truth about what happened? Never let it be said of me that I had a lick of sense when it came to women, especially when they spring a leak, he told himself. Maybe part of her tale is real and not some plea for an extra shilling or two. I'd not like to be back in those wilds with every hand turned against me, either.

"There, there," he soothed, stroking her back and keeping her close and snug until her sobs became less powerful.

"Hey, ahm sorry," she whispered, snuffling. "Ah don't want ya ta get kilt, ah didn't mean that. Hit's jus'. . . ."

"Well, I don't want to get killed, either," he said, and she shrugged in sad mirth against him. "No harm done. Tell me about it."

"Las' thang ah thought ah'd iver do's become a whore," she sniffed, now bereft of strong emotion, almost flat in tone. "Thought ah'd marry one o' the neighbor boys. Didn't know which yit, but that's the way o' thangs. He'd run a farm er a store, an' we'd have babies an' live a normal life, ya know? My daddy'd live a good long lahf, an' my momma wouldn't be owin' ever' meal ta the next man with silver, Rebel er Tory. Me, either."

"I am sorry things turned out this way," Alan said gently, feeling that he meant it, for all his native cynicism. He drew her back down on the bed where she nestled to him like a little girl.

"We weren't rich er nothin', jus' makin' hit from crop ta crop, same's ever'body else," she said in a tiny voice. "When they burned us out, we lost hit all, jus' the clothes we stood up in an' some stuff airin' on the line 'stead of in the cabin. Half the people wuz agin us 'cause they thought we wuz Tories after they hung Daddy, rest wuz agin us after what that Regulator said an' we got burned out. Only folks we could take up with wuz the soldiers."

"And you started following the army," he said.

"First off twuz Rebels." She shrugged. "They took us in over what happened on our farm, but they wuz chased all over hell an' we couldn't keep up, an' all we got wuz sore feet an' pore rations. Then the good people called us whores anyways, an' wouldn't give us a bye yore leave. Called us pore trash't needed runnin' from one parish ta n'other."

"Save us all from the smugly moral," Alan said, minding Treghues.

"Ran inta Tarleton's Legion an' took up with them, got a warsh tub an' some soap ta earn our keep, but soldiers never have much money, not rankers, noways. Told us we couldn't stay less'n we wuz doing more'n takin' in warsh."

"You *and* your mother?" Alan said.

"Momma weren't that old. Had me when she wuz sixteen, an' ah wuz the oldes' child. She took up with a foot sergeant who didn't mind the two other kids. Best of a bad deal, he wuz. Ah s'pose she's still with him. Least she's still eatin' well iffen she is, 'cause he's the biggest chicken thief in the Legion. A real hard man, but kind enough."

"And what about you?"

"Momma trahed ta stick me ta warshin', but twern't easy." She admitted. "Finally, a corp'rl give me a sack dress he'd stole if ah'd go off in the woods with him. Weren't much of a dress, at that," she said with a fleeting smile.

"And the corporal?" Alan asked, feeling her turn to a better mood than just a few minutes before.

"He weren't much, neither." This time she laughed aloud. "But we could get us money enough fer food an' beddin', an' Momma didn't ask where hit come from after that. I didn't whore fer jus' anybody, though."

"For the officers?" Alan asked, pouring them both more wine.

"Hell, yes," she snorted, now out of tears and laid back at ease. "This cap'n was all worked up 'bout the morals o' his men, but that didn't stop him from havin' me hisself. Then Tom Woods come 'round with an order ta move on, from that cap'n, if ah wasn't takin' up with jus' one of 'em. Anyways, Tom wuz from England and he looked sa *grand* up on his horse, an' sa clean all the tahm. Not lahk the soldiers comin' round. Ah had me on a new dress, had mah hair warshed an' a li'l scent an' ah could tell raght off he didn't want me run off lahk the cap'n said fer him ta do. He got down an' talked ta me, an' next thang ah knowed, he wuz offerin' ta take me on as his mistress, iffen ah'd a mind fer it. Hit seemed lahk a good deal, an' a way ta get back at the cap'n, sa ah said shore! Got some new dresses, a pony ta ride an' a cart an' pony fer Momma an' her stuff, too. Oh, mah Tom had a slew o' money! He wuz real proud o' me, lahked me ta look good an' show me off ta the other officers, even Colonel Tarleton. Colonel even come sniffin' 'round an' offered me a guinea to lay with him."

"And did you?" Alan asked, stroking her hips and thighs.

"What da you think," she said, smirking. "With the Colonel, hit's lay down're get knocked down. Doubt there's a girl in the Caralinas he hain't had, even he had ta rape 'em ta take what he wanted. Tom weren't too happy on me after that, got all upset, but he knew ah was whorin' when he met me. Maybe that's why he wuz sa eager ta leave me here in Chawlst'n when the army marched north. Momma went on with 'em ta Wilmin'ton, but Tom left me twenty pounds an' tole me he couldn't take no camp followers along as they wuz gonna march light an' fast. Raght after that, the money wuz runnin' out, so ah took up with Lady Jane an' come away with her hyuh."

Alan suspected there was more to Lieutenant Woods's rejection of her than she was telling, but it didn't really matter. She was out of her bad mood and still in bed with him, without a stitch on, and it was barely three in the afternoon. Alan stroked her into a better mood soon enough, and this time, perhaps from some gratitude she felt for his listening, or for his seeming concern, she was more properly passionate, and gave him the best rides he had known in months.

I feel like a fool, anyway, Alan thought as they left the house in the gloom of early evening. It was five, and they would barely be able to get back to the landing and take a boat out to their ship to report on time.

Alan had left her a crown, despite all his good intentions not to be gulled by the girl, and he carried a hastily written letter from Bess to her mother in the event they put into Wilmington or caught up with the army.

"And how was Della?" Alan asked David as they strolled loose hipped along the dirt road for the lower part of town.

"Damned interesting," David said. "Not as virginal as she seemed at first, thank God. Almost made me feel as if I were ravishing her for the first time for a while there."

"Lots of tears and entreaties?"

"There was that," David said. "I suppose that is something they all do."

"Only if it pays," Alan said with a lofty air of superiority in amorous dealings. "With an older man, she might have been a fishwife, if that was what was desired. Now you take that Bess. Started off acting like I was a great treat until she found all the acting wasn't necessary. They all have an air that appeals more to one than another. They're probably comparing tips and sharing notes about us to see what will make them more money from the next pair of fellows like us. Might even take turns playing the ravaged innocent," Alan said cynically.

"My God, what a hard bastard you are, Lewrie," David said.

"What did you think we bought back there, undying love?"

"No matter what you say, I think she truly liked me, beyond the coin we gave her and her mistress," David said stubbornly.

"She might have, David, but it don't signify once we're gone," Alan said. "Tonight she'll be just as nice to the next man with money in his purse. What difference? We got what we wanted. Now, someone you could set up as your mistress, that might be a different story."

"She was not some drab you rattle in an alley," David insisted. "She's more a courtesan, taking hours to please instead of a quarter hour and a quick wash. She has time to decide whom she truly likes or dislikes and is probably genuinely glad to see a favored customer again. I felt sorry for her, actually."

"Well, I can't think it natural that two such pretty girls have to take to that life except from sheer necessity," Alan said, realizing David would believe what he wished. He did not want to dispel all David's illusions or ruin his birthday remembrances with the brutal truth. And Bess had rung true, and had treated him with what felt at the end to be almost genuine fondness, and he did not think her so jaded or skilled.

"My sentiments exactly," David said firmly.

"Still, without necessity, there'd be a lot fewer available and obliging young girls to make sport with, so I think we should propose a toast to brute needs when we're back aboard," Alan said, tongue in cheek.

"Especially our brute needs," David laughed, tipping Alan's cocked hat forward onto his nose. "Remember what Wilkes said, A few good fucks and then we die."

"Speaking of brute needs," Alan said, looking up and down the street, and to where it joined a busier thoroughfare in the market area, "keep a sharp lookout while I pump my bilge on these . . . azaleas, or whatever."

He stepped into the weeds until he was out of sight and unbuttoned his breeches to make water.

"No worry, Alan," David told him softly. "No one coming but a pack of men with a cart."

"Fine. Be out directly."

"Jesus Christ!" David yelped. "Alan!"

"What?" Alan yelled back, aware of the sounds of running feet in the dirt of the road. He did up enough buttons to preserve modesty and stepped out into the lane, hand on his dirk.

There were three men on the road, big bruisers with staffs in their hands, all intent on beating David senseless, hemming him in as he stepped back with his dirk drawn. Two more faced the weeds, waiting for Alan.

"Get the Tory shits now," one man rasped.

"The hell you will," Alan said, drawing his own weapon. The man from the pair nearer him swung his staff. Alan leaped at him, taking the wood on his forearm and palm with a loud smack that almost paralyzed his left arm, but he was inside the man's guard, arm extended.

He buried his dirk hilt deep in the man's stomach, bringing a howl of agony, for it was a death wound, death for sure not too many days in future. He bulled over him as the man collapsed, using the body as a shield against the second man's staff. The man jabbed with the pole to keep him away. Alan fended off with his numb left arm once more, slashed at the hands that held the staff and nearly sawed off a couple of fingers. As the attacker flinched with pain, Alan shouldered up to him, shoving him away, and as he spun to turn, stabbed him in the kidneys, which brought another terrified shriek of pain.

David had been knocked down, though he had hurt one of his foes, a man clutching a slashed forearm. Alan gave a great shout and ran to David's assistance even as the remaining two prepared to brain him.

"Die, you bastards," Alan howled, brandishing his bloody blade.

"Leave it," their leader said, and they broke their circle about David to run back up the lane to the north, but they had Alan in their way. As they paused, David picked up a discarded staff and tripped the wounded one, and the others abandoned him as their courage left them. David slashed the last opponent across the back of the thigh as he stumbled to his feet, bringing him down once more for good while the other two made off at their best speed, abandoning their cart and their dead.

"You much hurt?" Alan asked, getting his breath back.

"Of course I am, you ass," David said, wiping blood out of his eyes from his head wound. "You think this is claret or something?"

"Go get the watch, then, while I keep an eye on these."

"Uh, could you do it, Alan?" David said, sinking to the ground. "I can hardly see straight. Sort of dizzy and weak, too."

"Help!" Alan yelled in his best quarterdeck voice. "Call the watch! Cut-purses! Murder!"

"I'll be alright, I think, if I can sit down." David sighed. "You go get some help."

"Lawsy mussy!" A black man spoke from the gloom. He was barefoot, dressed in a pair of discarded breeches, ragged shirt and straw hat, leading a donkey.

"You!" Alan bawled, freezing the man in his tracks. "Go get the watch, or help from the nearest store! We've been attacked by five men and my friend is hurt!"

"He sho is!" The black agreed, goggle eyed.

"Well, get with it, damn you!"

"Yassuh! Yassuh!"

Within minutes there was an army patrol on the scene, prodding the dead and taking the wounded foes into custody, taking notes on how the attack had started and binding David's head up in a shirt ripped from the back of one of the dead assailants.

"And they said 'Get the Tories'?" the young infantry ensign asked as they made their way toward the lit streets. "You are certain of it?"

"Exactly, sir," Alan replied, trying to find something on which he could wipe his dirk free of blood.

"Might have been an attempt to take your purses." The ensign pondered. "Where were you coming from?"

"The knocking shop up the road, Lady Jane's," Alan volunteered. "By God, it's nearly the end of the first dog. We have to get word to our ship we were set upon, or my captain'll have our hides off!"

"Lady Jane's, eh?" The ensign sneered. "You're lucky to get out of the doors with your heads still attached. We've been keeping an eye on it for weeks now. A little too much roughness going on there for my captain's comfort. You'd not be the first to be robbed after going there."

"You don't think they had anything to do with it, do you?" Alan asked, familiar enough with rough practices back in London to guess that they were indeed lucky to be alive.

"Not sure about that." The ensign shrugged in his trim red coat.

"But it's far enough out and dark enough off the main streets for footpads to be sure of easy pickings, not like some of the brothels closer in. Gets a better clientele, with heavier purses than most of the sailors' haunts, at any rate."

"Think you'd better see this, sir," his corporal said from the cart, which still stood in the middle of the road, the runty horse flickering her ears with supreme patience. The corporal held up ropes, grain sacks, two muskets and some old blankets. "Might have been more than robbery, sir."

"Corporal, send a man to the captain. Tell him we have three Rebel suspects who were part of an attack on two sailors."

"Midshipmen," Alan corrected, not wanting to be considered a mere sailor now that he had his equanimity back, along with his wind.

"Whatever." The ensign sniffed at being corrected. "Send another man to the wharf. Which ship?"

"The *Desperate* frigate sir," Alan replied. "Commander Treghues."

"However do you spell that?" the ensign asked.

"Commander the Honorable T-R-E-G-H-U-E-S." Alan replied sardonically.

"Ah, one of those, eh? Tell him to really foot it, corporal."

They were taken to the watch office near the wharves at the foot of the town, and while David's head wound was being staunched and sewn up they gave a more formal statement, interrupted by David's protests at the dullness of the army's surgeon's needle.

"I believe that should be all the information we need," a lieutenant said finally. "We have the prisoners to question, and we'll find the others quick enough, you can count on that."

"I believe we are sailing on the evening's tide, sir." Alan said: "Is there a possibility that Lady Jane's could have been involved with this? They treated us rather decent, really, and it would be hard to believe if they were linked to it."

"Doubtful at best. I'm a customer there at times myself," the officer confided with a grin. "No, it was most likely robbery they had in mind. Abduction, possibly, but that would have raised such a hue and cry, and for what purpose? If you were post-captains it would have made more sense. Not even Rebels would have a reason to take you off and pump you for information you most likely didn't have. Ah, there's a boat from your ship here to take you back. Hope your friend heals quickly. Your ship shall be going where, in case we need to send queries by letter?"

"At first to New York, sir. After that, God knows. The Chesapeake or the Delaware," Alan said.

They were escorted to the wharf and into a rowing boat in charge of the captain's coxswain, who was staring at them sadly. Once under way and the stroke was established, he turned to them.

"You done got yourself in trouble this time, sir," he told Lewrie.

"But it wasn't our fault—we were attacked and almost killed!"

"Not fer me ta say, Mister Lewrie, sir," Cottle told them sadly.

"Wonderful." Alan spat.

"Well, no matter what," David said, trying to fit his hat over his bandaged head and giving it up as a bad go, "you have to admit it was a memorable birthday celebration."

"There's that to savor," Alan remarked sarcastically.

"In case I did not mention it, thank you for saving my nutmegs back there. They'd have dashed my brains out in another minute if you had not gotten the upper hand with them."

"Think nothing of it, David, you'd have done the same for me," Alan said, taking his proffered hand and shaking with him heartily. "How's your head?"

"It hurts most sinfully. How's your arm?"

"Now that it's coming awake again it's throbbing away like a little engine."

"A proper shore leave, then," David laughed. "Eat our fill, topped up on wine, bulled a pretty girl into exhaustion and then had a fight to cap it all off!"

"Amen ta that, sor!" one of the oarsmen said.

"You keep that up an' you'll be real tarpaulin men, sirs!" another added.

"Everything but a cake with candles!" David crowed.

"We'll get something with candles, and that right soon," Alan said.

But looking back on it, now that the terror for his life was gone, it had been a proper run ashore, damned if it hadn't been.

CHAPTER 1

"THANK God we are back aboard," David said as they gained the entry port to *Desperate*. "If we run into more assailants, at least we outgun them here."

"Will you be quiet?" Alan said, sure of what was coming from their captain. "One would think your blow to the head had made *you* raving!"

"Mister Lewrie? Mister Avery?" Lieutenant Railsford called from the quarterdeck aft. "Come here, please."

Their youngish first lieutenant did not look his usual self; of course, he was stern as always. The life of a first lieutenant for even the most slovenly captain was a continual trial. What could go wrong to upset the usual ordered pace of Navy life kept most first officers biting their nails. In port, Railsford should have found a few moments of peace from the unending anxiety of what would go smash next. Now there they stood, disturbers of the lieutenant's only serene spell in days.

"Damn you to hell, Avery," Railsford snapped, his mouth screwed up as though he were chewing the words. "Damn your black soul to hell."

"Aye, aye, sir," David replied, thoroughly abashed and realizing just how bad it was if Railsford, normally the most forgiving and understanding officer he had, was vexed at him.

"And you, Mister Lewrie." Railsford spun on him. "*Very* stupid, I must say, Mister Lewrie!"

"Aye, aye, sir," Alan said, ready to be bent over a gun and given a dozen of the bosun's best as punishment. "But we did..."

"Silence!" Railsford roared. He stroked his lean jaws, perhaps to keep from turning his hands into fists. "I heard from the sergeant of the watch what happened. I have told the captain about the particulars, but he is...remarkably exercised about this. Whatever I could say to you shall most likely pale in comparison to what Captain Treghues shall say. Get you aft to his cabins at once, gentlemen!"

"Aye, aye, sir."

They followed Railsford below to the private companionway to their lord and master's chambers. A marine sentry in red uniform and white crossbelts was there, and was it Alan's imagination, or did he glare at them a little more evilly than most marines regarded midshipmen, and did he bang his musket butt on the deck with a little more enthusiasm and bellow their names to the waiting captain behind the door more loudly than usual?

"Enter!" Treghues yelled back.

They entered the captain's quarters, a fairly spacious stretch of deck in the stern of the upper gun deck, went past the coach where their captain dined, past the chart room and the berth space and met their judge and jury seated at his desk in the day cabin. He had on his best uniform, and a black expression—a devilish black expression.

He's so purple in the face he looks already hanged, Alan marveled as he came to attention before the desk. He had no sense of guilt for following his baser nature and had not provoked the fight with their assailants, but he was trembling with unease to be facing his captain in such a mood.

"So," Treghues said. Their captain was young and handsome, slim and manly and noble looking, as an aristocrat should be. In better times, he might have made a jolly companion, as long as one preferred hymn-singing and tea instead of caterwauling in the streets. But in the light of the swaying coin-silver lamps, he looked the very Devil incarnate, the sort of man one should rightly fear.

"That will be all, Mister Railsford," Treghues said, as though a curtain had fallen on his anger. "The tide shall slack four hours from now, and you shall stand ready to get the ship under way at that time. I shall inform you as to their punishment."

"Aye, aye, sir," Railsford said, departing, evidently hoping to be allowed to stay to partake in their chastisement, to savor the better bits.

"So, my two prize wretches have decided to return to us," he said after Railsford had gone. "After they had slaked their vile lusts to the full. Stuffed yourselves to bursting with food, did you?"

"Aye, sir," David ventured in a small voice. "It was my birthday..."

"Gluttony!" Treghues roared, back in his original demeanor, as when they had first entered. "Pigs-at-trough Gluttony, rolling about in your slops like Babylonian Pagans!"

We're going to catch Old Testament Hell, thought Alan.

"Washed it down with oceans of beer and wine, too, did you?" the captain continued, sitting prim behind his glossy desk with his hands on the surface, folded as in supplication for their salvation, even if he did privately consider them demon-spawn. "Got rolling drunk like some godless wretches in Gin Lane! Visited a house of prostitution, I'm told! Spent hours *spending*, weakening yourselves forever, risking the vilest diseases in the perfumed arms of...of... the Devil himself in disguise!"

"Uh, we did not get drunk, sir," Alan offered, considering that charge at least to be baseless; he could own up to the rest with pleasure.

"Did you not, sir!" Treghues said, slapping a hand on the mahogany with the crash of a six-pounder cannon. "You stand there swaying back and forth, barely in control of yourselves, reduced to the level of animals...reeking of putrefaction and...and...you dare to sass me?"

"No, sir!" Alan said quickly.

"The moment my back was turned, you gulled the first lieutenant to allow you to go ashore, knowing I would have not permitted it under any circumstances, inveigled your way into the purser's working party and took as your shield your own compatriot, used Mister Avery as an excuse to take all the pleasure you could gather!"

"It was my birthday, sir," David said, but not with much hope.

"And is that a reason to fall into the gutter with this poor example of a miscreant, vile, swaggering, crowing cock? I had better hopes for you, Mister Avery. I thought you were a God-fearing young man from a good family, and the moment I withdrew my gaze from you, you let Lewrie lead you astray into the swine pen as though you wished to join the Prodigal Son in his depravity and debauchery."

Try making an answer to that, why don't you, David, Alan thought to himself, amazed at Treghues's speech. Damme if David ain't going to get off with a tongue lashing, and the real thunder'll be saved for me.

"Well?" Treghues demanded.

"Sir, I asked to go ashore, and I requested Mister Lewrie to go as my companion because he is my friend," David finally said, after gnawing on the inside of his mouth for a long moment. "It was my idea, all of it."

"You take as a friend a caterwauling, dissembler who would force himself on his own blood? Then I tell you truly, Mister Avery, you are damned to eternal perdition unless you change your ways, and that right smartly! Well, that is the last time I shall allow either of you ashore for any reason except the good of our Service until I have decided that you have mended your ways and become the sort of Christian Englishmen I would like to have as midshipmen under me."

Treghues stopped, took a deep breath and sipped at a pewter mug of something. Tea, most like, Alan decided. Whatever it was, it seemed to calm him down, for he leaned back in his chair and almost, but not quite, made a smile—which was more frightening to them than anything they had seen as of yet.

"You both wanted shore leave. You both wanted to partake in all the sordidness this miserable town has to offer," he told them, and found no disagreement from either midshipman. "Then, on your way back, you fought with a party of men and killed two of them and wounded another. You both brought discredit on our Service, our uniform and our ship. Ten days' salt meat and ship's rations—no duffs, no spirits, no rum issue, no tobacco. Ten days' watch and watch duty. And a dozen each from the bosun."

"Aye, aye, sir." David said, letting out a sigh of relief. It could have been a lot worse.

"Aye, aye, sir." Alan said. He had spent nearly two years being deprived and degraded in the Navy; he could do ten days' minor deprivation standing on his head in the cross-trees.

"And, to improve your souls, you shall, when off watch, come to my cabins and read aloud a chapter of the Holy Bible each day. That you shall continue to perform until this ship pays off her commission." Treghues spoke with finality.

"Aye, aye, sir."

"Now get out of here and give my compliments to the bosun as soon as you can find him. I shall be listening." Treghues pointed to the open skylight over his cabins.

Once on deck, David gave a little groan.

"Go in peace, the service is ended," Alan whispered, removing his hat and mopping his brow. "Christ, what an asylum this ship is!"

"Well, the more we cry, the less we'll piss," David said.

"Speaking of." Alan sighed. "Bosun! Passing the word for the bosun!"

Two hours later, the tide began to ebb from slack water. The crew were summoned from below, where they had been napping, and began to let out on the bower cable to drift down on the kedge off the stern. Once at short stays, the kedge was tripped and brought in, the still night air having no chance to carry off the muddy tidal effluvia that the cable brought up as the damp thigh-thick cable was led below to the tiers to dry. They hauled back up to the bower and drew her in to short stays as well.

"Hove short, sir," came the call from the blackness up forward.

"Touch of land breeze, Mister Monk?" Treghues asked by the wheel, once more seemingly sane and rational, the very picture of an Officer of the King.

"Aye, sir, a light 'un, but it's there," Monk said.

"Hands aloft, then, Mister Monk. Hoist tops'ls, jibs, spanker and forecourse."

"Aye, aye, sir."

The first freed canvas began to fill from the softly soughing land breeze, heated during the day and now warmer than the sea breeze which had cooled to stillness. As that gentle wind found her, *Desper-*

ate began to make a slight way, beginning to stir dark waters.

"Weigh anchor, Mister Railsford."

The hands spit on their fists, breasted to the capstan bars and put a strain on them. The pawls began to clank as they marched about in a circle, and the anchor cable came in rapidly.

"Up an' down!" a bowman shouted. If the bower did not break free of the mud, if it was snagged on an old wreck or sucked deep into silt, a moment more could have the *Desperate* sailing over her own cable, bringing her to an inglorious halt, swinging her broadside and tearing the sticks right out of her.

"Anchor's free!" a bosun's mate called as the capstan pawls clanked rapidly, like a drummer's tattoo. In the feeble candles by the fo'c'sle belfry, one could see the puddened ring and upper stock of the bower and hands already over the side to cat it down. Raving, certifiable and leaping mad Treghues could sometimes appear, but no one could ever find a fault with his ship-handling. It was certainly a pity that their departure had taken place so near midnight that the town could not have turned out to gawk and marvel.

Steering carefully for the light, with the church spire squarely dead astern, they crossed the bar as the ebb began to gather strength but still had enough depth to carry them over in perfect safety. Once Railsford, the bosun and his mates and the ship's master-at-arms and corporal had made their rounds, the hands were allowed to go below to their hammocks, and *Desperate* became once again merely one more ship on a dark sea, lit up at taffrail, binnacle and belfry, but otherwise as black as a boot.

Alan and David were given the middle watch to stand together, from midnight to four, when the ship's usual day would begin, so they would get no rest until after the hands had scrubbed down the decks, stood dawn quarters, had brought up their hammocks and been released to breakfast. Across the bar, the sea was as restless as Alan's nerves. The quick phosphorous flash of cat's-paws broke all about them, though the air was still as steady as a night wind could be and showed no evidence of kicking up. A visit to the master's chart cuddy showed that their barometer indicated peaceful weather. There was a slice of moon ghosting through scattered clouds thin as tobacco smoke, and far out beyond them the trough glinted silver-blue when the clouds did not partially occlude that distant orb. If there was chop enough for cat's-paws, it held no malevolence, for the horizon was ruler-straight instead of jagged by clashing rollers. The wind sighed in the miles of rigging, the sails and masts quivered to the hinted power of the breeze, vibrated down through the chain wales, and set the hull to a soft quiver, as though an engine of some kind were operating below decks, an engine of the most benign aspect. Alan sometimes thought that the ship was breathing and purring like a contented cat by a warm hearth, rising and falling and slightly rolling with a deep and somnolent breath.

By God, that bastard hedge-priest can't take this away from me, Alan told himself, peeling off his short midshipman's coat and waist-coat. The day had been hot, and the area belowdecks before sailing had been stifling. He spread his arms to let the cool night wind explore every inch of his body that he could expose and still preserve modesty. He undid his neck-stock, unlaced his shirt and held it away from his skin for a moment. He felt a bit of breeze where one nor-mally did not feel breezes and inspected his breeches.

My God, I came back aboard with my prick damn near hanging out, he groaned. After those men attacked us, I never did up all my buttons. No wonder Treghues was thundering at me like he was.

Bad as the captain's opinion of him was at that moment, bad as it could get in the future (and Alan wondered if such a thing were possible), he could not restrain a peal of laughter at the picture he must have made.

"If you have discovered a reason for glee, by God I'd appreciate you letting me share it," David said from the darkness of the quarter-deck, almost invisible except for the whiteness of his breeches, shirt and coat facings.

"Did you notice that I was a bit out of uniform when we were aft?"

"No."

"Had my breeches up with one bloody button, that's what!"

David broke into a hearty laugh as well. "You mean to tell me you went in there looking like something out of The Rake's Progress and you didn't know?"

"Me and my crotch exposed, you and your head bandaged—we must have seemed like the worst Jack Nasty-Faces Treghues had ever laid eyes on!"

They went forward to inspect the lookouts and to get away from their captain's open skylight, in case he was still awake and now busily inscribing their names in his book of the eternally damned.

"God, I am laughing so hard my ribs ache," Alan said, stumbling about the deck over ringbolts and gun tackle and damned near howling, which upset the watch since they weren't in on the joke.

"I have tears in my eyes, I swear I do," David chimed in, pulling his bloody handkerchief out of his pocket and applying it to his face.

"Ah!" Alan heaved a great breath to calm down. He stopped laughing. "I would suppose we had better savor this. It's the last laugh we shall have for a long time."

"Worth it though, stap we if it wasn't. Here now, Lewrie, next leave is on me, my treat."

"Good. And I shall let you go first in the morning. In the beginning, the . . ."

"No, no, you'd be so much better at the Bible than me," David said, calming himself. "You've probably already violated half of it. Besides, why get us into more trouble by a report of blaspheming?"

"You're right," Alan agreed, leading them back aft.

"Um, Alan, what did the captain mean about you forcing yourself on your own blood back there?" David asked.

"Just raving, I expect. Think nothing on it."

"Did that have anything to do with the way he turned against you so quickly after Commodore Sinclair took over the squadron?" David said. "I mean you've never been really all that forthcoming about your past before the Navy. As your friend, it would make no difference to me, but . . ."

"Sir George knows my father, and like me thinks about as much of him as cowshit on his best shoes. And there's Forrester sneaking behind our backs to his uncle Sir George," Alan said quickly. "Put those two together and you get Treghues trimming his sails to suit Sir George."

"My father caught me with the cook's daughter," David confessed in a soft voice. "She was fourteen, I was eleven. I already knew I was down for the sea, but I thought I had another year before they sent me."

"You precocious young bastard!" Alan laughed. "Well, did you get into her mutton?"

"No, actually. Not for want of trying, though. And she was an amazingly obliging wench. So you see, I understand being sent off for something."

And now I am supposed to tell you all because you have shared a confidence with me, Alan thought, feeling weary and old for his tender years. Well, you'll not get an admission from me, no matter how much I like you and trust you.

"My father wanted me gone, David. I'll not go into the reasons, but he never loved any of us, not once. To this day I am not sure what I did to finally displease him," Alan lied glibly, "but displease him I did. And he packed me off to Portsmouth with Captain Bevan, Sir George's flag captain, in the Impress Service then. I doubt I'm welcome back home."

"But he supports you well enough, I know you have a yearly remittance, a pretty healthy one, near as good as mine," David said. "That doesn't sound too bad to me."

"David, do you love me?" Alan asked.

"Aye, I do, Alan. You're the best friend I've ever had in the Navy, the best friend I've ever had, period."

"Believe me that I hold the same fraternal regard for you as well, David," Alan said, turning warm as he realized that he really did hold David Avery as his closest and merriest friend. "But what happened back in London is dead and gone, and there's nothing to revive it. Nor do I care to. If you truly are my friend, please believe that it is nothing that I, or you, would be ashamed of, nothing to destroy a friendship."

"But you don't want to talk of it?" David sighed, partly in disappointment. "Well, there's an end to it, then. I shan't mention it again, or pry at you. And whatever passed between you and your father could never force me to lower my esteem for you."

"God bless you, David. Perhaps in future, when it is truly of no consequence or I have sorted things out and made something of myself, I shall tell you one night."

"Over a half-dozen of good claret and two towheaded wenches."

"Better throw in a stout auburn bitch, too."

"Done!"

* * *

At 4:00 A.M., the ship's day officially began. Bosun's pipes trilled the call for all hands, and the petty officers passed among the swaying hammocks, urging the men to wake and show a leg and form on deck. Pumps were rigged to draw up clean salt water to wash the decks, while the men rolled up their voluminous slop trousers above the knees and bent to the already pale timbers with holystones and 'bibles' to scrub, sanding off any graying of the decks dried by tropical suns, raising up the dirt of the day before and sluicing it off into the scuppers, slowly abrading the deck a tiny bit thinner than the day before. However, wood was cheap, and eventually, before they could ever wear enough away to harm the ship, *Desperate* would have been hulked long since or had her bottom fall away from rot and teredo worms.

With the pumps stowed away once more, the men brought up their hammocks, each numbered and carried to its required place in the bulwark nettings, having been wrapped up tightly and passed through the ring measure so that all were as alike as milled dowels and would serve as a guard against splinters or musket shot during battle. The hands then stood to their guns, the eighteen nine-pounder cannon that were *Desperate*'s main reason for existence, and the two short-ranged carronades on the fo'c'sle and the swivel guns on the quarterdeck. As dawn broke they were ready for action against any foe that appeared.

There was nothing in sight, not from the deck and not from aloft in the cross-trees of the masts. It might be halfway into the day watch before they caught up with the fleet, but for then, not even an errant cloud on the horizon could be mistaken for a tops'l.

"Fall out the hands from quarters, Mister Railsford." Treghues gave the order from the quarterdeck nettings overlooking the waist of the upper deck. "Pipe the hands to breakfast."

"Aye, aye, sir."

"Excuse me, sir, but who is midshipman of the watch?" Alan asked Railsford.

"You had the middle?"

"Aye, sir, both of us. And we shall have the forenoon as well."

"Get you below and eat, then." Railsford said. "Might as well get into working rig, too, or your shoregoing clothes are going to get too dirty."

They stumbled down to the lower deck and aft past the marine compartment to their tiny midshipman's mess, which was right forward of the master's cabin and the first lieutenant's. Young Carey was there already, digging into a bowl of gruel liberally mixed with salt meat and crumbled biscuit, slurping at his small beer with evident enjoyment. His eyes lit up as he saw them, not having had the chance to ask them how much trouble they had gotten into.

Midshipman the Honorable Francis Forrester was also there, round and glowing even though the morning was still cool, and also busily feeding. Cater-cousin to their captain, one of the original midshipmen from her commissioning, nephew to their squadron flag officer, Sir George Sinclair; an airily superior young swine they could have gladly dropped over the side on a dark night.

"I had hoped you had stayed in whatever sink or stew you had discovered in Charlestown," he said between bites. "Was it worth it?"

"We had a wondrous meal the like of which you would have considered a snack," David told him, stripping out of his good uniform. "We drank some rather good wine and then we repaired to a most exclusive buttock shop and rantipoled about until we had exhausted their entire stable."

"Don't waste a description of the women on him, Avery," Alan said as he dug into his chest for working-rig quality uniform items. "Didn't you know that Francis is still an innocent in that regard? Come to think on it, I cannot remember ever seeing evidence of his manhood, and there's not a scrap of privacy in this mess."

"Well, from what I hear, you'll be paying the price for your little escapade," Francis retorted hotly, but unwilling to try his arm against the two of them—they had bloodied his nose more than once in the past. "Hope you enjoy watch and watch. Hope you like watching me enjoy a good bottle of wine while you sip your water."

"You're a swine, Francine," David said. "A portly sow with two teats."

"Goddamn you!" Forrester roared, almost ready to rise, in spite of past experience.

"Blaspheme a little more softly, please," Alan said. "Before the captain decides to share the misery out. He's not in the best of moods today. Come to it, neither am I, so watch yourself and walk small about us."

They sat down to their bowls of mush and the mess steward set out a pitcher of water before them, eyeing them with a certain sadness.

"Have a heart, Freeling," Alan entreated. "Slip some small beer our way, won't you?"

"Oh, ah god a 'eart, Meester Lewrie, zur, bud iffen ah dew, ah won' 'ave no 'ead whan 'a capum 'ear of eet," Freeling responded.

"Bloody hell!" David said, taking a sip. "At least it's not wiggling today."

"Not even half brown. A good vintage," said Alan.

It was around three bells of the day watch, just after gunnery exercises, that *Desperate* caught sight of the fleet on the horizon to the northeast, after a good sail north along the coast with a soldier's wind. They were now roughly parallel with Cape Fear, slanting landward at a shallow angle to eventual landfall at Cape Henry and the mouth of the Chesapeake Bay, to peek in and see if the French had arrived.

Alan was in the rigging with a telescope, clinging to the shrouds with arm and knee crooked, leaning back onto the ratlines just below where the futtock shrouds began below the main top.

Well, no one's sunk while we were gone, he decided, counting the ships. There was Admiral Drake's small group of ships up from St. Lucia, now free of keeping guard on the French base in Martinique and very far from familiar waters; there was *Princessa*, the flagship, *Terrible, Ajax, Intrepid, Alcide* and *Shrewsbury*. Further north he could espy Admiral Hood's flag flying on *Barfleur*; also *Invincible*, the *Alfred, Belliqueux, Monarch, Centaur, Montagu* and *Resolution* riding in her wake. Fourteen sail of the line all told, and too few attendant frigates, as was usual. If the rumors were correct, and de Grasse had brought fourteen sail out of Port de France and had not picked up other ships at Cape Francois or Havana, then they would be evenly matched ship for ship in line of battle once they fell on their enemy.

It was so large a problem that his own paled in comparison, and he knew that he was looking forward to the battle with a certain relish, at that time in the uncertain future when upwards of thirty massive warships came up within pistol shot of each other and began to blaze away with every gun available.

Alan had seen single-ship actions since being almost press-ganged into the Navy, and such events as a fleet battle happened too rarely to be missed. He knew he had an extremely good chance to survive it, if it did occur, since frigates would not stand in the line of battle, but would be in the wings, repeating signal hoists and ready to rush down and aid some crippled larger ship. This battle, if it came soon, would truly decide the fate of the rebellion. Without the French fleet, there wasn't a ship on the coast that could stand up to the Royal Navy, and the blockade of their coast could check the last imports and exports that kept their miserable efforts in the field. This would be the crushing blow, and when it was over, everyone on the losing side would sue for peace and Alan could go home to England. Maybe not to London, not as long as his father was alive, but he could take off naval uniform and begin to live the life of a gentleman once more, so he had a personal stake in victory, and frankly, could not even begin to imagine any other result.

Then, no matter what career was open to him after getting out of the Navy, which had treated him so abominably, he could brag for the rest of his life that he had, by God, been there! Sword in hand, making every shot count, eye to eye with the Frogs, pistoling *moun-seers* right and left, or whatever else his imagination could do to enliven an observer's role as the tale grew with the telling.

I'll probably bore some people to tears with it. He laughed. There I was, hanging upside down from the clew garnets, four third rates on either beam! Harro for England and St. George and pass the bloody port if you're through with it! And the best part of it all is, I'll be safe as bloody houses for a change, instead of scared fartless.

Unwinding his limbs from his precarious perch, Alan clambered down to the starboard bulwarks along the gangway and jumped the last few feet to move back aft to the quarterdeck, where Treghues, Railsford and Monk were plying their own telescopes to survey the immense power spread before them.

"Still fourteen of the line, sir," Alan said to Railsford.

"Be more than that when we reach New York." Railsford

grinned at him. "Admiral Graves can add at least seven more, plus frigates. We shall have this Count de Grasse on a plate, mark my words."

"Mister Railsford, signal the flag there was no sign of the French at Charlestown."

"Mister Forrester!" Railsford bellowed.

"Sir?" Forrester called, running from the taffrail flag lockers.

"Signal 'negative contact.' Make sure *Princessa* or one of the repeating frigates replies with a matching signal."

"Aye, aye, sir."

The signal system, even with special contingencies included by Admiral Rodney before he departed the Indies, was meager almost to the point of muteness. Many signals were guns fired either to windward or leeward, ensigns hoisted from various masts, perhaps a certain colored fusee burning after dark. There were only so many signal flags, and each had a meaning mostly laid down in the Fighting Instructions, so anything that did not do with bloody battle took some ingenuity to convey. Usually it resulted in such confusion that ships sidled down to speak each other at close range anyway, and captains developed their lungs by shouting and bawling at each other through speaking trumpets, making their choler permanent.

Today was no exception. A red ensign hoisted from the windward foremast, and a blue signal flag at the gaff of the spanker was not understood as 'negative contact'; negative something, maybe, but what? The nearest frigate, the *Nymphe*, hoisted another flag that stood for "interrogative." *Nymphe* then lowered the interrogative and raised another which ordered *Desperate* to close with her. Since *Nymphe* was commanded by a post-captain and *Desperate* as a sixth rate boasted only a commander, not even a substantive rank, they had to yield their advantage to windward and come down to her, which would result in a long hard beat back to their assigned position once the message had been passed and understood.

"Play with your fancies: and in them behold upon the hempen tackle ship-boys climbing; hear the shrill whistle which doth order give to sounds confused," Dr. Dorne, their nattily attired surgeon was emoting as roundly as Garrick in Drury Lane. "Behold the threaden sails, borne with the invisible and creeping wind, draw the huge bottoms through the furrowed sea, breasting the lofty surge!"

Oh Christ, he must have aired his wig again, Alan thought.

"Henry the Fifth!" Railsford barked with glee. "Quite appropriate!"

"Oh, do but think you stand upon the rivage and behold a city on th' inconstant billows dancing; for so appears this fleet majestical, holding due course for Harfleur." Dorne ran on, now striking an oratorical pose, to the amusement of the assembled officers. Even cherubic Lieutenant Peck of the marines was smiling as though in fond memory, but being a marine, Alan was not sure that grin had anything to do with Shakespeare. Probably thinking on the last orange-vending wench he fondled in a theatre.

"Sounds most powerful like it, indeed sir," Monk agreed.

"Now you tell me, Captain, that the Bard did not do some time in the sea service," Dorne crowed.

"Follow, follow, grapple your minds..." Treghues began with some enthusiasm, but then stumbled and groped, not so much to remember the verse as to wander off the subject entirely, as though something else had caught his attention. He raised his telescope to look at *Nymphe* once more.

"Follow, follow, grapple your minds to sternage of this navy." Forrester recited, unable to resist the temptation to toady with his betters or show off his excellent education. "And leave your England as dead midnight still, guarded with grandsires, babies and old women, either past or not arrived to pith and puissance, for who is he whose chin is but enriched with one appearing hair that will not follow these culled and choice-drawn cavaliers to France?"

"Hah, hah, young sir, a scholard lurks!" Dorne shook with pleasure. "You are most familiar with him, I grant you."

"Aye, sir." Forrester beamed, trying to put on an air of modesty. "Especially Henry the Fifth, and that passage, which deals with the Navy."

"And when do you get enriched with that one appearing hair, Forrester?" Carey asked, with all the carrot-headed innocence that only the youngest midshipman could get away with.

"You would do well to grapple your mind to your duties and making something of yourself, young sir," Treghues said, shutting off their open enjoyment of Carey's dig. "Better indeed to emulate Forrester than be japing and frivolous! Or you shall never live long enough to grow that one appearing hair in my ship."

Poor Carey flinched as though he had been slapped in the mouth, and his eyes welled up in an instant. "I am sorry, sir," he quavered, on the edge of losing all control. Carey spun away and almost ran to leeward to be as alone as a completely humiliated and hurt thirteen-year-old boy can be on a ship.

Had discipline allowed, the assembled officers and warrants might have given an orchestrated chorus of groans at the harshness with which Treghues had chastised Carey for such a harmless re-mark. Even Treghues realized that he had gone a little too far, for he barked at them to be about their business and not stand about like cod's-heads.

Poor little get, Alan thought. Still, it's better him than me for a change, and he has been getting away with a lot lately.

"Don't stand there making gooseberry eyes at me, Lewrie," Treghues blustered. Alan realized he had raised his eyebrows in sur-prise at Carey's humiliation and Treghues considered it a reproof. "I doubt *you* know any Shakespeare at all, do you?"

"A little, sir," Alan replied, trying desperately to remember some.

"Let's hear it."

"Um, uh . . ."

"As I thought," Treghues said primly. "By the heavens, you're a rogering buck with no wit at all, aren't you? What was the last book you read? The guide to Covent Garden women? That Cleland trash?"

The last interesting one, yes, Alan had to admit, if only to himself. "A book, well, a chapbook really, about naval battles, sir."

"Who wrote it?"

"A man named Clerk, sir. A Scotsman. Avery's father sent it."

"A Navy officer?" Treghues asked sharply.

"No, I don't think so, sir, but it was a most interesting—"

"And I suppose you think that makes you equal to an admiral now, does it, just like this store clerk?"

"His *name* is Clerk, sir—"

"Fictional trash," Treghues sneered. "Bend your mind to your duties, sir! Take to heart what you read in the Bible this morning. Scotsmen, of all things!"

Since the morning's lesson had been from Genesis, there wasn't much that Alan could take to heart, unless he wished to re-create the human race, and he had already had a fair head start on that issue. Thankfully, Treghues turned away to more interesting things, allowing Alan to escape with a whole skin and to take refuge in what duties he could find.

He did not consider himself such a *great* sinner, not after all the examples in his life for comparison, so it was hard to reject the wave of self-pity that confronted him. When he had joined *Desperate*, even after a fatal duel for Lucy Beauman's honor, Treghues had not been so badly disposed toward him, not until that French gunner had smacked him with a rammer. There had been a time when Treghues had treated him fairly, decently, had thought him a 'comer.' To recognize that Treghues treated everyone oddly now was little consolation.

"Mister Lewrie," Railsford called from aft.

"Aye, sir?"

"Mister Cheatham requests your assistance with the ship's books in the holds. Do you attend him."

"Aye, sir, directly," Alan answered in relief.

Once below with their youngish purser in the bread room, Alan could relax a little, though he was sure that Cheatham had good reasons to despise him after his and Avery's escapade. But Cheatham put him at ease almost at once.

"The Jack in the Bread Room is aft in the rum stores at present, Mister Lewrie," Cheatham said. "We shall be opening a new cask of salt meat for noon issue and I need someone to attest as to its fitness."

"Aye, sir."

"Care for some beer?" Cheatham asked, waving a hand lazily at the keg in the corner.

"Beg pardon, Mister Cheatham, but Captain Treghues has me on water and ship's rations for the next ten days," Alan told him, licking his lips all the same. "After yesterday, I would not like to get either one of us in more trouble."

"Devil take it, Lewrie. Take a stoup," he commanded, which order Alan was only too happy to obey. He took down a wooden mug and poured himself a pint.

"Confusion to our foes, sir," Alan said, before taking his first sip.

"Hear, hear!" Cheatham acknowledged, tapping a pint for himself as well. "Now, Mister Lewrie, while we have some privacy, just what have you done that would turn the captain against you so badly?"

"I . . . I would rather that remain private, Mister Cheatham, sir," Alan said, wondering if he had to stand on the quarterdeck nettings and tell the whole world before they were satisfied. "It is not so much what I have done, but what has happened to Commander Treghues."

"I will allow that he has not been himself for the last month or so," Cheatham said, frowning between quaffs of beer. "There is a question as to whether he is in full possession of his faculties."

"Mister Cheatham, were we ashore in peacetime, Treghues would be confined to Bedlam, playing with his own spit." Alan grinned.

"No matter," Cheatham said. "He is our master and commander appointed over us by the Crown, and that is disloyal talk. Whether it is true or not," he concluded, ignoring his own remark, which could be taken for the same sort of disloyalty. "All of us . . . Mister Railsford, Peck, the sailing master, Mister Dorne . . . look you, Lewrie, you're a good sailor and you're shaping well as a sea officer. Before the captain's . . . misfortune . . . he thought well of you. It is without credence that he could turn on you so quickly without reason. You have friends in this ship, Lewrie, and we might be able to advert your good qualities to set aside whatever the captain has formed as to his opinion of you."

"David Avery did not speak to you, did he, sir?"

"Not recently, though he had expressed concern earlier," Cheatham said, closing the bread room door for more privacy and retaking a seat on a crate. "Perhaps I could be of some aid to you."

"On your word of honor that it goes no further, sir," Alan begged.

"I must discuss it with Mister Railsford, for one, but you may be assured of my discretion. My word on it," Cheatham assured him.

"I was accused of rape, sir," Alan began, feeling he had no one else to trust. He outlined how his father had snared him with his half sister Belinda, how he had been forced to sign away any hopes of inheritance from either side of the family, and to take banishment into the Navy.

"And you have no clue about your mother's side of the family, the Lewries?" Cheatham asked after listening to the tale.

"None, sir, save my mother's name . . . Elizabeth. They said her parents are still alive, but God knows where, or whether that's really true."

"Sounds like a West country name," Cheatham surmised. "I seem to have heard the name Lewrie before in some connection, but it does not have any significance at present. Tell me about her."

"She was supposed to have bedded my father, before he went off to Gibraltar in the last war, where he won his knighthood, but he left her with nothing," Alan said. "He always told me she was whoring before he came back and had died on the parish's expense. He found me in the poor house at St. Martin's in the Fields and took me in, and signed the rolls to claim me. I don't even know what she looked like."

"But you bear her maiden name."

"Aye, sir."

"So perhaps he did not marry her, but felt some remorse to learn that she had died in his absence and left him a boy child."

"Sir Hugo St. George Willoughby never had any remorse about anything, sir." Alan laughed without humor. "I remember a big man coming to claim me and taking me in a coach. First time I ever saw the inside of one. Next thing I knew I had the best of everything. Except for affection, that is."

Damme, I'm getting maudlin as hell just thinking about this, he thought, feeling a wave of sadness sweep over him such as he had not felt for two years.

"Perhaps you are worth something to somebody, else why keep you?"

"That might explain why I was set up with Belinda, and caught red-handed in bed with her by so many people, especially our solicitor and the parish vicar as well, sir!"

Alan thought a while. "You mean my mother's people may have had money?"

"No way to tell, not out here," Cheatham said. "But, my

brother works in the City, at Coutts' Bank. I could write him and let him make some inquiries on your behalf. If you were set up, as you put it, it would clear your repute with the captain and put your own mind to rest as well. If your father has recently come into money or land through your maternal side, that would be proof positive."

"It must be!" Alan was thrilled. "Why else would he send me off with an hundred guineas a year and force me to sign away inheritance on both sides? Sir Hugo never did anything that didn't show a profit. God, Mister Cheatham, if only you could do that! You don't know how miserable I have been, not knowing why I was banished. I admit I was a strutting little rake-hell. And given half a chance, I probably would be again, to be honest. But nothing as bad as they were, at any rate!"

"Then we shall attend to it directly." Cheatham smiled at him, and the smile automatically raised Alan's suspicions as to his motives. Damme, what's in it for him, I wonder? The life I've lived, there's no way to know when someone really means friendship, except for David.

"Um, I was wondering, sir, why would you . . ." he began.

"Because whether you can realize it or not, you have friends in this ship and in this world, Lewrie." Cheatham anticipated him: "Railsford thought you'd be squint-a-pipes about it. Do you really think yourself so base as not to be able to garner trust and friendship from others?"

"Yes, sir," he said without pausing to think, and felt his eyes begin to water with the truth of it. Until he had gotten into the Navy, he had never had a real friend, never had a word of approval from his father, his half-relations or tutors. Now here were people ready to make supreme efforts on his behalf to uphold his honor and good name—what there was of them—and go out of their way to settle all the nagging questions in his mind about his heritage. Too much was happening to keep his feelings in check.

"God, Mister Lewrie," Cheatham said, almost in tears himself, "I had no idea, my boy! Forgive me. You *do* have friends who care about you—not just people with influence who will be good for place or jobbery."

"I am beginning to realize that, sir." Alan shuddered. "Back home, there was no one I could turn to. Jesus!"

"What?"

"In a way this is so disgusting, sir." Alan smiled in self-depreca-tion. "Who would have thought that of all places, I would find . . . a home . . . in the bloody Navy! I've spent the better part of my service scheming to get out of it!"

"Why would you, when you're so deuced good at it?" Cheatham asked. "Oh, I suppose it is natural to be suspicious, growing up a London boy in such a household as you described, but there is good in this world, and you have some of it in you."

"A streak perhaps," Alan allowed. "A thin one, sir. I doubt I'll be buried a bishop."

"Who can say what you'll amount to?" Cheatham said, cuffing him on the head lightly. "No, I would not go so far as to say you could ever take holy orders. But you are who you make of yourself, not what others have told you you are. Think on what you have accomplished in the short time you have worn King's Coat—other than wenching and brawling your way through the streets of Charles-ton, of course. Consider the people you know that think well of you. You could not have earned their approbation without being worthy."

I don't know about all that, Alan thought. You've never seen me toady when I've my mind set on something. Still, there was the good opinion of Admiral Sir Onsley Matthews and his Lady Maude; also their lovely niece, Lucy Beauman, who was all but pledged to him. And then there were Lord and Lady Cantner, whose lives he had saved in the *Parrot*. There were probably as many others who hated the sight of him, but he wasn't particularly fond of those ei-ther, so to hell with them.

But with Railsford, Cheatham and, most likely, Dr. Dorne to improve his chances, and even Mister Monk's professional accep-tance as a seaman, and the willing cooperation of the other warrant and petty officers who took him at face value, there was suddenly a lot less to fear than he had thought. He took another deep draught of beer, and his prospects suddenly seemed that much brighter.

"I cannot tell you how much this means to me, sir," he told Cheatham. "I was despairing that I would be chucked onto the beach to starve if it was up to the captain alone. Maybe there's an answer in my past that would force me to think I'm someone better than the image I have formed of myself ere now. But I'm not betting on it, mind. What if I'm much worse than what I know of myself now?"

"That's our Lewrie," Cheatham said kindly. "As chary a lad who ever drew breath. Now let us take a peek into this salt beef cask to see if it's fit to eat, shall we?"

CHAPTER 2

O N the 25th of August, 1781, *Desperate* went in-shore once more, to Cape Henry in the Virginias, acting as the eyes of the fleet. Should she run into danger, there was another frigate with her with much heavier artillery to back her up, but being of deeper draft she wasn't much help close inshore.

"Passage'll be 'bout a mile off Cape Henry," Mister Monk said, referring to one of his heavily pencilled and grease-stained charts by the binnacle. He was partly teaching, partly talking aloud to himself. "Far enough offshore ta avoid the Cape Henry shoals, an' 'bout two mile off a the Middle Ground. Ya young gentlemen mark the Middle Ground? Silt an' sand shoal."

Forrester, Avery and Lewrie peered over his shoulder to mark it in their minds, while Carey, who was much shorter, wormed his way through to peek almost from Monk's capacious armpit.

"What about north of the Middle Ground, sir?" Carey asked, turning his gingery face up to their sailing master. "Up by Cape Charles?"

"No, main entrance is this'n, south o' the Middle Ground. To the north of it, ya'd never know how much depth ya'd have, wot with the scour. At high tide, ya might find a five-fathom channel, 'un then agin ya could pile her up on a sand bar in two, so deep draft merchantmen an' warships use the south pass. With our three-and-a-half fathom draft, we'd most like be safe up there, but anythin' big-ger'n a fifth rate'd spend a week gettin' off."

"It's big once you're in, though," Avery observed, looking at the chart past the entrance they were discussing.

"Like the gunner told the whore," Alan whispered.

"Let's keep our little minds on seamanship, awright Mister Lewrie?"

"Aye, Mister Monk, sir," Alan replied with an attempt at a saintly expression.

"Now look ya here," Monk went on, tapping the chart with a stub of wood splinter for a pointer. "Once yer in, there's Lynnhaven Bay. Un from Cape Henry ta Old Point Comfort, due west, mind ya, ya got deep water an' good holdin' ground. But—and mind ya this even better—from 'bout a mile north o' Point Comfort an' from there up ta these islands at the mouth o' the York River, ya got shoal water at low tide, and this shoal, they *think*, sticks out damn near thirty miles east, pointin' right at the heart o' the entrance. So ya can never stand too far in at low tide or on a early makin' tide without ya choose Lynnhaven Bay er bear off west-nor'west for the York, er up inta the bay itself."

"So the best places to base a fleet or squadron would be either in Lynnhaven Bay or in the mouth of the York, sir," Avery said.

"Right you are, Mister Avery, right you are."

"Which is why Cornwallis and his army have marched north from Wilmington in the Carolinas, to set up a naval base to control the Chesapeake." Alan said, marveling.

"Un right you are, too, Mister Lewrie." Monk beamed, proud of his students. "Either way ya enter, ya got ta choose Lynnhaven Bay, York River, er further up, but if ya take that route, ya gotta be aware o' this here shoal comin' outa the north shore o' the Gloucester Peninsula north o' the York, so that cuts yer choices down even more. I'd never stand in further than ten miles past Cape Henry afore choosin', and God help ya you ever do otherwise yerselves if yer ever in command o' a King's ship, Lord spare us."

"And there are no markers or aids to navigation?" Forrester asked.

"Nary a one, sir," Monk replied. "Mosta the shippin' roundabouts is shallow draft coasters an' barges ta serve all these tobacco wharfs on the plantations, er carryin' trade ta Williamsburg further up the James, so up ta now, there wasn't no need fer 'em. But, up the James er up the York, er way up the Bay, it's the world's best anchorage ta my thinkin' for a fleet."

"Then why haven't we set one up here before, sir?" Carey asked.

"There's not much ta the Continental navy, in spite o' that fight we had in the Virgins last month. Biggest threat was de Barras up in Newport, an' the North American Squadron covers them. Most o' the fightin' was around New York or down in the Carolinas. But now this bugger de Grasse is on his way here, we'll control the place."

"And with ships here in the Chesapeake, we'd be free to range from way up here on the Patowmac and Baltimore down to Norfolk and the entrance," Alan said, smiling. He could see what Clinton and Cornwallis had in mind. "We'd cut the communications from Washington and Rochambeau to his southern forces."

"A nacky plan, ain't it?" Monk said, as though he had thought of it himself. "So ya all look sharp as we work our way inta the bay, and y'll see the Middle Ground, all swirly like a maelstrom sometimes. Two leadsmen in the foremast chains by four bells o' the forenoon, now we're in soundin's. And we'll lower a cutter an' sound ahead, too, as we're comin' in on the ebb tide."

"Let me," Carey volunteered, almost leaping in eagerness.

"Aye, the boat's yours, Mister Carey. Ya put these younkers ta shame sometimes, so ya do!"

"And the leads, sir?" Alan asked.

"Do ya take yer copy o' the *Atlantic Neptune* an' place yourself in the foretop, Mister Lewrie. Mister Avery, y'll be with the hands in the forechains. Un Mister Forrester, I 'spect the captain'll wish ya ta be on the quarterdeck ta handle any signalin'."

"Aye, sir." Forrester said with a smug grin.

Desperate was ready for any trouble entering the bay. The hawse bucklers were removed and cable ready to run at bow and stern, both the best and second bowers seized to their lines, and a kedge and a stream anchor on the stern should she have to maneuver herself off a shoal with muscle power.

"Cape Henry, sir," Monk said to Treghues on the quarterdeck. "I'd feel better a point ta starboard if ya so mind, sir."

"Hands to the braces, stand by to wear a point to starboard!" Treghues shouted, then turned to Lieutenant Railsford. "Brail up the main course now and get a little way off her, but leave the tops'ls for now."

"Aye, aye, sir."

With guarded caution that to an outsider might still have seemed almost dashingly rash, *Desperate* made her way to the entrance, arrowing almost due west down the three-mile-wide channel, past the disturbed water of the Middle Ground, past the tip of Cape Henry into Lynnhaven Bay. Beyond, the Chesapeake was a sparkling sack of water, nearly devoid of shipping but for a few small British ships servicing the troops ashore, along with a large frigate, the *Charon*, a sloop of war just slightly smaller than *Desperate*, the *Guadeloupe* and some small armed cutters and store ships drafted from the coastal traffic.

Desperate finally idled close enough to *Charon* to be able to speak her, and from her commander Captain Symonds they discovered that the French were nowhere to be seen as of yet. There were some armed gunboats working further up the bay near Annapolis to keep some Continental infantry units from taking to the water in some homemade barges.

They also learned that Symonds and Cornwallis had rejected Old Point Comfort west of Lynnhaven Bay as the naval base. The bay would be too exposed to the coming hurricane season, and the land around Old Point Comfort was too low and marshy to be fortified—was barely two feet above high tide. A French ship, with her higher mounted guns, could drift right down on any battery established there and shoot it to pieces. Instead, Cornwallis would fortify the south bank of the York River just east of the town of York and the narrows at Gloucester Point. The land was much higher there, with steep bluffs to discourage any attempt to storm them, and batteries dug into the bluffs could return the favor to a ship of any force that attempted to get close enough for cannon fire. They would also be free of the marshes and their agues, and would have several choices of streams for fresh water if they had to hold out for any length of time.

So far, Cornwallis and his troops had had little trouble in these rebellious Virginias, raiding far west up toward Williamsburg and Jamestown, getting into one scrap on the James, but the enemy had been too daring and had tried to force a crossing into low marshland and forests right in the teeth of the field artillery and had gotten cut up badly. After scouring the neighborhood for victuals and harvesting what crops there were, the general was moving slowly back to Yorktown to begin his fortifications and was awaiting the arrival of the fleet into the bay. They had heard of the possible arrival of the French, and Clinton and Admiral Graves had promised to return troops south, so the possibilities were excellent for a grand battle which would not only destroy the French fleet in the Americas and knock them out of the alliance with the Rebels, but also destroy what men and guns that the Rebels were assembling from the south. Once what passed for an army in the Virginias was destroyed, the entire country was open to British troops as far west as the Appalachians, which would cut the rebellion in two. Symonds's news was electric, and reeking of confidence.

After a quick survey up north around the York River anchorages to be, *Desperate* wheeled about and made her way back out of the bay to carry the glad tidings to Admiral Hood and the Leeward Islands Squadron.

It was puzzling, all the same, to Lewrie, as to just where those French had gotten to, and he mentioned it to Lieutenant Railsford in the evening watch as their ship once more trailed the taffrail lanterns of the heavy units of the fleet, now on their way to New York to collect Admiral Graves and his line-of-battle ships.

"We have beaten them to the coast," Railsford commented.

"But what happens if the French are now busy retaking Charlestown and the Carolinas, sir?" Alan demanded, as much as a midshipman could make a demand upon a commission officer.

"The information all points to the Chesapeake," Railsford said, looking up at the set of the tops'ls that shone like eery shadow wings in the night. "So we must expect that the information is correct. Even if they did land south of us, they must know that their fleet could be bottled up in Charleston harbor and lost to the rest of the war effort. And it would only be a matter of time before our ships, with Admiral Graves's as well, and all of Cornwallis's army, would march or sail south and put them under the same sort of siege that won the place last year anyway. The Chesapeake is more vital at this moment, and closer for de Grasse to link up with de Barras's few ships in Newport. Like us, they could only stay on the coast until the equinox, and then have to flee back to the Indies, so here is the best place to effect something strategic. Cornwallis and his army is the magnet that will draw them, as it draws us."

"Well, sir, it seems to me that if de Grasse is behind us, then he could be sailing into the Chesapeake right now, and us none the wiser. Why not simply take our present fleet into the anchorage at the York River, or wait off the capes while we send a frigate to Admiral Graves and wait for him to arrive?"

"Because we would be only evenly matched without Graves and end up fighting a draw much like Arbuthnot did last year," Railsford said, grinning at Alan's efforts at strategy. "And if de Grasse came by way of Cape Francois, who is to say that he has not made combination with other French ships, or stirred those Dons out of Havana? They had ten sail of the line."

"By way of the Old Bahama Passage!" Alan was enthusiastic. "I thought that was the way they might come."

"But then we might be the ones outnumbered and overwhelmed," Railsford said.

"But if we cruised out to sea, sent frigates to scout, and could fall on the transports, even if we were outnumbered, we could cancel this de Grasse's plans overnight. If I were in charge, I'd... well, sir, *there* is a hopeful thought for you."

"You'd cost us the squadron," Railsford told him. "And then Graves would not have the force to do anything more. No, Cornwallis and his men and artillery can hold the bay while we assemble everything that floats to be sure we'll smash him when we come back. If he gains the bay while we are up north, then we can bottle him in anyway. He's most like brought troops as reinforcements, stripped the Indies to do it, and with him gone it'll be a year before the French could put together another fleet to send to the Caribbean, if then."

"Oh, that would be a different prospect entirely, sir," Alan said, seeing the wisdom of it.

"It's good practice, though, to use your mind as you have been doing. Good practice for when you really are an admiral, God help us." The first lieutenant chuckled.

"Now there's another hopeful thought indeed, sir!" Alan agreed.

Four bells chimed from the belfry; halfway through the evening watch on a dark night, as the moon waned further. Alan wandered to the lee rail of the quarterdeck and leaned on the bulwarks, for no one could see him there violating the rule that midshipmen never lean on anything, or slouch.

Someday when I'm an admiral. Alan gave a wry laugh. After we win this battle, the war will most like be over, so there won't even be time enough in service to gain my lieutenancy. I suppose the admirals we have at present know what they're doing, so there's no sense in my getting worked up about things. Still . . .

Somewhere out to leeward was a black shore, lost in the full darkness, and over the horizon from his vantage point. There was something nagging at him, but what he could not say; not fear this time such as he had felt when faced with the prospect of action against another ship. His role in this would be that of a properly enthusiastic spectator, then a paid-off veteran soon after—and that was about as valuable in England as a dead rat. Worse. One could always eat the rat and sell the pelt.

It finally came to him that Cornwallis's army could do nothing to stop the French from entering the bay and landing their armament, and that was what was bothering him. Even with only fourteen ships to face up to twenty-four French and Spanish liners, the real point was to deny the French an anchorage anywhere in the bay, and if it cost a squadron to do that, it would be worth it, for the army would still be in one piece, and whatever the French and Rebels put together in the way of field units would have been smashed or decimated before even stepping ashore.

The air was cool, almost chilly compared to the tropical climate Alan was accustomed to. He involuntarily shivered, and hoped it was merely the damp night that made him do so.

CHAPTER 3

EVEN if Alan Lewrie and his compatriot-in-crime David Avery had been blood relations to Commander Treghues, and in his best graces, they would have stood no chance for shore leave once *Desperate* anchored off New York. Alan thought New York a finer port for fun than Charleston, with its atmosphere seething with competing interests, the graft in military and naval stores, the spies and whispered confidences, and betrayals and the threat of the Rebel forces pending over all of it as if it were a besieged Italian city-state intent on survival in the time of the Borgias. It was a place that could turn a vicar into a pimp or fleshbroker and an honest man into a thief. It had most certainly turned many Loyalist women into grateful courtesans for the many handsome young men in uniform.

But Admiral Hood did not wish even to enter harbor, but anchored the fleet without the bar off Sandy Hook. However, the *Nymphe*, under Captain Ford, did cross the bar into the harbor, bearing despatches.

A flotilla of supply barges rowed out to them, but none of the many ships would be allowed out of discipline, pending a rapid assembly of the battle-worthy vessels of the North American Squadron, and an even more rapid return to the Chesapeake.

Boring, Alan decided, definitely boring. I've swung about out here before in the *Ariadne* and it was always deadly dull. And the way Treghues is acting lately, it's a wonder a boat full of clergy don't descend on us playing sad music, instead of us being allowed out of discipline.

"Bosun of the watch!" Railsford bellowed.

"Aye, aye, sir?"

"A boat for Mister Cheatham. Smartly now!"

Alan looked on hopefully, but it was Forrester who was entrusted with the duty of rowing their purser ashore. Cheatham shrugged eloquently at Alan by way of comiseration, but patted the large packet of letters he carried with him. So it was more than Alan's own letters to Lucy Beauman, Sir Onsley who was now ensconced in London with the Board of Admiralty and Lord and Lady Cantner. Cheatham was indeed posting a letter to his brother in London as well, regarding Alan's background.

The more Alan had thought of it since baring his soul to Cheatham in the bread room, the more he was certain that his father Sir Hugo had cheated him out of some sort of inheritance—nothing else made sense. Why else get him into Belinda's mutton and then entrap him with a ready-made pack of witnesses to force him to sign all those papers? He kicked himself for not asking for a copy to take with him. *Face it*, he thought, slapping his memory to life once more, you should have at least read most of them instead of merely scribbling your damn name to them.

He could console himself with the fantasy that somewhere in the near future Cheatham's brother would write back with proof positive of his father's perfidy, which he could dash into Treghues's leering face, at Captain Bevan and his master, Commodore Sir George Sinclair. They would fall all over themselves to take him into their good graces in atonement for their beastliness of the recent past. With their influence, and with the influence he had garnered from Lord Cantner and Admiral Sir Onsley Matthews, he would be well on his way to gaining that coveted commission, which would mollify Lucy's daddy and open all the doors to a peacetime future.

Interest was everything, if not second to outright jobbery and bribing his way to the top. Professional skill in ship-handling and seafaring were all right, but even the saltiest tarpaulin man could not advance without interest in those circles that abutted on the crusty older men at the Admiralty. Since he had so little interest as of yet, he was careful to curry to those he had.

May not make much difference anyway, he thought to himself. He must, according to the rules of thumb, be upwards of twenty, of two years' service as a midshipman or master's mate, and have been entered in ship's books for six years before he could even gain admission to an examination for his lieutenancy, and the war could end within a month after they beat de Grasse in the Chesapeake. Then where would he be in regards to Lucy Beauman?

Just the thought of her made him groan. She was so young, so delectably blonde, with startlingly blue-green eyes the color of a shallow West Indies lagoon. She idolized him, and each time he saw her, she had advanced just a bit closer to the softly feminine ideal of the age. She loved him openly and frankly. She was also as rich as Croesus; or her father was, which was much the same thing. And the match was not totally out of the question—if he cleared his name, if he made something of himself that her father would let in the front door, before someone more suitable came along. Or before Lucy met someone she liked better. It was a long sail to Jamaica, and she might as well be on the other side of the world at the moment.

Did he love her as well? He thought about that as he penned her long, continuous sea-letters. She was heart-stoppingly beautiful, desirable, sweet and unspoiled (in the biblical sense, at any rate). She was also his key to financial security after the war. No one else had ever fallen so head over heels in love with him (not anyone with that much chink). He had not had a major affair of the heart, having taken the usual route of paying silver for pleasure, or of taking advantage of house servants and country girls, just as any other young buck.

He felt something strong for her, but not knowing what love felt like as an emotion, he continually questioned it. He knew himself fairly well as a rake and a rogue, but this feeling for her was much greater than anything he had felt for a graceful neck, a well-turned ankle or a firm bosom. Yet damned if he could put a label on it. He puffed up with it when he wrote to her in short bursts between duty and sleep, and her rare letters filled him with pleasure and the passion of jealousy if she even mentioned another male. Frankly, her letters were only part delight, were misspelled so badly he could barely credit them—and damned if he could discover what was so fascinating about what she had worn to church or how her hair was fixed for a carriage ride, or how difficult it was to find a maid who could iron properly. Her latest screed had been a damnation of the French Navy, who seemed intent on denying her the right shade of blue ribbons, and a fervent wish that Alan would skewer all the bothersome pests as soon as dammit and let her get on with sartorial splendor.

So what if she's feeble? he asked himself. Most women are, when you get right down to it. That's not what they were created for. If I want someone to talk to about something that matters, I'll toddle off to a coffee house or a club. He remembered the night in London, just before a descent into the Covent Garden district for a run at the whores, when two educated men had almost come to blows at Ozinda's over whether women could be educated at all!

If one got a fortune and a termagant mort came with it, then one could always keep a mistress. In the better circles, which Alan fervently hoped he could soon rejoin, it was a matter of course that the wife was for breeding children, and the mistress for pleasure. The thought of domestic drudgery, of having to stay in and listen to the empty pratings of a woman night after night made Alan and most of his past friends shiver with dread.

God help the poor who have no outlets, he thought. And God help me should I turn out to be one of them.

No matter what happened, he had his reserve money—over two thousand pounds in gold coins lifted from their last prize, the *Ephegenie*. It was part of a much larger trove that had been hidden in a large chest in that ship's late captain's necessary closet. That gold was now deep within his sea chest, wrapped up in a discarded shirt so worn, mended, stained and daubed with tar that no one with any taste whatsoever would even look at it.

Ironically, he could not make much use of it, since to dig down to it would reveal its presence, and a midshipman's chest—even a locked one—was no safe place for anything. There were times that Alan regretted taking the money, and not settling for the roughly 125 pounds he would have received as a share out of the prize money once the main mass of coins—nearly 80,000 pounds—had been discovered. Admittedly those regrets were rare, but the thought had crossed his mind. Instead, he had to depend on the 100 guineas his father sent, and how long that arrangement would last, he had no idea, or any great hopes for in future.

His reveries were interrupted by seven bells chiming from the fo'c'sle belfry; eleven thirty in the forenoon watch. Almost immediately the bosun's pipes sang and the order was bellowed to "clear decks and up spirits." The hands lashed down their labors and queued up for their rum ration. Soon they would be allowed to go below to their dinner, while Alan would have to wait, his stomach already in full cry for sustenance. There was fresh food coming off-shore, but he would not share in it. There would be small beer and the last of the rum to savor for even the meanest hand, but he would not taste that fiery anodyne to the misery of a seagoing life.

"Lucky Forrester," Avery said, standing by the rum cask with the purser's assistant as the rum was doled out.

"He wouldn't know what to do with time ashore," Alan said.

"Might take two guineas to find a girl that'd let him put the leg over her."

"And she'd have to be beef to the heel, at that," Alan added.

"This is grievous to me," Avery said, looking at the rum.

"No grog fer ye today, sir?" the purser's assistant asked, waving a measure about toward them, knowing full well the captain's instructions and delighting in having power over the midshipmen in this regard.

"No, thank you," Avery said stiffly. "Carry on."

He and Alan made their way aft to the quarterdeck, unable to bear the sight of the hands smacking and savoring their liquor.

"Lots of activity," Alan said, indicating the fleet about them. "Damme, look there. Is that a load of lumber going into *Terrible?*"

"Lots of spare rope, too," Avery said, picking up an unused brass telescope. "I swear her masts look sprung. See what you think."

Alan took the glass and aimed it at *Terrible*. The third rate seventy-four did indeed appear badly worn, her masts slanted from the more usual slight forward rake. Except for closing with *Barfleur* a couple of times or sailing close to another, larger frigate, *Desperate* had been far out to windward from the fleet for the most part of their passage, unable to see much as to the condition of their fleet.

"Come to think on it, David, half of them appear they've just

come through a major storm. There's not a ship present that looks
well set up."

"Then I sincerely pray the French look just as bad," David said,
taking the glass back. "We seem more due a refit than a battle."

"We're more at sea than the French, usually—their big ships at
least." Alan was repeating common knowledge. "But what's this
delay in aid of? I should have expected this Admiral Graves to come
boiling without the bar at once and get us on our way. God knows
what the French are up to while we stew here. Any idea who he is
anyway?"

"Lord North's cousin, I am told." David said sourly.

"Is he, God save us!" Alan shuddered.

"Who knows, he may actually be good," David said, placing the
telescope back in the rack by the binnacle. "You know how people
feel back home. They wouldn't do a damned thing for the Hanover
Crown or the government unless they're damned near bribed by
promises of graft and jobbery. I expect they considered themselves
lucky to get anyone at all, the way all the so-called fighting admirals
have retired to their estates to sit this war out. It's not popular in the
first place, even if the government was, which it's not."

"This factionalism will do for us one of these days," Alan remarked.

"We were lucky to get Hood and Rodney together with one fleet
for a while. I'd feel better with Rodney back out here, but . . ."

"Once he clears all his creditors, perhaps he shall come."

"How many ships did Mister Railsford say de Barras had up in
Newport?" David asked suddenly.

"Eight sail of the line, I think," Alan answered. "Why?"

"What if he and de Grasse combine in the Chesapeake?"

"Then we smash both of them together," Alan said firmly.

"Perhaps Graves cannot leave New York uncovered. We might
have wasted our time coming to him for assistance. God, I wish we
were both post captains right now," David said, with some heat.
"This not knowing anything is driving me to distraction."

"Don't believe that the post-captains know much more than we
do now," Alan cautioned. "All we have to do is fight. They'll point
us at the foe like a gun and all we have to do is discharge at the right

time. We shall either do something glorious, or look like a complete pack of fools—so what is there to worry about?"

"God, you are an unaware bastard," David said, grinning and shaking his head in wonder at his friend's attitude.

"I dare say," someone drawled, and they spun about to see if the captain had caught them at their speculations. David pointed to the open skylight over the captain's quarters.

"Oh, damme," Alan whispered.

"I shall be on deck directly, and I trust I shall see two midshipmen doing something more profitable with their time than second-guessing their betters!"

"Aye, aye, sir," David called back as they made their escape to the bows, far away from that disembodied voice before Treghues made good on his threat.

"Now will you look at that!" Alan exclaimed. "Mister Avery, will you join me on the foredeck? Look at the state of that carronade slide. Not enough grease to let it run freely, I swear!"

"Thank you," David whispered. "I was about to remark on the forebraces, and there's nothing wrong with them."

"Summat amiss, sirs?" Tulley, the new gunner's mate asked them as he ascended to the bow chase guns to join them. He was a recent replacement for poor Mister Robinson, who had been shot in the knee and discharged a cripple from his position a bare three weeks before in their fight with the Continental Navy brig-of-war *Liberty*. Tulley was too new in his berth and warrant to feel safe even with midshipmen, especially in a ship run by a seeming lunatic, and was as nervous as a cat to be found lacking for the slightest excuse.

That was the main reason he did not treat the midshipmen with the usual patient disdain that was the customary usage of human existence, and The Fleet. He was also big, bluff and hearty, a plug of oak with flaming ginger hair and a permanently sun-baked complexion. He had, so far, appeared no brighter than he had a right to be.

"Might have a word with the quarter-gunner about this slide," Alan said. "The captain said he would be on deck directly."

"Aye, thankee, Mister Lewrie," Tulley quailed. "Did he, by God? Mister Sitwell? Call yerself a quarter-gunner an' roon one a my guns fer the lack o' some tallow?"

"Me, Mister Tulley?" the quarter-gunner barked, deeply offended.

As Alan and David waited for their own meal to begin, drab as it promised to be, they could delight in hearing Tulley berate the offending Sitwell, hear Sitwell roar for Hogan the carronade gun captain and pass on the grief. By the time Treghues appeared on deck, he was drawn to the ado and paid no attention to them as they betook themselves below out of danger.

"That is one thing I absolutely love about the Navy sometimes, David," Alan said as they sat down to their dinner. "You can stir up such a shitten storm for other people over the slightest trifles."

It was later, during loading of stores scared up by Cheatham from the warehouses, that the wind shifted into the east and began to blow dead foul for any of Admiral Graves's ships to work their way down harbor and cross the bar to seaward.

They spent three more days swinging at their anchors, gazing at the shore with fond regard and wondering what was to occur before the wind at last veered favorable and the signal to weigh broke out on the flagship, Admiral Graves's ninety-gun second rate, *London*.

Treghues had gleaned a little information from other captains, and had passed it on down the chain of command, and by the time it had reached the midshipmen's mess, it was frankly disturbing.

The frigate *Richmond* had come in from the Chesapeake on the twenty-ninth with the information that so far no French ships were anywhere near the bay.

De Barras in Newport had sailed—no one knew where, but it did not take an educated guess to discern the final destination. De Barras had transports with him, and the French had nearly 5,000 troops around Newport, with heavy siege artillery. Should he combine with de Grasse, that would make up to a supposed twenty-two French ships to face theirs.

And they would only be nineteen ships of worth. The North American Squadron could contribute no more than five, since the *Robust* was in the careenage undergoing repair, and the *Prudent* was lacking spars and masts enough to sail.

Admiral Graves brought out *London, Bedford, Royal Oak, Amer-*

ica and *Europe*—the *Europe* so in need of careenage and repair herself that the fifty-gun fourth rate *Adamant* also joined the fleet to take *Europe's* place if she had to drop out, and that would leave a dangerously weak gap in the line if *Adamant* faced a line of battle ship, for she was more suited to commanding a light cruising flotilla than fighting a major battle in the line. She was an over-sized cruiser, not meant for heavy punishment.

"Now what's he signaling," Treghues snapped, pacing the deck in a fit of nervous energy. "Mister Carey?"

"Um . . ." Carey fumbled with his slim signals book and a telescope nearly as tall as he was. "Can't quite make it out, sir. The flags are blowing away from us."

"That is what the repeating frigate is for, young sir," Treghues reminded him sternly. "Now what is the signal?"

"'Engage the enemy more closely,' sir?"

"Does that make sense even to you?" Treghues replied. "Where is the enemy in the first place?"

"Uh, no, sir." Carey blushed, turning red with embarrassment.

"Those two flags together, in Admiral Rodney's signals book, *are* 'Engage the enemy more closely,'" Railsford prompted from the sidelines, "but in Admiral Graves's system, they mean . . ."

Carey tumbled to his mistake and almost dropped the telescope in his haste to fetch out the proper sheet of signals. "'Make easy sail,' sir," he said, with an audible gasp of relief.

"Now this one," Treghues said, as a new hoist went up their flagship's yards. "You, Lewrie."

"'For *Solebay*,' sir, 'Captain Everitt.'" Alan was reading even before the frigate named in the signal hoisted a reply. Immediately a second hoist was made on the *London*. "'Proceed ahead to leeward,' sir."

"Is that what you think, Mister Forrester?" Treghues asked.

"Um . . . I *believe* that is correct, sir," Forrester replied, most unsure of himself, but not wishing to grant Lewrie any competence.

"Hah . . . hmm," Treghues said, slapping his hands into the small of his back and stalking off toward the starboard gangways.

"Wish to God we were using our own signal book and not Admiral Graves's version," Railsford muttered, taking off his hat to smooth back his hair. "We have the more ships, so it would only be fair. This is confusing in the extreme."

"Only natural," Alan whispered to Avery, "the Navy's spent the last two years confusing the devil out of me!"

"There's another hoist!" Treghues cried, coming back aft in a rush. "Last miscreant to read it gets to kiss the gunner's daughter."

"'To *Barfleur*,' sir," Alan said quickly as soon as he saw the single flag. "'Send boats.'"

All of them stumbled out almost at once in their haste to avoid a caning. A second flag had appeared.

A third, explanatory hoist went up *London*'s yards. Alan read it as number forty-eight, which would be . . . "I am sinking"? Couldn't be, he thought. But maybe it could be. No, maybe it's ninety-eight. That's . . . "Take on excess supplies."

"'Take on excess supplies,' sir!" Alan was beaming, glad to be the first to answer, but barely ahead of Avery, who gave the same answer barely ahead of Carey, who did the same barely before Forrester began to say something else and ended up not saying anything at all, merely flapping his lips like a boar at a slop trough.

Treghues had promised a caning and he could not play favorites in public. Forrester got the gentle attention of the bosun's strong arm for a half-dozen with a stiffened rope "starter," after which Treghues decided that signals lessons were over for the day. Forrester looked absolutely betrayed and aggrieved, which pleased them all to no end, and he grumbled that he would get his own back.

For all the urgency with which they had finally departed New York, the cruise down the coast of America was remarkably leisureable. The line of major warships made no more than four or five knots during the day, taking in sail during the night to crawl even slower, while the frigates dashed ahead and dashed back to report what little they saw, stirring about like cockroaches scuttling around a parade of snails.

The time passed as it always did in the Fleet; hands up to scrub decks, lash up hammocks and stow, breakfast, gun drill in the forenoon, rum issue and dinner. Sail drill, fire drill, evolutions for passing cable, musket practice and cutlass drill. Evening quarters, down hammocks and more rum before supper. Stand down the overhead lookouts, lights out and sleep. All the mind-numbing routine of a ship of war that ground the men down to mere numbers and parts of a watch, a division, until they could act without thinking at all—there was punishment in the forenoon watches for those slow to learn. Perhaps for a little relief there would be music and exercise in the second dogwatch, a little make-and-mend in the fresh air after the sun had lost some of its heat; fiddles and tin whistles and bare-footed young men dancing hornpipes because they were young and strong and still full of energy. Not that they did not think about things to come anyway, when given half a chance. There were too many warlike preparations to be ignored, like all the extra cartridge bags that the sailmaker and his crew were making up for the master gunner, Mister Gwynn, and his mate Tulley; why gun drill was a touch more earnest than usual and the men practiced leaping from one battery to another as though they might be called to fire on both beams at once; the rasp of the grindstone from dawn to dusk putting wickedly keen edges on cutlass blades, pike points, bayonets, board-ing axes and officers' swords. For those that were well churched, there was a lot of muttering over prayer books and Bibles. Those that could read and write—perhaps a third of the crew—wrote letters, just in case, and wrote last notes for the others less fortunate. Dr. Dorne, his apothecary assistant and the loblolly boys brought out the stretchers and carrying boards and refitted them, a most ominous sign, and when Dorne went to the armorer to have his surgical tools honed, everyone shrank away nearly in terror.

"I can make out Cape Henry, sir!" Forrester bawled down from the foremast cross-trees high in the rigging. "*Solebay* is closing the shore!"

"Very well," Treghues said in a conversational tone that could not have carried much further than his immediate circle. He was turned out in his best uniform coat, as advised by Dr. Dorne, and dressed in clean white shirt, neck-stock, waistcoat and breeches. His fingers drummed on the hilt of his ornate smallsword.

Desperate and *Solebay* were in advance of the fleet line of battle. *Desperate* was flying everything she could from aloft to keep up with the larger frigate in order to serve as the communications link between *Solebay* and *London*. Even with her deeper draft, Captain Everitt's ship had been selected to lead, since Everitt knew the Chesapeake well and had aided Cornwallis and Symonds in selecting the proposed fleet anchorage on the York River.

Alan caught himself yawning, his jaws creaking with the effort to keep them shut. He had been in the middle watch, and had not had much of a chance for any rest after the morning call for deck scrubbing and dawn quarters. He had been lucky to get below long enough to choke down some gruel and change into clean linen and silk stockings. Dorne advised that silk was easier to extract from leg wounds than cotton. He shrugged to settle himself more comfortably into his waistcoat and jacket.

He had seen men yawn before battle; a sure sign of fear and nervousness, he had been told, and he wondered why he was affected in such a manner. *Desperate* would be little more than an observer, and they would be safe as babes in bed, unless something disastrous occurred.

Am I frightened, or just excited by the thought of battle? he asked himself. God knows I've seen enough blood and powder to last me a lifetime. This should be mere rote by now.

Still, the news about de Barras, the lack of information about the whereabouts of de Grasse and the seeming poor condition of their fleet, all contributed to his anxiety. He had read the Fighting Instructions and then once more perused Clerk's little booklet and had gotten a glimmer of something beyond simple tactics and the movement of a single ship of war.

I was better off before, not knowing how much goes into this sort of endeavor, he thought. I am as nervous as a virgin at a hiring fair and I am certain Graves, Hood and Drake are ready to jump out of their skins in comparison. Hah. Even given the chance, I would not have gotten a wink of sleep for worrying today.

He yawned again, and his jaw muscles shot pain down his neck as he tried to restrain himself once more. Let's get it over with! Anything but this miserable ignorance and waiting for doom to come.

He turned to study how the other officers on the quarterdeck were comporting themselves. Monk was doodling on one of his personally marked charts, humming a tune to himself softly. Treghues was a study in self-control, languidly seated on the nettings and railing over the waist and only the movement of his fingers on his sword hilt betraying concern. Lieutenant Railsford was rocking back and forth on the balls of his feet, passing his brass speaking trumpet from one hand to another. Peck, the marine officer, was making bubbling noises through flaccid lips, totally unaware of his actions.

Trust the bullocks to show great calm, Alan thought with secret delight, nudging David to turn and witness Peck's behavior.

"If he had a beard, he'd be eating it," Avery japed softly.

"Signal from *Solebay*, sir!" Forrester screeched. "'Enemy in sight'!"

"Oh, shit," Alan whispered.

"Oh," Treghues said, getting to his feet, but otherwise showing no emotion. "Mister Avery, repeat that signal, will you."

"Aye, aye, sir!"

"Can you see any ships from the masthead?" Treghues bawled, his hands cupped around his mouth.

"No, sir!" Forrester replied, his voice breaking with the effort. "Lots of bare trees, sir!"

"Damned foolishness," Treghues sniffed.

"Settlers here 'bouts strip pine trees, sir." Monk commented, going to the captain's side. "Then they fires the slash 'round the base ta smoke the tar out while they're still standin'. Mayhap that's what they sees."

"Perhaps," Treghues said, nodding. "Has the signal been acknowledged?"

"Aye, sir," Avery answered.

"Very good," Treghues said. Judkin, his steward, came on deck to bring Treghues a mug of something to drink and he sipped at it thoughtfully, looking up at the rigging. "Mister Railsford, we shall stand on to the capes as long as *Solebay* does, but I would admire if you reduced sail. Get the stuns'ls off her to begin with."

"Aye, aye, sir. Topmen aloft! Trice up and lay out to take in stuns'ls!"

"Might as well strip down to all plain sail," Treghues said casually. "Get the royals off her, too."

"Aye, sir," Railsford agreed, anxious to be doing something other than stand around and fidget, and glad for some hard toil to take the men's minds off the possibility of battle as well.

"Signal from *Solebay*, sir!" Forrester howled.

"Speak, thou apparition!" Treghues barked back, almost in good spirits, making Alan wonder just what it was that was in that drink and wanting some if he did not have to sell his soul to the devil to get it.

"Enemy is French, sir!"

"Well, I sincerely doubt it would be the Prussians!" their captain erupted, which brought a welcome bout of laughter to the decks to loosen the tension.

"De Barras, do you think, Mister Monk?" Alan asked their sailing master as he sharpened a piece of charcoal for a marker.

"That lot from Newport?" Monk surmised, speaking heavily. "Mayhap. They sailed 'round the twenty-fifth, so they'd have plenty o' time ta get here by now. Iffen they is, we're gonna have 'em fer breakfast."

"Sir!" Forrester shouted down once more. "The count is twenty-eight sail of the line!"

"God's teeth, Mister Monk." Alan said. "It's the entire French Navy!"

"Repeat the signal, whether it is accurate or no, Avery."

"Aye, aye, sir."

As they closed with the coast, *Solebay* continued to feed them news. There was a large group of ships anchored in Lynnhaven Bay, identified for certain as warships. There were three flagships present, one the gigantic three-decker first rate of over one hundred guns, de Grasse's reputed flagship, the *Ville de Paris*. But as of yet, none was stirring.

Having gotten as close as they dared to the entrance, *Solebay* finally hauled her wind and came about back toward them, which required *Desperate* to tack as well in order to retire toward the tops'ls of their own fleet on the northeast horizon.

"This shall be a grand opportunity," Treghues said, almost capering like a young seaman about the quarterdeck. He was so energetic he reminded Lewrie of the Treghues he had known when he first signed aboard. Still, it sounded more like a good opportunity to get a lot of men killed. But, Alan realized, Treghues was odd enough to regard his own crucifixion as a blessed event.

"The tide is making, and with this nor'easter breeze, they'll not make it out past the Middle Ground or the Cape without a lot of short tacking. Some will run aground or foul each other." Treghues explained the situation happily. "We have but to fall on their van and chop it to bits as they emerge, throwing the rest into total confusion."

"We have trapped them," Forrester said, once more restored to the deck and the presence of his mentor. "It shall be a glorious day!"

"Indeed it shall, my boy. We shall shatter a French fleet, snap up their transports and all their artillery, crush them between Cornwallis and ourselves and eliminate the French either on land or sea in the Americas. Not only will this rebellion finally be confounded, but the Indies shall lie open to us with one stroke."

Desperate came within sight of the fleet later that morning, and it was impressive to see those nineteen great beasts rocking along under all plain sail in perfect alignment. *London* signaled for an early meal so that galley fires could be doused long before battle was joined, and *Desperate*'s crew tumbled down to their mess deck with a hearty appetite. In honor of the occasion, Treghues relented in his firm instruction concerning Avery and Lewrie, and they were allowed the last of the fresh bread and some not-quite-rancid butter to accompany their salt pork and peas, washing it down with a glass or two of wine for the first time in days. They toasted victory noisily.

But it took time, time to move that line of ships across the sea at six knots, time to align the formation perfectly, with the thrilling signal flag for "Form line of battle" flying from *London*. Still in the lead, *Solebay* reported that the French were scurrying to ferry their crews back aboard from duties ashore, and were cutting their cables and making sail. As the tide began to ebb and flow outward, they began to get under way, now not so limited in their ability to make the open sea. The French van was not in any particular order; it looked like a panicky scramble to escape the confines of the bay before being penned into it.

Alan was still yawning, this time from lack of sleep and the fumes of the wine he had imbibed with his dinner. He longed, though, to have the use of a telescope to see just how disordered the French were. Even from the deck it did not resemble a fleet so much as an informal regatta of small boats all trying to beat their way into the same narrow channel. Some of them were moving, some were dead still with their sails hanging limp as old rags, winded by the more weatherly vessels and unable to gain enough air to do much more than maintain steerage way. To everyone, it looked as if the French were offering their van up for destruction.

"God," he muttered, "this is going to indeed be glorious, and I can't see a tenth of it. This is going to be worth all the canings and cant, all the humbug and the stupidity!"

Desperate was to windward, almost due east of the capes, and even without a glass, they were close enough on the disengaged side of the fleet to see that *Alfred,* one of Hood's ships in their own van, was just about to enter the passage between Cape Henry and the Middle Ground.

"Signal from the flag, sir," Avery called.

"Damme, what is this now?" Monk cried with as much pain in his voice as if he had just been run through.

"'Wear together to the port tack due east'!" Avery shouted, unable to believe what he was seeing.

"Goddamn my eyes, that can't be the signal!" Railsford bustled to read the hoist himself.

"I should think you should know my feelings best about people who blaspheme, Mister Railsford," Treghues said, chiding him harshly.

"Sorry, sir, but this puts me beyond all temperance."

"He's letting them come out!" Alan fumed, beside himself with the sense of a sterling opportunity lost forever.

"Of course he is," Treghues said. "Admiral Graves is not rash enough to put his own ships in peril on the Middle Ground. He is letting at least their van exit the passage, where we shall fall upon them. Why fight in the mud flats and shoals around the Middle Ground?"

"Because that is where the enemy is, sir," Alan observed, without thinking, lulled by Treghues's too-good mood of the morning.

"Ah, you alone know better how to handle fleets, I see," the captain said with a bitter relish, back to his usual self once more. "You are criticizing the officers appointed over you by the Admiralty and the King, but then, you always know best, do you not, Mister Lewrie."

Oh, fuck it, Alan thought. I shall not knuckle under this time. And I shall not run in fear of speaking my own opinions for any man, even if it costs me. After a moment's reflection however, and the realization that he was dealing with one of God's prime loonies, he tempered his resolution.

"Would it not be better to bear down on him at this instant, sir, and smash his van now?" Alan asked, trying to couch his complaint as a question to be answered in the reasonable tone with which it was offered. "Once the van is thrown into disorder, the center shall have to bear away and end up on the Middle Ground or the shoals around Cape Henry, would they not, sir?"

"And violate the Fighting Instructions?" Treghues asked contemptuously. "One never breaks the unity of the line of battle until the foe is flying. To bear down we must needs break the line, wind our own ships as they are doing and overlap our fire. With you in command, we would lose the fleet. How foolish and precipitate you are."

"Impatience o' the young, sir," Monk chortled, trying to defuse the captain's evident anger.

"Thoughtlessness of the headstrong," Treghues countered. "But Mister Lewrie does a lot without considering the consequences, do you not, Mister Lewrie?"

"I have never done anything without forethought, sir." Alan spoke back gently, trying to allay the hell he was expecting to catch. Damme, there was never a truer word spoken! How often can I damned near get my arse knackered since I was out of swaddles without scheming and planning to get anything out of life?

"You are swaggering deuced close to open insolence, sir!"

"I truly mean no disrespect, sir," Alan said.

"Do you not, sir!"

"The fleet is coming about, sir," Railsford reminded Treghues, who was lost in the passion of his pet.

"Very well, hands to stations to wear to larboard," Treghues said, reluctant to leave the subject, but forced to by duty.

The next two hours, until about four in the afternoon and the start of the first dogwatch, were almost heartbreaking to witness.

The fleet took up the new course due east, Hood's strong division now the rear of the battle line, with Drake's few ships as the van, backing and filling. Given the grace period, the French were beginning to sort themselves out into a line-ahead of their own, the van now in perfect order. Their center was beginning to exit the bay, and the milling rear division was also sorting itself out of chaos as well.

Desperate was by then near the head of the British line, with the ships of Admiral Drake, almost on the beam of *Shrewsbury* the leader. She backed and filled as well to maintain rough station well in sight of the divisional flag in *Princessa* and in sight of *London* far to the rear. Finally, when it seemed hours too late, Graves signaled to bear down and engage the opposite ships. But for some reason he left the signal for 'Form line of battle' hoisted as well.

This resulted in all ships turning slightly to starboard to bear down on a bow-and-quarter-line oblique approach, what Clerk's booklet told Alan was named a "lasking approach." Since the fleets were converging at a slight angle already, the vans would come together first, then the centers, and the rear divisions in both fleets would remain out of contact or gun range til late in the day, unless something was ordered to change it.

It was a daunting prospect to see all twenty-eight enemy ships in one ordered line-ahead, a line much longer than theirs, with many more guns ready to speak thunders; a line that they could not match ship for ship as usual practice, for the French could bring more ships from the rear to double on them once they were engaged.

Alan was on the gun deck with his men when the first ships tried firing at the range of random shot. He could not see anything below the bulwarks and the gangways, aching as he was to witness what would transpire. All he could see were masts and sails and then growing clouds of powder smoke as more and more ships began to trade broadsides. *Desperate* was at quarters, the men swaying easily by their light nine-pounder guns, which in this battle would be as useful as spit wads at thirty paces. No matter how stiff the discipline, everyone craned his neck for a view, or took little excursions atop the gun barrels or the gangways when the officers were not watching them. Even upwind of the fighting, though, Alan scented the powder smoke and saw the grimy gray-tan wall of smoke climbing higher than the liners' masts and cross-trees. Hiding himself behind the thick trunk of the mainmast, Alan furtively scrambled up on the jear bitts, his favorite vantage point, so that his head was above the line of the bulwarks and hammock nettings. The sight that met his eyes filled him with awe.

"What do you see, Lewrie?" Carey called out below him, hopping up and down in excitement.

"God, what a sight," Alan breathed. "It's glorious, it truly is! They're all in range for good practice now—Drake's ships and the French van. You can see only the topmasts and tops'ls of the Frogs, now and then a stab of flame from a gun barrel through the smoke. Our ships are so full of powder fumes they look like they're on fire!"

As the officers aft were too busy with their telescopes to care if anyone was standing still like a draft horse, Lewrie reached down and lifted Carey into place with him.

"Good Lord in Heaven!" Carey exclaimed in wonder. "Oh, I shall remember this all the days of my life."

The cannonading increased in fury and volume as he spoke and more ships came within range, and the guns slammed and boomed and barked in an unending storm of fire and metal. As far as they both could see, there were many ships—a forest of ships—with their courses brailed up to avoid the risk of flames, their tops'ls shot through like rags, upper masts hanging drunkenly here and there in both dueling lines of battle. The air quivered with the shock of broadsides, rattling their internal organs, setting their lungs humming with the power and terror of modern warfare. In the British line closest to them, they could witness shot ricocheting off the sea and raising tall waterspouts, could see hard-flung iron balls smashing home to tear loose clouds of paint chips, wood splinters and spurts of ingrained dust and dirt, striking great sparks when encountering metal and shattering on impact with something as solid as themselves.

"The French line is much longer, isn't it," Carey said, tears of passion streaking his smutty face. "Why does not Admiral Hood engage back there?"

"They might double on him if he did," Alan said. "They could cut across the end of his line to windward and fall back down to fight on both sides of his ships at once. Perhaps he is waiting for them to try, and he will rake them across their bows when they turn up."

"Alan," Carey said, suddenly dead serious. "I know that war is a terrible thing. But is it so terrible that it is wrong to feel as though we are seeing something grand?"

"I don't think so, it's what they pay sailors for," Alan japed.

"So it would not be wrong to say that I love this?" Carey pressed.

"No." Alan smiled. "I confess I love it, too."

"Good, 'cause so do I," Carey said fiercely.

"Mind you, young Carey, I only say that because we are not being shot at personally," Alan admitted wryly. "You can cheer all the fame and honor and glory you like when you're seated in the balconies."

Men were dying over there, ships were slowly being torn asunder by the shocking weight and power of iron; gun carriages were being overturned and their crews pulped in agony, riven by splinters or swatted dead like flies. The hideous reality was, however, over there, and not here in the *Desperate*, and even with prime examples of butchery not a month in the past to use as an example and a warning, Lewrie could not deny the fact that he was choking up with a pride he had never expected to feel in the Service. His eyes were moist and hot, his throat tight with emotion.

Marine captain Osmonde back in *Ariadne* was right, he decided grimly. This is brutal and bloody and cruel and horrible, and it can eat a man up but I swear to God above that I truly do love it! They have made me into a sailor, damn them all, and now I shall make an officer of myself if I live to accomplish it.

Shrewsbury, lead ship of all the British line, came reeling out of battle, surrendering her place of honor as she could no longer maintain control over herself. Her rigging was shot to pieces so badly that she had barely a shred of sail aloft. Her gangways and bulwarks on her engaged side were pockmarked and shattered with shot holes, the oak stained black with spent gunpowder. *Desperate*'s people gave her a rousing cheer as she retired, having done all she could do. Sadly, *Intrepid,* the next ship in line, looked in about the same poor condition; her rudder hanging in tatters from her stern posts, she was being steered by relieving tackle below decks, but she still fought. Next, *Princessa* was missing her main topgallant mast and the spanker over the quarterdeck. Her lower shrouds were shot through, threatening the stability of her masts as she rolled. *Ajax,* to her rear, had hardly any top hamper left, and *Terrible* was listing noticeably, her lower gunports dangerously close to the water, and her foremast spiralled back and forth as though it would go by the board at any moment. The other ships astern of her could barely be made out in the pall of smoke.

But there was Hood's rear division, now almost dead astern of *Desperate,* nowhere near firing range, maintaining a maddening line ahead and showing no eagerness to engage, almost parallel to the French line.

"Why does he not bear down," Lewrie said, almost wringing his hands in frustration. "Damme, he's throwing away the last chance we have."

"Get down from there, now," Mister Gwynn suddenly ordered, up from his magazines to survey the battle with the freedom his warrant gave him. "Set a good example for the hands, Mister Lewrie."

"Aye, Mister Gwynn," Alan replied.

"Twas this very way with Byng in the last war in the Mediterranean," Gwynn commented as softly as he could once he had strolled aft by Lewrie and young Carey. "Back when I was a raw rammer man. The way sea battles are. Half the ships never get a chance ta fire a shot."

"You'd think there was a better way." Alan complained. "To bear down and break through the other line or something."

"Not for the likes of us to say, Mister Lewrie."

"Goddamme, what a waste."

"War mostly is a waste," Gwynn grunted, cutting himself a plug of tobacco to cram into his cheeks. "Anythin' that takes a man outen a woman's bed and away from easy reach of a bottle *is* a waste, to my thinkin'."

By half after six in the evening, Cape Henry was far astern and almost under the horizon. The action still raged, though the broadsides were becoming very ragged and slow, the gun crews decimated and stunned into numb exhaustion from the continual roar and the shock of horror piled upon horror on those gun decks.

It was also possible that ships were running low on powder and shot; a battle that long would have emptied *Desperate*'s magazines hours before.

They had not fired a shot themselves, but had stood down from quarters after rendering what aid they could to the crippled *Shrewsbury*. Alan rotated to signals duty on the quarterdeck as cold food was issued, and small beer or American spruce beer was passed liberally to quench the dry throats among the crew.

With a better vantage point, Alan noted that the worst-damaged French ships were able to slip away to leeward to allow fresh vessels to take their place from that reserve in the rear, still untouched by Hood, who had not budged from his role of disinterested spectator. Alan felt a cold anger seething in his breast at an act which he could only describe as that of the ultimate poltroon. He lifted his telescope to see better as the light began to fade. *London* was not looking good, nor did any British ship that had managed to engage, and Alan could imagine the letter of rebuke that Graves would send Hood once he had a chance.

There was something different about the *London*—what was it?

"Signal is down, sir!" he shouted, having discovered what was missing.

"Watch her closely," Treghues said, almost at his elbow. Alan took a sideways glance at his young captain and was shocked. Treghues looked a dozen years older. He was gray in the face and barely a shadow of himself. He held his mouth in a bitter arc of disapproval, and Alan felt that for once the displeasure he evinced was not toward him personally, but toward the entire conduct of the day.

About five minutes later a single flag hoist went up a halyard, a blue and white checkered flag. Lowering his telescope, Alan consulted the short list to find the meaning. "Goddamn and blast," he whispered sadly, almost drained of emotion or the ability to be surprised by anything. "Signal, sir: 'Discontinue action.' Yeoman, hoist a repeat on that."

"I see," Treghues said. "Thank you, Mister Lewrie."

There was no groan of disappointment heard on *Desperate*, no low curses or signs of reaction. Perhaps men slumped just a bit more on hearing the import of that one colored bit of bunting. The battle had been fought, and it appeared from where they stood that they had just lost it.

CHAPTER 4

ERHAPS Midshipman Carey's *geste* against Midshipman Forrester was not the most aptly timed event in the continual war of wills in the mess that Alan had seen yet, nor was it particularly bright to jape so soon after such a galling failure as the Battle of the Chesapeake. The repercussions did not bear thinking about, and had Lewrie or Avery had a chance to talk Carey out of it, they most definitely would have. But, given Lewrie's own recent history and the series of misadventures that seemed to dog his existence, it was much of a piece, and therefore seemed almost fated.

Once full dark had fallen, the galley stoves had been lit and the steep-tubs began to bubble and boil to prepare the crew's dinner, though few men or officers who had eaten with such gusto at dinner in the forenoon watch had much of an appetite for their plain-commons supper. Avery was in the evening watch, which left Carey, Forrester and Lewrie in their small mess compartment to be served boiled salt beef and biscuits, livened only by a communal pot of mustard and the watered-down issue of red wine come aboard in New York, with a redolence of varnish. There were only four men in their mess, and the normal issue for a seaman's mess of eight was a four-pound cut of meat. Minus gristle and bone, it might make a third of a pound of meat for each man. Theirs, however, was even tougher than most, composed of more useless junk, and had the consistency, even after boiling, of old leather.

"Freeling, if you do not deal sharply with the mess cook when they choose the joints, I shall see you at the gratings," Forrester threatened, throwing his utensils down in disgust. "This is inedible!"

"Aye, zur," Freeling answered noncommittally. He was half dead already, a toothless oldster of forty who appeared over sixty from a hard life of seafaring, herniated from hoisting kegs with stay tackle once too often, shattered by too many years aloft in all weathers. He had seen too many midshipmen come and go and turn into officers, and held a particular abiding hatred for each and every one of them. Even bribes could not move him to charitable efforts in their behalf.

"I mean it this time, damn your eyes," Forrester snarled.

"You're not going to eat that?" Carey asked, eyeing his plate and the raggled strands of meat. Carey would eat anything.

Forrester did not answer but picked up his utensils once more and began to gouge at the beef to carve it into bite-sized pieces. It was much like trying to slice old rope with the edge of a fork the only appliance.

"Why not just pick it up and gnaw?" Alan said. Forrester was the only person he had ever seen who seemed to prosper on ships' rations. The lad had been fat as a piglet when Alan came aboard in spring, and now was in such fine and obese fettle as to excite the fantasy that soon some villagers would trice him up by his heels and bleed him for the fall killing. It was September after all, almost time for the first frosts and the slaughter of excess animals for the salt kegs or the smokehouses.

"That would be more your style," Forrester said. "I leave it to you. Such a lot of peasants! God rot the lot of you!"

"Did you hear some snuffling and rooting, Carey?" Alan jibed. "My ears definitely did. Or was it human speech after all?"

"Oink, oink," Carey said through a mouthful of biscuit.

"Do not row me tonight, Lewrie," Forrester snapped. "Perhaps this performance of ours today did not affect you, but, by God, it angered me!"

"But it did not seem to affect your appetite," Lewrie said, happy to have Forrester to abuse to alleviate his own sense of gloom concerning the battle. *Desperate* had been short two midshipmen when he had come into her—one had drowned, the other was a raging sponge who had been drunk most of the time and was finally dismissed, a hard feat to accomplish at any level of English society in these days. Forrester had been the tyrant of the mess until Avery and Lewrie had sided with Carey and played one prank after another on him until Forrester had been driven almost to distraction. It enlivened the usual drabness of their existence, and there was little that Forrester could do about it. One did not complain to superiors that one could not hold his own against the spiteful cruelty of his peers. It was their rough and tumble microcosm of society, where lads as young as ten or twelve became men along with becoming potential officers, and if one could not cope, one could not hope to prosper. It had come to blows a few times, at which point Forrester could only snarl and withdraw and scheme to gain his revenge, an event that so far he had never achieved, for with three against one, he had no chance. His not being the brightest person ever dropped also had a great deal to do with Forrester's frustrations.

Angry or not, Forrester managed to clean his plate and call for the cheese after Freeling had removed the joint to save the last of it for Avery.

"A small slice for me," Carey said as Forrester cut into the hoop of fairly fresh Cheddar recently shipped from England.

"Cut it yourself," Forrester replied, still sulking and taking the equal of two men's shares.

"Oink, oink," Carey said again.

"Damn you, will you stop that stupid noise!" Forrester barked, rising from his seat and taking a swing at the younger boy with the back of his hand. Before Lewrie could respond and deflect the blow completely, he had succeeded in cuffing Carey on the head.

"How would you like me to kick your nutmegs up between your teeth, Forrester," Alan warned, grabbing the offending hand and holding it immobile against Forrester's best efforts to free it. "By God, it's blow for blow in here, and well you know it, just like a Scottish feud."

"Goddamn you, Lewrie, unhand me," Forrester commanded, squirming with the effort to free himself. "I'll square your yards for you!"

"The hell you will," Alan said laughing cruelly. "You may inherit your daddy's title and rents, but you'll always be a churlish, craven pig."

Alan let go of Forrester's arm with a shove that almost unseated him. Forrester glared at him hard while Alan cut himself a slice of the cheese and poured a glass of Black Strap in lieu of port. He knew Forrester's type from civilian life, the bullying sort who would try to get even backhandedly, but would never face an enemy in a fair fight, and he enjoyed taunting him with a merry grin of physical superiority.

"How sadly is our aristocracy fallen, Carey, since the days of the Crusades," Alan scoffed. "Or when they faced Caesar's legions painted blue with woad."

An hour later, the master-at-arms and ship's corporals came about to see that all lights were extinguished for the night to lessen the mortal danger of fire, and they turned in. Alan took a moment while Forrester was forward in the heads to warn Carey to be on his guard in days ahead.

"He doesn't frighten me," Carey said with a smirk. "What can he do to us? Three of us against him."

"But he might get to you when we're not here."

"No matter, you'll settle him for me," Carey said, full of young confidence in his older mates to protect him. "But I'll make him pay for that slap."

"Carey, I think—given the captain's mood—that you leave well enough alone for now." Alan frowned. "Let it go, or you'll get us all in trouble, not just Forrester."

Carey had only smirked at him once more, then skinned out of his clothes and sprang into his hammock to curl up and sleep, and Alan thought no more about it, eager to get to sleep himself for a few hours before his midnight-to-four tour of duty in the middle watch.

Perhaps it was something about blue woad that set Carey off, for at dawn quarters the next morning, all the midshipmen turned up on deck to await the rising of the sun and the possible renewal of the battle with the French fleet, whose riding lights had been visible all night on the southeast horizon, still headed out into the Atlantic under easy sail.

As the grayness of predawn began to lessen the darkness, and the binnacle, belfry and taffrail lanterns began to lose their strength, some of the men began to titter into their hands and almost bite their tongues to keep from laughing out loud about something.

Must be a grand thing to get them going, Alan thought wearily after another night on deck with only three hours' sleep. There's not all that much to be amused at in this fleet.

"Silence on deck." Lieutenant Railsford snapped, unusually out of sorts.

"Whatever is with the people this morning?" Treghues growled, stalking by the windward rail, unshaven as of yet and unfed.

"Don't know, sir," Railsford replied.

"I'll prove to them they have nothing to laugh about after yesterday, by. . ." Treghues said, almost blaspheming himself.

I like him better when he has a mug of whatever that stuff is, Alan thought, planning to ask Dr. Dorne if the captain was under any medication; not that he really expected an answer, but he was intrigued anyway by the sudden change in behavior that Treghues evinced whenever he partook of it.

A man next to him on the gun deck began to laugh softly and Alan went to his side. "If you wish to be at the gratings in the forenoon, go ahead and laugh, why don't you?"

"Sorry, sor," the man replied, much too brightly.

"Just what is so all-fired funny to you?" Alan queried, and the gunner jerked a finger in the general direction of the starboard gangway and screwed his mouth shut, trembling with the effort not to laugh.

Alan looked up at the gangway. Nothing funny up there; the yeoman of the sheets looked about as stupid as usual, the marines were mustered properly at the hammock nettings with their muskets, and the landsmen and brace-tenders all seemed normal enough. Lieutenant Peck was pacing slowly, as was his wont, with his burly sergeant in tow just as every morning.

"Oh, my God!" Alan gaped at Forrester as he came aft from the fo'c'sle belfry. Carey, you little shit, you've done for us, by God if you haven't. It had to have been Carey. Avery has more sense.

Forrester had had his countenance adorned during the night. There was blue paint on his face, large dots on each cheek, a false mustache a Hessian guardsman would be proud of, great arching false brows, a streak down the nose and two quarter-circles on the jowls to emphasize their roundness, with a final large blot on the slack chin.

"Jesus," Coke, the bosun, commented as he spotted Forrester. "We're for it now, Mister Lewrie!"

"Amen to that," Lewrie whispered back.

"When'ud ya find the time, sir?" Coke asked once he was past them.

"Me?" Lewrie replied. "By God, it wasn't me."

"Merciful God!" A wail came from aft on the quarterdeck as Railsford spotted Forrester's phyz in the lightening gloom. "Mister Forrester, what is the meaning of this?"

"Mister Railsford?" Forrester snapped back, too sleepy to be wary, too surprised by Railsford's tone and totally unknowing the nature of his sin.

"Just what sort of harlequin are you to appear caparisoned so?"

"Sir?" Forrester replied, on his guard now and feeling about his body to see if he was properly dressed after donning his clothes in the darkness of the midshipmen's mess with no time for a peek in a mirror.

"You . . . clown!" Treghues shouted in his best quarterdeck voice as soon as he spotted the miscreant. "How dare you turn out like that! Get below and wash that . . . that foolishness off at once, do you hear!"

"Sir?" Forrester begged, aware that he was in trouble for sure.

"And I'll thank you to keep a civil tongue in your head when addressing the first lieutenant," Treghues said.

"But, sir . . ."

"Now, idiot!" Railsford commanded.

The word "wash" alerted Forrester to the possible nature of his offense. As he saluted and spun away to disappear belowdecks, he felt of his waistcoat, his breeches, then his face as a last resort, and was appalled to bring his fingers away still sticky-damp with blue paint.

"Mister Lewrie, get your miserable carcass up here instantly!" Treghues bawled, and there was no denying the summons. With a bitter shrug he scampered aft to a quarterdeck ladder and faced his irate captain.

"Sir," he said, doffing his cocked hat in salute.

"I know your brand of deviltry by now, Lewrie, and this time you shall pay for it in full measure," Treghues said, spittle flying from his lips.

"I did not do it, sir."

"Don't bother to lie to me, Lewrie!"

"On my honor, sir, I did not do it," Alan persisted.

"Avery, Carey, come aft at once," Railsford commanded.

"There's no need for that, Mister Railsford. I know who the biggest sinner in my own crew is, you can be assured of that."

"Sir, Mister Lewrie had the middle watch all night."

"Sir," the other midshipmen said as they reported and saluted.

"On your honor, did you paint Forrester's face blue, Avery?" their lieutenant asked of him. Avery had seen Forrester's new appearance and had said nothing, but even the seriousness of the situation could not keep the smirk off his face as he swore up and down that he had not done the deed.

"There's nothing to laugh about," Railsford barked, his own lips quivering at the edge of humor anyway, which did nothing to keep Avery from grinning even broader. "Carey, was it you?"

"Oh, this is a waste of time," Treghues grumbled. "Mister Coke!"

"I did it, sir." Carey said, pleased with his handiwork.

"You?" Treghues gaped.

"Aye, sir. Forrester cuffed me at supper last night."

Forrester reappeared on deck, the sharp edges of his new make-up now smeared, but still bright blue.

"I told you to go below and wash!"

"It won't come off, sir," Forrester admitted miserably. "It's paint, sir. I tried, sir, honest I did!"

"Did you strike Carey last night?" Railsford demanded.

"I . . ."

"Did you or did you not?"

"Lewrie stopped him from doing more," Carey stuck in mischievously.

"Sir, they were . . ."

"Did you strike a fellow midshipman?" Railsford reiterated.

"Aye, sir, I did, but they . . ."

"Bully!" Railsford roared. "To think of a young man of your size, cuffing a little boy about. You disappoint me, Mister Forrester."

"Vile wretch," Treghues said, frowning heavily at his relative. "I had thought better of you until now, boy! And you, Carey, playing at shines as men such as us bleed and die yonder. All of you, shame on you for being such a spoiled pack of unfeeling prodigals. What did we do yesterday? Watched a battle being lost, good ships shot to pieces, good men shot to pieces, and you dare to cut such a caper and still call yourselves gentlemen-in-training as professional Sea Officers. Well, you'll pay for it. Mister Coke, a dozen of your best for Forrester and Carey, and a halfdozen for Lewrie and Avery as well. Mastheading for Forrester and Carey until I remember to let them come down. And get that . . . stuff, off your face. Carry on!"

"Aye, aye, sir."

Once Treghues was gone below and the strokes had been given out, Railsford turned on them as well. "Goddamn you all for this childish . . . shit. I shall have the next fool flogged again, so help me!"

The sun was fully up after quarters were stood down, a day of calm seas and light winds. The sixth of September could have been a marvelous day to be sailing, were the circumstances different. The British fleet still sailed in easy column towards the southeast, pursuing the French, who were perhaps five or six miles off to leeward, drawn further and further away from the Chesapeake and the coast. But there was no question of battle being rejoined; too many ships had been roughly handled and needed urgent repair. The light winds were a blessing, allowing shattered topmasts to be struck so they could be fished or replaced with what few spare spars had been available from ships less hurt.

Admiral Drake's van ships had taken the worst of the pummeling; the *Intrepid* and *Shrewsbury* looked as though even an easy swell would roll the masts right out of them. But *Terrible* was the worst off, nearly in sinking condition, and her many wounded being parceled out to the less damaged ships for medical attention. The chain pumps clanked continually to stem the inrush of the sea from her bilge and lower decks.

The frigates still dashed back and forth on their ceaseless errands to scout dangerously close to the French and to keep an eye on their intentions, to carry spare timber and spars from well-endowed vessels to those most needy and to pass messages too complicated for the meager signaling book.

Or messages too vitriolic to be shared, Alan thought grimly. He could imagine the choler with which Graves might be penning a despatch to the Admiralty about the debacle, dashing off irate questions and accusations to Admiral Hood; Drake might be pouring out pure bile about the near destruction of his ships in the van, thrown away without proper support by the rest of the fleet, especially Hood's rear division. Hood and Drake might be countering with invective about Graves's incredible decision to let the French form beyond the Middle Ground and the waste of a splendid opportunity that Providence did not give grudgingly to any admiral.

How long does it take to become an admiral, anyway, Alan wondered as the usual ship's day proceeded to spin out its ordered sameness. Even with a newly like me in charge, we'd have accomplished more yesterday than what this pack of fools did. And if I should ever make flag rank, will we still have a navy at this rate? We should have stood on into the bay and cut the Frogs' gizzards out of them! Even I know that.

The day before, the sight and sound of battle—in the early stages at least—had raised in him a martial ardor and pride in his uniform that he could scarcely credit as coming from such a churl as himself, and now it all seemed like a fever dream. What was the point in becoming an officer in such an inept Service? What sort of honor and credit would it bring him, and what sort of glory was there to reap with such an addled pack of bunglers?

Why are we still following that damned de Grasse like a cart horse on the way to the stable? Alan wondered. There was a French army in the Chesapeake now landed in Lynnhaven Bay, an army that would force Cornwallis to withdraw within his siege-works sooner or later. The fleet needed to go back and aid the army. Let de Grasse bottle them up in the bay. He would be denied entrance until after the hurricane season began, and had no force of note still with him other than his ships to threaten New York or Charlestown or any other port on the coast. A fleet, even a large one, had never succeeded in taking and holding a garrisoned and fortified location on its own with only marines to put ashore. By God, I don't believe one of these ridiculous jackanapes in charge over us has the slightest idea what to do with the fleet now. We'd do better with that damned Frog to lead us."

In the afternoon a flag hoist from the *London* summoned *Desperate* to attend her. Once near enough to hail, *London*'s hard-pressed sailors had a chance to laugh at the sight of Forrester at the main masthead, still blue in the face as a Pict, for the paint indeed would not come off.

"A talisman, is your ancient warrior?" a lieutenant from *London* asked Treghues by way of greeting as he gained the quarterdeck with the usual canvas-bound packet of despatches under his arm.

"Your japery is out of place, lieutenant," Treghues said with icy harshness.

"Your pardon, Commander Treghues," the lieutenant stammered, taken off guard and remembering his place in the scheme of things when facing a senior officer, even if the lieutenant was blessed to be the senior in the flagship of a major fleet. "Admiral Graves sends his most sincere respects and directs you to make the best of your way into the Chesapeake to deliver despatches to Lord Cornwallis and then return to the fleet."

"And where shall the fleet be, I wonder?" Treghues asked of him. "Halfway to France? Still tagging along behind de Grasse?"

"I would not presume to know, sir. We shall still be at sea, certainly, to the east'rd of the capes."

"Hmm," Treghues sniffed in a lordly manner. "My deepest compliments to Admiral Graves and I shall assure him the safe arrival of despatches or die in the attempt."

"Very good, sir. I shall take my leave, then, and not detain you."

"Good day, sir." Treghues said. "Mister Railsford! Mister Monk! Stations to tack ship and lay her on the most direct course for the Chesapeake. Drive 'em, bosun. Crack on all the sail she can fly."

Before the lieutenant from *London* had even regained his seat in the flagship's cutter, *Desperate* was boiling with activity as every reef was shaken out, as she wore about to pinch up close-hauled preparatory to tacking across the wind to a course opposite that of the fleet.

Even with a light northeast wind, she began to fly like a Cambridge coach with the wind broad on her starboard quarter, one of her fastest points of sail.

"Be in soundin's agin by around two bells o' the evenin' watch, sir," Monk announced after they had taken several casts of the log. "We're nigh on nine knots. Will ya be wantin' ta enter the capes afore dawn, sir?"

"High tide should be making around then?"

"Just the start of the flood, sir. But we'll be off the entrance 'bout six bells. Be full dark, sir, and no moon ta speak of. Even so, I wonder if ya wants ta stand in under full sail er plain sail, what with no idea of what the Frogs left behind."

"Might not be a bad idea to reduce sail, especially the royals and topgallants before sundown, sir." Railsford stuck into the plans. "Even if the sun is going down behind the French watchers and we'll be out in the gloom, they'd shine in the last light."

"You'd have us loiter off the channel til dawn and the turn of the low dawn tide, Mister Railsford." Treghues countered, "And our orders brook no delay. Royals down in the second dogwatch, topgallants down after we fetch the coast, but we'll enter just as the tide is beginning to flow inward. We shall just have to chance any French warships."

"Aye, aye, sir."

"I'll have the ship at quarters, no lights showing, as we enter."

Treghues looked about the deck once more, then went below to his quarters, bawling for his steward Judkin to attend him.

"Probably wants to look his best when he sees Symonds or Cornwallis," David whispered once he was off the quarterdeck.

"He'd have to wear coronation robes to sugarcoat this disaster," Lewrie observed. "What a shitten mess."

"Oh, don't be such a Cassandra," David sighed. "Once Graves gets his fleet in any sort of order, he'll turn about and come back into the bay, and where will de Grasse be then?"

"The only reason they harvested Cassandra's liver is because she was always right," Lewrie said, grinning. "Keep that in mind, my lad."

"I love you dearly, Alan, but there are times when you have

absolutely no faith in our superiors," David replied, withholding most of his vexation. "If you weren't so jaundiced in your outlook, you'd fare all the better. Think on this: there's a clutch of French transports in that bay, most likely without decent escorts, what with de Grasse and de Barras off ahead of Admiral Graves. We could snap one or two of them up tonight on our way in."

"What if Symonds and his frigates have already done so?" Alan countered. "They might not have left much for us. At least, for once, I hope they haven't."

"God, you're hopeless," David grumped.

"But still alive and prospering," Alan retorted.

The seas had begun to rise once they got in soundings. They reduced sail bit by bit as it got darker and darker, so that not even the faintest reflection of the setting sun would gleam from the upper yards. Just before entering the black channel near midnight, they even brailed up the main course to reduce the chance of fire if they were intercepted by a lurking French vessel. They then went to quarters.

Not a light showed above the gangways, and the slow-match in the tubs by each gun was shielded from sight and the gunports still were tightly closed so they would not give themselves away.

"Ships in the bay, sir!" The message was passed down from the topmast, from the lone lookout to the maintop to the quarterdeck staff. "Ridin' lights aburnin'!"

"Three men to each gun, excess crews stand easy amidships," Mister Gwynn the gunner ordered softly. "Be ready to leap to it on either beam."

"Lewrie?" A disembodied voice called from the quarterdeck. Lewrie recognized it as Railsford's.

"Aye, sir."

"Do you go forward and remind the boy at the belfry to ring no bells but only turn the half-hour glass at the change of watch." Railsford thought a moment as it neared midnight. "Then take charge of the fo'c'sle."

"Aye, aye, sir."

He went forward, stumbling over men and gun tackle in the

stygian darkness until he reached the belfry at the break of the fo'c'sle, where one of the ship's boys stood by the bell.

"You ring that damned thing and the first lieutenant'll have your head off," Lewrie said. "Turn the watch glass, hour glass and all when the small glass runs out, but no bells."

The other two were peering almost eyeball-close to see when the last of the sand ran out of the half-hour glass and did not answer, but only snuffled in anticipation. Alan went on up to the fo'c'sle and the carronade gun crews, making sure the slow-match for the pair of short-ranged "smashers" was safely out of sight on the gun deck first.

"Sitwell," he whispered into the gloom.

"'Ere, Mister Lewrie."

"Stand easy."

"Aye, sir."

Once on the foredeck, Alan could see much better in the night, and the assembly of anchored ships ahead of them were quickly evident by their riding lights in the taffrail lanterns. There seemed enough ships there for a couple of brigades of troops, perhaps enough supplies for a full season of campaigning. The French were in the Chesapeake to stay, certainly. And where they were, there would be Rebel units as well.

"Sitwell, send a man aft to the quarterdeck and request a glass," Alan said. "Neither of the lookouts has one up here."

"Aye, aye, sir."

The hand returned via the gangways with a day telescope instead of one of the precious night glasses. It was better than nothing, but did not gather the light as well. At least I don't have to look at everything upside down and backwards. Lewrie thought, extending the tube and raising it to his eye. Expecting some kind of guard ship at the mouth of the main channel that led to the precious merchantmen, he looked instead off to either side of the bows for a darker, harder shadow in the blackness. Even a rowed cutter could give the game away, and if there were indeed French warships in the bay, it would summon one of them up in a moment.

"Summat ta starboard, sir," one of the bow lookouts exclaimed in a harsh whisper. "Looks like a ship, sir, four points off the bow."

Alan swivelled about and lay the telescope on the man's

shoulder to let his arm guide his eye. "Yes, it's a ship, alright, under tops'ls and jibs only. Going away?"

"Cain't tell, sir."

"Sitwell, send a man aft. Enemy ship to starboard, four points off the bow."

"Aye, Mister Lewrie."

Within minutes the messenger was back, a little out of breath from making two trips to the quarterdeck in as many minutes. Even before he could lean back on something to rest, Alan was snapping fingers for him again.

"Run and tell the captain the ship to starboard is slipping aft and appears to be going away. She's six points off the bow now."

"Aye, aye, sor!" the man gasped.

The minutes passed agonizingly slowly as the French guard ship went her unwary way further off toward the Middle Ground and the north end of the ship channel until she was lost in the blackness, her slight wake not even discernible any longer against the pattern of the few cat's paws.

"Guard boat, sir," the lookout called, "dead ahead. A cutter o' some kind, Mister Lewrie."

"Sitwell, pass it on."

"Maple," Sitwell hissed. "Go aft an' repeat the message."

"Agin, Mister Sitwell?" the now weary man complained. There was a meaty sound much resembling a bare foot connecting with someone's nether anatomy and the messenger staggered off along the gangways once more.

Alan could make out the enemy, a large cutter with a single mast and a gaff sail and jib winged out for a reach across the wind. She was crossing left to right ahead of them, perhaps two cables off, but *Desperate* was slowly falling down on her and it would take a crew made up of blind men to miss seeing her.

"Anything to larboard?" he asked.

"Nothin' yet, Mister Lewrie," the other lookout replied.

"Sitwell, another man aft. The cutter is heading north towards our starboard, about two cables off at right angles."

"Aye, sir."

They could feel *Desperate* alter course slightly a few minutes later, angling to larboard closer to the coast, where she would be merely another dark shadow against the hulking darkness of Cape Henry and the shore of the bay, while the cutter went blithely on without spotting them.

"By God, we're in the anchorage," Alan muttered. "Too close in for anything but rowing boats. Everyone watch the surface close in."

Desperate wore to starboard, altering course again as she got too close into the shore, probably at Mister Monk's insistence. They were now closing in on those tempting transports that slumbered with only an anchor watch, thinking themselves protected in a secure harbor. Hands came forward to brail up the forecourse to reduce their ship's top-hamper, lessening the chance that anyone would spot her. With the taffrail lanterns throwing long glimmering troughs of reflections on the sea, they could now spot any oared guard boat rowing about the transports much more easily, could catch those flashes from oar looms and the splashes they made. It did indeed look as though they might have some of the enemy as prizes before morning!

Anchored tantalizingly close, the French transport fleet looked like a small seaport town with all its street lighting burning in a peaceful evening. Further beyond the transports, the shore was also lit up with the campfires of a newly landed army, adding to the impression of a town.

Desperate took in all her sails, laboriously reloaded her guns with grape shot and langridge instead of solid shot to repel any boat expeditions that might want to return the favor on her, and hoisted out the boarding nettings. The nets were hoisted loose and sloppy from the ends of the course yards and cro'jack yard on the mizzen to prevent easy entry over her bulwarks by enemy sailors intent on her capture, and draped in unseamanly bights so that no one scaling the nettings could count on any sort of firm foot or handhold before he was picked off or skewered by the men on *Desperate*'s decks. Finally, the boats were led around from astern and the first lieutenant given parties of men for each boat to form a cutting-out expedition against the nearest French transport.

Lieutenant Peck the marine officer joined Railsford in the place of honor, along with half his platoon of marines, four to each of the boats. Cottle took charge of the captain's gig, with six hands and a steady quartermaster's mate in command. Railsford took the barge, Avery the cutter and Alan the jolly boat; only Carey remained aboard ship along with the older and less spry hands who could not be expected to scramble up a ship's side in the perfect darkness and continue on into unfamiliar rigging to put sail on a prize.

Railsford's barge led the short parade of four; the night was so black without even a sliver of moon that it was hard to see the boat next in line unless they were almost touching. The hands stroked as softly as they could, the rowports muffled with old tarpaulin or worn-out sail scraps. The natty white-painted oar looms had been hastily daubed with tar to lessen their gleam. The stroke was slow to cut down on any splashes that might be seen as reflections from the enemy's riding lights, and to save the mens' strength for battle. The making tide did as much to propel them forward as their efforts at the oars.

Alan sat on the sternmost thwart of the jolly boat, tiller bar under his arm, and peered intently into the blackness. The rumble and thump of the oars was maddeningly loud and he licked his lips continually in concern and a little bit of fear as well. It was not merely the unseasonal chill of the night that made him shiver this time. It was the first time he had ever been on a cutting-out, and he was on the water in the dark, remembering once more that he could not swim. Under the circumstances, he could not even cry out for aid if he fell into the water, but would most likely be expected to drown in perfect silence. Sitting in the open boat was bad enough, but worry about how he would gain the deck of a French ship in the night was uppermost. Once he reached the dubious safety of an enemy deck with steel in hand to fight whatever presented itself was almost a happy afterthought.

What if there are still troops aboard, like the *Ephegenie?* he wondered, gnawing his cheek unconsciously. We could end up tumbled back over the side at bayonet point. Given a choice of being skewered or shot, I'd take either one over drowning.

More to the point, had *Desperate* been spotted despite all their caution, and were they now rowing into a well-laid trap which would result in many deaths, most significantly his own?

He noticed that he had clamped his jaws so tightly shut to avoid chattering teeth that his mouth was beginning to ache, and though he was not exerting himself at an oar, he was breathing about as hard as the two men nearest him.

What the devil is the matter with me? he chid himself. It's not like me to be so skittish. Of course, it's my first time for this sort of expedition, but that don't signify. Mayhap it's because I've seen enough in the last two years to know there *is* something to fear. What if I get killed?

He felt the muscles of his back twitch at the thought and had to shake himself to settle down. I'll try to go game, of course, like a gentleman should. But not to tussle with a wench again, or lift a bottle or two—God, how hellish. Wonder what the world would be like without me?

Probably much better off, he decided after a moment of rueful cogitation, and smiled in spite of his feelings and the circumstances. Lucy Beauman would weep over him until some other swaggering buck came along, which might not be too long a period of mourning, if he knew anything about impressionable young tits like her. No one in London, certainly; he was already dead and gone to anyone he had known there, anyway. David Avery and little Carey might miss him, a few former shipmates from his first ship *Ariadne*, such as Keith Ashburn and . . . no, the rest of them had hated his overachieving guts, and it had been pretty much mutual. Treghues? The captain might do a short hornpipe of delight before he remembered what a fine Christian he was and put his solemn Sunday face back on.

A faint sound intruded on Lewrie's musings; the sound of one of his oarsmen moaning softly, a moan of the truly lost with each oar stroke.

"Just who is that ass who's fucking the manger goat?" he snapped, unsticking his tightly lashed jaw muscles.

There was a soft titter of relief from all his hands as their own fears were momentarily forgotten in disgust for some faceless and nameless shipmate more fearful even than they, someone they could despise most heartily because he could not control his fear like a stalwart English seaman, and they could.

"Ecstasy with the French camp-followers will have to wait," Alan said, shifting his numb posterior to a more comfortable position on the hard thwart.

"They'd bring women, sor?" someone asked from up forward with an interested gasp of surprise.

"Who knows," Alan answered wryly. "They're Frogs, ain't they? Do be quiet now, and mind your stroke."

A few moments later, they almost went up the stern of the next boat in line, Avery's cutter. The thought of women carried aboard a French ship had indeed lengthened and strengthened their work at the oars.

"Damn you, Lewrie," Avery hissed. "Ease off, there!"

But they were almost at their destination. Out of the black night they could hear wavelets lapping, could hear the faint groan of ship timbers as a vessel rode to her anchors not far from them. This vessel's taffrail lanterns were not burning; only a faint glow from her binnacle by the unmanned wheel was lit and barely threw the loom-hint above her bulwarks, as a coastal navigation light or the glow of a coastal town will appear just below the horizon. All four boats drifted into an ungainly pod with upraised oars pointed skyward, trying to fend off with their hands quietly.

"Forrester, take the stern," Railsford said in a whisper as they drifted closer together. "Cut her stern cable and guard her watch."

"Aye, sir." Forrester piped.

"Silence, damn you! Avery, do you take the starboard main chains and go for the wheel. I shall go to larboard and send my people aloft to set sail. Lewrie, do you take the fo'c'sle and cut her bow cables. Do not any of you load a musket or pistol until you are on deck. Use cold steel if you have to put anyone down, and try to do it quietly."

"Give way, gently," Lewrie ordered after the other boats began to drift away far enough to reemploy the oars. He put the tiller bar over to steer alongside the French ship in Railsford's tiny wake. They both ducked under the jutting jib boom and bowsprit, ghosted to a crawl in a tight turn just under the rails of the beakhead, eyeing the loose bights of line from the brailed up spritsail as a possible way up.

"Hook on," Alan mouthed almost silently. "Boat your oars."

Railsford's boat faded out of view into the night and Alan waited, not sure exactly for what. The sound of Railsford scrambling up the side? Or would that be too late? A response from the sleeping French?

"Let's go," he whispered finally, after the tension began to grow on him to almost unbearable proportion. His men sprang into action, going up hand over hand by the bight of line to the beakhead rails, using the bulge of the gunwale termination as a footstep. Alan had no choice but to try and follow clumsily. He was weighed down with a pair of those awfully inaccurate Sea Pattern pistols in his jacket pockets, a cutlass on a baldric over his shoulder, and his dirk hung by a belt frog from his waistband. If I fall in, I'll sink like a stone, he told himself fearfully.

He stepped on the bow of the jolly boat, hauled himself upward with both hands on the bight of spritsail brace until he could hook one claw over the lowest beakhead rail, which was slimy with night damp and the excreta left behind by French sailors. He almost lost his grip as he used the rails for a backward-leaning ladder, but there was a horny hand on his wrist and a great tug that pulled him up and over the rails with ease to the grated platform atop the cutwater.

"Las' shit that turd'll drop, sir," a harsh voice whispered to him with great glee, indicating the Frenchman who was sprawled ungainly like a sack of scrap canvas at his feet. The man had his slop trousers down by his ankles and had obviously had his throat most efficiently and silently cut as he sat musing at his ease.

"Jesus!" Alan gaped in awe, feeling like a very green and unblooded cod's-head at the sight, which he had not expected. "Any alarm yet?"

"No, sir. Caulkin' like lumber, sir."

"Load your musket," Alan ordered. "Watch my back while I load my pistols."

He had already tamped down powder, ball and wad into the barrels but had left the pans empty and the hammers full down. Fumbling for powder flask around his neck, he snapped open the frissons of first one gun and then the next to prime his pistols, dribbling powder into the pans. He could not see what he was doing, but hoped that he was being accidentally liberal. He shut the frissons, drew the hammers back to half-cock, and stuffed them into his jacket pockets once more. He drew his cutlass, looped the short lanyard around his wrist and touched the man with him on the shoulder to let him know that he was ready.

They advanced to the outer doors to the bulkhead roundhouses where petty officers took their ease when called by nature. There was no one there. Passing through the bulkhead, they emerged on the fo'c'sle. In the faint light of the fo'c'sle belfry lantern, they could see that their men had preceded them and had slit the throats of several Frenchmen sleeping on deck in preference to the close air below-decks. Their blood gleamed wet and black in the gloom.

"We've got her," the man said in triumph, baring his teeth in a wide grin and turning to beam at Lewrie, who wasn't sure of anything at that moment.

Then they heard a shout from aft, where Forrester's people should be ascending to the poop deck to take charge of the stream anchor cable and the officers' sleeping quarters, where the small arms would be kept.

"*Qui va là?*" the shout came.

"*Pont de la gard!*" a voice called back full of confidence.

"Oh, you unspeakable, ignorant ass!" Alan hissed.

"*Merde, alors, c'est l'Anglais!*" someone in command screamed. "*Aux armes!*"

A pistol discharged and somewhere in the dark a man who had been the target—French or English, it was impossible to tell—yelped in agony as he was hit, followed by a large splash.

"At 'em, Desperates!" Railsford bellowed over the sudden alarm and bustle.

"Get that anchor cable cut and set one of their jibs," Alan told the man with him. "Bow party to me. Head aft by the starboard gangway." He knew that Railsford would be on the larboard side, Avery aft by the main chains to starboard and trying to take the wheel from the awakened French watch party, and most in need of assistance. There were Frenchmen everywhere, as though they had stirred up a hornet's nest, as men who had been asleep on deck in hammocks or bedding on deck rose up and took in hand what weapons they could.

There was a hammock slung before Lewrie, and a man trying to exit the cocoonlike sack. Before he could get one foot on deck, Alan swung his cutlass with all his force and took the man across the neck and chest, bringing forth a howl of pain as the man tumbled out of his hammock to the deck to twitch and thrash in his death throes.

Several sparks gleamed in the night, then came the ragged crash of muskets or pistols and more cries of anguish. A marine loomed up in front of Lewrie, bayonet lowered and blood in his eyes, howling some wordless shout as he drove for his ribs.

"English, dammit!" Alan cried, forced to step aside from the glittering bayonet point, and the musket shoved between his arm and his side as he ended up close enough to count the marine's remaining teeth. "Stop that!"

"Oh, 'scuse me, Mister Lewrie, sir!" the marine said, once more in possession of his faculties, spinning about on his heel and plunging aft into the fight once more without a backward glance, leaving Alan shaking with the closeness and stupidity of his near-death.

"Alan," Avery called, coming out of the night with his uniform facings flashing. "Are you hurt?"

"Scared so bad I wouldn't trust mine own arse with a fart," Alan said. "That damned bullock almost knackered me."

"Well, this is turning into a bloody shambles!" Avery spat, wiping his cutlass blade on the swinging hammock that had lately contained a man.

There was a deep boom off in the night, a cannon fired as an alarm to wake the other ships to the danger of raiders in their midst. Lights began to appear on the distant decks as crews came up on deck to peer into the night to see where the danger was.

For the moment, anyway, the fighting was over, for the small French civilian merchant crew had surrendered, and those few who had been below were being chivvied on deck at sword point. Very few people really had been killed or hurt. They were not paid to take the risks of naval seamen and had caved in almost before they had rubbed the sleep out of their eyes, the only resistance being the anchor watch around the wheel and binnacle and those mates that had gotten on deck from the officers' cabins aft.

"She's empty," Railsford told them as he came up on the gangways. "They've already unloaded her. Looks like she was carrying troops. Nothing of value. Who was that idiot who said *pont* of the guard?"

"Somebody aft, sir." Avery said.

"Forrester, I'll be bound," Railsford said. "Only a perfect little Latin student could cling to *pontis* instead of *bateau.*"

"Ship or boat was *classis*, sir," Avery advised. "*Pontis* was bridge."

"And fuck you too, Avery," Railsford growled, going aft to the men by the wheel.

"If the truth be known, Avery," Alan drawled, wiping and sheathing his own cutlass, "*classis* was fleet; *navis* was ship, and *boat* would be a *linter, cymba, scapha* or, in rare usages, *navicula.*"

"Do tell," Avery snapped.

"And to compound the error, *pons* was the singular, *pontis* the plural..." Alan went on, as though nothing had happened of any consequence to their chances for prize money, and escape.

"Yes, Dr. Dorne," Avery cried, exasperated. He walked away.

"Cables're free!" The shout came from the fo'c'sle.

"Avery, Lewrie," Railsford called. "Attend to getting the ship under way!"

The foredeck party had already gotten a jib hoisted and had let fly the spritsail under the jib boom to get a forward way on their prize so the rudder could get a bite and allow them steerageway. Alan led three men aloft onto the foremast to cut loose the harbor gaskets from the foretops'l for more speed. Before they could even gain the foretop, however, the hull drummed to several cannon balls fired from the ships to their lee.

"Warship off the starboard bow, sir!" the foredeck party called.

There was something out there, something not too big—another of those damned cutters, perhaps, or a sloop of war.

"We're in the quag now, sir," one of the hands told Lewrie as they gathered in the foretop ready to scuttle out the tops'l footropes.

Small as the enemy might be, they would have artillery which could punch through the frail scantlings of a merchantman, and a crew of trained men ready to board and retake the ship from them.

By God, I'm beginning to wonder if we can do anything right any more, Alan cursed to himself.

"Burn her!" Railsford announced. "Lash the wheel and set her alight. By God, they'll not have her!"

"Back to the deck," Alan ordered. "Daniels, secure our jolly boat!"

"Aye, sir!" the man replied. "We're gonna be needin' it."

They scrambled back down to the deck and began to gather up anything they could find that was flammable, which on a ship was considerable. Within minutes they had a fine little fire going below decks in the waist, made from the straw bedding the soldiers had used before being disembarked.

"Lash the wheel!" Railsford yelled. "Make sure we leave no one behind, now. Into the boats and abandon ship!"

"Anyone hurt from our party?" Lewrie asked his most senior hand by the larboard foremast chains.

"All here, sir," the petty officer informed him. "Even the marines is here!"

"Into the boat, then, hurry," Alan said, looking over his shoulder at how the fire had spread already and was beginning to leap above the gangways to gnaw at the rigging and the base of the masts. He was last to leave the deck after looking around for anyone he recognized still standing or left wounded and discarded in a dark corner. Before he spun away, the French warship had already opened fire with her bow chasers, and one iron ball slammed hard into the merchantman's hull and flung broken wood everywhere, making him duck and scramble over the side. With a slashed forebrace for a manrope, he lowered himself close to the waiting jolly boat and jumped the last few feet, landing roughly on some of his men who were struggling to ship their oars, making them all curse and grumble.

"Shove off," he ordered, stumbling over their legs and feet to his place at the tiller. "Out oars, there! Give way all!"

As long as they were in the lee of the burning prize, they were safe from the warship's attentions, but that situation could not last long.

The ship was now being pounded to matchwood by the French sloop of war, and was well alight but still under way heading west on the making tide and the slight wind for the rest of the anchorage, while their hope of rescue lay east, and within a moment they would lie exposed on the open waters to the guns of the sloop of war, and would be hopelessly vulnerable targets. Taking Railsford's course as a fine example, Alan steered for the darkness to the south and the black shore beyond the other ships.

"Gawd, they got guts, sir," Daniels said in awe, pointing aft.

When Alan looked over his shoulder he could see that the sloop of war, a fine brig-rigged ship of at least fourteen guns, had come about to run down on the burning merchantman, either to nudge her out of the way or put a crew aboard to put her helm over to steer her away from the rest of the threatened transports.

"May they roast in hell for their pains," Alan said, but it did give them a chance to escape, which Railsford took at once, waving an arm and pointing them back east toward where *Desperate* was anchored, away from the transports and the possible guard boats that would be gathering to intercept them.

"Row like Satan was after you!" Alan encouraged. "Put your backs into it like you never did before."

They tried, he gave them credit for that, but it was a hard row. The tide was against them and splash and dip as they might, sending the boat surging forward with each stroke, they seemed to make no progress at all. He was almost despairing of them keeping up such a furious pace when a gun discharged somewhere and sent at least a six-pound ball humming over them close enough to wind them with its passage and splash a cable off.

"Who goes there?" an English voice called into the night.

"*Desperate!*" Railsford shouted back. "Ahoy, the ship!"

"Come alongside!"

"Thank Christ," Alan breathed. "Easy all."

Desperate had raised her anchors at the first sign of alarm to come to their rescue, since nearly a full third of her crew was off on the raid. She loomed out of the dark, a hard shadow still showing no lights and let her boats nuzzle up to her by her chainwales and entry ports even as she continued to gather way.

"Quickly, now!" Treghues's voice could be heard urging them from the quarterdeck. "Lead the boats astern after the people are on deck. Mister Monk, lay her nor'nor'west. Mister Toliver, hands to the braces to wear ship. Mister Gwynn, we can use some of your gunners on the sheets and the braces."

Life on the *Desperate* could be drab and dull, the food could approach swill at times and Treghues could be an unpredictable martinet, but every man jack was exceedingly delighted to get back onboard.

"I shall expect your report in the morning, Mister Railsford," the captain said as the ship turned onto her new course and the confusion of overworked hands and frightened arrivals began to sort themselves out to their duty stations. "What a muddle!"

Lewrie went to the larboard gangway for a moment before joining his gunners in the waist. The French prize that had almost been theirs was now turned crabwise and though still burning fiercely was no longer any danger to her consorts, some of which had cut their cables in their eagerness to avoid being set on fire. However, the sloop of war was heading their way.

There were other warships to seaward of them, but of no immediate concern, and by the light of the fire they could espy no ship of any strength that could beat up to windward on the light breeze against that tide to reach them before dawn.

"Mister Gwynn, draw grape from the larboard battery and reload with solid shot," Railsford called from aft. "We shall be having company soon and must give him a proper greeting."

Alan dropped down into the waist and supervised his gunners as the bags of langridge and grape were wormed from the barrels and tossed aside.

Gun captains rolled nine-pounder balls around the deck to find the most perfectly cast that would fly true when fired, then had them rammed down the muzzles and tamped down. Arms raised in the air to indicate each gun's readiness.

"Run out yer guns," Gwynn ordered, and the crews hauled on the side tackles to trundle their charges across the slightly canted deck to the port sills where the carriages thumped against the hull. Side tackle was laid out for smooth recoil with no snags; train tackles were overhauled as well.

"Prime yer guns." Gun captains reached down with prickers to poke holes through the serge cartridge bags. They inserted powder-filled goose quills into the touchholes and stood by with their slow matches.

"Wots'e got, Mister Lewrie?" the nearest gun captain asked.

"Six or seven guns per broadside, six-pounders most like; that's what they felt like when they were shooting at the prize," he answered.

"Wuz she worth much, sir?" another man asked.

"Empty. Usual Frog trash—filth and no cargo."

To get close enough to make his lighter guns do damage, the French commander had to beat up to them close-hauled on the starboard tack. Since *Desperate* was still making for the mouth of the York River, that meant that the French sloop would spend long minutes almost bows on to them, hoping for a convergence. But this would leave her open for raking fire on her own bow. And when the range was about two cables, and the target barely recognizable in the darkness now that the burning prize had burned out or sunk, this was what *Desperate* proceeded to give her.

"As you bear . . . fire!"

One at a time, starting with the larboard carronade on the fo'c'sle, the guns barked harshly, flinging themselves backwards to the center line and stabbing long amber flames into the night. The hands threw themselves on their artillery, sponging out the barrels, inserting new cartridges, ramming down fresh shot and running out, as well-drilled as clever little German clockwork toys freshly wound up.

The French sloop of war replied, aiming high as was their practice, but the angle of convergence was getting more and more acute and her guns could not bear, so most of the storm passed overhead and to sternward on the first broadside.

He'll not cut us off, Alan decided, looking at the way his own frigate was headreaching on the Frenchman. He shall have to haul his wind or pass astern of us and we shall get clean away.

The shadow of the enemy vessel did lengthen as she turned, seeing that she was not fast enough to intercept *Desperate*. But as she did so, she got off another broadside, and this one brought all her guns to bear. There was a loud crash from aloft, and things began to rain down.

"Jesus Christ!" A gun captain yelped in alarm as he was almost beheaded by a heavy halyard block that crashed to the deck beside him. Rope snaked down to droop over the guns as braces, stays and sail-tending lines were torn loose.

"Look out below amidships!"

The main tops'l yard came swinging down like a scythe to smash into the larboard gangway, scattering the brace tenders and sheetmen, who had to dive for their lives.

"As you bear . . . fire!" Gwynn yelled. "Lewrie, take three men and cut that raffle away. Save the yard if ya can. We'll not see its like in the Chesapeake."

"Aye, sir." Leaving a party from the gangway to anchor the free end, he went aloft to see what was holding it and found it resting on the edge of the maintop, snagged by its starboard rigging into the shrouds. The topmast and topgallant mast above it were leaning drunkenly over the starboard side, ready to let go themselves.

"Yeoman," he called down, "work the butt end forrard by the shrouds and begin lashing down." He turned to the bosun's mate, Weems, who had come aloft with him. "We'll have to get a gantline on this end and just lash her to the shrouds. She'll lean there alright for now, do you not think?"

"Aye, sir," Weems replied, sending a man further aloft to haul in a surviving parrel and preventer backstay to secure the upper end of the yard. "But, that up there . . ."

"Topmast is shattered halfway up, looks like," Alan agreed.

"Might save it an' fish it. Topgallant mast, though. Don't know what's keepin' it aloft as it is. 'Bout ready ta let go."

There was another broadside from *Desperate*, and a ragged cheer which made them turn to look. They had the French sloop of war at roughly musket shot now, half a cable away, and had just punched some holes into her, making her stagger in the water as though she had run aground on an uncharted reef. Her foremast leaned over drunkenly and she began to slow down, now unable to keep up with *Desperate* even on a parallel course.

"We'll need more men." Alan said, removing his baldric and cutlass, unloading his pockets of the weight of the pistols, which were still at half cock. He eased the hammers forward for safety, laid everything in the top platform and gritted his teeth to make the ascent to the topmast to see how bad the damage was. It was ex-pected of him, God help him.

There was a great groan of tortured pine, and the damaged masts leaned over to starboard even more, the topmast beginning to split down its length as the weight of the topgallant mast tore loose from whatever last shred had been holding it.

"'Ware below!" Weems boomed.

Alan had no choice but to slide back down the topmast he had been scaling until he fetched up at the lower mast cap and the trestletrees, clinging for dear life to avoid being pitched out of the rigging or torn asunder if the mast split off at the cap. With a final shriek, the entire topgallant mast and half the topmast split off and went over the side to raise a great splash of water alongside, and Alan exclaimed in terror as standing rigging and trailing rigging slashed about him like coach whips.

"I'm sorry, I quit!" he shouted, not caring who heard him. "I've done just about bloody enough tonight, thank you! If you want to kill me, you'll find me in my hammock belowdecks!"

"Damme, we've lost it!" Weems cried, in anguish at the hurt to his precious rigging and masts. He scrambled up to the cap with Lewrie and surveyed what little he could see in the night. "Not a shred left of it. Ripped every stay, every shroud right out. We'll be the next week makin' repairs, an' where'll we get spare spars enough, I'm wonderin'."

"I am well," Alan told him, his voice dripping with sarcasm. "Thank you *very* much for asking, Mister Weems!"

"Goddamn French bastards, the poxy snail-eatin' sonsabitches!" Weems continued to lament the scarred perfection of his masts, shaking an angry fist at the French sloop of war that was, as Alan finally noted, being pounded to pieces by *Desperate*'s heavier fire. Her own damaged foremast went by the board over the farther side, and must have still been attached, for she slewed about as though snagged by an anchor cable, which threw such a shock to her remaining rigging that Lewrie saw for the first time a ship slung about so violently that she indeed had all "the sticks" ripped right out of her, her other mast crashing down in ruin to cover her decks in timber, rope and canvas.

"Serves ya right, ya duck-fuckers!" Weems howled.

"May I go down to the deck now, Mister Weems?" Alan asked, picking a rather large splinter out of his palm from the shattered topmast.

"Aye, nothin' left doin' aloft, not on this mast. Hurt yeself, did ya? Best let the surgeon see ta that. Might get a tot of rum outen it if ya talks sweet to him," Weems said.

That's the best offer I've had all day, Alan decided.

CHAPTER 5

UNTIL dawn *Desperate* made her way painfully to the anchorage at the mouth of the York River. There had been few men injured in the fight with the French sloop of war, even fewer in the abortive attempt to take the merchantman; even so, Dr. Dorne and his surgeon's mates had been busy until that time sewing up cuts and scrapes, taking off an arm here that had been shattered, amputating a leg above the knee on a young gunner who had had the bone smashed into permanent ruin by a musket ball. The low tide slacked and the sea breeze died just before first light, so that the frigate was for a time becalmed, drifting for a piece slowly sternward out to sea once more before she anchored. Once the land breeze sprang up, she could find enough steerageway to work close-hauled up the York to join her sister ships already in the bay.

"Now, damme, will you look at that," Railsford muttered as he stood by the taffrail, peering into Lynnhaven Bay with a telescope.

Alan was swaying by the binnacle and compass, ready to pass out with fatigue. He had been up all night, like all the hands, tending to what hurts to the ship could be put right immediately, and at that moment could have cheerfully murdered someone for hot tea or coffee. Railsford's words brought him out of his stupor enough to join him at the rail.

"There's that Frog transport we burned out last night. And look you at what the others were." Railsford spat, almost beside himself.

Alan took the heavy tube in both hands and applied it to his right eye, the weight of the instrument making his weary limbs shudder.

"Coasters!" Alan exclaimed. "Potty little oyster boats and such!"

"And not a full dozen of 'em," Railsford moaned. "We were tricked."

"They looked like ships last night, sir. All lit up and chiming the watch bells."

"At the least, we burned out the only decent ship they had and put the fear of God into a French sloop of war." Railsford shrugged, taking the telescope back. "They must have carried all those troops in the line-of-battle ships and larger frigates, crammed 'em in any old how. God, if we could have just caught 'em at sea before they landed, we could have done 'em into fried mutton. So many men aboard in each other's way..."

"So, except for that sloop of war and a cutter or two, there are no French present as of yet, sir," Alan said, wondering in his fogged mind what that might mean, if anything. The effort was almost beyond his power to reason any longer.

"If we had but known, we could have had all of those scows!"

"And I almost got killed for nothing." Alan grumbled half aloud, a sentiment that Railsford either pretended to ignore at that ungodly early hour or actually did not hear from sheer exhaustion. The first lieutenant scratched his chin and Alan could hear his fingers rasping in his stubbly beard.

"Mister Monk, would you be so good, sir, to take charge of the deck for a moment while I apprise the captain of something urgent?" Railsford asked.

"Aye, sir." Monk drawled, his face drawn with fatigue and looking a lot older than his thirty-five-odd years.

Railsford left Alan the telescope, which he rested on the taffrail for a while, reminding himself that he must remember to stay awake enough to not drop it over the side from nerveless fingers.

The last time I was this exhausted, he thought, I'd walked ten miles before dawn, ridden cross-country with those damned county boys all day, partied and played balum-rancum with a pack of whores all that night and had to ride back home the next morning. And that was a whole lot more fun than last night!

He went to stand by Monk and used the telescope to check out the anchorage up the York. There was the frigate *Charon*, the sloop of war *Guadeloupe*, a smaller sloop of war—little more than a ketch, really—the *Bonetta* and a small gaggle of gunboats. They looked as peaceful as Portsmouth Harbor on a Sunday morning, and he bitterly wondered what they had been doing while the French had been landing their armament.

The York peninsula between the York and the James was pretty low country, much of a piece with most of the American seaboard that he had seen in his few trips to the continent. The land was higher towards the narrows of the York, up where the little town was reputed to be, and the bluffs ended up being quite steep, but not particularly high. There was some high ground of much the same sort on the Gloucester side, which rapidly tapered off into salt marshes and low ground the further east one could go past the narrows.

"See that house yonder?" Monk said. "Moore's House. Rather fine landmark."

"Where is the town?" Alan asked.

"Around the bend from us, right at the narrows. Not much of a place, by my reckonin', ner anybody else's," Monk added. "Deep water just offshore, mayhap thirty-five ta forty fathom, 'bout a cable out. Closer in, ya got only six fathom, but that's right under the bluffs an' at low tide, too. Lotta tobacco comes outa here. Even outa the Gloucester side. Virginia's famous fer it. If the army ain't burned it fer spite, I'll get me some ta chew."

"Looks pretty low over there, sir," Alan noted on the north shore.

"Aye, once past Gaines Point goin' back ta sea, ya get inta some salt marshes and swamps an' bottom land—Guinea Neck, they calls it. They's farms in there, even so. Corn, tobacco an' such like. Some pines fer pitch an' tar an' board."

"So the scour of the tide, and the current of the river, lay to the suthr'd, sir, below the bluffs and runs sou'west along the shoals."

Alan said. "With Moore's House on your larboard bow. . ."

"Aye, so it does. Keep the House ta yer larboard, 'bout five points an' no closer, ya'll not tangle with the shoals, an' you'll have smooth sailin' right inta the York and firm anchor. Til the tide turns, o' course."

Treghues emerged on deck, lips pressed tight together in obvious dislike for the bad news Railsford had given him about their wasted effort of the night and how badly they had been fooled. That ended the lesson from Mister Monk on how to get into the York.

"I have the deck, Mister Monk," Railsford said, coming to stand by him to leeward of the wheel, giving the windward, now the landward, side of the deck to the captain. "Stations for anchoring, Mister Coke. We shall require the captain's gig led round to the entry port as soon as the hook is on the bottom, Mister Weems."

"Passin' the word fer the captain's cox'n!"

In contrast to everyone else's appearance, Treghues was freshly shaved and washed, his linen clean and white and his coat brushed free of lint and dust.

You're hating it, Alan thought. You're going to have to tell the bad news about the battle to Symonds and Cornwallis. And admit you failed last night. I must be awesomely tired—I almost feel sorry for the poor bastard!

Still, Alan felt that it was a lesson. A landed army obviously meant large transports, so that was what Treghues wished to see and that was what he thought he had seen. He had risked the ship for nothing, and if they had succeeded in getting into the anchorage and burning all those coasters and local scows, they would have been trapped by the guard ships, including the one frigate they had seen just at dawn up the James, and *Desperate* would have been destroyed for an exchange that would not have made a decent stake at The Cocoa Tree on a throw of the dice. Not only was Treghues mistaken about the transports, he was mistaken in wanting to attack them at all. Their primary duty had been to deliver despatches and they had almost lost the chance to do that as well.

Maybe he feels like he has to prove something, to make up for a bad admiral or a lost battle, Alan thought. By God, it's one thing to make the best of what Providence drops in your lap, but quite another to try and force the issue and make your own luck.

"Stations for wearing ship!" Treghues called. "Prepare to an-chor!"

Desperate plodded on into the tiny fleet gathering and rounded up into the wind, backing her tops'ls to bring her to a complete halt, at which point the best bower splashed into the bottom and she began to stream back from her mooring. The side boys and officers assembled as Treghues went over the side, saluting amid the squeal of bosun's pipes until their captain's head had dropped below the level of the upper deck.

"Not much to the place, is there?" Avery said, walking over to Lewrie by the entry port which now faced the small town of York. "I hear it aspires to be called York Town, but York Village is more like it."

"I've seen better villages back home, even on Sunday." Lewrie smiled. "Looks half deserted."

"You'd leave, too, if you were about to be stuck into the middle of an army encampment surrounded by the French," David said. "By God, we shall get shore leave here, see if we don't. It looks so damned dull that an entire troop of devils couldn't raise enough mischief to wake a country parson."

"I don't know, David," Alan replied, feeling that odd dread come over him once more whenever he was in close proximity to the place. "I think there will be some fine mischief raised before we see the last of it."

Three more British frigates came in from seaward during the day; *Medea, Iris* and *Richmond,* bearing despatches both from Graves still far out to sea and from Clinton in New York. They had been sent in just a few hours after *Desperate;* evidently Graves had had more to say, or had forgotten some important items in the first place.

Their arrival brought no cheer to the small flotilla anchored in the York; when they had left the fleet, the wind and sea had been getting up, and *Terrible* was taking so much water in her bilges that Admiral Graves had been considering taking her people off and sinking her. They still had not caught up with the French fleet under de Grasse and showed little sign of really wanting to, with their own ships so badly cut up in their top-hamper. The last bit of bad news was that none of the newly arrived frigates had any spare spars for *Desperate*. Nor did any of the few ships of worth in the anchorage, so repairs would take longer than they hoped, unless they could find some decent timber ashore and cut it down themselves.

"Take a good tree ta make a new topmast, sir," Coke the bosun told Treghues that afternoon. "Trestle-trees on the mainmast top were sprung an' need new timber, cross-trees gone ta kindlin', tops'l yard is saved but needs fishin' with a lighter piece er some flat iron. New royal an' topgallant yard as well, sir, not ta mention a new topgallant mast."

"But the shore fairly bristles with good pine, does it not, Mister Coke?" Treghues said, once more seemingly in good cheer and normal state of his faculties. "We could send a working party ashore to hew what we need."

"Aye, sir," Coke agreed. "But where we'd get the horse teams ta do the draggin', I don't know. Army might have some ta spare."

"Artillery beasts, aye," Treghues said. "Mister Railsford, I would admire if you would go ashore with the bosun and a working party. See Captain Symonds and discover who in the army we need to talk to about getting some help in felling trees with which to make repairs."

"Aye, aye, sir," Railsford said. "How many men, Mister Coke?"

"Carpenter an' his crew, sir, mayhap a dozen more hands ta do the strippin' an haulin', some what knows horses," Coke speculated. "Maybe twenty all told, sir, at best."

"We shall take the barge and cutter," Railsford decided. "You and I, Weems and . . . Lewrie in the other."

Alan had been standing near enough to hear and Railsford's eye had fallen on him first. Treghues was in another of his more complaisant moods and made no objection.

"Perhaps I should go ashore now, sir, to liaise with the 'lobsters' first," Railsford said. "It is late in the day to organize any aid from shore and select proper trees before dark."

"Aye, my compliments to Captain Symonds," Treghues said. "See him first, and then talk to the army. We shall put the working party to their labors after breakfast."

"Lewrie, get a crew together for the jolly boat and we shall go ashore now."

"Aye, Mister Railsford, sir." Alan said. He hustled up Weems, who quickly got him a boat's crew and led the towed jolly boat around to the entry port.

They put in at one of the town docks, leaving the boat's crew at the landing under a petty officer, a quarter-gunner with strict instructions to avoid trouble, and walked down the dirt street toward the house that had been indicated as the naval shore party's office. The town teemed with troops in various uniforms of green, red and blue of the various regiments in Cornwallis's army, even the tartans and kilts of either British or Loyalist Highlanders, Carolina Volunteer units, German mercenaries and regular line units.

"Quite a muddle, sir," Alan observed, pointing at all the men and horses active around the town. "One hopes Lord Cornwallis knows what he is about."

"Our role is not to question, Mister Lewrie," Railsford said, almost rolling drunkenly after spending months on an unstable deck and foxed by the steadiness of the land. "We must obey and . . . and *hang* the larger issues."

"Aye, sir," Alan said.

"There is still time to win a victory over the French and the Rebels, Lewrie," Railsford told him. "Were I you, I would try to put the best face on it before the hands and not let them see their officers looking distressed. You shall get in a lot less trouble with the captain if you do. At this moment he needs all the enthusiasm and cheerfulness he can get from his people. He would be most cross with anyone that showed any signs of worry or defeatism. You are already in trouble enough with him."

"Aye, sir," Alan agreed with a humorless laugh. "Too true."

"That is why we attacked those transports last night," Railsford said unexpectedly.

"Sir?"

Railsford went on, mopping his brow with a colored handkerchief against the late-summer heat. "There *were* larger transports, further up the James River, along with some frigates, as we were later informed. We did, in fact, burn a ship to the waterline. But, more to the point, we *did* something, an act of retribution to put heart back into the crew so they could feel we could still strike back on an even basis against our enemies. That is why Commander Treghues took the risk. Not for glory-hunting, and not because he is out of his wits, as you believe. A captain must keep his men in their best fettle, not just in victuals or discipline, but in spirit as well, and you had best remember that if you ever hope to gain a commission."

"I see, sir," Alan replied, crestfallen at the implied rebuke.

"A crew that doubts its own abilities is a crew ready to strike the colors at the first broadside, or when they are hard pressed," Railsford said solemnly.

"But what does one do when recent events are so disheartening?" Alan asked. "When there is no way to put a good face on things?"

"Then hope that discipline and pride will be enough," the first lieutenant said with a smile. "We drill their little minds into rote behavior so they respond without thought, calm or tempest, day or night, peace or war. And we appeal to their pride in themselves as Englishmen and as sailors. We appeal to their pride in their own ship, in their Service. Nothing else much matters outside the bulwarks. All this talk of King and Country is so much moonshine when you get right down to it. People facing death or dismemberment don't care much for the so-called 'patriotic' reasons. They die for their shipmates, to go game before their peers."

"So what must we do to keep the men inspired, sir?" Alan asked, seeing what was necessary over the next few days until they could get out to sea once more.

"Hard work to take their minds off things, for one," Railsford told him as they reached the porch of the house in question. "If we did not have serious hurts to mend in *Desperate*, we would invent some form of labor to keep them busy. Idle hands and idle minds begin to conjure up the worst in the human spirit. Straighten your hat."

They entered the house and conferred briefly with an aide to Captain Symonds. Railsford was given a letter to take to the army headquarters for draft animals and an escort for the next day so they could go beyond the newly dug perimeter fortifications for their timbers. Then they had to walk out into the country beyond the town to seek out the army before dark. They spoke with a major of light infantry, got passed to a colonel named Yorke, finally to a senior officer from the Brigade of Guards named O'Hara and got their request approved. They would be allotted the use of two horse teams for only two days, the needs of the army for the placing of artillery coming first, and would get some provincials for an escort, all to meet them at the docks at an appointed time the next morning.

"Warm work, sir," Alan said as they made their way back towards the town and their waiting boat. "Think we could—"

"No, we cannot, Lewrie," Railsford intoned solemnly. "Did you not get into enough trouble the last time you were ashore?"

"Not of my own making, sir," Alan protested.

"Trouble is your boon companion, Lewrie. You do not have to seek it out; it always finds you. Were we to stop into what passes for a public house around these parts for a pint, you'd have a brawl going within half an hour."

"Sir!" Alan said, much aggrieved by the accusation, but thinking that the first lieutenant was correct; he had gotten into enough trouble in the past with the most innocent of beginnings. Still, it was pleasing to be thought a bellicose sort of rake-hell by his first officer, for the reputation held no malice from Railsford; rather the opposite in fact.

First light found them once more at the main landing in the town, with two boats full of men and tools, men eager to step ashore, no matter what the reason after months aboard one ship. They were looking forward to a new face or two, new tales to hear, the possibility of actually touching something green. The work would be no harder than anything required of them aboard the *Desperate*, perhaps a lot less with horses to do the major hauling once they had felled their choice of trees and stripped them of bark and limbs. It was almost like a picnic outing, complete with rations and drink prepared for later consumption.

They were met by two six-horse gun teams, decent sized horses rather than the usual runty animals found in the colonies, which had made the poor beasts captured on the *Ephegenie* so valuable. There were teamsters dressed in the blue coats of the artillery, and a platoon of men in short red infantry jackets with dark blue facings, light infantry of some sort wearing wide-brimmed black hats adorned with a black silk ribbon, bow and a clump of dark feathers for a plume on the left side of their hats. All of them looked as though they had seen rough service, for the original pristine condition of their uniforms was patched and resewn to orderliness, their white waistcoats and long trousers permanently marred with ground-in dirt, and their lower legs encased in muddy dark gaiters, known as "half spatter-dashes."

"You would be from the *Desperate?*" the young infantry officer asked of Railsford as they alighted on the dock.

"I am, sir," Railsford replied. "Lieutenant Railsford, at your service."

"Lieutenant Chiswick, sir, of the North Carolina Volunteers," the lanky, harsh-looking officer said.

"Midshipman Lewrie, my assistant," Railsford said. "Our bosun, Mister Coke, and his mate, Mister Weems."

"Delighted, sirs." The officer showed no sign of delight at all at that early hour. "This is my ensign, also a Chiswick. We are at your orders, sirs. What is needed?"

"To go inland and find suitable trees to fell for repairs to our ship, lieutenant," Railsford said. "Pine trees, for our top-hamper."

"Whatever that is." Lieutenant Chiswick yawned. "Not much left around the town. We shall have to go outside the defense line to find good stands of pine. I suppose a naval officer can ride, sir? I have a spare horse for you."

"Thank you very much. This naval officer was raised in hunting country in Dorset," Railsford said, grinning.

Railsford mounted expertly and the two parties fell into a rough column, with an advanced party under a corporal leading off, their weapons at high port, ready for anything, even in the midst of an English army encampment. Railsford and Chiswick followed, with the wagons in their wake, and the sailors in a clump behind. Almost without orders, one squad of infantry went to either side of the road, and the rest brought up the rear, as though the sailors were under arrest for some crime.

Alan was galled that he had to walk instead of getting a horse to ride. He had worn his cotton stockings and his worst, cracked pair of shoes in case of mud and damp, and they were not the best fit he had ever ordered from a cobbler. He hoped they were not going far, or his feet would suffer. He fell in at the head of the rough grouping of men from the ship, alongside the young infantry ensign named Chiswick.

"Whatever the devil is that?" Alan asked, seeing the weapon the young man carried.

"A Ferguson rifle, sir." The ensign replied. "Breechloader."

"How does it do that?"

"One rotates the screw-breech, which removes the rear estopment from the user's end of the barrel, sir." Chiswick explained, taking hold of a large lever behind the trigger and guard. The whole thing screwed down revealing the screw behind the breech. "One loads it muzzle down from the rear. One can fire four shots a minute, and it is accurate out to nearly two hundred and fifty yards."

Alan noted that the breech of this weapon was already loaded with a powder cartridge, supposedly also fitted with a ball in the chamber.

"You people are most cautious, sir," he observed, "to load here."

"If you had fought in the back-country in the Carolinas, you also would be loaded and ready round the clock as well, sir," the ensign said with stiff pride.

"Ah, I see," Alan replied, trying to ignore the two unloaded and useless pistols stuck into his pockets. "Seen much action, have you?"

"Quite a bit," Chiswick boasted. "We're light infantry. The Lord Cornwallis uses us for scouting and skirmishing—first in and last out of a battle. We can keep up with Tarleton's Legion when the line infantry would be worn out."

"Ah, Tarleton," Alan said, "I have heard of him. Something of a hard man, I'm told."

"These are hard times," the ensign said. "The Rebels in the Carolinas are not exactly gentle, either, I assure you."

"So a girl once said."

"And where was that, sir?"

"A whorehouse in Charlestown." Alan grinned.

"Really? Which one?" Ensign Chiswick asked, with a first sign of humor lighting his face.

"Lady Jane's, just off the Cooper River."

"I am not familiar with that one."

"Well, Maude's had moved to Wilmington and t'other had been shut down for brawling," Alan said.

"I am familiar with Maude's, however." Chiswick grinned broadly. "Too bad she and her girls could not accompany us, but Lord Cornwallis had us strip to the bone for this march into Virginia, and we had to leave most of the camp followers behind. Damned shame, really."

"So there is no sport to be had hereabouts?" Alan asked.

"No, more's the pity." Chiswick spat. "You may get your laundry done but that's about all, and Yorktown is nothing much."

"Speaking of laundry," Alan said, reminded of the letter he still bore in the tail pocket of his short uniform jacket. "Do you know of some woman named Rodgers? Her daughter Bess bade me carry a letter to her. I believe she associates with a Sergeant Tompkin in Tarleton's Legion."

"I know both of them," Chiswick said. "They are across the river on the Gloucester side. No need for cavalry over here yet. Simcoe's Queen's Rangers and the Legion are both over there. Look here, where does a midshipman stand in the scheme of things?"

"Damned low." Alan had to confess with a rueful expression. "Petty-officer level, an officer in training. I have been in two years almost."

"An ensign is the most junior officer one can be," Chiswick said, offering his hand. "My name is Burgess, by the way, Burgess Chiswick."

"Alan Lewrie."

They established that Burgess was a year older, nineteen, and had been with the colors for a year with the North Carolina Volunteers. By a fortunate fluke, he had not been at King's Mountain with Major Ferguson, the inventor of the superlative firearm he bore, but he had been at Cowpens attached to Tarleton's Legion and the light infantry that accompanied that body.

"And what happened at Cowpens...lord, what a name for a town?"

"Wasn't a town," Burgess informed him. "Just a big meadow, a clearing used for cattle feeding and selling. And they beat our arses there."

"Who, the Rebels?"

"Of course, the Rebels," Burgess said. "They're good as informal fighters, sniping from ambush and all of that, but we mostly had beaten them in more formal battles. The hardest part was catching up with them and bringing them to action, or pursuing them once they were beat. But lately, they've been beating us. Wiped out Major Ferguson and his command at King's Mountain in the Piedmont, mostly Loyalist troops with him but good ones. And then at Cow-pens. Took our charge like regulars and then charged us. Governour and I were happy to see the light of day next morning."

"Governour?" Alan wondered.

"My brother, our lieutenant," Burgess said proudly. "He joined up three years ago, being the oldest. I had to stay home until . . . well, when we lost our lands, there didn't seem to be much point of me not taking the colors any longer."

"What happened to them?"

"Damned Rebels burned us out!" Burgess glared angrily. "Shot all our livestock or drove it off, fired our crops or trampled them flat. Set fire to our barns and stables, torched the house, ran most of the slaves off except for a few house servants. My family had to flee to Wilmington with nothing much more than the clothes they stood up in. Thirty years of work, all gone."

"Where was this?"

"Below Campbelltown, in the lower Cape Fear country."

That did not tell Alan much more, since he was not familiar with anything in the Carolinas beyond the harbors, though he had a rough idea from the description that it was in North Carolina, be-hind Wilmington.

"Perhaps you can regain your lands when we have beaten the French and the Rebels," Alan offered, trying to think of something hopeful.

Burgess turned to stare at him as though he was the featured act in some traveling raree show. "Where the devil have you been lately? We shall never get our lands back, nor do I have any hopes for victory any longer, not with a French army over on the other side of the James from us at this moment and God knows who else gathering on this place. What did you fellows in our wonderful Navy do with them?"

"They beat us." Alan frowned, dropping his voice to a whisper to avoid sharing his thoughts with his crew, which was still trudging along in his rear. He sketched out the progress of the battle which had taken place a few days before, expressing his own distaste for the way it had transpired.

"Well, perhaps there is hope your admiral can get back to grips with this Frenchman de Grasse," Burgess said, mellowing a little. "We could do nothing to stop the landing. They had put four ships in the mouth of the York to keep our ships in while they were landing their troops and guns."

"So that is why no one interfered with the transports. I thought Captain Symonds was shirking or something to not try for them."

"Who's he?"

"Senior naval officer present, in command of the frigate *Charon*."

"Then he could not have done anything in any case," Burgess said. "They landed all his artillery for the fortifications, all eighteen-pounders. We only have field artillery with the army. You'll be fortunate to get out of this as soon as your ship is repaired. We could be hard-pressed for a few weeks as long as the French are present."

"Well, if there is no sport to be had in this Yorktown, I shall indeed be grateful to put back to sea," Alan said as their senior officers called a halt.

They had left town on the main Williamsburg road to the west and had crossed the line of fortifications and entrenchments before what Burgess had informed Alan was the Star Redoubt, and had crossed Yorktown Creek, a sluggish body of water indeed. Burgess gave him the further information that it had not rained in weeks and all the creeks were low, which was limiting the efficiency of the mills in the area where they had hoped to grind the corn they had confiscated on their march up the James River. Many of the cavalry and draft animals were grain fed, and were already suffering from the long march from Wilmington and the peregrinations of the army in the Virginias so far attempted. The troops had also been forced to eat their corn green—which had not done their digestions any good—soaking it and frying it in their mess kits instead of baking it to make a more palatable bread.

Once cleared through the lines, men from the North Carolina

Volunteers spread out into ragged skirmish order, ahead and to either side of the road as they continued their search for wood. After about another mile of travel, they reached a fork in the road, the fork bending back to the southeast and the main road continuing onward inland to the west. Another halt was called for while the officers consulted.

"Most of this is second growth an' damned scrawny, sir," Coke said, peering about them. "Whatcha think of it, Chips?"

"Trash," the carpenter replied. "Musta been cut over a long time ago."

"If we take the fork, we shall end up in mostly cleared land," Lieutenant Chiswick pointed out, gesturing with his riding crop. "And the army most likely has cut over the area before the outlying parallels for materials to stiffen the entrenchments and clear lanes of fire."

"What about out that way?" Railsford asked, shifting his sore behind in the saddle. It had been years since he had spent any time mounted, no matter how rural his upbringing.

"The Williamsburg road?" Chiswick frowned. "We did not come that way on either of our marches in this area, so I am not familiar with it. Though there are some steep hills in there, as we can observe. I am told there is a creek thereabouts."

"Aye, a creek, sor." The carpenter brightened. "They'd be timber as thick as cat's fur along a creek, and in them little hills. Ye can see pine from here, sor."

"That sounds like our best prospect, then," Railsford decided.

"Your men are armed, sir?" Lieutenant Chiswick asked.

"We brought cutlasses and a few muskets, yes, sir."

"Then if it is your intention that we proceed into those hills by the creek, off the main road, I would strongly suggest you load your muskets and tell off a portion of your party for protection, sir."

"There may be Rebels this close?" Railsford asked, reining his mare closer to the army officer to converse more softly.

"There are Virginia Militia and some few regulars about, sir, under a Frenchman named Lafayette," Chiswick told him, not without a wolfish grin of delight to have the much-vaunted Navy at his mercy in their ignorance of land fighting. "Were I a Rebel officer,

God forbid, I should be at the business of scouting the whereabouts of my foe at this very instant."

"An' wild Indians, too, sir?" Coke asked, peering about with new fear.

"I should not be a bit surprised, sir." Lieutenant Chiswick said, hiding his glee at the stupidity of his fellow man. Every newcomer from England expected to be scalped or skewered by painted savages as soon as he or she alighted from his ship, right in the middle of a major town, and as a lowly Colonial, Chiswick was only too happy to play the game of scaring the bejeezus out of superior home-raised Englishmen.

"Surely not," Railsford scoffed, only half convinced that Chiswick was having a jape at their expense.

"No organized bands, sir, but they still live in the Piedmont and some have sided with the Rebels as scouts and irregulars," Chiswick assured him, pursing his lips to control his grin. "Either way, it's best not to be too lax. We're a small and tempting morsel beyond reach of our lines."

"Mister Lewrie?" Railsford called.

"Aye, aye, sir."

"Tell our people to load muskets and keep a wary lookout, but no firing at anything without direct orders from either me or you."

"Aye, aye, sir." Alan said, turning to speak to the men in a low voice. "Load your firelocks. Check your flints carefully. Prime, but do not carry your pieces at cock or half cock. Do not even think of taking aim unless you hear it from me first, or I'll see the man who did dancing on the gratings, hear me?"

The picnic outing mood was gone now as the men check-snapped their firelocks, plied their gun tools to ram down powder cartouches and ball, primed their pans and closed frissons.

They were beyond the sounds of axes ringing as the army built up defenses, and they were in wild country, a lot wilder looking country than anything they had ever seen at home. The clearings were not orderly and terraced fields full of crops, bound by stone walls or hedges, but openings in the woods laced with rank growths of weeds and high grass. The woods themselves were not picturesque nests of trees on hilltops above verdant farmland but brooding, dark forests that sloughed down almost to the dirt road, full of secondary growth and bushes where the sun did not penetrate except in dapples here and there. Even the sound of the native birds were different than what they were used to from their youth, making the land alien, too full of threat and almost too large and uncivilized to be understood. It truly was not Surrey or Kent—more like the sort of place that could harbor thousands of half-naked savages intent on taking their lives from ambush at any moment.

"It *is* sort of ominous, isn't it?" Alan said to Burgess as he loaded his pistols.

"Definitely not a game park." Burgess grinned. "Are you a good shot?"

"If one can be a good shot with these Sea Pattern monstrosities," Alan said, closing the frissons and blowing excess powder off, "then yes, I am. I am much better with a musket."

"Hunt much?"

"Some. Birds, mostly," Alan said. "But I must warn you, I am a London man."

"God help us," Burgess said, "but, if you can be successful at fowling, you may not do much harm. Don't let your sailors shoot at any of my men. We shall be out skirmishing. I have to go now. Good luck to you."

Lieutenant Chiswick made a hand signal to his men, and his sergeants and corporals took off silently, leading a party of wary troops to either side of the road to melt into the woods, another party to advance down the road almost in the bushes on either side, well spread out so that a single volley would not strike all of them. A corporal took five men back the way they had come to back-trail the column to avoid any surprises from that direction, leaving Railsford, Lewrie and their men alone with the artillery teams and drivers. Railsford took out his pocket watch and studied it, to follow Chiswick's last whispered instruction that he wait a full two minutes before following his advance scouts.

"I cannot hear them any longer," Alan said, marveling at the silence with which the North Carolina Volunteers could move through the thick brush and timber.

"Backwoodsmen, I'll wager," Railsford said. "As good as any

Indian at this sort of thing. Rather inspiriting to think so, at any rate."

Railsford dismounted suddenly and rubbed the small of his back. "Been a while," he sighed, stretching a kink from his posterior.

And a mounted man is automatically a target for some Rebel sniper, Alan thought grimly.

"Care to ride for a spell?" Railsford offered, evidently thinking the same thing. To a partisan hiding behind some bush or rock, he could not appear to be anything other than an officer, even if the man did not recognize a naval uniform from an artilleryman's.

He is not intentionally trying to get me killed, Alan thought. And I cannot look suitably senior enough to be shot, even mounted.

"Happily, sir," Alan decided, springing into the saddle.

He was cautious enough, however, to remove his unadorned cocked hat and toss it into one of the gun caissons, believing that a bareheaded man would be even less tempting.

"Hoppy, give me your musket," Alan ordered the nearest armed sailor.

"Sir?" The man said, quailing at the thought of being unarmed.

"Take one of my pistols in exchange," Alan snapped, offering one of the useless damned things. "With these wild Colonials about you in these woods you're as safe as houses anyway, and I might see something to pot for supper."

Satisfied by Alan's innocent lie that he was intent on hunting up a deer for the men's mess, Hoppy surrendered his musket and took the pistol from him. Alan slung the musket over his neck and shoulder so that it hung across his back, muzzle up like an infantryman on the march, which would make him look even more menial to any lurking sharpshooter in the woods.

"Some venison'd go down right tasty, sir," Hoppy said with a smile of relief, wanting to be convinced.

"I hear one deer in the Virginias will feed twenty messes," Alan said loud enough for the rest of the men to hear, understanding what the first lieutenant meant about keeping the men in good spirits. "Mayhap we can get one or two, even if we have to go shares with the 'lobsters'."

He turned and cantered back up to Railsford, who was still intent on his watch.

"Should have been long enough," Railsford said, snapping the case shut. "Off we go. Lead off, Mister Lewrie."

"Aye, aye, sir," Alan replied, heading down the road. The walk so far had been hell on his feet, and he was glad to get a chance to ride.

He soon caught up with Lieutenant Chiswick, who, a Ferguson rifle in his right hand, was leading his own horse. As soon as he caught sight of the red tunic, he slowed his mount to a plodding walk and tried to keep separation from the infantry officer. Chiswick, however, stopped his own roan and waited for him to catch up, cocking a wry eyebrow at him.

"Your lieutenant prefers discretion over valor, I see," Chiswick smiled briefly as they drew even with each other.

"Not on his own decks, sir," Alan answered a bit more sharply than he would with a naval officer, but Chiswick took no offense at his tone, merely shrugged and turned back to lead the horse up the road once more.

"If you are going to carry a musket, let it rest on your saddle and not hang useless on your back, Mister . . . Lewrie, did he say?"

"Aye, sir, Lewrie," he said softly, slipping the musket to a more quickly usable perch across his lap, pointing to the left side of the road.

They proceeded in silence for some time, with the more experienced Chiswick listening intently to the sounds of the woods, which so far seemed benign in the extreme, for all the foreboding that was hinted in their lush and wild dark jumble.

"Do all your men have Fergusons, sir?" Alan asked almost in whisper. The road opened up on either side in rough clearings, and he could espy some of Chiswick's men in the woods ahead by their red coats and white breeches.

"Mostly," Chiswick said, peering into the woods still. "When our company was raised, my father helped outfit them and thought Major Ferguson was onto a good thing. Some of the other companies had to make do with the Brown Bess or their own guns from home. Do you like it?"

"Aye, sir," Alan said. "I'd like to try my hand with one someday."

"Pity poor Patrick Ferguson could not convince the army to adopt it," Chiswick commented, looking up at Alan for a moment. "Now he's dead and his rifle will most likely die with him."

"It would be perfect for use at sea, though," Alan observed. "To fire at long range with aimed fire would play merry hell with officers on a quarterdeck."

"As long as the enemy did not play merry hell with you," Chiswick grunted. "I cannot imagine just standing there out in the open like you do in sea fighting."

"Mostly you are behind a bulwark or a barricade made of rolled-up hammocks, sir," Alan said. "For my part, I cannot imagine standing out in the open like regular infantry does, trading broadsides or volleys or whatever at a hundred paces."

"Let the *line* troops do that." Chiswick sneered. "We're riflemen, by God—out on the flanks where we can do the most good, screening the advance or covering a retreat."

"So your brother informed me, sir."

"Well, there are some pines for you." Chiswick pointed to the low ridge ahead with his rifle barrel. "Do you believe they would suit?"

"It is not for me to judge, sir, but I will fetch the carpenter and the bosun," Alan said, looking at the trees growing up the hill to the right and left of the road. "They look tall and thick enough."

"I shall halt my skirmishers at the top of the hill until you have made your decision, then," Chiswick offered.

"Aye, sir." Alan said, and wheeled his horse about to canter back.

It seemed that those trees would suit admirably, being both tall enough, straight enough and thick enough to serve as new masts and spars once they were trimmed of limbs and stripped down. The limbs were not so low on them that the best parts of the trees would have too many knots or knurls once they were cut to the right lengths.

"Ya chose well, sor," the carpenter allowed to Chiswick.

"We used to mill timber and float it down to Wilmington on the river," Chiswick told them. "They looked suitable to me."

"Let's get to work, then," Railsford said, all of a bustle to get something accomplished so they could get out of those woods before dark. "Lewrie, have the hands stack arms and start felling those trees the bosun and the carpenter indicate."

"Aye, sir," Alan said, dismounting. "Perhaps we shall finish in time to get a little hunting done, sir."

"What do you say to that, Lieutenant Chiswick?" Railsford said.

"I'd not stray too far if you do," he cautioned. "The fewer men the better, and the less shots as well. We do not know who is out here, and do not want to draw too much attention to our party."

"Yes, I suppose so." Railsford frowned. "Still, some fresh meat'd be welcome."

"With a rifle instead of a musket, I could bag something, sir," Alan said, hoping to get out of standing around supervising the working party. "I would not fire until I was sure of my target."

"Yes," Railsford said, "and you're about as useful at this as tits on a man. Bosun, have we a good woodsman to accompany the midshipman?"

"Cony, sir, twas caught poachin' afore he joined."

"I would have to send some of my men, regardless," Chiswick said. "Poacher or not, this is not some squire's private preserve."

"I could take Mollow, sir," Burgess Chiswick volunteered. "And we could use the horses to carry anything we bag."

"Right," Chiswick said after a moment's thought. "But do not go too far or stray too far from the road. If you meet up with any trouble, strike for the river to the north and get into the open. No wild firing, or I'll have your hide, see?"

"When did I need more than one shot, dear brother?" Burgess chided.

"True enough," the elder Chiswick had to admit, albeit grudgingly. "Mollow do you see the sergeant for the trumpet. Give us a blast on it if you run into any enemy troops."

"That I will, 'pon my honor," the private said, slouching over the barrel of his rifle as no English regular would ever be allowed.

"You wished to try a Ferguson," Lieutenant Chiswick said to Lewrie as his private dashed off on his errand. "Here, use mine."

He offered the rifle and a cartouche pouch, taking Lewrie's in exchange. "If you think twenty rounds shall be enough?"

"If not, perhaps I shall be able to pester a deer to death, sir," Alan replied.

"Everyone ready?" Burgess asked once Mollow had joined them along with Cony, the wiry young ordinary seaman. "Here, leave your sword behind. You'll only trip on it in the woods. Got pistols just in case?" Every man carried at least one, with the army man armed with a pair of long barreled, and probably more accurate, dragoon pistols. Chiswick took off his own sword and tossed it to his orderly, retaining a bayonet.

"Along the creek, or over the hills?" Alan asked the ensign.

"Too late in the morning for game along the creek," the younger Chiswick decided. "They'd come down to drink at dawn and then go back up into the woods. Best cross the hill and see what's on the other side. We'll lead the horses."

CHAPTER 6

AFTER the first hour they had covered only a mile, creeping like slugs through the woods to the south of the road. Mollow and Cony were out ahead on the flanks, almost out of sight, while Lewrie and the ensign formed the central pair, within a long musket shot of each other. Alan was enjoying himself hugely as he picked a way through the underbrush wide and high enough for the led mare to follow. He had not been this far away from uniforms and naval discipline in months, even though he had to admit to himself that he did not know what the hell he was doing. He was not a trained hunter, not like Mollow, Cony or Chiswick, who had been at it almost since birth. He was indeed a city man, only exposed to hunting in the summers on his father's not-so-large estate, more at home with bird shooting or riding behind a pack of hounds over open fields.

This silent crouching and stalking, listening for the sounds of game and trying to limit one's own clumsy crashings and slitherings was foreign to him, but he was getting into the spirit of it although it was damned dry work. The ground was too dry to see much in the way of a sign, or to recognize it as old or new if he had. Face it, I am not a red Indian he thought. Still, it was so close to play instead of work that he could easily lose himself in the process, not being dependent on what he shot to be fed that night or not.

The woods began to open up before him, and he could see signs that the trees had been thinned at one time; some stumps were still sticking up. He could stand up fully, and he halted to survey things. There was less shrubbery, and what was evident was low and fairly new. He looked to his left to see Cony halted as well, merely a flash of red-and-white checkered shirt between the trees. He looked to his right to see Chiswick, who was coming towards him without his horse. As Alan watched, Mollow brought up the rear, leading the animal. Chiswick waved at him and pointed, as though shoving him away, and Alan got the idea that he should turn and go south towards Cony. They carried on this silent dialogue until he determined that that was indeed what the officer intended.

They carried on south for some time until Cony waved them to a halt and motioned them down while he snuck deeper into the woods to the right, their original direction before the turn. Alan sat down behind a tree and brought his rifle up to his side, glad for a chance to get off his aching feet in the cracked and pinching shoes. Chiswick came on down to him from the north to join him.

"We're on someone's farmland," Chiswick said softly, taking a seat near him with his rifle ready as well.

"How can you tell?"

"Stumps, for one," Chiswick said, as though it was self-evident. "And I ran into a rail fence and a lane heading down this way. You would have, too, in another minute. Low, sunken lane. Great place for an ambush. And there was a pasture and another fence on the other side of that."

"Did it look occupied?" Alan asked, crouching by a sturdy bush to tie the reins of his horse so both hands would be free to use his rifle.

"Couldn't tell." Chiswick shrugged.

"Well, is that good or bad?" Alan persisted, a little put off that he had to ask so much information. Damme, I spend nigh on two years getting the lore right at one thing, and here I am a rank amateur again! And the galling thing is, I don't know enough to even ask the right questions. He's going to think me a complete slow coach.

"No way to know until we discover it," Chiswick said with a grin. "If it's a Rebel farmstead, we can take what we like. Might be abandoned after the armies came through here in the summer, and we can still take what we like, loyalties be damned. On the other hand, we could run into a battalion of troops already using it."

"In which case, we fade away like startled deer and head back to the working party," Alan said.

"There's the truth of it," Chiswick replied, very much on his guard from hard field experience, but reveling in danger. "Ah, I see your man wants us."

They rose to a crouch and headed down toward Cony, motioning Mollow to bring the other mount down to where they had waited. Mollow understood his ensign's signal and tied both horses to the same clump of brush, then came to join them so that all the party were together.

"Fence, sir." Cony grinned as though he was at home sneaking into his squire's rabbit runs. "They's a farm t'other side o' this fence. They's somethin' movin', too, sir. Don't sound like men. Cow, maybe."

"Supper, maybe." Alan grinned in return. "And without firing one shot to attract attention."

"Don't eat it before it's skinned, sailor," Burgess chuckled. "I and Mollow will scout ahead. You wait here with your man. If you hear any to-do, get back to the horses quick as a wink and head for the main road. Don't worry about us."

Burgess pulled his rifle back to half cock and went off to the left, pointing the private dead ahead. Alan thought about cocking his own rifle, but demurred, not sure enough of himself in case there was a problem until it had presented itself in true colors.

"Smelt like a farm, though, sir." Cony said almost in his ear, taking dangerous liberty with ship's discipline and the separation expected between a common seaman and a midshipman. "Cain't hide that from my nose, sir."

"We shall see directly, then." Alan said, trying to appear as stoical as a post-captain, while ready to squirm with anticipation. It was five minutes before Mollow came sneaking through the brush to them almost on his hands and knees.

"We're in luck, that we are," Mollow said, showing the same lack of formality to Lewrie that he had to his own lieutenant before.

"Was it a cow?" Alan asked, still whispering.

"It's a whole damn fuckin' Ark over thar," Mollow said. "Farm paddock an' pastures. They's a cow with two calves, coupla sheep an' two half-grown pigs. Mighty skittish, so we don't wanta spook 'em. Mighta been turned out wild. No sign o' life from the house yit. Mister Burgess is a'checkin' that out now, but we can move up. Mind ya do it quiet, now. I'll fetch the horses."

They followed Mollow's trail through the woods until they reached a rail fence made of split pine logs stacked zig-zag atop each other waist high. Mollow had very quietly taken a stretch of them down to let room for the horses to be led through. There was a dry dirt lane before them that led to a wider clearing to the left and the hint of a house and some outbuildings. In a pasture directly ahead of them, there were some animals grazing or rooting about, warily distanced to the far side of the pasture near the trees, but showing no real signs of distress.

"Put a halter on that cow, an' the little'uns'll tag along quiet as mice, Mister Lewrie," Cony said, taking his musket off half cock. "Pigs might be a problem, though, sir."

"We could pack them back on the horses once they're dead."

"Better'n venison any day, sir," Cony said, slinging his gun and heading off for the farmstead to the left.

Ensign Chiswick met them in the middle of the road, his rifle also now slung muzzle down and a rag wrapped around the lock to keep dirt out.

"Place looks abandoned," he said in a normal tone of voice. "The barn's been burned down and the house appears to have been looted. The doors and window shutters are off and the yard's full of castoffs."

"It's not hunting, but we'll take something home for the pot," Alan said, glad that they did not have to take aim and fire at something that would draw attention to themselves.

"And look what else I found," Chiswick said, holding up his left hand in triumph.

It looked like a rough lump of candle wax, which made Alan wonder just what a colonial thought valuable.

"It's soap!" Chiswick chortled. "Homemade soap. Might take the hide off you, but it'll get you clean enough for a burying."

"I'd pass on the burying," Alan said quickly, "but it has been a time since I had a full bath."

"I had noticed," Chiswick japed, wrinkling his nose as though he thought Alan stank worse than most people did. "There is a small creek in the place, dammed up below the barn for a stock pond. Once we get these animals rounded up, we may bathe before heading back."

"Is that safe, way out here?" Alan asked.

"Nothing ran those animals off, so it should be. Now, how are you at roping wild pigs?"

It turned out that Alan was terrible at roping wild pigs. It was easy enough to get a rope around the neck of the mother cow, for they had not been running wild very long. Once she was led into the barnyard, her calves followed along docilely enough. The sheep could be hemmed in with much shouting and waving into a corner of fencing, where Alan could dive onto one and hold it down until a lead could be placed on it. In the barnyard they found two chickens and a rooster, which were despatched with a piece of light wood and gutted on the spot to tie them on the saddles.

The pigs, though. The pigs were devils in disguise, squealing and snorting and making mock charges at them, almost impossible to grab and fast as the wind for being built so low to the ground. A man on horseback could not keep up with their bursts of speed or match their twists and turns. Mollow was an expert with a length of rope, forming a noose at one end and throwing it in a whistling arc to settle over any target's neck to draw snug, making it look like an effortless skill. Even that did not avail over the thick necks of the pigs.

"The devil with it!" Alan gasped after his fourth trip at a dead run across the pasture. "Why don't we . . . just shoot . . . the buggers?"

"Suppose we'll have to," Chiswick said, panting on his knees by Lewrie. "Hate to do it, though."

"I *hate* the bastards," Alan growled. "I'll do it!"

"The noise is what I meant. Look out!"

One of the pigs had raced back straight for them, evidently wanting to get his own back. He was not a wild boar with tusks to slash a man open, but he had a mean set of teeth anyway. Chiswick jumped free, but Alan could not move in time and could only roll away as the hog slammed into him at full tilt, almost knocking all the wind out of him, rooting with his snout at Alan's crotch.

"Damned if you do!" Alan cried, drawing his dirk with one

hand and grabbing a forefoot with the other. He stabbed down, up, sideways, as the hog rolled him like a slopbucket around the pasture and began to squeal in pain. Alan had a chance to roll on top and get a few more strokes in with his dirk while the blood flew like a fountain. Finally, assured the animal was dead, he gladly got to his feet and backed away.

The other pig succumbed to a rifle shot, and their course in animal husbandry was over for the day, leaving them time to laugh at Lewrie's appearance. He was pig blood and pig shit, old, dried cow pats and grass stains from head to foot, his stockings torn down to his ankles, one shoe missing, and the seams of his jacket ripped open. The black ribbon that bound his clubbed-back hair was gone and his hair hung lank and dirty on either side of his face.

"Hurrah, you done fer 'im, sir!" Cony roared, taking an opportunity to get a laugh on an officer-to-be.

"Might be needin' this," Mollow said, offering him his shoe.

"Still have that soap, Chiswick?" Alan glared, his chest heaving for air after his battle to the death with an enraged porker. "I think I'll take you up on your offer of a bath."

They slit both pigs' throats, dragged them into the farmyard and hung them up to bleed fully after slicing their bellies open and gutting them. Mollow made a drag from two fence poles depended from one of the horses' saddles and laced them together so that the carcasses could be carried. Then Chiswick gallantly offered to stand guard while Cony and Lewrie got an opportunity for a wash in the stock pond.

Cony was having little of it. He took off his shirt, socks and shoes, rolled up his slop trousers and waded in for a quick splash, not having much use for soap. "Tis unhealthy ta take too many baths, sir, so it is," he said firmly. "One at yer birthin', one at yer weddin', one at yer dyin', that's all a good Englishman needs."

Alan, though, was happy to shuck his clothes and let them soak in the pond while he waded in with soap in hand, naked as the day he was born.

There was little enough fresh water aboard ship, rationed at one gallon per day per man, and most of that used for boiling rations in the steep-tubs, with only a pint a day for sponging or shaving, so it was heaven to lie back with his posteriors resting on the shallow bottom and lave himself with water warmed by the sun. He scrubbed with the hard lump of soap until all his saltwater boils and chafes stung, but it felt like a healing sting, like staunching a cut in sea-water. He stood up knee deep and lathered his whole body, then dunked and rinsed. He soaped his scalp and rubbed and scratched with his fingers until his hair felt almost squeaky between his hands.

"A little bit of heaven, is it not?" Burgess asked, squatting by the bank with rifle in hand to stand guard for him.

"Maybe it is dangerous to staunch one's perspiration, or bathe too often, but now and then, it's marvelous!" Alan sighed happily.

"I told your seaman to scrub out the worst from your uniform."

"Thank you right kindly, Chiswick. Let me know when this is maddening to you and I shall spend another twenty minutes in the water."

"Take your time." Chiswick waved as if it did not matter. "I had a dunk two days ago in a creek closer to the town. Don't forget to do behind your ears. Your momma would not allow that to pass un-washed."

"Never had one," Alan replied. "I've always had dirty ears. No one would know me without them."

"For dear old nurse, then," Chiswick shot back. He rose to his feet and took a long look around. "This must have been a nice farm once."

"Really?" Alan said, wondering what had been so nice about a cabin made of pine logs with no mark of real civilization to it.

"For this part of the world, yes," Chiswick said, changing his tone, which made Alan swivel to look at him. "More than half the farmers in the Colonies would give dearly to look so prosperous or orderly."

"What was your own place like?" Alan asked, raising one leg to give it equal treatment with the soap.

"Oh, we were proper squires in the Carolinas," Burgess said, smiling but not much amused by the remembrance. "Had a brick house and some columns out on the portico. Painted barns and out-buildings. We grew tobacco, corn, rice and timber, and had the mill, too. Tried our hand with indigo, but never got the hang of it, not like some closer to the coast. We had a decent herd of cattle and sheep. And some really fine horses."

"And I hope you killed all your pigs . . . painfully," Alan said.

"Never asked 'em." Burgess grinned.

"So you were what my whore in Charlestown called Tidewater people?"

"Charleston," Burgess corrected without thought. "Yes, we were, in a way. Sort of betwixt and between Piedmonters and Tidewater, not fully one or the other. People firmly established in the Tidewater put on more airs than we could afford."

"I'm sorry you got burned out," Alan said, rising and dripping water as he waded the few paces ashore. "Regular troops or Regulators or whatever?"

"You did learn a lot from that whore of yours," Burgess replied, tossing him a scrap of cloth with which to dry himself. It had been some woman's sack gown once, a light blue linen worked with white embroidery in a pattern that was now hard to identify, evidently something that Burgess had found in the house or the yard, smelling strongly of mildew and leaf mold. It was fairly clean and dry, though, so he used it without another care.

"No, twas a troop of horse rode through while the army and the militia were away over toward Charlotte," Burgess said, his hazel eyes narrowing in anger. "Wild as over-mountain men, not even an organized troop, most of 'em. Some local hothead Patriots, too, as they like to style themselves. *Most* of our neighbors were Scots, loyal to the Crown."

"Were you there then?" Alan asked, sitting down in the sun to finish drying with the scrap of gown across his lap for modesty.

"Aye, I was there." Burgess winced, his hands growing tight on the rifle. "My daddy and momma, my sister Caroline and my younger brother."

"Did they harm any of you?"

"They shot George." Burgess glared. "Shot him down like a dog. He was just fourteen; he didn't know. They were taking his favorite horse and he went after them and . . . they just shot him down. And they laughed. He bled to death before we could do anything for him."

"My God, I'm sorry, Chiswick," Alan said, shocked in spite of all the deaths he had seen in his short time in the Navy.

Burgess went on. "Could have been worse. Their leader, one of the local Rebels, was a gentleman. Else we'd have all been killed, and my momma and sister raped. Their leader had that man beat half to death right on the spot. But then, he went on looting the place after that, so it wasn't much comfort to us. We all got used pretty ill, anyway, what with all the shoving and pushing. Couple of our house servants got shot, and they ran off the rest, along with the stock. Then they allowed us some time to gather what we could, and torched the place."

Alan didn't know what to say, so he finished dressing. Cony had done a fair job as hammock-man and had gotten out all the worst smuts.

"I'll stand guard for your bath now," Alan offered.

"I knew that bastard, Lewrie." Burgess almost moaned.

"That Rebel neighbor?"

"It was one of our cousins," Burgess said, on the verge of tears.

"Holy shit on a biscuit!" Alan gaped. That proves it. The whole bloody country's mad as a lunatick in Bedlam, he thought.

"I grew up with him, played with him, hunted with him, sported with him and his family," Burgess said. "They were better off than us, real squires of the county. They had no use for more land, but they've got ours now, and some of our slaves and our stock. From Momma's side they were, in the Carolina's longer than we were, closer to Wilmington, and the town turned into a hotbed of rebellion until we occupied it. Their daddy was at all the meetings and conventions, saying he was for the King and only wanted his rights as an Englishman, but then they all changed and turned on us 'cause Daddy was a newcomer and stood up for King George. God, I cannot tell you how much I hate them. How I want to see them suffer and die. You cannot know what it is to be betrayed by your own blood!"

"The hell I can't," Alan said without mirth. "When we get back I shall tell you about it, if there's time. But if we got our wishes, a battalion of people would be consigned to Hell. Now stick your head under water for a while to cool the heat of your blood."

"I guess they used us for an example, of what would happen if any more of our neighbors stayed Loyalist." Burgess muttered on as he stripped away his uniform to take a scrub. "Like I said, most of our neighbors were Scots. They came over after Culloden, and when they give an oath, they never break it. Most of the lower Cape Fear is like that, around Cross Creek and Campbelltown. I suppose we were just too good a target. Daddy had helped Colonel Hamilton outfit the Royal North Carolina Regiment, our unit, so they had to do something to punish us, what with Governour already with the colors and all, and half the men away fighting. But we felt so safe there, with our neighbors of one mind with us to support the Crown. And with the Fannings and Cunninghams and Tarletons on our side raiding the Rebels, they had to respond. But everyone in the county loved George, Lewrie. He was the best horseman and hunter going, not afraid of anything. I'd rather it had been me, sometimes."

"But your family is safe, now," Alan said, trying to change the subject. God, he thought, and I believed I had a vicious set of relations.

"For the moment," Burgess said, wading into the water and sitting down in the shallows. He did duck his head and came up spluttering, and it seemed to calm him. "Wilmington, though, is full of Rebels and sympathizers. Were it not for Major Craig and his garrison, and Fort Johnston at the tip of the peninsula, I fear they'd be slaughtered in their beds. Daddy's not been the same since, Momma's not a strong person and only poor Caroline with what blacks we haven't been forced to sell to keep body and soul together to run things. She's a strong girl, is Caroline, but I doubt even she can cope if things get worse. Prices are high, higher for Loyalists from those Rebel townspeople. We left what money we had, but we haven't been paid in months. They were going to seek cheaper lodgings, last we saw them before we marched north. Sorry, Lewrie."

"Sometimes it helps to talk. Go on and bathe. I'll guard."

While the army men splashed in the sun-warmed water, he wandered up to a higher vantage point above the stock pond by the burned out barn and outbuildings. Cony had gone to see to the stock they had captured, and was using a seaman's knife to cut some grass for the cows, once more back in the peaceful world of animals and farm chores he had left God knew how long before to take the joining bounty and enter the harsh world of the Navy.

"Keep a sharp eye peeled, Cony," Lewrie had to remind him.

"Aye, sir," Cony said, as he ruffled the becoming tuft of woolly hair on one calf's skull. "Poor beasts. Shoulda been weaned long ago, I 'spects, but nary a soul about fer months ta do it, most like. Nearly a yearlin' now an' still nuhsin' 'is momma."

Reluctantly, Cony took up his musket, cartouche bag and powder horn and headed off toward the edge of the woods to the west, where they came down almost to the edge of the stock pond. Watching him go, Alan could see that the fence between the pasture where they had seized their livestock and the stock pond had been torn down; perhaps by the raiders that had looted the place, or perhaps by the animals in their thirst once things had settled down and they had returned to the farmstead from the woods where they had fled.

Alan went off toward the yard of the house to keep an eye on the dirt lane that ran down from the Williamsburg road, and the wider expanse of the pastures and fields. There was corn growing there, rows of beans and potatoes of some kind, which might have been ripe enough to pick, and Alan reminded himself that they might want to gather some before going back to the working party. He hunted about for a sack or keg for carrying.

Further north up the road there was another fence, beyond the home garden enclosure, and there were broad-leaved plants there, some already turning brittle and brown under the hot autumn sun; tobacco, he surmised, never having seen it growing before, or having much use for it up until then. He did know that tobacco fetched high prices in London shops, so perhaps Burgess was correct that this had been a fairly prosperous farm once.

Alan was dressed informally in breeches and damp shirt—his waistcoat and short blue jacket were still drying after a good scrubbing—so he was concerned that he stood out too prominently against the greenery. He went back from his vantage point to the shadows of the house to where he could still see a long distance should anyone attempt to sneak up on them, but not be as easily spotted.

The house was not as rude as he had first thought, either, being well-made and chinked, the timbers adzed flat instead of the logs being laid round or still furred with bark. There had once been precious glass in the windows, and the door and shutters that had been ripped off had once been gaily painted and of good milled lumber, most likely done by the owners themselves. The porch was neat, the supporting posts made square and solid and white-washed still, the floor of the porch planed or sanded and close-fitting as a ship's deck, and nearly as white. There were overturned chairs with cleverly rushed seats scattered about, and he righted one for a rest on the porch near one of the windows.

After a few minutes, however, he became bored, and began to peek into the open window more and more, wondering if the raiders of whichever side had left anything worth looting.

He rose and scanned the area of the stock pond. The soldier Mollow was out of the water and dressing, near his rifle and ready for immediate danger while Burgess Chiswick was toweling himself dry and already in his breeches and stockings.

Thinking there would be little danger, he rose from the chair and entered the house. It was a lot grander than he had thought inside as well. There was a large room with a plank floor that had been oiled or varnished at one time, and was still shiny under the dust of neglect that had gathered. There had been a cleverly made fireplace and hearth on one wall, and a neat mantel. There had been a bookcase, now smashed into kindling, and perhaps a dozen books scattered on the floor. The furniture was heavy and European made, either brought by the emigrants or ordered with profits from the farm's produce, though the cabinets and chests were empty. One of the books that lay open took his interest, one of Fielding's novels— *Joseph Andrews*—which he had heard was a merry story.

"God, what a smell," he whispered, now that he was in the house.

Folding the book closed and sticking it into his waistband, he prowled towards the overturned dining table. The glint of metal caught his eyes, and he knelt to pick up a discarded pewter knife, a pair of spoons and a fork, which went into his breeches pockets. They could use them in *Desperate*'s midshipmen's mess, if only to replace the ones that their steward Freeling had lost over the months. He found a pewter mug smashed flat by something, another fork which was in good shape and a ladle, which would come in handy for dipping out soup or rum toddies.

Then he tried the bedrooms, which both opened off the main room.

"Oh, my God!" he screeched once he had the door open to reveal what had been hidden. The stench of long decomposition rolled over him like a channel fog.

He dropped the ladle and almost dropped his rifle as he backed away. But it was the sight that had forced him to retreat; there was a nude woman on the high bed, long dead and eyeless. She had been ripped open like a slaughtered hog and had stained the sheets black with her blood and entrails. And pinned to the wall . . .

At the horror Alan lost what little breakfast he had had.

Pinned to the wall with a bayonet, a tiny baby too small to be a suckling babe—perhaps ripped from that ravaged belly before birth —now with parchment-dark skin and tiny little bones and leathery looking stains on the whitewash. Beside it, written in blood: THOU SHALT NEVER BIRTH ANOTHER REBEL.

"Jesus Christ!" Alan was gagging, bent almost double but unable to take his eyes from the sight. "Oh, my merciful God in Heaven!"

Burgess burst into the cabin with his rifle ready for firing. He came to Alan's side and dragged him away and gave him a firm shove toward the door and the fresher air on the porch.

Alan clung to a porch post and continued to heave, though his stomach was empty. "God, I never saw anything like that! No one should ever see such a sight! God in Heaven!"

He emptied his pockets of his loot and flung the utensils into the dirt of the yard, threw away the merry book and felt he could use one more very long bath to get the oily, cold-sweat feel of putrefaction off his skin, to be cleansed of what he had seen in that bedroom.

"Here," Burgess said, shoving a small, stoppered flask at him. He tore off the cork and took a long pull at whatever it was, which almost choked him. It was alcoholic, that he realized, but hot as fire and twice the bite of neat rum—at the moment he needed it badly.

"What the devil is this stuff?" he managed to choke out.

"Corn whiskey," Burgess said, dragging him free of the porch and walking him over to the well on the other side of the yard. "You'll not see its like in England, but it's popular here—and cheap."

"That could take your mind off your *own* death," Alan said.

Burgess cranked up the bucket from the bottom of the well, sniffed at the water to see if the well had been fouled, then offered him the bucket in lieu of the missing dipper. Alan took a sip or two, but felt better dumping it over his head and shoulders and swiping his face with both of his hands.

"Wot was it?" Mollow asked, now dressed in full uniform and ready for a killing, his Ferguson at full cock.

"Dead woman and baby in the house," Burgess said tightly. "Poor Mister Lewrie saw it and near lost his wits."

"The usual sort o' thing, Mister Burgess?" Mollow asked.

"Worse than the usual," Burgess replied.

"Should I be booryin' 'em?"

"Much too late for that," Chiswick said with a shake of his head.

"The usual?" Alan demanded, after another long pull at the flask. "The *usual?* What's so bloody usual about seeing a woman gutted and her unborn babe stuck to the wall with steel?"

"They were Rebels," Chiswick told him.

"Damn you to hell, Rebel or savage, no one deserved that!"

"I'm not saying anyone ever deserves that, Alan," Burgess insisted, taking back his flask now that Lewrie looked human once more and full of normal, righteous anger. "But like your whore must have told you, this is the worst sort of civil war. It's not flags and trumpets and regulars going at each other like a war in Europe, not here in the South, anyways. It's partisan fighting, and horrors like this on every hand. Families turned on each other, neighbors turned on each other, and after a while the decent spirit of Man gets lost in the tit-for-tat."

"How would you know they were Rebels?" Alan asked.

"You read that . . . epitaph on the wall," Burgess said. "And you'll notice there's no men's bodies about the place. Off with the fighting in the spring and summer most like and not coming home again, or still bearing arms and not had the chance to discover what happened to their people. Arnold and Phillips were through here; Tarleton was through here scouting and foraging with us as well. Who knows who did it, or when?"

"If that's the sort of war we're fighting, then God damn us all for

murdering cowards!" Alan raged. "Women and little babies, for
Christ's sake! It's one thing for a man to be punished for rebellion,
but this!"

"Like my brother George." Burgess spat. "This could just as easy
be a Loyalist farm and those innocents slain by the Rebels!"

"And it still wouldn't make it right," Alan declared.

"No, it would not." Burgess softened, laying a firm hand on
Alan's shoulder to steady him. "And I hope the officer and the men
who did this die just as painful and as gruesome a death, no matter
what uniform they wear. All we can do is make sure we would not do
such a deed."

"God, get me away from this hateful country and back to sea
where I belong," Alan prayed. "Where the fighting is clean and
upright and a man can keep his honor!"

"Speaking of that, we'd best be getting back to the others," the
young infantryman said. "Mollow, find that seaman. We'll be leaving."

"Aye," the soldier replied. "Be takin' the road, I 'spect? Cain't
lead no stock through the woods."

"We shall have to. You shall scout ahead once we're ready."

Alan went back into the sun to fetch his waistcoat and jacket,
still damp but a lot cleaner than they had been before, and donned
them. He hung his military accoutrements about him and took up
the rifle once more as Mollow and Cony gathered the stock for leading. He was happy to shake the dust of the place from him and
unable to smell anything else than the sick and copper odor of death
that clung to the farmstead. The fresh blood smell of the 'spatched
cocks and the hogs almost made him start gagging all over again, and
he walked as far from them as he could, letting Cony lead the horse
with the drag as they started out.

He trudged along, stumbling over shallow wagon ruts and loose
rocks in the lane between the fences, too shaken to care where they
were going.

God, how could any human being with any honor at all do such
a murthering thing? he asked himself. Bastard, I may be, but I could
never raise my hand against a woman. Maybe Cheatham is right—I
am not the basest person that was ever born after all. The Navy
would never do such a deed or allow it to happen. Thank God Fa-

ther shoved me in the Fleet and not some regiment bound for the Colonies, or I'd have run screaming into the backwoods by now, sick of it all.

He tried to harken back to all the women he had known who had done him dirty, trying to discover one who might have deserved such a death, and was amazed that even the Covent Garden whore who had pinched his purse of nearly ten pounds when he was a feckless fifteen could not engage his rage enough to wish her such agony.

And the babe. God, in heaven, how could he ever sear that fiendish sight from his memory. He hated babies, usually; squawling little bundles of nastiness best kept out of sight with a nurse and trotted out at bedtime for a cuff on the head. The getting of them was enjoyable, but the keeping of them was not, a matter best left to the sluts who dropped them.

Then there was Lucy Beauman. What if it had been her slashed open like that? What if he and Lucy married someday? And what if it had been *his* child, his heir, nailed to the wall by some rampaging fiend?

I'd hunt the bastard down and kill him slow, Alan vowed, suddenly full of anger instead of sickness. Whoever did that deserves to die, and to die horribly. I wish I could find him and make him pay, and I don't care if it's that hero Tarleton, or that turncoat Arnold or Cornwallis himself. The regular army would make him roast, by God.

They reached the main road, Alan never being aware of the dread and anticipation with which the soldiers had walked that sunken farm lane, sure an ambush would occur at any moment. In his anger he was oblivious.

"You are looking positively wolfish," Chiswick commented as they waited for Mollow to scout west against any party advancing on Yorktown to their rear.

"Must be your . . . what did you call it . . . whiskey?"

"Liked it, did you?" Chiswick grinned. "There'll be plenty more in camp. The soldiers can brew it themselves from corn, and this country is full of that. Easiest way to get corn products to market from up in the Piedmont, and no taxes to pay for import of claret or port."

"It helps," Alan confessed. "Look here, Burgess. You said to the private that it was the usual, or worse than the usual. So you have seen such an atrocity before?"

"Yes, more than enough, unfortunately."

"Has your unit ever..." Alan asked, wondering what a band of Loyalist volunteers could do in reprisal to the people they ran across who supported the rebellion.

"No, we have not!" Burgess snapped, his eyes narrowing. "How dare you accuse me of such a thing. I've half a mind to call you out for it. We may not be an *English* unit, by God, but we're not a pack of thieving and murthering poltroons like the Fannings and 'Bloody Bill' Cunninghams."

"My apologies, then, Burgess," Alan said, seeing that Chiswick was indeed ready to kill him for the slur on his unit's honor, and on his own personal honor.

"That is not good enough, sir," Burgess said.

"I must humbly beg your pardon, Mister Chiswick, for by the asking of a question meant in all innocence, that you might have felt that I had cast any aspersions upon you or your company," Alan said in the most formal tone of complete and abject apology, amazed at himself to be backing down from any man, even someone he was beginning to like. He would not have done it in London, and they would have met and crossed swords or stood and delivered a volley out of sheer pride and honor.

He shifted the rifle to his left hand and offered Burgess the right, which Burgess took after a moment. "I am sorry I was so quick to take offense, Alan, but damme, that was a little close to my feelings. We've flogged and hung before to prevent that sort of thing."

"Then I shall be easy in my mind that we are still decent Christians, no matter what sort of service we have seen." Alan smiled as they shook hands heartily.

"Well, not well-churched Christians, I think." Burgess smiled.

"But never capable of such as we saw, so that says something for our salvation." Alan said. "For being a pair of rake-hells?"

"Amen to that."

* * *

Once determining that the Williamsburg road was clear of enemy activity, they led their menagerie east, back to the working party just in time to see the end of labors. Two stout pines had been cut down for replacement masts, trimmed of limbs and laid out to be skinned clean of bark and knurls. Two lighter timbers had been selected for replacement royal and topgallant yards. Other blocks from the butts had been shaped roughly into new trestletree pieces, which the carpenter and his crew would finish later aboard ship. Not being content merely to satisfy the ready needs of the ship, they had harvested several spare spars as well for future service, the entire gathering slung between the two caissons and the twelve horses reharnessed into a single large team ahead of both wagons.

"Good God above, it's Noah!" Railsford laughed loudly as they hove into sight leading the cattle and sheep, dragging the pig carcasses.

"Sure you do not want to join the army, Mister Lewrie?" the elder Chiswick asked as he surveyed their small herd. "I could use a good forager such as yourself."

"Though the foraging proved rough on your uniform," Railsford said as he saw the state of Alan's uniform and the stockings which were little higher than his shoe tops, leaving his legs bare below his breeches.

"The fortunes of war, sir," Alan replied, offering the Ferguson back to Lieutenant Chiswick, who opened the breech and checked the flint professionally in an automatic response to see if the user had fouled it or done something dire with a good gun.

"We heard but one shot," Chiswick said.

"That was Mollow killing the second hog." Burgess grinned. "After our sailor here had wrestled and stabbed the first to death, like Samson slaying the lions in the wilderness. That's how he got skinned up."

"Any sign?" his brother asked.

"Quiet as church on Monday. Looted farmstead, where we found all this, but nothing of the enemy. I shall tell you the rest later."

"Good." Lieutenant Chiswick nodded. "You missed dinner, but we've no time to feed you now. I'd like to get back across Yorktown Creek before dark."

"I shall cope," Burgess replied with a shrug.

I shan't, Alan thought, but no one was asking him, and he realized that it was already midafternoon and he had not had a bite to eat since before dawn. Mollow could get a crumb or two from his fellow soldiers, Cony could depend on his mates to have saved him a morsel or two, but Alan had to go without, and it was a long, slow trek back in the heat and humidity with only stale water for sustenance.

By the time they reached the boat landing and began loading the boats with their prize, it was nearly dark. The army encampments were lit up with squad fires and they could detect the tempting aromas of individual messes in the process of cooking their meals, the smell of bake ovens and the sight of game and domestic meats being roasted for the officers in front of their pavilion tents.

"You would be welcome to eat with us," Burgess offered as he came to Lewrie's side near the docks. "Would your captain allow you?"

"You do not know my captain." Alan grimaced. "I am his prime case of sloth and sinfulness, not to be let out of his sight long enough to get into more trouble."

"A man after my own heart, you are," Burgess chuckled. "But perhaps in future, before you sail, I and Governour could send an invitation aboard for you to dine with us. We shall kill one of those calves for you."

"Don't wait for me for an excuse, but I'd enjoy continuing the pleasance of your company indeed, Burgess." Alan said, sure that he had made himself a new friend, if even for a short acquaintance. "I shall get you some wine, even if it is a poor sort of rough-and-ready issue."

"Then you should be doubly welcome. I shall say good evening to you, then, until next time."

"Until next time, aye," Alan replied, shaking hands with him once more and adding his warm respects to the elder brother as well. Then it was into the boats and a row out to *Desperate*. He would not be going empty-handed, even so. The North Carolina Volunteers had gotten one of the sheep, one of the hogs and both calves, while *Desperate* got the cow, one hog, one sheep and the chickens, one of which Alan still possessed for his own mess.

By the time they had lashed their new spars and masts aboard for hoisting the next morning, it was full dark, and the few buildings in the town were lit up, as well as the ships in the anchorage. A cool sea wind had sprung up to blow away the heat of the day, and the cook and his assistants were busy boiling the cow for supper. With the news of their good fortune at foraging, everyone had a good word for Lewrie as he strolled the decks, sniffing at the good smells and almost slavering like a famished dog for his fresh meal. Even Treghues had been kindly in his praise, for he had gotten a chicken out of the encounter.

"A good day's work, was it not, Mister Coke?" Alan said as he met him by the larboard gangway, where the bosun and the carpenter were assaying their precious lumber still.

"A fine day indeed, Mister Lewrie," Coke replied. "Though I'd be easier in my mind ta soak these spars in a mast pond fer a few weeks ta season 'em. Guess a dash o' tar'll have ta do."

"Anything to get us off this wretched coast and back to the fleet," Alan said. The chime of the last bell in the second dog-watch freed him from the deck, and he went below to partake of his dinner, knowing that even Freeling could not make the chicken that awaited him unpalatable.

"A tasty looking dish," Avery said as the roasted bird was placed on the mess table alongside the fresh joint of beef that had also resulted from the trip ashore.

"Wish you could have found some potatoes, though," Carey said.

"You ungrateful little whelp! I put my life on the line for this, and you want something else!"

"I like potatoes with all this good gravy," Carey said.

"But it wasn't much trouble, was it?" Forrester stuck in, none too eager to give Lewrie much credit for his pains, even if they shared in the largesse. "I mean, you were escorted and all."

"But in the middle of Rebel country," Alan reminded him. "Woods as like as not full of enemy scouts way beyond reach of the lines. Miles out in those dark woods like nothing you've ever seen."

He laid it on thick, stressing the alien nature of the forests and the dangers even the skilled troops of the North Carolina provincials had worried about. As he talked, though, he took a breast and leg from the bird and a large slice of roast beef, dripping juices and piping hot, to leave the rest of the bird to them. They had wine, more pease pudding, and biscuits fresher than ship's issue from the naval stores ashore. There were whole ears of boiled corn that even rancid ship's butter could not ruin—as much as they liked for once. Carey's face was glinting with the greases as he crammed himself full as only a perpetually hungry midshipman could when offered a decent chance. Even Forrester shut up and wolfed his victuals with more than his usual evident relish.

Not wishing to spoil anyone's supper (even Forrester's) with the account of what he had seen in the farmhouse, he kept silent on that subject, trying to dismiss it from his own mind as much as he was able.

"What smells of rough spirits in here?" he finally asked, wondering if anyone had been painting belowdecks in his absence.

"Forrester's face." Avery smiled. "Still won't come off, Francis?"

"I am still laying for you, and I shall have my revenge."

A day's scrubbing with paint remover had not done much for the splendor of Forrester's countenance.

"When pigs can fly," Avery grumbled through a particularly tasty bit of biscuit soaked in steak juices and mustard.

"What's for dessert?" Carey asked, leaning back from the table and displaying a belly taut as a drumhead. "Any apples left? Freeling?"

"Apple dowdy, zur," Freeling said, making even that welcome pronouncement like an undertaker's greeting. "They wuz gone over zo noothin' ta dew but smoosh 'em un' make a dowdy."

"How appetizing you make it sound," Alan replied as a bowl of hot dowdy was put down before them. Half flour, some crushed biscuit, mashed apples with molasses and a toasty crust that might have been also sprinkled with some sugar. Alan was sure that if Freeling had had a hand in it, the cores and stems and seeds were still there, along with the peels, but he was game enough for something sweet to sort out the odd bits.

"Then yew wooden be warntin' any, ah takes it, zur," Freeling said mournfully, but with a glint to his eyes, which meant that he had been planning to eat what was left of it. Damned if he would!

"Dish me a goodly portion," Lewrie said, gleaming back at him. "A goodly portion, mind you, Freeling."

"Aye, zur."

When spooned out, it was evident that a fair measure of rum had made its way into the dowdy as well, which made them all smack their lips.

"You know," Alan began between heavenly bites, "I wish we could get together with those soldiers again and go back out to that farm on the Williamsburg road. There must be other farms that have been abandoned. I saw beans and potatoes going to waste in the fields, fodder for whatever stock that survived the looting around here. Must be orchards, too."

"Then they may as well be the Golden Apples used to lure Diana," Avery said, frowning. "We'll be at sea day after tomorrow after we refit. And I doubt if Captain Treghues would let us ashore for any more scavenging."

"Not us, perhaps, but if I know anything about those Chiswick brothers and their men, they'll be scouting out there at first light for anything they can grab." Alan laughed easily, now getting very tight in the middle and wondering if he had room for two more bites of the dowdy, even in such a noble effort as depriving Freeling of a single morsel. "I could send a letter ashore at first light and let them know we would pay well for anything they could bring us. They did invite me to dine with them, too."

"No large hopes for that with all the work we'll be doing," Forrester said, scooping his spoon around his bowl for the last crumbs and streaks and licking the spoon thoroughly. "But, if they could provide us with some fresh fruit and vegetables, I'd gladly go shares on it."

"Might be dear. They're a famished lot," Alan warned.

"What else do we have to spend our money on?" Forrester countered. "What would they be worth—a peck or two of potatoes, some peas or beans and a keg of apples or something sweet? A pound altogether?"

"The thought is intriguing," Avery said. "Otherwise, we shall be back at sea with Graves and Hood, and God knows when we shall put into port again. This might be our last chance for weeks."

"I had better write the letter now, before lights out," Alan said. "Even if I cannot accept their invitation to dine. Mind you, now. I said I'd supply some wine for them. What have we left?"

"Four bottles of red, one of claret, but we were saving that."

"That's good enough for soldiers, provincial soldiers at that," Forrester sneered. "Let's send them a half gallon of Miss Taylor for their swill."

"If we did that, we'd not survive our next reencounter with them," Alan said. "They'd kill us on sight after one glass!"

"Have to be the red, then." Avery summed up: "Two bottles of the red . . . and the claret, too."

"Here, now," Forrester protested.

"A good trade, don't you think? We could even get some meat on the hoof. Surely there is more where this livestock came from?"

"Freeling, bring me ink and paper," Alan said. "And some rum."

CHAPTER 7

THE next morning, the ninth of September, dawned with a light fog and a chill to the air, which none of the men were accustomed to after long service in the Indies. It was a welcome chill, though, for they would be put to very hard labor during the day, and under tropical conditions it would have wrung the sweat from them until they left as much water on the decks in their shadows as they could imbibe.

Alan's quickly penned letter went off with Weems, who wanted to secure some new cordage from the other ships in the anchorage, if there was some to spare. In his absence Toliver filled in, with Feather the quartermaster's mate, who had done the chore a dozen times in his career.

First, the newly carved and formed trestletrees and cheek pieces were hoisted aloft into the maintop, to be lashed and bolted to the upper butt of the mainmast ready to receive the new topmast.

"Ahoy, there!" Coke bellowed. "Ready ta tail on the yard purchase! Haul away handsomely, now! Mister Forrester, do ya ready yer people on the stay tackle as she leaves the deck."

Slowly the fresh new mast rose from the horizontal until the butt end was all that kept it on deck. A party of men took up tension on the stay tackles to either side and aft to keep it from rolling, swinging or dashing forward to do hurt to the doublings of the lower mainmast.

"Haul away, my bully boys! Haul, boys, haul!" Coke ordered.

"Now walk yer stay tackles forrerd, handsomely now!"

He was in his element and enjoying every minute of it, leaving even Railsford and Treghues on the sidelines to keep silent and only jump in if something untoward happened.

"Up an' down, Mister Coke!" Toliver cried, leaning down to eye the alignment of the topmast with the lower mast and lubber's hole in the top.

"Snub ya well yer preventers! Hoist away all aloft!"

Up the new topmast went, one foot at a time until it threaded through the gap in the trestletrees and cheek pieces where it was to rest. The new foot piece was inserted, and the roving of the doubling bands was wrapped firmly about it even as other hands began to set up the newly made upper shrouds. With everything torn away, it was a lot more labor to reset the topmast than the usual drill, for the fore and aft stays had also to be installed and then fiddled with until everyone in charge was satisfied with their tension and the upper mast's angles.

It was halfway into the forenoon watch before the old tops'l yard, now "fished" with one of the precious, seasoned stuns'l booms and lashed about like a giant splinted bone for rigidity, could be rerigged with all the blocks, sheaves and hardware for the braces, clew lines, halyards and jears. They rove it to the top tackles first to be hoisted aloft to the top platform, then secured it to the new halyards and jears to hoist it firmly into its proper position so it could be overhauled for complete trim and reef control. Once in place, the sailmaker and his crew fed the resewn and patched original tops'l up through the lubber's hole into the maintop where the sail handlers could bend it back onto the yard, apply new sheets to help draw it down to its full length and then brail it up.

As the process was being repeated to begin swaying up the new topgallant and royal masts to their own trestletrees, cheek pieces and waiting doubling bands, one of the men on the tops'l yard gave a shout and pointed out to seaward. Lewrie was higher than he at the topmast cross-trees, which had just been correctly cross-tensioned by the shrouds, and he turned carefully on his precarious and half-finished perch to see what the excitement had been about.

The morning haze had burned off with the heat of the autumn sun, though the day was still pleasantly cool, which made for almost ideal viewing conditions. As Alan shaded his eyes against the morning sun in the east, he could barely make out an unnatural-looking cloud on the seaward horizon, somewhere just inshore of the Middle Ground and the main ship channel into the bay, he suspected. Certainly it could not be a ship in the passage—that was near forty miles off, below the horizon.

"Riyals an' t'gallants!" the impromptu lookout declared firmly.

"Looks to be only a cloud to me." Alan said, with a shrug.

"'Tis ships, Mister Lewrie, sir," the man insisted.

"Might be *Iris* and *Richmond,* then." Alan said. "They were out to pick up all the bouys the Frogs left when they cut their cables a few days back."

"Mebbe our fleet acomin' back fer us, sir," the man went on, nodding his head with the rightness of that thought. "See, sir, that gunboat of our'n out there is headin' out ta check on 'em."

Alan looked closer in. Perhaps ten miles off, almost under the horizon herself, there was a ketch-rigged patrol craft that had come down from higher up the bay at dawn after taking or burning almost every boat or watercraft still on the upper reaches of the Chesapeake, so it would be impossible for the French over on the James to amass any shipping that could threaten the army on the York. Symonds's small flotilla had not left a rowing boat for the Rebels to use above their anchorage.

"Aloft there!" Coke's voice boomed. "Stand by yer top tackles ta take the topgallant mast!"

"'Old yer water, Norman, 'old yer water, damn ye," the carpenter griped, still rasping that last little bit of smoothness between the assembled trestletrees which would receive and hold the butt of the topgallant.

"Go down and tell the captain there are unidentified ships in the bay, and that one of our gunboats is investigating," Alan said to the seaman who had made the first sighting.

"Oh, Lor', Mister Lewrie, I couldn't do that, sir!" he pleaded.

Cool day or not, the work was hard enough, and with so few people aloft Alan had had to do some of it instead of merely supervising, so he turned on the man quickly. "Damn you, go on deck and report to the captain as I instructed you, or the bosun'll have the hide off you tomorrow forenoon!"

"Aye, aye, sir," the man replied, trying to hide his worries about how he might be received by their captain in whatever mood God had seen fit to give him at that moment. Just by trying to weasel out of going he had come close to insubordination and back talk, which could cost him a full dozen at the gratings from a cat-o'-nine-tails. He swung out of the rigging with lithe skill and scrabbled down a newly rigged and tarred backstay to the deck before Alan could think of another word to say.

"Haul away on the top tackles," Coke commanded, and the blocks began to roar and squeal as the topgallant began to make its way up the mast.

There was enough to do to take everyone's mind off the sighting in the next hour, and the seaman reported back quickly and fell to work with a will, evidently glad to have survived speaking to a quarterdeck officer instead of Treghues directly. Anyway, it was no concern of theirs as long as *Desperate* was not ready for sea in all respects. Had the strange cloud been a host of angels come ready for Armageddon, they would have had to wait until the bosun had the ship restored to "Bristol Fashion."

By the time the fore and aft stays had been rigged for proper tension on the topgallant mast and its yard had been hoisted aloft to be refitted, the seaman had a higher perch over the bluffs and trees of the York peninsula and the outlying islands, almost into Lynnhaven Bay itself, and once more he called out for attention to seaward.

"Now what?" Alan frowned as he balanced on the footrope of the topgallant yard to aid in brailing up the new sail to the spar.

"Take a look now, Mister Lewrie, sir," the man said, trying to keep vindication from his tone, though it was a given that the man had been right, had known it all along and was pointedly *not* calling all officers and midshipmen fools for ignoring him.

Alan leaned into the yard to free his hands to shade his eyes once more, and this time he stiffened with intense interest. "Stap me!" he said.

The strange cloud was a lot closer now, well inside the Middle Ground, high enough up over the horizon to reveal the graceful curving shapes of royals, topgallants and a hint of tops'ls. The little gunboat was coming up over the horizon ahead of the cloud, as if she were leading. The cloud had split, part of it advancing toward the mouth of the York.

"Deck there!" Alan bawled. "Send up a telescope! Ships in sight!"

"Hood an' Graves?" the carpenter asked from the cross-trees below them. He was not as spry as he had been in his youth, and going aloft was no longer one of his required duties, so he was taking no chances on any unsafe handhold over one hundred feet above the deck.

"Can't tell, Chips," Alan replied.

"Musta caught up with them Romish bastards an' give 'em a good drubbin'. Mebbe run 'em halfway back ta Brest!" The carpenter chortled. "Now we kin go back over ta the James an' shoot the Frog sojers ta shit."

If it was indeed the return of the British fleet, Alan realized it would be late in the day before they made their stately way into the fleet anchorage in the York, and nothing could change that, so there was no reason to be impatient. On land or at sea, things moved at their own speed, which was usually damned slow, like a four-hour dinner party. Patience was one of the prime virtues of the age, so Alan felt no hectic desire to have that telescope within the next blink of an eye. He was getting anxious, however; that old shivery prickling feeling was back plucking at his heart strings and knotting up cold in his innards.

It could be Graves and Hood, he told himself as he steeled himself to show outward calm. *If de Grasse decided to sheer off now he's landed his troops and guns. I've not heard the Frogs really ever risk too much with their fleets. But Graves was such a tremulous poltroon t'other day, he more like simply turned about and let them go in peace. Best, in the long run. He's finally here, and he can seal the bay. Even a halfwit can accomplish that.*

"Glass, sir," a nimble young topman offered, panting from his long climb to the topgallant yard with the telescope. Alan slung it over his shoulder like a musket and scaled up to the cap of the topgallant mast for a better vantage. Hugging the mast, he drew out the tube to its full extension and steadied himself for a look-see.

The first thing that caught his eye was the little ketch-rigged gunboat, now heading straight for the mouth of the York and the passage between the two outlying shoals. She was flying all the sail she could safely carry still hull down. Beyond her, only royals and topgallants were showing—ships of some kind. It was still too far to make out any identifying details, but there were at least eight to ten large ships headed for the York—they overlapped so much it was hard to get an accurate count. He swiveled to look over at Lynnhaven Bay and saw another pack of sails headed in for the old French anchorage, merely a gentler hint of ships, since they were much further away from him, even with *Desperate* anchored the most easterly of the ships in the base. But he could make out two ships closer to him, two ships that he took to be *Iris* and *Richmond*. Was it his imagination, or were they also headed in to join their sister ships in the York? Bows on to him, they were now.

"Pass the word to the deck," he suddenly said. "At least ten sail of the line bound for the York, and an unknown number of sail headed for Lynnhaven Bay. No identification yet."

While he clung to his perch, topmen came up around him and began to haul up the royal mast and the light royal yard to secure them into position and link the braces to the lower yards and drop new rope down to the deck and the handling tackle.

By eleven-thirty in the morning, *Desperate* was a whole ship once more. The lifting lines were flaked down or coiled away for future need, and the crew dismissed to their rum ration and the prospect of hot food. Alan could have joined them, but he remained in the rigging, now almost to the peak of the royal mast so that nothing on the peninsula would block his view, not the bluffs around the town and harbor and not the lower land out near the islands and shoals. There was a meal on the mess table for him, but he could not go below without knowing for sure, so he remained out of a perverse sense of duty, swaying back and forth as the ship gently heaved and rolled and the masts slowly spiraled against the bright blue sky. He would have to go down soon, for Treghues still insisted on him and Avery coming to his cabins and reading aloud from the Old Testament; after the paint incident, they were all there now.

The ships bound into Lynnhaven Bay and the James he would never be able to identify—they were simply too far off. But it did seem as if several of them—dare he call them frigates?—had separated from the mysterious main body and were closing in on what he took to be *Richmond* and *Iris,* and that was damned ominous.

Closer in and now almost to the east, the little gunboat was now nearly hull up; she was close enough to spot her national ensign, and with a strong telescope almost catch the whip of her long commissioning pendant. Behind her, with all sail plans above the horizon, there appeared now a full dozen ships of the line and what appeared to be a couple more frigate-sized vessels.

There was a puff of smoke from the gunboat, a tiny bloom of gray torn away almost at once into a light haze. It was too far away to hear the cannon shot, but it was a signal nonetheless.

"Oh, Christ, no," he muttered.

On the ketch's foremast, there rose a signal flag. It was from Admiral Graves's book, of course, since the local patrol craft were a part of his North American Squadron, and he had seen this particular flag hoist in the last few days aboard the *Solebay* as she had led the fleet down to the Cape Henry entrance to the bay on the fifth.

Enemy In Sight.

"Goddamn them," he growled. "Just goddamn the incompetent shits." He tried to read his feelings; would it be more suitable to scream and rant, to be petrified with fear for the future, to play up game as a little guinea cock? He was surprised to feel absolutely nothing, none of the emotions others might consider appropriate to match the situation.

"Deck, there!" he yelled as loud as he could, and saw several white faces turn up to look at him from the quarterdeck. "Enemy in sight! French ships in the bay!"

He did not have to repeat it.

That ought to spill some soup on the mess deck, he thought. Christ, we are well and truly fucked!

Desperate relayed the hoist to Symonds in the *Charon,* and the little gunboat was ordered back out to sea to scout. She was not gone for long, and was forced to come scuttling back to the safety of the river two hours later, bearing bad news.

Richmond and *Iris* had been overwhelmed and taken as prizes by the French. There were at least eight sail of the line in Lynnhaven

Bay with several more ships that might be transports in company anchoring to the abandoned buoys. There were four command flags that she had spotted, one in Lynnhaven Bay, two vice admirals' flags in three-deckers and a full admiral's flag flying from a huge three-decker that was most likely the *Ville de Paris,* de Grasse's flagship. There was a two-decker and three frigates anchoring out by the islands at the mouth of the York, and the main passage between Cape Henry and the Middle Ground was most likely to be blocked as well. And all the ships present were flying the white banners with the golden lilies of Bourbon France.

In midafternoon, the closest French frigate in the York fired a single gun to leeward as a challenge, daring any ship or combination of ships in the English flotilla to come out to fight.

They were trapped.

"He wants our powder?" Treghues scoffed, shocked to the depths of his prim and addled soul.

"Aye, sir," Railsford said with a shrug. A flag lieutenant from Captain Symonds stood on the quarterdeck with a military officer in the buff, blue and red of the artillery. "And we are also instructed to dismount our carronades and half our swivel guns and deliver them ashore, with all spare shot."

"That would render us unable to fight!" Treghues barked. "One might as well ask for all our nine-pounders, too!"

"You have nine-pounders?" the artilleryman asked. "Long nines? They might prove useful as well."

"Then we would truly be disarmed!"

"With the French fleet blockading the river and the exits from the bay, Captain Treghues, your armament is at present nugatory, is it not?" Receiving no answer, the artillery officer went on, patting the breech of one of the quarterdeck swivels in appreciation. "Until your Admiral Graves returns we shall have to fortify, and we have nought but field pieces, none over a six-pounder. And should it prove a long siege, we shall be short of powder and shot for counter-battery fire. Your Captain Symonds has already stripped his vessel of all her eighteens, powder and shot."

"Why do we not simply lay her up in ordinary, strip her to her tops and gantlines," Treghues fumed, "or just burn her outright and turn her crew into... *soldiers?*" There were few things lower to a Royal Navy man—"farmers" was the common epithet for the clumsy, but for the clumsy and stupid in the bargain, "soldiers" expressed a sailor's indignation quite well.

"You have at present eighteen long nine-pounders, captain," the naval aide pointed out. "A very long-ranged and accurate piece, and they would be more useful in the present circumstances ashore in fortifications than aboard the *Desperate*. Your carronades at extreme elevation could deliver bursting shot as well as any howitzer or mortar barrel, and the swivels could break up any raiding party. Surely, you must see the sense of my captain's request. Perhaps you could dismount half your ordnance to form three half-batteries, and you could be left with a few *en flûte*."

It did not take a genius to discern that if Treghues refused to grant the request, then it would come back before the end of the watch as an order, which would leave him nothing.

"I could retain two as chase guns forrard," Treghues mused, his brows knurled with repressed anger. "And three in battery on each beam. I can spare no more than ten."

"At present, sir," the flag lieutenant said, reminding him that circumstances could indeed demand *Desperate's* stripping and burning sometime in the future should the siege last a long time.

"My gunners would be most grateful, sir," the artilleryman added. "We shall take good care of your pieces, see if we shan't."

"Naval artillery in the hands of soldiers?" Treghues reared back, ready to go on another tear. "Nay, sir, I shall depute my own gunners for land service!"

"That would be most welcome, Captain." The army gunner nodded gratefully, unaware that Treghues's truculence was anything more than the usual grudge match between army and the sea service.

"We could have barges alongside for the powder and shot by the beginning of the day watch, sir," the naval aide assured him. "Perhaps only the first tier of powder to begin with, and all prepared cartridge bags and shot garlands."

"Aye, if you must," Treghues said, rubbing the side of his head that had been the target of the heavy rammer. "See to it, Mister Railsford. I shall be aft. Judkin?"

"Aye, sir?" his steward replied, stepping forward.

"Pass the word for Dr. Dorne, would you?"

"Aye, sir."

The barges came alongside within the hour while Treghues sulked in his cabins. They were barges slapped together from green pinewood locally harvested, and minus all the attention to detail one usually expected from a good boatwright. They were broader than normal and of shallower draft, still pierced for a dozen oars, with a raised stern post and tiller head. It was fortunate that they were being used on a river, for they looked unhandy in any sort of seaway, even to the less experienced hands. They began to look even more unhandy as they were loaded thwart deep with kegs of powder and rope nets full of ready-sewn powder bags, or stacked with round shot, canister and grapeshot.

The shot went down the skids to either beam, thick and smooth ramps that could cradle a beef cask or water barrel as it slid up or down the ship's side. The powder, though, had to be hoisted out one keg at a time, checked most carefully for dust or dribbles, slung into a net and then swayed up with the main yard and a series of gant-lines to check any swing or sway. They were lowered into the waiting barges as carefully as eggs would go into a farmgirl's straw basket; one shock and . . .

The artillery was no more easy. The gun tools, and the carriages were fairly light and went quickly, but the barrels themselves were sinfully heavy and hard to handle. A barge could take only two barrels before it began to settle down so low that water began to lap near the gunwales and rowports, and the boat was then rowed gingerly to the town dock for unloading with jury-rigged spars set up as cranes.

"Looks naked as a whore's belly," Mister Gwynn the gunner commented as he surveyed his bare decks. For the first time, below the gangways on either beam, the gun deck was free of tackles, blocks and sheaves, free of guns, rope shot garlands, netting bags for practice shot, and water tubs for the slow-match, or firefighting. There were now two nine-pounders on the fo'c'sle forward as chase guns, and only three abeam remaining with which to fight; one pair just forward of the mainmast, and one pair just under the break of the quarterdeck for balance fore and aft. With her gunports empty, she did resemble a flute waiting to be played, instead of a warship. There were times that larger frigates had been disarmed or had given up half their guns to ease the burden of carrying troops, which was where the term *flûte* had arisen, but no one had ever imagined that lithe little *Desperate* would ever be called upon to surrender her guns til she was finally decommissioned. It was ironic that her commissioning pendant still flew from the mainmast truck under the circumstances.

"This is getting serious," Alan decided.

"Aye, so tis." Gwynn replied, ruminating on a wad of tobacco in his cheeks. He leaned over expertly and spat into the kid by the foremast. "Fuckin' army got themselves trapped, so they did."

"And us with 'em," Alan said.

"I ain't no man for land fightin'," Gwynn growled, chewing hard at his almost dead plug. "Lice and fleas, sleepin' rough on the ground 'stead of swayin' in a comfy hammock and caulkin' easy nights. Takes a pure fool to be a soldier, and not much of a man, neither. Nobody worth a damn ever took the King's Shilling and put on a red coat."

"At least they don't have press-gangs," Alan said. Poor as the life of a soldier could be, and with such little regard from the citizens towards them, no one had to scour the seaports and coastal towns to drag people into the army.

"Takes a superior kinda man to make a seaman." Gwynn smiled. "But he's the kind that needs a little *prodding* to sign aboard, like."

"A one smart enough to run, sir?" Alan said. "Caught anyway."

"Then how'd we get you, Mister Lewrie?"

"Damned hard luck all around, Mister Gwynn." Alan grinned.

"Get your gear together, then. See what sort of damn hard luck we have ashore."

Gwynn could joke about it—he was a senior warrant, a man who was retained in peace or war aboard ship. In war he was in charge of all the artillery, powder and shot. In peacetime he could live aboard ship with his family in *Desperate* as long as she was laid up in ordinary and her guns stored in some warehouse ashore. A gunner's mate like Tulley would be turned out onto the beach to make his own way, but a man with a warrant from the Admirality had a lifelong living if he so chose, since his skills were valuable, more so than those of a lieutenant, who would go on half pay once he was no longer needed.

So Gwynn was not going ashore, much as he might crab about the conditions they might face. He was staying aboard ship.

Tulley was going ashore, though, along with Lieutenant Railsford, who would command Desperate's batteries. There would be full crews for all guns, which would require a gun captain each piece, a quarter-gunner for each half-battery of three guns, a rammer, powderman, shotman, a ship's boy to fetch powder cartridges and only two hands for tackles, since they would not be trying to roll guns up a sloping deck to firing position. That was still seven men per gun, and represented nearly half of Desperate's allotted 160-man crew.

Of the midshipmen's mess, only young Carey would stay aboard to help supervise the remaining crew with the sailing master and the captain. The quartermaster would stay, but his mates were available as senior petty officers. The bosun, Mister Coke, would stay, with his mate Weems, along with the sailmaker and his crew, cooper, carpenter and the mast captains and able seamen from the tops.

Leaving the ship presented a problem for Alan beyond the wrench to his soul at going into siege warfare on land, for which he was so unprepared; what was he to do with the contents of his sea chest?

A locked sea chest was fair game in the holds to anyone with a clasp knife and a little privacy. Even if left in the midshipmen's mess it was vulnerable to pilfering. Alan had valuable writing paper in it, books and shirts and silk stockings, his prize money certificates and the records of his meager sea career, which he would have to present some time in the future to gain his money. And there was that gold. All the rouleaux of guineas—one-guinea, two-guinea and beautiful five-guinea pieces that could vanish in a twinkling! They were much too heavy to carry on his person, and much too valuable to leave behind.

There was no way he could confide in anyone aboard to safeguard the gold for him without admitting he had pilfered it from the French prize Ephegenie, and that was damned near a hanging offense.

Even the mild and supportive Cheatham would not countenance it should he learn of it.

What was worse, he had no confidence in ever returning to *Desperate*. The French fleet was blockading the bay and the mouth of the river, and it would be storm season before they departed. There was a French army on the James shore of the York peninsula, and Cornwallis was going into fortifications to withstand a siege that might result in the surrender of the British army if Graves and Hood didn't get their act together soon. *Desperate* could end up a French prize of war and his sea chest could end up looted. He could become a prisoner of war, confined to a hulk or dungeon by sneering Rebel or French captors, stripped of every possession on his person except his clothes. *Desperate* might be burned to the waterline to prevent her use by the victors.

Damn Treghues, I wouldn't put it past him to set fire to her, he thought in an exquisite agony of indecision. Then I am once more as poverty-stricken as a pregnant bawd. And in prison to boot. Oh, God, I should never have pinched the stuff. I knew it at the time, but I did need it so devilish bad. If I'm not killed in the battle, I'm stuffed in irons until the war's over and out of the Navy without a hope, and out all my money, too. What's to happen to me then? What career would be open to me without prospects or sponsors or gold enough for security?

Still, officers were usually released on their own means if they gave their parole to no longer bear arms against their captors, and their personal property was usually respected. There might be a chance.

Taking great care not to be seen, Alan, in packing a canvas seabag of things to sustain life ashore, slipped into his hoard and stuffed a deal box of two hundred guineas in one-guinea coins into his bag. If all else failed, he would have enough to survive confinement.

Might be enough to bribe my way into better quarters or something, he thought ruefully. Anyone thrown into debtor's prison could find good treatment and victuals if he had money enough on his person; how could a French or Rebel prison be any different? Besides, if he was ashore and in the tender mercies of the army long enough, a little gold could come in handy for delicacies or drink. His whore in Charleston had sneered at the Rebel Congress's currency as "not worth a Continental," so a gold piece could command a lot of clout in an economy starved of specie.

"Ready ta play lobsterback?" Mister Monk asked, rolling through the small midshipmen's mess from his quarters aft in the officer's wardroom. He smelt pleasantly of rum.

"Aye, Mister Monk," Alan replied, drawing the strings taut on his seabag. "Though I fear I don't know the first thing about it."

"Anythin' ya need ashore?"

"A telescope, perhaps, sir. I doubt a sextant would prove useful. Or any of my books."

"I've given the first lieutenant two o' the day glasses, an' one o' the night glasses," Monk said. "All we kin spare, in faith."

"I fear for the contents of my chest, though, sir," Alan ventured hesitantly. "Tis all I own in this world, like any sailor..."

"We shift 'em inta the wardroom fer safe-keepin' once yer gone," Monk announced. "An' y'll be back aboard now an' agin ta fetch fresh."

"That would be most kind, Mister Monk, indeed," Alan said with a lively sense of relief. Monk would keep a good eye on things, as good an eye as he could until something dreadful happened to the ship.

With a lighter burden on his mind, Alan shouldered his seabag and went on deck to muster with the hands to board the boats for shore.

CHAPTER 8

FOR days on end their tasks were easy. The army
had already dug the fortifications for them—
raised banks of earth shoulder high. For the bat-
tery of naval guns, the rampart was only waist high, and the native
earth had been left in place like a ramp that spanned the trenches.
On this they constructed "decks" of pine lumber, set up their trucks
and slung their artillery pieces.

The soldiers had already prepared the ground before the ramparts as well, having sewn nasty *abatis*, sharpened stakes driven into
the ground to slow down and channel onrushing attackers into fire
lanes before the guns and the few swivels allotted them. The ramparts themselves also bristled with sharpened stakes to prevent their
being crossed by even the rashest Rebel soldier. Not that they represented a real defense, even with the fascines and gabions to stiffen
them.

They were nakedly in the open. On their right was York River,
and the so-called Star Redoubt to their right rear. There was a long
and connected fortification on the right on their side of the Yorktown Creek and its steep ravine. Far away on their left, there were
some other redoubts, small oblong semiforts, but none of them tied
together by any connecting trenches or earthworks. The army officers who had sited them in position had assured them that there
was nothing to fear, for a determined foe had little hope of climbing
the hills to get to their portion of the outer defense line. Far away on

their left was the best approach route, across the lower-lying Worms-ley's Pond and Wormsley Creek, where there were more redoubts and connected trenches.

Lewrie was pretty much on his own most of the time, since once he had come ashore the efforts of the *Desperate's* crew had been dissipated by the needs of the army. Lieutenant Railsford and two half-batteries had been sent over to the Gloucester side, where the nine-pounders formed the core of Tarleton and Simcoe's artillery other than light field pieces suitable for dragoons and cavalry units. Happily, Midshipman Forrester had gone with him. Gunner's mate Tulley, Sitwell from the fo'c'sle and most of his men had gone into the inner defense line with the carronades and one of the nine-pounders to make up a full battery of guns stripped from lighter naval units of the same caliber. Unhappily, Midshipman David Avery had been assigned to those guns and that battery. Alan had been sent out to this rashly exposed and isolated fortification on the far bank of Yorktown Creek, and it wasn't even a redoubt with four or more solid walls that made one feel safe. It was merely a redan, two walls connected at an angle of no more than thirty degrees. One of his nine-pounders was at the apex of the two walls, and one on each end. In between, there were two light six-pounders from the army on their large wheeled field limbers, with only a grizzled—and forbid-dingly evil-looking—sergeant in charge. He had four light one-pounder swivel guns on the low rampart for use against troops in the open. Once they were in close, he had the support of two dozen Hesse-Cassel Jagers, and if the artillery sergeant was an evil gent, then the Jagers were very devils incarnate. Each one sported a mus-tache nearly the size of a marlinspike, on which they paid more keen attention than upon their uniforms. Alan was beginning to distin-guish them by which way their facial hair pointed; the officer in charge of the redan wore his curled down, then up at the tips like a bow wave—that was Feldwebel-leutnant Heros von Muecke, and how Alan could pronounce that was pretty much anyone's guess. Not that it mattered much; von Muecke could barely rumble one complete phrase in English before reverting to his native tongue and spitting saliva over the person addressed.

His sergeant—a *real* sergeant (or feldwebel) instead of a bastard hyphen such as von Muecke—was a white-blonde lout named Kniemeyer, and his hairy lip appliance stood straight out, as the whiskers on a cat that was intently interested in something that moved. It was also bright red and could be recognized on a dark night. There were two corporals who were addressed only as "unteroffizier," and if they had names, Alan had yet to discover them (not that he was all that eager to make their acquaintance—they stank like badgers), but he could recognize them by the color of their mustaches.

Alan had Cony with him from their previous excursion into the forests, a quarter-gunner and three gun captains, three powder boys and eighteen other men. They had been issued muskets, cutlasses and boarding axes for their own defense should they prove necessary, but there were only so many muskets to go around, so a round dozen would have to do, and they would have to depend on the Jagers to keep the enemy off them. And that was something that the Jagers were reputed to be very good at, even if they did look somewhat silly in their red and white ticken-striped long trousers so tight around the knee and lower legs, their yellow-buff waistcoats and the shabby rifle green tunics with the red facings. As a light company, they at least wore a recognizable tricorne hat instead of a fur cap with the metal front plate of a battalion company or guards unit. Altogether a scruffy lot, who scratched a great deal and whose idea of a bath was to smoke themselves by a fire while their clothing was smoked as well to get rid of the "gentlemen's companions." Alan was sure that they were steady fellows, but if they ever got the wind up and decided to flee, whatever they said in parting would be totally unintelligible, and the naval party would be left holding the redan by themselves without a clue.

Behind the redan's walls, and safely out of reach of the guns, they had dug some pits which they had walled in and covered to store the powder cartridges and kegs of powder they had been allowed. To keep the elements out, they had covered the mounds with scrap sails that had been tarred to make them waterproof. Behind the magazines, there was a small hollow that had been expanded into a dugout for von Muecke and Alan.

With enough pine boughs and cut grass Alan could make a passable bed with his hammock spread over it for a ground cloth. There were some ditches to keep water from flowing into the hollow, and it was roofed with excess pine boards and scrap limbs, with another piece of sailcloth over it as well. Not that it was Alan's idea of a great way to live, half in and half out of the ground. But it was the best quarters they could find to assert their rights as officers and gentlemen, and the men in both the army and navy expected officers of the gentleman caste to keep up their appearances and their separation. Von Muecke had made great expostulation about the *dignitat* he was due as a Feldwebel-leutnant, which was, like the rank of midshipman, half noncommissioned officer, half gentleman. To have to share quarters with a navy man, he had had to be convinced that Alan was indeed a gentleman of suitable *ton* and of a rank high enough so that it would not be demeaning for him to share food, company and farts.

He had also, once assured of Alan's bonafides, insisted on the disguising of their dugout to the point that it was hard to find after dark if a fire were not burning at the uphill lip and entrance.

"Gewehr!" von Muecke had spluttered, wetting down his mustache in explanation. "Die Amerikanische Jager geschutze und . . . pif pif! Sie sind todt, verstehen sie?"

"Please speak the King's English, you hairy twit."

"Ach, der English, jah! Reppel oder Franzosiche . . . sniper! Pif pif und you shot dead, verstehen sie? Oder der artillery zink zis der kommando hauptquartier . . . nein? Ah, der command post, jah. Und zey into us a feldhaubitze feur. Grosse boom, grosse todt gentlemenner, jah?"

"Gross indeed," Alan had said.

Conversation was so difficult that they seldom attempted it after that beyond the usual line of duty, and Alan was careful to stand back far enough to avoid the tiny explosions of moisture after every tortured *umlaut* or guttural tongue trill. Come to think of it, von Muecke didn't smell like a bottle of Hungary water himself.

Below their position, there was a broad open plain that once had been carefully tilled farmland surrounded by the low, but steep, hills at the edge of the creek behind them. To their right was a cul-de-sac that led between two fingers of ridges, too steep to assault and only guarded by a redan of light infantry with no guns for support. Their own position was on another cul-de-sac route, a fairly open and flat dome between two more ridges, with a final bulge of land to their rear perhaps six feet higher than their walls, and with two escape routes to the rear that swept round the dome. Immediately behind the dome of land there was one route down, not over a thirty-foot drop, but fairly steep, steep enough to require lots of horses to hoist the guns up into position onto the flat space. Behind that by perhaps thirty yards was a small bench with another drop-off as one headed east for the creek, and then the steep banks of Yorktown Creek itself. They had come down from the north to emplace their guns through a narrow cut in the first cul-de-sac, and if challenged on their front, would never get the guns out of there.

Mayhap that is why we have so little round shot up here, Alan thought. And so little powder. The army might get their light carriage guns out in a hurry on those big wheels, but we'd play hell with the nine-pounders on their little trucks. And if we're so all-fired important up here, where are the supporting troops to back us up?

They had food enough for a week or so, all hard biscuits and salt meat from either army or naval stores, some rum to dole out each day at midday, and could be resupplied from the rear if one didn't mind half-killing a packhorse or a mule in doing it. Alan and von Muecke both had the use of a mount should they need to communicate with the rear, but the more Alan had ridden about in the last few days, the less he thought of their usefulness and the hill on which they were emplaced. Oh, they had a great field of fire, but no one in his right mind would attempt to climb up in the face of the guns, not when they could go into the first cul-de-sac to the north, where the ground was easier. Certainly no cavalry would try it.

So he slouched on the inner side of the rampart by the hour, looking for a foe that never came and showed no signs of ever making an appearance. He became extremely bored, perhaps more bored than he could have ever become aboard ship.

The days slipped by until a week had gone. That night, it finally began to rain, after being dry for weeks. It came down in sheets and the wind rose, soaking the ground and the men huddled under their blankets. And when it no longer rained so hard that the droplets slanted into the mouths of the gun magazines, it started to pour continually, hour after soaking hour. By dawn the creek behind them was rising and making rude noises as the banks filled with the runoff.

"Be able ta grind corn now, Mister Lewrie, sir," Cony told him as he served him a cup of bitter "Scotch coffee" in the officer's dugout the next morning. "All the creeks'll be up enough."

"Be able to drown in mud as well, Cony," Alan grumbled.

"That, too, sir." Cony smiled. The man was blissfully happy; off the ship and away from the harsh discipline, out in the woods and in his element again, which was heaven for a former rustic and poacher. He was short and slim, a dirty blonde young man only a few years older than Lewrie, and claimed that he was from the West country, born and raised east of Offa's Ditch near the Welsh border, but didn't have the irritating burr of Zedland, only the lilting, musical accent of a Welshman. That was perhaps where he got his hawk's nose and sharp features. Yet he was handsome in his own way, as handsome as a common lad could expect to be. He was baked and seared a light teak color like everyone else in *Desperate* after two years at sea. Still rated for service on the guns and the decks, he was barely considered an ordinary seaman.

Alan had never really noticed him before. Cony had never stood out at anything, believing in the safety of mediocrity and the center of his own mob instead of standing out. Yet Cony had a certain intelligence and had latched onto Alan after the harrowing experience at the Rebel farm, perhaps hoping to strike for mess steward to replace the awful Freeling. He had almost unconsciously taken up the duties of hammock man, seeing to Alan's needs and comforts once they had gotten ashore.

"Beggin' yer pardon, Mister Lewrie, but would ya admire a hare fer yer breakfast, then?" Cony offered out of the blue.

"Rabbit?" Alan gaped, now fully awake. "I would think hunting in this rain would be terrible."

"Set some snares back on t'other side of the hills, sir," Cony said.

"A poacher on two continents are you, Cony?"

"Aye, sir. You'd have to share with the hairy gentleman, but 'tis a fine, fat rabbit."

"And I expect you have a second laid by for your own breakfast?" Alan teased.

"That I do, sir," Cony replied without shame, showing the natural guile of the admitted scrounger and woodsman.

"In that case, it sounds hellish good."

"Tis on the spit at this minute, sir."

Alan nodded his thanks and Cony slipped out of the dugout, leaving Alan to finish his burnt-bread imitation coffee, which was at least hot enough to get him started for another morning of drudgery. He dressed quickly and threw a tarpaulin watch coat over his shoulders for a rain cover and went outside to inspect his battery and the redan.

The cook fire was burning for the men's morning meal and the iron pots were simmering up gruel and chunks of salt meat. The artillerymen and Jagers had individual squad fires burning. The smoke lay close and heavy to the ground like a morning mist. The rain no longer poured down in buckets, but now drizzled endlessly and miserably from a pewter sky. Only half the open fields could be seen below them, and the far woods were lost in fog or mists.

"Mornin', Mister Lewrie, sir," Knatchbull the quarter-gunner said as he emerged from the dugout.

"Morning, Knatchbull. How do the hands keep?"

"Damp right through, sir," the man replied, knuckling his forehead in rough salute. "We could use some sailcloth er tarpaulin, sir, ta kivver up the sleepin' spaces."

"I shall request of some after breakfast," Alan said, studying the small tents the Jagers and the army artillerists had erected. "Perhaps some tents would keep the rain off. How about our guns?"

"I'm that worried 'bout the breechin' ropes, sir," Knatchbull said. "Iffen ya could take a squint, sir. Them posts we sunk ta serve ta attach the breechin' ropes an' side tackles an' sich're in mud now."

"Are they shifting?"

"Not so's ya'd notice, Mister Lewrie, but they will iffen ya sets light ta a powder charge ta fire a gun."

"I doubt if we could find a dry cartridge this morning, anyway."

"Aye, sir, sich a day it is."

"Guten morgen, herr mittschiffesmann Lew-rie," von Muecke dribbled. "Eine schreckliche tag, nicht wahr?"

"It is when I have to decipher that," Alan mumbled under his breath, but saying out loud, "Good morning to you, Mister von Mooka."

"Muecke," the soldier corrected. "Fon Mehr-keh, verstehe?"

"Whatever." Alan shrugged and waved it off with a hopeless grin. "Any sign of the enemy this fine morning?"

"Nein, mein herr. Ich habe . . . I have der scouts aus also."

"Powder dry?"

"Jah, oder zuh primings sind . . . sput!"

If he does that one more time he'll hit my coffee, Alan thought, protecting his mug from the small shower of spit that had accompanied the sound effect of a squibbed priming.

"My hammock man Cony has a rabbit for us to share, Mister . . . Fon Mee-key. We shall have a decent breakfast, at any rate."

"Ah, eine rappit? Eine hase? Wunderbar!"

Alan wandered off to the forward artillery piece of the redan to look over the bleak countryside, shivering slightly. It had seemed like summer over the last week, not as fierce as the Indies, but warm enough during the days. Now, with the rain coming down as though it would never cease and the fogs blanketing those sharp hills and tree tops, it felt more like true autumn, more seasonal for the last of September. It also made those far hills and trees seem more forbidding than before, more wild and uncivilized. Every good Englishman that got a plot of ground, an estate or a farm spent countless hours shaping and weeding, cutting back thickets and removing underbrush, reforming Nature into gentle and civilized gardens and fields as orderly as a Roman villa. It was Man in charge of Nature, announcing his sovereignty and superiority over the dumb beasts and the wildness. But here, there was so much Nature, it was inconceivable that anyone could even begin to make a dent on it, and it made Alan feel puny and insignificant. And there were thousands of miles of this sort of wilderness stretching off to the Piedmont and beyond, into God knew what sort of savage remoteness, a country that might just stretch to Asia; limitless as a map of Russia, as wide as the mighty Atlantic Ocean and just as trackless and harsh, deluding the traveler with its lush or rugged beauties just as the sea deluded the unwary.

"God, get me out of this beastly place," Alan said softly. "It's driven the Rebels mad, every one of them and it's out to get me!"

After half the hare for breakfast, Alan had his mount saddled and took a long ride to the north to seek out supplies for his battery.

He came down off the front slope and rode at the edge of the hill line into the next cul-de-sac north, perhaps a quarter mile, seeking the small draw at its north end for passage through the convoluted terrain.

"Halt, who goes thar?" a voice challenged from the mists.

"A damned wet sailor!" he called back, after he had gotten over his sudden fright. Under his tarpaulin coat he had his pair of pistols, the ones bought nearly two years before in Portsmouth, but they had lain unused except for a cleaning and oiling, because midshipmen could not wear their own iron except for a useless dirk, and once battle was joined he had never had a chance to go below for them. They were still next to useless under the folds of the tarred coat, but he had reached for them.

"Watch wot yer adoin' with yer hands, thar, sailor," the invisible watcher shouted back. "Ride up an' be reco'nized!"

"Ride up where, damn you?" he said. In reply, a soldier got to his feet from the bushes not thirty paces away to his right, holding a rifle at full cock and ready to fire.

How can a man in a red coat be so invisible? Alan marveled, reining his horse about to walk up near the man. He thought that he recognized the uniform. "North Carolina Volunteers?"

"That we are. Now, what in hell're you?"

"Midshipman Alan Lewrie. I am from the redan to the south."

"Open that coat an' let's see yer true colors."

Alan unlaced the coat and pulled it back to reveal the navy uniform, the white collar tabs of a midshipman and the anchored buttons.

"Guess yer wot ya say ya are. Where ya agoin'?"

"To find some tents for my men and tarps for my guns."

"Gonna ride through that thar draw, wuz ya?"

"I am an officer," Alan reminded the man, stretching his rank.

"I kin see that." The man nodded in agreement, lowering his rifle and taking it off cock. He began to wrap an oily handkerchief about the firelock and frisson to keep his priming dry. "But ya ride up thar an' somebody'd put a ball in yer boudin's afore ya could say Jack Sauce!"

"Then how am I to get through the draw...private?" Alan asked, his blood rising.

"Get on down an' I'll lead off."

Alan had to dismount and squelch through the wet grass and mud behind the soldier, who did not give him a backward glance until they were almost in the notch of the draw.

"Corp'ral o' the guard, thar! Gotta horse an' rider with me!"

More men popped up from the thickets and Alan was waved on past.

"Mister Lewrie," someone called. "Come to accept our invitation?"

"Ah, Burgess Chiswick!" Alan grinned, happy to see someone that he knew. "On my way past, really."

"Surely your errand is not so important you could not break your passage, as I believe you sailors say, and have a cup of coffee with us."

"Real coffee?"

"The genuine article," Burgess boasted.

"Then I shall accept with pleasure."

He was led into camp behind the draw, where life was lived more openly than in the forward face of the position. Tents were slung under the trees or stretched like awnings over lean-tos for shelter and concealment. Very small fires burned, with a lot less smoke than Alan could credit.

"Brother, look who I found tramping in the woods," Burgess said as they got near the shelter he shared with his sibling. "I promised him some coffee if he'd bide awhile with us."

Alan was made welcome under their rude shelter while his mount was led off by an orderly. He shed his tarpaulin coat and sat down on a log before the fire, which was damned welcome after a morning in the cool damp. A large mug of coffee was shoved into his hands and when he took a sip he made the happy discovery that it had been laced liberally with brandy, which made him sigh in pleasure.

While he took his ease, he explained where he was set up, what his errand was and related his experiences with the Hessians.

"Poor bastards," the elder Chiswick said. "Sent over here as a ready source of money for their prince or whatever he is, no idea of the country or what the fighting is about. Even have to supply their own rifles."

"Didn't look like yours," Alan commented.

"No, it's more like a rifled musket or one of these Rebel Pennsylvania rifles," Burgess told him, adding a top-up of brandy into the mug. "Poor work but more serviceable than what the Rebels have."

"I thought the Rebels had a wickedly good gun."

"Damned long ranged, and most of 'em can shoot the eyes out of a squirrel at two hundred paces." Burgess shrugged. "But, it's slow to load because of the rifling in the barrel, a lot slower than a musket, and the stock's too light to melee with hand-to-hand."

"Won't take any sort of bayonet, either, unless you shove a plug down the barrel," Governour stuck in. "And then where are you?"

"Then why make them?" Alan asked.

"Because they were light enough to carry in the woods, accurate enough to drop game with one shot when that's all the chance you get to feed your family, and long ranged enough to avoid having to sneak right up on a deer or what have you. It was never meant for a military use. You put a line of Rebel riflemen up against a line of regular infantry and you'll get your much-vaunted riflemen slaughtered every time once the regulars go in with the bayonet," Governour confidently said. "We and the Jagers can fire three . . . four times as fast as they and give them cold steel after the last volley."

Governour and his younger brother were good-looking fellows. However, even the younger Burgess had a ruthless look. They both had sandy hair and hazel eyes, but those eyes could glint as hard as agate, so Alan assumed they truly knew the heart of the matter when it came to skewering and slaughtering Rebels.

"So I may depend on the Jagers?" Alan said.

"Absolutely," Governour assured him. "They're highly disciplined and crack shots, near as good woodsmen as we. And Heros von Muecke can be relied on to stand his ground like Horatius at the Bridge. He's a bit hard to take—thinks he's some German blood royal and can get his back up over the slightest thing—but we've skirmished beside him before and he and his men have always been bloody marvels."

"That is reassuring, since I don't know the first thing about land fighting," Alan said, leaning back on the wall of the lean-to. He described where his battery was and how the redan was laid out, until he began to notice how the Chiswick brothers were both frowning.

"Tis a bad position," Burgess said with finality.

"Why?" Alan asked, once more beholden to someone for knowledge and slightly resenting the necessity of it, of being so unprepared for what he was being called upon to do. Damme, I was getting right good at the nautical cant, and here I am an innocent lamb again, he thought.

"We rode over that last week, Alan," Burgess said. "You only have what . . . a ten-, fifteen-foot rise to your front, and you're set in the open before that last bit of ground. Steep hills on either side, higher than you but not unscalable."

"A *regular* officer would think unscalable." Governour spat.

"Rebels'd be all over you like fleas on a dog. Come at night, most like. I would," Burgess said.

"No way down the back side, and if you do get down, you're stuck on one bank of the creek with no way down, or across," Governour added.

"Never get your guns out of there if you have to withdraw," added the younger Chiswick.

"Never get your own arse out of there, either."

"Well, what about you and your troops, then?" Alan sputtered.

"We cover both sides of the defile in a cross-fire, and the front of both little fingers of the ridge." Governour sketched in the dirt with some kindling from the small fire. "If overwhelmed, we fall back and skirmish to the marshes of the creek to the northeast. We can fall back on the fortified parallel on the river or into either the Star Redoubt or the Fusilier's Redoubt. Really, I don't know what the officer who sited you was thinking of," he concluded, tossing the stick into the fire. "There is no reason to cover that ground, 'cause no one could ever use it."

"Because it is too steep and wooded on the east slope, and goes right into the deep ravines of the creek," Alan said, seeing the sense of it. "They could not bridge it, or find boats to cross it."

"Exactly." Governour smiled briefly. "Might find sites for mortar or howitzer batteries in there, but you'd be much better placed up here with us. If they did set up in there, we could butcher their flanks."

"But the ground is so boggy now, it would take fifty mules to get one gun shifted." Alan groaned. "Mayhap those army guns could move in all this, but mine would not."

"We could make a strong-point with our battalion and Lewrie's guns, Governour," Burgess enthused. "We would not have to fall back as we planned if assaulted. And with von Muecke's Jagers to flesh us out . . ."

"Aye," Governour said, getting to his feet stiffly. "Do you entertain our naval compatriot while I see Colonel Hamilton about this. He could get the battery resited for us."

Lieutenant Chiswick shrugged into his coat and squared his hat, then stalked away on his long legs to see their battalion commander while Burgess lifted the lid of a stewpot.

"Have you breakfasted, Alan?" he asked.

"My man Cony snared a rabbit last night. Yes."

"Mollow shot a deer yesterday. Care for some venison?"

"Well, I'd not say no to a slice or two." Alan beamed.

It did indeed take nearly four dozen mules to shift the guns to a better site over the next two days, after Lieutenant Colonel Hamilton had made his protestations to Cornwallis's aides. The rain still came down to sullen showers, clearing for a while and warming up just enough to make everyone steam below gray skies, then starting in again for an hour or two, so that Alan was constantly shifting into his tarpaulin coat and out of it, constantly checking the priming of his pistols and his musket, and learning the value of an oily rag wrapped around a firelock, or the worth of a whittled pinewood plug in the muzzles to keep the loaded charge fairly dry. At a suggestion of Governour's, Alan sought out a wagon-wright to see if he could get field-gun wheels and axles attached to his gun trucks, with some longer timbers to serve as trails and limbers. There was only one dry path across the marshes to their rear, the one the guns had negotiated the week before, and he was damned if he would surrender his artillery for the lack of proper carriages when finally placed in a position he could hope to evacuate.

They tore down the *abatis* and loaded them on muleback to be redug into the new position, shoveled down the ramparts into the shallow trench and filled in the magazines and dugouts, leaving only bare patches of earth to show that they had ever been there. The area looked like mass graves when they were finished destroying the redan, and the ease with which it went down gave everyone a squeamish, impermanent feeling.

There came a time, eventually, when Alan could have killed for a clean set of linen, and there was little that Cony could do to keep his uniform presentable in the field, so Alan asked permission to go back to *Desperate* for some fresh things from his sea chest, and it was granted. Burgess was curious about shipboard life, so he came along as well and they had a pleasant ride back to the town and the docks.

"Boat ahoy!"

"Aye, aye!" the bowman shouted, holding up one finger to indicate a very low rank to the deck watch of the frigate and the need for only the smallest side party. Under the circumstances, the bosun's mate did double duty of piping them aboard and representing the ship as watch officer. There were few enough people on deck, at any rate.

"Permission to come aboard, Mister Weems," Alan said, doffing his hat and nudging Burgess to emulate him.

"Aye, Mister Lewrie," Weems said. "How're things ashore?"

"Only half misery, considering, Mister Weems. This is Ensign Chiswick of the North Carolina Volunteers. I suppose that is much like a warrant rank, possibly an acting lieutenant."

"Yer servant, sir," Weems said, knuckling his brow.

"And yours, sir," Burgess replied.

They went below to the midshipmen's mess, where only little Carey resided at present. He was glad to see Alan, and was full of questions directed at both of them, seeming in full, childish awe of the soldier.

Alan rapped on the light, temporary partition between his mess and the officer's wardroom, and was bade enter. He led Burgess in to meet Dr. Dorne, Cheatham, Lieutenant Peck of the marines, and the sailing master, Mister Monk.

"Had enough of soldiering, have you, Lewrie?" Peck drawled,

taking his ease on the transom settee with a clay pipe fuming by the window.

"And learned sweet damn-all, sir," Alan agreed. "I would not presume to enter the wardroom, but I believe my chest is stored here, and I need fresh linen and things."

"Aye, so it is." Monk nodded. "Mister Chiswick, sir, take a seat an' have a drop with us while ya wait."

"Thankee kindly, Mister Monk," Burgess said, shying his hat at a peg and drawing up to the scarred mess table.

"Ya bring yer laundry, too?"

"No, sir. Just my thirst," Burgess said easily. "And a curiosity about your ship."

Alan dumped his jute bag of soiled linen, hoping a hammock man could eventually tend to it, and dug down into his chest for clean shirts and stockings, a more presentable neckcloth, and a second pair of shoes that he could rotate with the only pair he had been wearing in all the muck over the last few days of rain and sogginess. He was intensely relieved to see that nothing had been disturbed in his absence and that a very torn and stained shirt in the bottom was still in the same position and gave off a muted, heavy clinking sound as he shifted it. He packed himself a fresh pair of breeches and a pair of working rig slop trousers as well and relocked his chest.

"Sit down as well, Mister Lewrie, don't stand on ceremony," Monk ordered. "They's grog, there, an' some decent red as well. Top up an' share a glass with us."

"Thank you for the wardroom privilege, sir."

"Big doings ashore, then, Mister Lewrie?" Dr. Dorne asked as he straightened his eternal tiewig, and peered over his tiny spectacles.

"Nothing much yet, sir. No sign of the enemy to the west of us."

"Well, they are up on the Gloucester side," Peck said. "Lafayette and some Frogs. Lauzun's Legion, I'm told. Lancers, dragoons and foot, along with some unit called the Virginia Militia. Some of 'em marched in, some boated in from the French camp on the James."

"And we could not stop them, sir?" Alan asked, filling a glass with the red wine. Rum he could get ashore, and it was getting tiresome.

"The French're absolute masters o' the navigation now. Not one British craft c'n swim but by their leave," Monk said.

"Well, there's the spy boats," Peck stuck in.

"Sneakin' in and out at night with letters to an' from Clinton an' Graves in New York ain't challengin' the French, sir," Monk retorted.

"Any word on when we may expect relief, sir?" Burgess asked.

"None yet, lad."

"It is not like Cornwallis to sit so idly, I assure you, sirs," Burgess said out of pride. "In the Carolinas, we marched like . . . like foot cavalry, active as fleas. There is still a chance to march inland to Williamsburg and cross over into better country. And with enough of these small transports I saw here in harbor, we could cross to the Gloucester side. Tarleton is a Tartar—he could cut a way through for us."

"There's to be an attempt to cross the bay to the eastern shore soon, I have heard," Cheatham volunteered. "A solid enough rumor of it, in faith. Heard it from the supply quartermaster ashore. Send fireships downriver to frighten the French away and cross before they can respond."

"I wish they would tell us," Alan ventured, thinking that he was too far from the harbor to reembark on that experiment, and fearful of being left behind as a forlorn hope or rearguard. "It would take some time to get our guns back aboard for the attempt."

"Yea, well." Monk coughed in embarrassment and looked away to busy himself with a large swallow of grog.

That's exactly what would happen, Alan realized with a cold shudder under his heart. Some regulars would get off, but the Volunteers and my people would be sacrificed. Goddamn and blast the bastards!

They shifted to cheerier topics; the good state of health of Lieutenants Railsford and Forrester over on Gloucester, what Avery was doing with the heavy guns closer around the town, but it was a gloomy mess.

Wardroom privileges did not extend to supper, so Alan and

Burgess excused themselves as the mess cloth was spread and no one made any noises of invitation to dine with them. Dr. Dorne was good enough to see them out on deck, taking the need of air as an excuse. But once on deck, they met the gloomy presence of Commander Treghues, who swooped up like a wraith in the dark.

"Mister Lewrie, is it?" he said.

"Aye, sir. Come aboard for fresh linen, sir. May I present Ensign Burgess Chiswick of the North Carolina Volunteers, sir."

"Mister Chiswick, give you joy, sir. I hope Mister Lewrie has not let the reputation of the Navy down?"

"Indeed not, sir," Burgess replied. "He has been a most resourceful fellow and a good companion. His battery is attached to our redoubt just on t'other side of the creek. Good artilleryman, he is, sir."

"Yes, he likes the sound of guns. Good work, Mister Lewrie," Treghues said with a small chuckle which was so out of character from the harsh and bitter man Alan had come to know that he strongly suspected the captain had totally lost his wits, even if it was a startling improvement.

"Who would have thought it?" Alan whispered after Treghues had quit the deck for his cabins and his own supper. "Dr. Dorne, sir?"

"You'd not notice in the dark, Mister Lewrie, but I performed a slight trephination upon him after you left the ship," Dorne said softly enough so that even Burgess could not hear. "There was pressure upon the cranium from the occluded blood resulting from the blow he received, which I relieved, and he is remarkably restored to his former self thereof. He has little memory, however, of the last few weeks."

Dorne slipped him the wink to let Alan know that he had forgotten even his grudge against his least-favorite miscreant rogue.

"Thank bloody Christ!" Alan breathed.

"There is, however, a slight problem," Dorne continued. "He was dosed with a tincture of hemp, a decoction from the South American plant cannabin, more correctly *Nicotiana glauca,* in wine for pain. That led to some lucid moments before the trephination, and he has grown quite . . . fond of it, I am afraid. Since my supply is gone, I do not know what he shall be like in future. But we shall see. Perhaps it is best that you are ashore at present, and cannot rekindle any unfortunate memories."

"God, yes," Alan agreed. "I'm off like a hare."

"More like a fox, if I know you well at all," Dorne said. "And good luck to you in our shared misfortune."

"Aye, Dr. Dorne, and good fortune to you as well."

Once ashore and on horseback once more, Burgess was most complimentary in his opinion of Commander the Honorable Treghues, and of the people in the wardroom.

"A most charming gentleman is your captain," Burgess said.

"As long as he has his wits about him, yes," Alan replied, and spent the next few minutes of their ride filling Burgess in on how the captain had behaved before his surgery and how brutally he had treated everyone. Alan did not go into Treghues's reasons regarding himself; he liked Burgess and wanted him to remain a friend.

"You're a lucky fellow, Alan," Burgess opined.

"How do you come by that, Burgess?" Alan asked, mystified.

"When you are on shipboard, you have your fellow midshipmen in a snug mess with a steward and a hammock man to see to your table and your kit, never have to sleep out in the wilds in all weathers and you are assured where your next meal is coming from. What more could you desire in time of war?"

"Going back to London and raising merry hell," Alan said, laughing, "and letting some other person fight the damn thing."

"Well, had I the choice to make, I would have preferred the navy to the army," Burgess said. "Like that wardroom where your officers live and dine—it looked damned comfortable."

"Burgess, all the partitions are deal or canvas and come down when the ship is piped to quarters," Alan explained. "There normally would be artillery in the wardroom, and when the iron begins to fly there is no safe place aboard a ship. They shovel the dead— what's left of 'em—and the hopelessly wounded over the side to make space in which to keep the guns firing. Trust me, there is nothing desirable about being aboard ship then. There's more safety ashore where one may dig."

"We do not dig," Burgess replied. "We are light infantry."

"Then we both stand an equal chance when it comes to getting our deaths," Alan said. "Not much to choose between them."

"You speak from experience, sounds like." Burgess sobered suddenly. "Tell me of it."

Alan did not mind bragging on himself, so the rest of the ride passed on the way back to their position in the hills as he related his successes in *Ariadne, Parrot* and *Desperate,* even touching on the duel with the infantry lieutenant on Antigua over Lucy Beauman's honor. By the time they dismounted and turned their horses over to an orderly before seeing to their own supper Burgess Chiswick was mightily impressed with his new companion as a fighting man who had seen more action than Burgess or even his older brother Governour, who had been with the colors longer. But then Alan was, by that time, pretty impressed with his own prowess as well. And after a filling game pie and a mug or two of Burgess's corn whiskey, he was absolutely convinced of the fact that he was a devil of a fellow.

CHAPTER 9

"THEY are still there," Alan said, borrowing Burgess's telescope to stare downriver. They had gone for a morning ride over to the river bluffs near the Star Redoubt to survey the work of the fireships. Cornwallis had filled four schooners entrapped in the anchorage with all the straw and flammables he could find, and had placed them under the command of a Loyalist privateer captain. The fireships had gone downriver and had frightened the hell out of the French for a time, driving them away from the mouth of the York, but the privateer captain's schooner had been set alight much too soon, and all the others lit themselves off at the same time as though it were the correct signal. One had blown up, one had gone aground in the shallows after being abandoned by her very well-singed crew of volunteers and the total effect was nil.

"Well, it was a brave effort, damme if it wasn't," Burgess said.

"We might try it again in a few days, though I doubt if they'll stand for it a second time," Alan said, closing the telescope with a heavy click of collapsing tubes and handing it back to Ensign Chiswick. "Wouldn't have done us much good, anyway. No one had called us to fetch back the artillery or prepare to evacuate with the fleet."

"The bulk of the army would have gotten away to the eastern shore, but we could have still crossed over to the Gloucester side in barges and joined Tarleton to cut our way out," Burgess informed him. "Lauzun's Legion is perhaps six hundred men. Mayhap eight hundred French marines landed from the ships, and the Virginia Militia surely can't be much. Our troops used them like so many bears back in the spring. Still, I don't see what is stopping us from going down the river. There are only three ships."

"A third rate seventy-four and two large frigates," Alan recited. "They are anchored so they could sweep the main channel. And what you see as open water is really shoals. Even at high tide it is not enough to float a ship of any size. You can see where that schooner went aground, and she didn't draw a whole fathom, loaded as she was. And if we did force the guard ships to cut their cables, they would fly off signal fusees and we would never make that far shore before the main fleet near Cape Henry caught up with us."

"But they cannot come up the river."

"Thank Providence for small favors. I'd not attempt it without an experienced pilot, and then only in the smallest craft."

"Then there is nothing for it but to put our trust in Clinton and your Admiral Graves to get back here and rescue us," Burgess said.

"Whenever that may be." Alan spat, tugging at the reins of his mare to turn her about to face inland once more.

"Any guesses on that?" Burgess asked. "I heard Colonel Hamilton say that General Clinton had assured Lord Cornwallis that over four thousand men were ready to embark from New York now there is no threat to the city."

"Hmm . . . Graves departed the coast on the tenth or so," Alan said as they walked their mounts down from the bluffs to the Williamsburg road. "With favorable winds, he would have gotten to New York on the fifteenth, even beating into a nor'east breeze. Ten days to refit and embark those troops . . . if he can work back across the bar off New York with all his ships. He could have departed yesterday on the twenty-fifth, and could be here by at least the thirtieth. Say the second of October on the outside. But he would still have to fight his way into the bay against the French as he should have the first time."

"So by the second, we shall have four thousand more troops, more artillery and supplies and might succeed in forcing the French fleet to take shelter up the James River, reversing the odds against us."

"Bide a minute, Burgess," Alan said, pulling his mount to a stop. "What did you mean about New York no longer being threatened. De Barras and his troops in Newport never threatened New York directly."

"Oh, I am sorry, I thought you had already heard," Burgess apologized. "Washington and Rochambeau have abandoned most of their positions around New York and are reputed to be on the march for Yorktown."

"Jesus Christ!" Alan shrieked, startling both mounts, who jumped about for a few minutes before they could calm them back down, tittuping and side-paddling and farting in alarm.

"I wish you would not frighten the horses so, Alan. This plug is skittish—not my usual mount," Burgess complained.

"Fuck the horses. You just frightened the devil out of *me!*" Alan shot back. "Is there anything else on the way you have not told me about? No expeditionary force from the Grand Moghul of India with fifty war elephants? No Mameluke cavalry from the Ottoman Empire?"

"From Clinton's letters, which were passed on to the colonel for his information, we should be about even in numbers and much stronger in cavalry should we needs break out," Burgess said.

"Jesus Christ," Alan repeated, though much more softly than before. "We're going to get our arses knackered. We're going to lose this damned war if we keep this up. This is the last army of note in the Americas."

"And the last Parliament would raise, most like," Burgess agreed, so stoically calm about their future chances that Alan felt like hitting him. "So there is no way that Graves or Clinton would leave us hanging in the balance for very long, is there?" Burgess reasoned. "We can hold until relieved and sooner or later the hurricane season will force the French to sail away, and all this affair will be just another campaign that almost achieved something but didn't. Washington shall have to go back north to the New York area eventually or stand still for General Clinton to rampage all over the upper Colonies and destroy all their work."

"That sounds... logical, at any rate," Alan had to admit, though he remembered his talk with Lieutenant Railsford in *Desper-*

ate on their way to New York, and Treghues's rant about fleet strategy before the Battle of the Chesapeake. That had sounded emi-
nently logical, too, and look where that had gotten them.

Regardless of the circumstances, there was still duty to be done.
The half-battery had to be manned, patrols had to go out to forage or
to scout, their position had to be constantly improved and watches
had to be stood much as at sea, with some of the gunners by their
pieces at all times. Knatchbull was not an imaginative man, but he
was a competent one and practically ran the battery for Lewrie,
presenting a going concern to his midshipman each morning with all
the care of a first lieutenant doing the same for his captain. Sighting
shots were fired with round shot out across the fields to let the gun
captains find how far they could reach and improve their chances
when a real foe presented himself. Gun drill was carried out every
morning, just as aboard ship, and the midday rum ration was doled
out at eleven thirty in the morning, corresponding to the seven bells
of the forenoon watch, followed by dinner. Alan led cutlass drill
himself to keep the hands sharp and out of trouble with so much idle
time. A corporal from the North Carolina Volunteers led the musket
practice, and the men, with nothing other to bet on, began to improve at targets, being forced to load and fire faster than they ever
had before.

Alan kept the men working on his gun carriages. Using the
trucks as the base, he found enough seasoned wood to form axles and
trails, and the more creative gunners did the rest. There was little
that an English seaman could not make with his hands, if properly
stimulated to the work, and soon he had spokes and greenwood
wheels abuilding. The wheels would not have iron rims—they could
not aspire to that with limited materials—but he could shift his guns
more easily once the labor was finished.

The camp rang with hammering and sawing and the rasp of
carpenters' planes and files. The naves began to sprout spokes as new
platforms were nailed to the bottom of the trucks, and the trails were
bolted on.

"Lookin' proper, Mister Lewrie," Knatchbull informed him. "I'd still use the breechin' ropes an' the side tackles an sich, just in case. That's greenwood an' pine at that. Takes good oak're ash ta do it right."

"Still, it eases the work of running out to the gunports in this redan." Alan was pleased with the handiwork of the first piece to be converted and emplaced. "We could cut down two men from each gun crew and send them back aboard ship."

"Aye, sir, but iffen we had ta get outa here in a hurry, I'd not be sendin' 'em back ta the ship anytime soon," Knatchbull said.

"I shall write the captain a letter about it, anyway," Alan decided. If Treghues was in a better mental state, it didn't hurt to piss down his superior's back and let him know that at least one of his midshipmen was being diligent and creative in adversity—one he could not quite remember clearly since his trephination, but one whom he should get to know once more on much better terms.

"Guess we better test-fire the bugger, Mister Lewrie," Knatchbull said. "Full cartridge an' round shot."

"There is nothing at present to our front. No scouts out this morning this late. Let's do."

A gun crew came forward, while the rest of the men and some of the Hessian Jagers and North Carolina troops who were free of duties came to gawk; at a reasonably safe distance, Alan noted. Since it was his idea, there was nothing for it but to stand beside the gun crew as the piece was loaded.

"Charge yer gun," Knatchbull intoned. "Shot yer gun. Prime yer gun. Quoin in. Don't wanna hit no poor bastard off in them woods."

"Aim for that clump of shrubbery three cables off," Alan ordered. "Excess crew take cover. I shall touch her off."

The side-tackle men and the powder boy scuttled to the rear, and the rammer man, shot man and gun captain headed out to the flanks in the trench on either side of the gun platform.

Alan lowered the smouldering length of slow match gripped in the claws at the end of the linstock to the priming quill and took a deep breath. He touched the quill and there was a flash of powder smoke and a sharp hissing sound as the fine-mealed powder in the quill took light. Then there was a sharp bang, and the piece recoiled to the back of the platform right smartly, snubbing at the extent of the breeching ropes and slewing a bit on the new high wheels. It reared a bit on its trail, then thumped back down heavily, but after the smoke cleared Alan could detect no cracks or splintering of the new carriage.

"Check her over, Knatchbull," Alan said, letting out his breath. Still got my nutmegs intact, he exulted.

There was a ragged cheer from the hands and the onlookers, and Alan took a theatrical bow to his audience while Knatchbull and several of the men closely involved in the carriage's construction looked it over.

"Sound as a fifty-guinea horse, so tis," Knatchbull judged.

"Musta skeered that fella ta death, Mister Lewrie," the gun captain laughed, pointing off into the fields where a rider could be seen at full gallop heading their way.

"We didn't put a ball near him, did we?" Alan worried.

"Nah, didn' come nowhere close, sir," the gun captain told him. "Put the ball dead square in that clump, mebbe a furlong shy, anyways."

Alan unslung the telescope by the gun and took a look at the approaching stranger. He was wearing the uniform of a British officer, but that was about all that could be discovered until he had reined in his mount by the outlying sentries and shouted his news, panting dramatically as though the world hung on his next word.

"Washington's army," he gasped. "On the Williamsburg road. On the way here, about ten miles off. They shall be up to these positions by nightfall! Have you a fresh mount? Mine's done in."

"Good God a-mighty, Mister Lewrie," Knatchbull muttered, his craggy face dark with concern at this new development.

"Yes, Knatchbull," Alan replied calmly, having been apprised of the possibility days before. "Now, even more reason to continue work on the new gun carriages, is it not? Rum ration at the usual time."

He took out his pocket watch and opened the face as though the question of rum was really more important.

"Aye, sir."

"And I want the second gun mounted by nightfall at the latest. So work 'em hard after dinner."

"Aye, aye, sir." Knatchbull nodded, calmed by the sangfroid of his immediate superior, and went off to do Lewrie's bidding without another thought.

There, that'll show the bastards I can be as cool as a post-captain, Alan thought grimly. Mister Railsford, wherever you are over there on the Gloucester side, thanks for the warning about showing calm.

After dark, Alan could hear the enemy army on its approach march. He was certain that the army could be heard as far back as Yorktown itself. Chains jangled from artillery caissons, axles squealed and screamed as heavy guns and supply wagons made their way over the poor roads. Even the grunting and neighing of horses could be heard, and the bawl of oxen in their yokes being goaded forward and now and again when the wind was just right the solid tramp of many marching feet. There was nothing to be seen to the front, even with a fairly full moon; only the silent hills and the silvered forests that brooded in their alienness.

"Think they'll attack tonight, Mister Lewrie?" Knatchbull asked.

"They've covered at least ten miles today, maybe twenty," Alan told him, repeating what little he could pick up from the talk at supper with the Chiswick brothers, their captain and the Jager officers in a pavilion back near the end of the draw. "We would know if they had attempted to scout us, so it's sure they do not know where our fortifications are for now. They'll scout tomorrow, but we've nothing to fear for this evening. Still, make sure the guns are loaded with round shot and canister to boot, run out ready to fire with tompions in to protect the charges against the night damp until time to fire. Post two men from each gun crew as sentries with muskets. They are not to fire on anything unless strictly ordered, or I shall have the man that did it flogged tied to a tree if a grating cannot be procured."

"Four hour watches, Mister Lewrie?"

"Aye. You can use a watch?"

"Ah, I ain't no scholar, Mister Lewrie," Knatchbull admitted in the darkness. "But I got the hour glass."

"Good enough, then," Alan said, making a production of yawning for Knatchbull's, and his men's, benefit. "I shall turn in. Send a man to wake me if there is any alarm, and without fail at the end of the middle watch."

Alan wandered back from the ramparts of their new post and found his small tent tucked away under a grove of trees snuggled up on the right side of the draw. Cony had a small fire going that was barely flaming to see by as he stripped off his coat and waistcoat, loosened his neckcloth and slid off his shoes.

"You turn in, Cony," Alan told him. "Knatchbull will send someone to wake you for lookout before dawn."

"Aye, Mister Lewrie," Cony replied, spreading a hammock for ground cloth by the fire and arranging his blankets.

Alan crawled into the tent and found his own bedding. He stretched out and flung a rough blanket over his body so he could lie in the dark and watch the tiny flickers of the fire on the wall of the tent, wide awake and staring up at the faint shadows of the boughs over his head as they swayed in the faint wind and moonlight.

"Sir?" Cony said softly from beyond the tent flap.

"Aye, Cony."

"They's a flask o' rum by yer head, sir, ta help ya caulk the better," Cony told him, already rolled into his own blankets against the damp night chill.

Thank God, Alan thought, fumbling about until his hand fell on a small leather bottle and withdrew the stopper. Neat rum was not something he normally preferred, but tonight it was welcome. He took a small sip and winced at the bite of the rum and its sharp odor.

The bedding rustled as he lifted the bottle to his lips once more, and Alan could swear he could already feel the tiny movements of the many bugs drawn to him by his warmth, his scent and the hope for blood. That was one of the worst parts of serving on land—being awakened by the bite of something too small to be fought, or finding the welts in the morning and feeling the fleas begin to shift about in his clothing. He had already had several ticks withdrawn from his skin; each time he was filled with loathing at the brutes and the way they had swelled by feeding on him. At least the Navy did not have to put up with the bastards and could fumigate and rid a ship of most lice, fleas and other insects. Roaches were the main worry on a ship, along with the occasional brave rat that ventured out of the orlop and bilges.

Damme, I wish I could scream and become demented, instead of being such a little paragon of equanimity, he thought silently. I am so distraught by all the filth and ordure, the bugs and the sleeping on the cold ground that if I ever do get back inboard of *Desperate* and out to sea, I shall never complain about the Navy again.

Realizing how desperate he was to make such a vow, he could have pinched himself to see if he was not already dreaming. But he had to wait a long time for sleep to come that night, while the ground trembled ever so gently with the vibrations of the approaching army.

"Pull out?" Governour Chiswick spat. "Damme, that's a wrench."

"Pull out to where?" Burgess asked.

"Back into the inner fortifications closer to Yorktown," Governour informed them, waving a feeble hand toward the east.

"Bah, das ist . . ." Heros von Muecke searched for the right word in English but failed to find anything suitable. "Sheiss!" he finally spat. "Ve here der bastards can skin!"

"The Star Redoubt can control the western approaches to the town and everything else is either marsh or ravine," Governour said. "They do not think our position is favorable. It is not just us, mind. The whole outer defense line is being withdrawn. On the other side of the creek's ravines there is high ground again, where we may dig in. Lord Cornwallis does not believe he has enough men to man the outer line properly."

"The hell we can't!" Burgess bragged. "Just let the shits try!"

"We have our orders," Governour said.

Alan, who had been sitting back in the pavilion and listening to the argument, had only one thought: to get his artillery evacuated. Then there might even be a chance to reembark the guns into *Desperate*, take a much-needed bath and get aboard ship and away from this nightmare.

"My guns," he said. "I need horse teams and limbers."

"Will those carriages hold up?" Governour asked.

"Of course, they will," Alan snapped. "For the two guns mounted on them, that is. The third gun needs a heavy wagon to take the barrel and a second to take the truck and gun tools."

"I shall send a rider to request of them, then," Governour said. "That means we shall have to stay until Mister Lewrie's guns are out of here. I shall tell the staff that as well."

This time there would be no thought of dismantling the ramparts.

The tents and shelters were taken down and folded up, the personal gear was bundled into field packs, the magazines emptied once more and the guns rolled out of position ready for the horse teams to arrive. But the third gun could only be held in abeyance. It took the effort of all the naval party to lift the weight of a long nine barrel from the gun truck with heavy tackle slung below the piece, then laid out on the ground on a section of heavy netting.

When the teams did arrive, it was a scrawny pack of beasts that had been despatched. The grazing had not been the best, and the corn and oats were directed to the troops' diet instead of the horses. With the third barrel in the wagon, finally, it took a double team of eight of the horses to draw it, and the men had to assist the remaining animals with their own muscle power, up through the draw, down the back side, along the edge of the marshes to the main road, sometimes unharnessing some horses to double up whenever a gun bogged down.

They rolled into Yorktown and were left on their own after the North Carolina troops and the Jagers were sent off to their new quarters. Alan bade everyone a hearty good-bye, even von Muecke, and then sat down by the side of the road to wait for instructions since the army staff seemed to have forgotten about them completely. After getting thoroughly bored with an hour of inactivity, Alan wandered off to the docks.

"Excuse me, sir," he said, doffing his hat to a naval lieutenant who was directing the work of a party loading barges to supply the troops across the river.

"Yes, what is it?"

"I am in charge of three guns from *Desperate*, sir," Alan said. "And we were posted on the far bank of the creek until this morning. Now no one has a clue about what we are to do with them.

There are three long nines, two on field carriages and one still on a naval carriage."

"Well, why do you not ask the teamsters?"

"They only want their animals and wagons back and have no instructions as to taking us anyplace else, sir."

"Damme, what a muddle!" the lieutenant swore. "Trust the army to have the brains of a crop-sick dominee do-little! See the headquarters, back of the town."

"Aye, sir."

He had not gone a hundred yards, though, before he ran into David Avery and gunner's mate Tulley, and gave a great shout to get their attention.

"Alan!" David cried back. "How do you keep?"

"Full of fleas but main well, considering," Alan replied, very glad to see someone from the ship once more. "Look here, the army has no idea about what to do with my guns, and . . ."

"Gawd a-mighty, Mister Lewrie, wot ya been doin' wi' my guns?" Tulley exploded, seeing the impromptu field carriages.

"I wrote the captain of them," Alan snapped. "He seemed most impressed, Mister Tulley." Treghues had indeed replied to Lewrie's letter with a most kind answer, giving faint praise for his initiative and creativity, but it was praise nonetheless, and that from a man who had recently been willing to feed Lewrie to the fires of hell and help shovel some good, hot-burning sea-coal into the bargain, so Alan was having none of it.

"Damn, there's two guns wot we'll never get back now!" Tulley spat.

"Get back?" Alan asked, perplexed.

"Captain Treghues asked for some of his artillery back, since we were the only ship left in harbor of any size that was even partially armed," David explained. "When Cornwallis decided to withdraw into the inner defense line, the staff said we could have them, since they were on naval trucks and unsuitable for a siege work. But now . . ."

"Even the smashers?" Alan wondered, asking about the carronades.

"Well, no, they do want to hold onto those," David said, taking a keen interest in the field carriages himself. "Even so, we are leaving four pieces on the Gloucester side, but we got my nine-pounder back aboard this morning, and we can refit your third gun. But these . . ."

"What if we can get them back aboard right away?" Alan pressed, eager to get off the land. "We can knock the trails and limbers off, put them back on their own small wheels and axles. What would you wager the army doesn't even know of them?"

"They know," David said sadly.

"Damn."

"They thought it most clever, and if we still had access to all that timber across the ravines, they might convert more. So these two guns stay with the army."

"Damn!"

"Along with the nacky cock who came up with the idea."

"Oh, hell!"

I have done it again, Alan cursed himself. I was too fucking smart for my own good again. There's no bloody justice in this world, I swear. Damme for being clever, damme for doing something stupid, it's all one. If I tried to do something dumb, I'd get a caning for it anyway!

"Surely, one midshipman is much the same as another," Alan said. "They could bring Forrester over. Let him take some glory."

"You want to appear keen, do you not, Alan?" David queried, looking at him askance. "Captain Symonds put it in his reports and asked for you by name."

"Oh, did he?" Alan said, raising hs eyebrows.

Well, perhaps that is a different kettle of fish. When the fleet gets here to relieve us, I could gain favorable interest from Hood and Graves. That could not hurt my career.

"I am told," David Avery told him in a softer voice and from a much closer distance, "that the captain is in his right mind once more, and was flattered that Symonds asked for you. Even commended you for the effort to convert the pieces to field use. Much as he may have liked to do something good for Forrester, you are the one in favor at present. I should make the most of it."

"It's simply that land service is so depriving, so dirty and full of

bugs and such," Alan insisted, finding another reason for his reticence to stay ashore. "I could use a good delousing, David. Our army
is not the cleanest lot I've ever served with."

"I spent a few nights sleeping rough myself, so I can sympathize." His friend laughed. "It's most fortunate we ran into you so we
can take the third gun back aboard ship this evening. If there is
anything you need from your chest or from our mess to lessen the
burden, do let me know and I shall see that you get it."

"That's very kind of you, David," Alan said, hiding the bitter-
ness he felt at being the ship's perpetual orphan, banished ashore
until old age, it seemed, while Avery could loll about with few duties
onboard *Desperate*. Tulley was still incensed about this gun, but he
was glad to take charge of the disassembled piece and move it toward
the docks, along with a third of Alan's shore party. Alan had no
choice but to sigh and direct the teamsters to tow his converted field
guns into town where an army artillery officer was expecting his
arrival. They were shoved into the line on the east side of the town,
overlooking the river and the docks, almost on the edge of the bluffs.

The inner defense line, for all the work done on it by slaves and
soldiers, wasn't much better than what he had seen out in the hills.
The rampart was low enough to jump over, and the trenches behind
it were not very deep, either, though they were rooved with scrap
canvas and tents to keep the rain and sun off the men and there were
small zigzagging trenches about waist high that snaked back into the
town through which rations and relieving sentries could communicate with the ramparts. The line was also zigzag for much of its
length facing the enemy forces, which would lead attackers into
cross-fires from front and sides. In some places easier to approach,
the fortifications had been given a crenellation in the form of a small
redoubt that jutted out onto a higher piece of ground, or one in-
dented to take advantage of a ravine where the foe could congregate
and be struck from three sides instead of only two.

The walls, though, were not three feet high anywhere, barely
able to shelter a man standing in the trenches, faced with *abatis*,
strung with *chevaux-de-frise* to deter cavalry in the easier ground.
There were also some outlying redoubts beyond the ramparts as
strongpoints, especially on the southeast end of the town, nearest
the French landings on the James River, a few clustered to the south

corner above the ravine by the Hornwork, a large redoubt that over-looked the open ground around Wormsley's Pond and the creek of the same name, and even one still across the York Creek, but better sited than anything Alan had been involved with.

The town was just behind them, close enough to retire to from the ramparts through the communications trenches and to rest there in the abandoned buildings or homes that had not already been commandeered for use already.

"Your guns shall go in here," the army officer instructed, show-ing Alan two vacant gun ports in the east wall. There the wall was mostly straight, with an extended crenellation to their left. The area of the rampart around the gunports had been built up with fascines and gabions, and wooden ramps were already in place so the guns could rest or recoil smoothly. "Nice work you did, getting these naval pieces converted for field use."

"Thank you, sir. What do we do here, though?"

"Cover the river," the officer shrugged.

"I cannot reach the French ships from here with a ball, even at maximum elevation, sir. Unless they come farther up . . ."

"Then you can fire to your heart's content."

"Well, I was thinking that we would be more use further west or on the north face, sir. A long nine could drop shot into that big battery the French are building. Or cover the Star Redoubt."

"No point in that. The Star Redoubt is being abandoned as well. And we have mortars of our own to deal with that battery."

"With a long nine, sir, I could reach Gloucester Point as well. With so much artillery being put in on this side, it would seem reasonable to expect that we could use our more accurate pieces to provide a counterfire. On solid land, naval gunners can be devilishly accurate."

"And they could teach their grannies to suck eggs." The officer frowned. "We have six-pounders and infantry redans to cover the road from the Star Redoubt, and guns enough to cover the river above the town and strike that battery they're building. So why don't you just get your guns into position and leave the planning to your betters, eh? There's a good lad. More experienced men than you have already made allowance for any contingency, so why not just obey orders?"

Burgess and Governour have the right of it, Alan thought sourly as his gunners began to wheel their charges into the emplacements. Our regular army is a pack of idiots. I don't think they've had an original idea since Cromwell died. We ain't fighting on the French border with Marlborough. We're surrounded and short of powder already.

Still, once in place, Alan was relieved to find that the troops who supported him were mostly marines who could be trusted, so he would not have to share the same rarefied air as the army.

It is a truism that warfare consists mostly of marching off to the possible site of battle, and being thoroughly miserable in the process. And once there, it consists of waiting for that battle to begin and, depending on the climate, the availability of amusements and the amount of worrying one does while waiting, a pretty miserable process as well. Each morning, they rose early and stood to their guns, much as at dawn quarters. Each morning, the sea was empty beyond the capes and only the French ships could be seen from the town bluffs or the top of the ramparts; the ones beyond the shoals at the mouth of the York, or the ships far out in the bay blockading the entrances. . . Inland, they could watch the enemy march into positions; positions in the outer defense line that they had abandoned days before and were now redug and improved to their own detriment, and the joy of their foes.

September ended, and Graves did not come. The first days of October passed by in enforced ennui, with the town now thoroughly invested by both French and Rebel troops. More and more artillery wheeled into position, whole parks of guns. Not just light field pieces, but heavy siege guns and howitzers and mortars that could throw fizzing shells of up to sixteen inches that would burst with great thunderclaps should they ever cut loose with them.

The American Rebels made a brave show from the ramparts, marching in what seemed very good order, their muskets slung precisely and their step quick and lively, their striped Rebel banner with the starry blue canton and their regimental flags flying. The drums rolled and the fifes whistled thinly, like a man sucking air through his teeth; mostly they played "Yankee Doodle," which was about the most nonsensical song Lewrie had ever seen written down, even dumber than most, such as "Derry Down" or "When the World Turned Upside Down." The French troops wore white with rose, purple, green or black facings. The Rebels looked natty in dark blue and buff with white breeches and various regimental trim.

The Rebels and French bands serenaded them as their troops dug and countermarched and drilled, or toiled with improving artillery positions, and the marines paraded before the ramparts as well, playing "Hearts of Oak" and "Rule, Brittania," until Alan was sick of hearing them.

At night, the land across the ravine of Yorktown Creek, the woods and the fields were swarming with small squad fires in a glittering arc from the York River down to below Moore's House, out of reach of rifle fire or small arms. Strangely, both sides held their fire, even though the artillery could have put the fear of God and British gunnery up the Rebels and their allies. There was a rumor making the rounds that those insane Rebels had gotten up on their own ramparts of a freshly dug parallel and performed the manual of arms in Prussian style and it was such a good show that not a shot had been fired, though their Colonel Alexander Hamilton could have been handed his arse on a plate for forcing his troops to do such a stunt. And through it all, Graves and Hood and General Clinton and his four thousand reinforcements were also only a rumor, for they did not come. The skies clouded up and rained occasionally, and the nights were becoming chillier, the days less warm—more like home back in England in late summer, when the apples were ripe for the plucking, ruddy with the first frost.

The forage situation for the thousands of horses was getting desperate, and with too many animals in the fortifications providing a sanitary problem, many were turned out to crop the late summer grass on their own between the lines. They would not be called upon to haul guns or wagons, not for weeks to come, it looked like, and they were already half famished for want of good corn or grain. Come to think of it, so were the troops, and their needs came before horses and mules.

Making the situation even worse when it came to rations, there were thousands of black faces in the fortifications; slaves from the many plantings in the Chesapeake and the Tidewater region who had been dragged off as moveable property confiscated for the Crown, or had escaped from their masters and were hoping for eventual freedom from their Rebel owners if the British were successful in withstanding the siege. Their labor was handy to dig and improve the defenses or serve as bearers from the warehouses and armories to the guns.

Alan ended up with half a dozen to help tail on the tackles to run out his guns and to keep a supply of shot and cartridges coming from his magazines. A more miserable lot he had never seen in his life; the blacks in the Indies were freemen, at least the ones he had seen around the ports. There were many who had signed aboard King's ships after their European crews had succumbed to the many fevers, and they were rated as landsmen or ordinary seamen, paid the same wages as an English sailor. Some of the younger ones even made damn good topmen and able seamen after a few years. But this lot were as thin as wild dogs, clothed tag-rag-and-bobtail poorer than even the worst-off gin drinkers in some London stew. They responded to the cheerful friendliness of the British sailors with caution and cringed like whipped pups if anyone even looked sharp in their direction; Alan thought that had a lot to do with the lash marks on their backs that their thin clothes could not cover. When he allowed them a scrap of sailcloth to make a snug lean-to near the battery, their gratitude was so humble and heartfelt that he was almost repulsed by their suddenly adoring neediness.

For his part, Alan had the use of a bedroom in a small house within one hundred yards of his battery on the rampart, shared with an officer with Symonds's marines from the *Charon*; the house itself full of officers sleeping three to a bed, on the floors and furniture, even bedding down on top of, and under, the dining table. They were all young and junior and had access to lots of spirits and personal stores they shared together for their informal mess. Alan could return to a dry bed, Cony's ministrations with his uniform and kit, a glass of hock, rhenish, red wine, brandy, corn whiskey or rum toddy. There was cider, some captured local beer and plenty of food and condiments to make it palatable as long as their caches held out. There was a privy in which he could take his ease (which was rapidly filling up, though, with so many people using it). There was an outhouse with a large wooden tub where Lewrie could take an occasional bath in warm water when the stewards and orderlies were not using it to wash clothes.

So he waited like the others, rising for the rare alarums and diversions as a battery would fire on the enemy digging a parallel down southeast, or light off a rocket at night, sure that a party of infiltrators had appeared, but for a desperate war, it was a chore to even keep interested in it most of the time.

WHEEE-BLAM!

Alan jerked involuntarily in his sleep, savoring the most lifelike dream of fondling and undressing Lucy Beauman. Her father was at the door, crying out for his daughter's virginity and slamming his fists on the door. WHEEE - BULAMM!

"Sufferin' Christ!" His bedmate said, rolling off the high mattress and taking refuge under the bed frame with the chamber pot. The other officer who shared their bed had already gone out the window. "Lewrie!"

"Umm?" Alan mazed sleepily. It had been so warm and snug, bundled in between the other officers, each wrapped in a good blanket with a quilt spread over all three of them. WHEEEE - BUB-LAMMM!!

This made the entire house shudder, and Alan came awake in the afterglow of the explosion of a large-caliber mortar shell that felt as though it had struck in the next room.

"What the hell is it?" Alan said testily. He was never at his best just awakened, and the dream had been *so* damned good.

"Well, it sounds mighty like the end of the world." His bunkmate said from below him. WHEE-BLAM! A strike farther off, but still close enough to blow in the drapes and stir the air in the room.

"Who opened the fucking window?" Alan said. "It's cold in here."

"Gad, but you're a cool'un," the marine told him.

"Holy shit on a biscuit!" Alan suddenly realized what was happening. "Where are you?"

"Down here," the marine said.

Alan tried to disentangle himself from his bedclothes as the WHEE of another descending shell could be heard in the distance, rapidly drawing closer with a menacing wail. He finally gave it up and rolled out of bed like a human caterpillar and thumped heavily to the floor to wriggle under the bed as well, just as there was another apocalyptic BLAM!

The house shuddered once more, and the sound of running feet was making the floor bounce like a drumhead. Voices shouted what sounded like arrant nonsense in a cacophony of questions, statements, yells of terror and demands for silence and order. Trumpets brayed in the camp, the Highlanders got their bagpipes working and filled the air with the hideous screech of war marches and drummer boys beat loud but shaky rolls to call the troops to arms, as if they had not considered a shelling enough incentive to head for the ramparts and the guns.

"Mister Lewrie, sir?" Cony called, bursting into the room. There was another shriek in the air as one more shell descended, and Cony found room under the bed for himself as well. "You alright, sir?"

"Bloody grand, Cony," Alan muttered as the shell struck close enough to raise the dirt and dust puppies around them. "Let's get the hell out of here."

He dressed in the dark, Cony passing him waistcoat, shoes, neckcloth, coat and hat, one item at a time, like a conjurer who knew exactly where the chosen card was all the time. His pistols were shoved into his hands, and while he was stuffing them into his breeches pockets Cony was hanging his dirk on the frog of his waistband.

"Yer hat, Mister Lewrie," Cony said in the darkness.

"Seen my orderly?" the marine officer asked.

"No, sir, I ain't," Cony replied, flinging open the door to the dining room and parlor. "They's the flask in yer coattail pocket, sir, an' I'll see to yer breakfast later, if ya don't mind, Mister Lewrie."

"Not at all." Alan headed out into the darkness. Well, it was not entire darkness. There were fires enough burning to light up the encampment where a fused shell from a high-angle piece such as a mortar or howitzer had set fire to the hay stands for the remaining animals, or shattered a house and set it on fire.

"God!" Alan gaped at the night sky. There was some low cloud that night turning pale gray on the bottom from the fires already set and from the bright bursts of flame of the guns in the artillery parks and redoubts that had finally begun the bombardment of Yorktown. Hot amber meteors soared up from the countryside and howled across the sky under those clouds to arc down and burst with horrendous roars and great stinking clouds of expended gunpowder. It was an awful sight, of such complete and stunning novelty that he stopped short and just stared for the longest time. Solid shot could almost be seen as quick black streaks that crossed the eye before they could be recognized and followed. Heated shot moaned in all colors, depending on the bravery of the gunners who had rolled it down their muzzles; either blue-hot or yellow-amber like a half-made horseshoe on a forge, but sometimes a dull red from those careful souls who did not want to deform the shot in the barrels or set the propellant charges off with the heat of the projectiles before the crews could stand back for safety.

Fused shells, those filled with powder and designed to burst and rend anything near their impact with shattered iron balls, came flicking in slowly, their fuses glowing like tiny fireflies as they descended to the earth to thud into the ground, hiss malevolently, then blow up and raise a gout of clay and rock. Sometimes the fuses were cut too short and the ball exploded before it hit the ground, scattering death about it below the burst, and no one in a trench could be safe from such a blast.

The guns worked over the north end of the town for a while, then shifted further south, allowing Cony and Lewrie to run for the safety of the trench beside their gun platforms.

"Everyone well, Knatchbull?" Alan asked his senior gunner. He had to take hold of the man's shoulder and almost shout into his ear. Either Knatchbull had been concussed or deafened or frightened out of his wits.

"Two samboes gone, sir," Knatchbull finally replied. "Shell damn near got 'em all back there. Daniels had ta go ta the surgeons. Hit with splinters, sir."

Daniels. Alan remembered that he had been in his boat crew the night they had burned the French transport. "Is he hurt much?"

"In the lungs, sir."

So much for Daniels, Alan thought grimly. A lung wound was sure death within days . . . perhaps even hours, if Daniels was fortunate. He could get drunk one last time on the surgeon's rum and go quickly.

"Nothing on the river?"

"Nothin', Mister Lewrie," Knatchbull said with a shake of his shaggy head. "They kin keep this up fer days afore tryin' us direck."

"Then what's all the fuss about, then?" Alan said with a smile he did not feel. He went along the parapet to his gunners, those keeping a watch with muskets and those clustered by the nine-pounders, clapping a shoulder here and there, telling them to rest easy and keep their heads down until they heard something, assuring them no one in their right minds would try a frontal attack, not tonight at any rate.

Their own guns were firing in response, flinging shot and shell into those artillery parks out in the darkness, measuring the fall of shot by the glows of their own fuses, though it seemed that Cornwallis's batteries were not as numerous, or not firing in such a hasty volume as the enemy's. It would make sense, Alan realized to conserve the powder and round shot they had in the fortifications until they could find a good target, for they could not be resupplied until their relief force arrived, and the French had most likely brought tons of the stuff and could get more from the thirty-six or so warships in the bay.

There was nothing else to do but wait some more, no longer in so much suspense, but wait in terror and trepidation for the next burst of shell. Narrow ramparts were hard to hit with mortars and howitzers firing blind at night at high angle, so except for that one lucky shot (which was all it would take) they would stew and fret at every wailing infernal engine that the enemy fired in their general direction, squat down when it sounded close and stand up and grin foolishly after it had struck away from them. Had it not been for the screaming, it would have been almost a game that they were watching.

Hideously wounded soldiers were screaming their lives away back in the town in the surgeries and dressing stations. Horses and mules were screaming in terror as they dashed back and forth through the fortification's enclosures, dashing from one end of their pens to another, or were out in the open, galloping away from each new sound and bloom of dirt and smoke, only to be hewn down by the shells and then bleed to death, with broken spines, broken legs, spurting wounds in innocent dumb bodies, entrails hobbling them as they tried to run; always screaming and neighing in fright, wondering why their masters did not make the noises and the lights stop, why no one could make their screaming stop.

At first light Alan called his gunners to quarters to stand by their guns and parapets. He kept his blanket over his shoulders to ward off the early morning chill and joined them from the trench in which he had tried to rest during the night.

From their eastern wall he could see the Star Redoubt, not much pummeled and still flying a French flag, and the huge battery further west. With a glass he could see that the positions on the Gloucester side had gotten the treatment, too, but not as heavily. Those positions had not changed much.

The town, though, had suffered from the shelling, and crushed buildings showed like newly missing teeth from the order of the day before. The fires had burned out and a haze of sour smoke lay over the entire encampment, thick with the stench of charred wood and expended gunpowder.

Going on tour along the north and west walls, Alan could see that there was nothing to their fronts. The redans guarding the road into town were still there, as were the ramparts, battered but still whole, and the fields before their positions were empty of threat. Nothing stirred in the ravines of the creek, and not a bird fluttered in the woods.

"Knatchbull, see to breakfast," he said upon returning.

"We're a might short, sir," Knatchbull told him. "Nought but gruel an' some biscuit, an' this ain't no Banyan Day, Mister Lewrie."

"Nothing left from supper?"

"Nossir, they ain't." Knatchbull was almost accusatory.

"Send two men back for meat, then. Enough for the slaves, too."

"Ain't none o' ours, Mister Lewrie," Knatchbull complained.

"By God, they stood by as scared as the rest of us, and if they serve powder and shot to my guns, they are ours, even if they were creatures from a Swift novel," Alan snarled, too testy and exhausted with a night of fear to be kind. "Feed 'em. Ration for a half mess."

"Aye, aye, sir," Knatchbull quavered, never having seen Lewrie on any sort of tear against another man. He had been too junior, too hard pressed himself by the officers and warrants in *Desperate*, but now Lewrie had the look of a quarterdeck officer, and the grime of the night did not improve his looks much, either.

Knatchbull returned half an hour later with a sack filled with meat, two four-pound pieces to be shared out by the two gun crews, another four-pound piece for Alan, Knatchbull, Cony and the four remaining blacks.

"Tis horse, Mister Lewrie," Knatchbull apologized. "They's shorta salt beef're pork. Ain't never eat horse afore."

"Ever go to a two-penny ordinary in London?" Alan teased.

"Aye, sir."

"Then you probably have eaten horse, and in worse shape than any you'll sink your teeth into today." Alan laughed. "Boil it up."

"Yer coffee, Mister Lewrie," Cony said, seeming to pop up out of the ground with a steaming mug in his hands. It had been battered in the bombardment, but Alan recognized it from the house.

"Goddamn my eyes, Cony, this ain't Scotch coffee!" Alan said, marveling at the first sip. "This is the genuine article!"

"Them marines fetched it offa *Guadeloupe*, Mister Lewrie, an' I sorta fetched it offen them in the rush an' all, like." Cony grinned.

There was a sudden loud shriek in the air of an incoming shell as French or American gunners began to work over the north end of the town once more. Everyone ducked as the sound loomed louder and louder and changed in pitch, howling keener and higher like a bad singer searching for the right note. BLAMMM!

They stood up to see the ruin of the kitchen outhouse of the abode Alan had been using as his quarters. The entire back porch of the house was gone in a shower of kindling, and there was a new crater in the ground that steamed furiously with half-burned powder particles.

"I hope you liberated a power of it, Cony," Alan said, brushing dirt from his sleeve. "That may be the last good coffee I'll see for some time."

"Never fear that, Mister Lewrie. I made off with nigh about a pound an' a half. Might have ta make do with that corn whiskey fer yer spirits from now on, though."

"I imagine I could cope."

Cony was waiting for Lewrie to say something more, such as "Cony, what would I ever do without you; be my steward in the midshipmen's mess and my servant when I am commissioned." It would be a soft job for the young man, but Alan was not about to promise that much, especially since getting back aboard ship and out to sea where he could pursue his career was looking more like a forlorn hope each day. Besides, he did not want the man to feel he was too beholdened to him that early on. Cony would make a fine gentleman's servant, but one did not let them know it until one could settle on a decent wage and conditions.

"Ye'll be needin' a shave, Mister Lewrie," Cony volunteered. "I have yer kit safe an' snug, an' can put an edge on yer razor while yer breakfast is acookin'."

Alan was not so far advanced in his adolescence to need a daily shave, but his chin did feel promisingly raspy, so he nodded his assent.

Flattery will get you nowhere, Cony, Alan thought happily, glad to have a domestic situation to think about rather than the anonymous terror of the continuing bombardment. And when it became plain that the main effort of the enemy gunners was on the south and west corner of the town ramparts, he could almost enjoy his breakfast in peace, looking forward to a clean shave and another cup of real coffee.

Besides, if Admiral Graves did not come from New York soon, his domestic arrangements might be the only thing he could contemplate with any hope as he lounged in some Rebel prison after the whole horrible muddle fell apart.

CHAPTER 10

THE brutal cannonading went on for days, and the French and American batteries were prodigal with shot and shell. During the day their guns began to strike directly on the ramparts from a range of only six-hundred to eight-hundred yards, pounding the earthworks into ruin, smashing the fascines and gabions that reinforced them and dismounting guns that attempted to return fire. At night, high-angle shells burst with regularity in a fire-storm horrendously loud and unceasing, shattering the night and everyone's nerves, flinging men about like straws if they happened to be too close to an explosion, sheltered in a trench or not.

Alan had been into town along with the marine officer he had once shared quarters with to search for fresh horsemeat for their men. They had located two once-magnificent saddle horses, now reduced to skin and bones, their heads hanging low in utter exhaustion. Hard as it was going to be, they would lead these once-proud blooded steeds back near their positions to be slaughtered for food. The corn and oats were almost gone, so dinners would be mostly fresh meat and biscuit, what little of that was left. What they had gathered and foraged had been eaten days before.

They had barely taken charge of the animals when there had been a manic howl as a huge sixteen-inch mortar shell came whistling down nearby, and Alan had dived to the ground in mortal terror. There had been a huge and deafening blast of sound, giving

him the feeling that he was swimming in air and being pelted with
rocks, and then he had found himself several yards away from where
he had lain, covered with damp earth and blood, his uniform in
tatters. The horses were splattered about the street like fresh paint
and his companion had been shredded into offal as well, only his
lower legs remaining whole. His smallsword was turned into a cork-
screw that smoked with heat.

Badly shattered by the experience, Alan had almost crawled all
the way back to his battery to find what comfort he could in others
of his own kind, no matter how menial they were in the naval order
of things. Cony tended him, fetched out fresh togs and put him to
bed to sleep it off, which he did, in the middle of the deafening roar
of bombardment.

It was the ships burning that finally broke his spirit.

After two days and nights of steady terror, *Charon* and *Guadeloupe* took advantage of the fact that they had been ignored so far
and tried to maneuver further out into the river to make a stab at
escaping, hoping that *Charon*, minus her artillery and stores, would
be shallow enough in draft to make it between the shoals.

With twenty-four-pound guns and heated shot, the big French
battery on the enemy left on the York River had opened fire. *Charon*
had been hit and turned into a heart-breaking torch, burned to the
waterline. *Guadeloupe* had gotten under the town bluffs into safety,
but several outlying small warships and transports had also been set
on fire and abandoned. Their own ship *Desperate* had been hit twice
with red-hot shot, and smoke had billowed from her, but there had
been hands enough to put out the fire and work her up alongside
Guadeloupe, where she would be safe.

If Alan's morale had finally given way, then he was not alone.
He could not cross the camp without discovering drunken British,
Hessian or Loyalist soldiers who had broken into spirits stores and
were deeply drunk for what they felt was the last time before death.
Troops still held in better discipline by their officers served as field
police to keep the vandalism and defeatism from turning ugly, but
one could smell the fear on every hand, see the stricken expressions,
the sense of loss in every eye. Cornwallis's force was an army waiting
to die.

There were caves below the town bluffs and eastern entrenchments, where many well men sheltered from the continual fire-storm without shame among the wounded. Even Lord Cornwallis and his staff had moved into a cavern, surrounded with their lavish creature comforts.

Had there been any liquor left within reach, Alan would have happily gotten besotted as the lowest sailor or soldier. He had worried before about the possibility of capture and imprisonment; now that was a fond wish, preferable to being blasted into so many atoms by the impersonal shells that drenched the garrison round the clock. The money he had hidden in his sea chest could not buy him a single moment of life more, and his sense of loss about it was nothing more than a pinprick. There would be no escape from this debacle, and all he could do was curse the fools in New York who had not yet come, who now looked to never arrive in time to save the army or the remaining ships.

His men were not in much better condition. No amount of japery was going to put much spine back into them, and he knew it. They had that same haunted look he had seen in the soldiers and only went through the motions of duty, diving into the bottom of the trench and their new additional dugouts below the earthworks every time a shell came anywhere close and stayed there underground as long as possible, no longer even much interested in the rum issue, not if it had to be taken in the open.

Alan himself was in the bottom of the trench, just at the edge of one of his gun platforms. So far, they had not suffered a strike so near that their guns had been dismounted, but that was not for want of trying on the part of the foe. They had been concentrating on the western wall and had reduced it to an anthill from which a stubborn flag still flew on a stub of pole, though its guns had been mostly dismounted and its continued usefulness was much in doubt.

"Lewrie?" an older marine captain called. "This army officer has need of your remaining powder. Give it to him."

"But what shall I defend my guns with, sir?" Alan asked, his voice a harsh rasp. The fog of powder smoke that seemed much like a permanent weather condition did not help.

"Doesn't matter much." The marine shrugged. "Keep back enough charges to fire a dozen canister shots to repel a landing. Let them have the rest."

"Aye, aye, sir," Alan said, rising from the trench.

The army officer mentioned was the same goose who had so blithely positioned them alone in the hills in their first days of the occupation, still a dandy prat in clean breeches and waistcoat, his red coat still unstained and his gorget and scarlet sash bright as the day they were made. Alan took a sudden and intense dislike to him.

"I have to retain some charges pre-made for my swivels, sir," Alan said wearily. "And my hand's personal powder horns and cartouches. I can give you the rest."

"Hurry with it, will you?" the man snapped. "We're running low on every wall and no one would attack *this* rampart."

"Knatchbull, open up the magazines and supply this gentleman with all our kegged powder."

"And your gun cartridges," the officer added. "You have no need for them. There are no other nine-pounders still in action, so they will have to be emptied and resewn to proper size for our guns."

"Retain a dozen, Knatchbull."

"I ain't no scholard, sir," Knatchbull said. "Could ya count 'em out fer me, Mister Lewrie?"

"My God, how did you become a gunner?" the artillery officer said. "I said I want them all."

"My immediate superior said to retain a dozen, and that is what I must do, sir," Alan told him, almost too weary and too lost in a really good case of the Blue Devils to argue. He just wanted the man to go away so he could silently contemplate his chances of survival til the morning meal and perhaps perform his litany of revenge on his father who had put him into the Navy so he could end up in such a mess.

"Goddamme, you'll give me all or I'll have you put under close arrest," the officer threatened. He motioned to his gunners to aid him.

"With the best will in the world I could not, sir. How could I destroy my guns without charges when the time comes?"

Not that they've been worth a groat the past few weeks, Alan thought. He had dragged them from pillar to post and done nothing of value with them since; never fired a round in anger—for lack of opportunity at first and then for lack of powder and shot in the second instance. Might be satisfying to burn the fuckers and unbush them at that.

"When what time comes, sir?" the artilleryman shouted over the sound of the barrage. "What do you mean by that sort of croakum?"

"When the Rebels and the French have pounded us to bits, sir, and come over the walls," Alan calmly said.

"Never heard such insufferable nonsense. Now order your man to give me all your powder, all of it, mind, and be quick about it."

"Will you also give me a signed order to destroy my guns at the same time, sir?" Alan demanded.

"Who is your captain, you puppy? What ship?"

"Treghues . . . the *Desperate* sir," Alan replied, thinking fast. "If you take all our powder and cartridges, then there is no point in keeping two valuable naval guns ashore. Would you object to our taking the pieces back aboard without powder?"

Go on, Alan thought, give me an excuse to get out of this before it all falls apart.

"Damn you, and damn your insolence!" the officer raged, his hands straying near his pistols. "Sergeant, take everything in the magazines to the carts. I'll thank you not to hinder us, if you shall not help."

"Take what you like, then, sir," Alan said.

The army officer's party made quick work of scavenging everything in the magazines—all the small kegs of loose powder, all but a handful of firing quills, most of the tin canisters of musket balls for antipersonnel shot, all the bundles of grapeshot, leaving only three charges per gun with the useless round shot. They trotted away with it in their small carts, dodging the shell bursts.

"And may you be blown to Perdition!" Alan called after them, once they were almost out of earshot and he was finally able to vent his true feelings.

"Thort he wuz gonna shoot ya, so I did, Mister Lewrie," Knatchbull finally said after he had regained his normal breathing.

"Not *his* kind," Alan sneered, very relieved that the man had not done that or had him dragged off to a summary court, which would have resulted in the same thing. "Who do we have who's a good runner?"

"Runner, sir?" Knatchbull cogitated. "Well, Tuckett's not bad, sir."

"Have him come up here while I write a note to our captain," Alan said. He sat down next to his small jute bag and dug into it for some scrap paper and a stub of pencil. "How would you like to get back to our ship, Knatchbull?"

"God, that'd be grand, Mister Lewrie!" The man beamed. "Kin we do it?"

"We serve no useful purpose here any longer, not without powder. We can't help the marines, except to leave them the swivels. There's a chance we may be ordered to take these two guns of ours back into *Desperate*. And us with 'em."

"Right away, Mister Lewrie!"

Cornwallis's harried staff saw no sense in two useless guns left ashore to be captured, so they spent the rest of the day knocking the extemporized field carriages apart and taking the guns and the re-maining round shot back aboard.

Desperate still was shy her carronades and the four nine-pounders on the Gloucester side, but she had fourteen guns back in place should she be called upon to fight her way out, with enough reserve gunpowder from the bottom tier kegs to make a short but spirited engagement of it.

Everyone from Lewrie's party, and Alan most of all, was greatly relieved to be back aboard. The men were once more in the bosom of their mates in relatively more comfortable surroundings; though the rations had deteriorated in quantity and quality there was still enough rum. They felt oddly safe in the understandable world of the Navy instead of in the dubious clutches of the army, eager to em-brace the rigid discipline of a ship of war, especially one that was not being fired at. Under the bluffs and free of direct observation by French or Rebel batteries, they could sit out the bombardment with-out fear for the first time in days.

Alan found his sea chest and clean clothes, a hammock man ready to tend his needs and wash up the clothes off his back, a bucket of hot river water in which to scrub up and a peaceable sit-down supper with Carey and Avery, with the last of their personal wine stock to drink in relative quiet. The barrage continued through supper, petering out for a while as he rolled into his hammock and bedding and discovered all over how easy it was to sleep snug and warm free of the ground.

Almost before his head touched the roll of sailcloth that was his pillow, he was dead to the world. So he slept through the assault by the French Royal Deux-Ponts Regiment and an American regiment under the ambitious Colonel Alexander Hamilton that took Redoubts number Nine and number Ten, the last bastions before the smashed ramparts on the southeast end of Yorktown. He slept through the counterbattery fire from the British lines, snoring so loud that Carey tried to wake him to make him stop, but Alan was too far gone to even respond to vigorous shaking.

It was only at 4:00 A.M., when all hands were piped on deck to begin the ship's day and scrub down her decks that he awoke, and the barrage was so loud that he did not hear the British sally to try and retake the redoubts, for drums and musketry could not carry over the roar of the cannonade. Events on shore, even unsuccessful ones, touched him no more.

I should hate this bloody ship like the plague, Alan thought as dawn painted the decks with faint light, revealing the sameness of a warship that held no surprises after long service on those very decks. But damme if this don't feel hellish good.

"Good mornin' ta ya, Mister Lewrie," Monk said.

"And a good morning to you, Mister Monk," he replied cheerfully, even glad to see Monk's ugly physiognomy and ungainly bulk.

Treghues was pacing the weather side of the quarterdeck deep in thought as he usually did, speaking to no one until he had had his coffee and breakfast. He seemed much leaner than before, but Alan put that down to the plain commons everyone had been reduced to lately. He met Alan's eyes only once and nodded a silent greeting, which Alan returned with a doffed hat, but there was no malice in those haunted eyes for once.

Temporary the respite might be; the army was on the very last dregs of endurance, and the best defenses had been ripped away during the night. The enemy guns still did terrible duty on the bluffs above their heads, and it was hard to determine if any British guns were still firing in response. Another day or two might see the end of everything, and *Desperate* was still trapped in the river, and in the bay. Yet she still seemed safe and womblike. Over one hundred guns were in action, but she drifted in a sour haze of powder smoke and flung dirt as though nothing could ever touch her, or hers.

Around ten in the morning, Lieutenant Railsford came aboard from his post on the Gloucester side, bringing some of his gunners with him. There were only two nine-pounders left in operation now with Tarleton and his dismounted cavalry troopers in their fortifications, and the other two had been smashed. Railsford conferred with Treghues, and then they both went over to the shore to talk to Symonds.

"Something is up, I fear," Avery said softly by Alan's side.

"Surrender," Alan surmised. "There's nothing left of the fortifications that a lazy cripple couldn't scale."

"Is it that bad ashore?"

"Yes, by Heaven, it is," Alan told him, wondering where the hell David had been the last few days. "I wonder how anyone still lives at all."

"That will mean our surrender as well." Avery shuddered.

"Most like," Alan replied.

"This has changed you terribly, Alan, I swear. You are so cold and hard now, I hardly know you any longer."

"I believe it has, too," Alan said, thinking back on his behavior of the last week or so. "Well, you cannot be a child forever. I hope it's merely something that will wear off when I get enough sleep and some decent food. Perhaps a few weeks in a prison before being paroled will do it."

Treghues and Railsford were rowed back to the ship just before midday and went aft immediately, passing the word for Mister Monk and his charts of the York River. Shortly after, all senior warrants and midshipmen were summoned aft to the captain's cabins.

They found their officers peering at a chart, and were bade to draw near and look at it carefully.

"Lord Cornwallis has ordered Captain Symonds to put together boat crews enough to transfer the army to the Gloucester shore tonight," the captain began, tapping on the chart with a brass ruler. "We shall be evacuating Yorktown before the enemy overcomes our remaining defenses. Here, at ten o'clock tonight, at the docks and on this beach, we shall start embarking troops. The artillery has to be abandoned, along with all the stores remaining, but we can save the troops and their personal weapons. With so little resistance against Tarleton and Simcoe there is hope we can break through and head north into Maryland or Delaware, and with a quick march with little baggage, may get closer to our own troops before the French or the Rebels can begin pursuit. Carry on, Mister Railsford."

"Here on the right of our positions," Railsford lectured, gesturing at the map, "there are French marines there, with artillery enough to break up any landings, so you had better not venture into this inlet or risk being shot to pieces. Steer west of north for the point, or the cove just to the west of the point. You'll want to be careful of the boats; it's a rocky shore thereabouts. At ten o'clock there will be a making tide, but the York flows swift enough to almost cancel it out. Once out from behind the bluffs at the tip of the town, remember to put a little starboard helm on, even if it takes you farther west than you think proper. The Virginia Militia is on the left of the lines, not far past the entrance to the cove, so don't bear too far north. There is to be a small light at the back of the cove to mark the entrance for you. Look for it, for your lives."

"What about the ship, sir?" Coke the bosun asked.

"We have Captain Symonds's permission to try and break out after most of the troops are across," Treghues said. "So don't be late in getting back here once you have ferried your last load. I doubt if any of you want to spend any more time with our army than you have in the last few days, so if you do not want to march right out of your shoe leather or end up eating bark and berries, you shall return to *Desperate.*"

Treghues was in fine spirits once more, making his little jokes and exercising the use of his voice, which he had always been most fond of hearing during his briefings and lectures and Sunday services.

"But, if we cannot break out past the French ships at the mouth of the river, we shall have to burn her to keep her from capture," he said soberly. "The ship's boats are not big enough, for the most part, to take as many troops as necessary, so we shall be using those recently constructed barges."

There was a groan at that. A few weeks in the water had not done anything to improve their watertight integrity, or their handling. They were heavy, ungainly, hard to steer and row, even with a dozen oarsmen aboard, and they leaked like a sieve. What was worse, they were fairly flat bottomed compared to a boat built with love and care, and made leeway as fast as they could be propelled forward on a windy day.

"I would admire that Midshipman Forrester be called off shore to help with the barges," Treghues said, making sure that his cater-cousin would be close to him at the end, whatever transpired. "He shall take one boat. Mister Lewrie, you take another. Avery takes a third, and Carey shall supervise a fourth. Mister Coke, the cutter and the launch from *Desperate*'s complement shall be employed as well. Give one to my coxswain, Weems the other. Mister Monk, it would be best if your master's mates stay aboard ready for departure, but the midshipmen could use the quartermaster's mates to assist in pilotage."

"Aye, sir."

"No outward preparations until after dark, which shall be before seven this evening. No sign of what we are attempting must come to the attention of the enemy, or there is no point in trying. The army is counting on us to save them." Treghues concluded, saying, "I do not intend to let them down for the last time as . . ."

Treghues choked off his possible comments about Graves and the other leaders who had never even shown a royal yard over the horizon in all that time and had muffed the battle at sea that had led to this hopeless condition.

"We'll get 'em safe across, sir," Railsford promised.

"We must," Treghues said vehemently, his eyes clouding up with emotion. "We must!"

"The night seems perfect," Railsford said, sniffing at the wind by the entry port soon after the hands had been fed an early supper. "Be as dark as a cow's arse."

"Just as long as we can see where we're going, sir," Alan said. "If we cannot show a light, even to peek at a boat compass . . ."

"Steer for the shelling and you'll come right," Railsford told him, clapping him on the shoulder. "Off with you now, and pray God for our success."

"Aye, sir, thank you."

Alan scrambled down the battens by the manropes and dropped into place at the stern of one of the hastily built barges. The night was indeed perfect for clandestine activities; there was no moon, and if it had been even a sliver, would have been lost in the thick cloud cover that had blown in during the afternoon. There was a slight breeze from the west that predominated over the sea breeze as well, which would require careful balance on the tiller to counteract it and the current of the York.

"Toss your oars," Alan commanded softly. "Ship your oars. Quiet, now. Who is senior hand here?"

"Me, sir, Coe." One of the older men spoke from the darkness, leaning forward to be recognized.

"Rowports muffled with sailcloth?"

"Aye, sir."

"Very well. Shove off, bowman. Out oars. Give us way, larboard."

Desperate was lying athwart the river, anchored with bower and stream hooks, her guns manned to prevent any French spy boat penetrating the upper river. Leaving her starboard entry port, the barge was quickly taken by the current, and by the time they had come about to aim for the town docks, they had lost over a hundred yards downstream.

"Gonna be 'ard rowin', sir," Coe commented from his position of stroke oar, near Alan's knees.

"The tide's making," Alan told him. "The rowing will get easier as the night goes on."

They reached the town docks about nine-thirty in the evening and joined a formless pack of ships' boats and barges that were queuing up to the various piers and gravelly beaches to pick up troops and load them for the trip across the river. By companies, the battalions and regiments were lining up to depart. To avoid confusion, only one regiment or battalion was permitted near the docks at any given time. There were artillerymen whose pieces had been smashed to ruin or who had run out of powder and shell, now armed with muskets taken from the dead and wounded and most uncomfortable in their new role as "light infantry." There were troops from the Brigade of Guards—the 17th, the 23rd, the 33rd, and the 71st Highlanders, those that had survived the bombardment and the sickness that had finally struck the camp, as sickness would decimate any large military gathering sooner or later. There were troops from the brigade of light infantry, the 43rd, 76th and 80th regiments. There were German and Hessian mercenaries from the two battalions of Anspach, the Hessian Regiment Prinz Hereditaire, Hessian Bose Regiment, the Jagers, now not much more than a company of about sixty men remaining, and the provincials from Alan's friends, the North Carolina Volunteers. But nearly two thousand men were in hospital still in Yorktown, and they would not be evacuated since they could not march and fight, nor survive on the poor rations or forage expected after the army had cut its way through the French and Rebels on Gloucester. They would be left behind to the mercies of the victors.

Alan's boat ground ashore on the beach with a rasp of sand and pebbles, and he was immediately swamped with troops intent on escape.

"Avast, there a moment," Alan said as loud as he dared. "Now, this barge is a lump of shit, and I can only take thirty men with the usual kit and gear or we'll founder out there. Is there an officer or sergeant here?"

"'Ere, sir," a red-coated non-com answered from the darkness. "A comp'ny o' th' 23rd preesent an' haccounted fer, sir. Thirty-h'eight privates, one corp'rl an' me, sir."

"Give me your corporal and twenty-nine men then. Count 'em off and the next boat shall take the rest," Alan said. "Tell 'em to sit in the middle on the bottom and not get in the way of the oarsmen."

"Right, sir," the sergeant replied, disappointed that he would not find immediate rescue, but still in charge of his poise and his men.

"Wy we gots ta wait, sarge?" a plaintive voice wailed from the night. "They's plenny o' room!"

"My arse on a bandbox there is!" Alan said sharply. "Want to drown out there wearing all that kit? Now hurry up and get aboard with the first thirty."

Once in the boat, and the boat back out on the black waters, the troops sat still as mice, breathing shallowly as they sensed how unstable and ungainly the barge really was in the grip of the current.

This is going to be a muddle, Alan thought sadly, realizing how companies were going to be separated upon landing. Even with one regiment or battalion transported at a time, where they would land on the far shore was up to the vagaries of the individual coxswains of the boats involved, with part of one unit landed in the cove, on the point, to right or left of the area still held by Tarleton and Simcoe. They would also be landing into the teeth of a shelling, and it would be hours before each unit sorted itself out into proper military order for the breakthrough at bayonet point. It would be dark and regimental facings and distinctive uniform trim would be almost lost to the harried officers, who would be searching for their people. Alan was supposed to link up with all the boats under command of a lieutenant from one of the disabled ships who would lead all the boats bearing one unit to a single landing, but in the almost total darkness, he would be lucky to tag onto any group of boats.

"Twenty-third over here," a strained voice called over the sound of the continuing cannonading. "All boats with 23rd regiment here!"

He could only take a vague guess as to the direction of the voice, for sound could do strange things on the water at night, as he had already learned to his detriment from his first experiments in boats. Hoping for the best, Alan put the tiller bar over and steered in the wake of a gaggle of boats who were already under way. The current would not allow any stop for cogitation. Sitting up on the high stern thwart of the barge, he could barely espy the boat ahead and the boat astern of him.

Once the tide began to flood and counteract the current of the river, the rowing did become much easier. They made two round trips in the first hour while the men were still strong and unwearied, but that slowed down as the night drug on. The only rest was on the beach or beside the pier, and the troops loaded too quickly to allow much.

"Easy all," Alan called as they drifted into the York side of the river for the third time. With the barge empty, it was not so hard to row, but the very devil to fight across the current. The tide was now pushing them upriver without his having to countersteer, and when Lewrie dipped a hand into the water, he could scoop up a mouthful of very salty water instead of the fairly fresh water of earlier.

"Boat your oars, stand by to ground."

Men splashed into the shallows to take charge of the bow and drag it up onto the strand. His crew slumped down in exhaustion as the hull ground and thumped against the shingle.

"Everyone ashore," Alan said. "Coe, break out the barrico of water. We need a rest."

"Aye, aye, sir," Coe said with some enthusiasm.

"Might rotate the larboard men for the starboard men, too, Coe," Alan ordered. "Keep 'em from cramping."

"Aye, sir, 'at it would. Water, sir?"

"Aye, I'd admire a cup."

Another boat ground alongside his, its crew bent low over their own oars with weariness, and seeing what Alan's crew was doing, went over the side for a rest as well.

"Here, stop that!" a thin voice cried.

"Carey?" Alan asked out of instinct.

"Lewrie? They just got out of the boat!"

"They're worn to a frazzle. Let 'em take a rest for a few minutes. How are you doing so far?"

"Main well, I suppose." Carey sulked on his stern thwart, still too unsure of himself to exert much authority with the hands, and smarting from being countermanded.

"We're making good progress." Alan sighed, sipping at his water. "Most of the Brigade of Guards across by now. My last trip was light infantry, I think. Hard to tell in the dark."

"Mine, too," Carey said. Then, in a wheedling tone, "Lewrie, may we trade boats?"

"Is yours sinking?" Alan chuckled, stepping ashore and looking as close as he could at Carey's barge. Carey scrambled ashore to stand with him so he could speak privately.

"They won't work for me, Alan, not like they'd work for you. I have Fletcher as senior hand, and he simply ignores me half the time. I . . . I think they have some rum. I could hear them giggling and getting groggy."

"Fletcher, that farmer," Alan said. "I expect the troops have some small bottles on them and they're sharing out. You put him straight right now."

"Who's your senior man?"

"Coe. One of the foresheet men. Good and steady."

"Then why don't we trade boats? I can get along with Coe, Alan, but I can get nothing out of Fletcher, he's such a surly bastard."

"No," Alan said, after thinking about it for a long moment.

"But, Alan, I . . ."

"Look here, Carey," Alan whispered, reaching out in the dark and taking the younger boy by the upper arm. "Most of the seamen I've ever met *have* been surly bastards. They're not your favorite uncles, so one senior hand is just as good as another. If they won't work for you as chearly as you want, then it's up to you to make 'em do it. You're not in the mess now. You're a midshipman in the King's Navy, so why don't you start acting like one? Avery and I are not here to cosset you anymore. You're on your own bottom, and you have a job to do, so you'd best be about it the best way you can."

By God, I'm sorry I said that, Alan told himself as Carey took himself off, for a quick weep most likely. But it had to be said sooner or later. We've been shielding him long enough and letting him get away with his puppy shines, 'stead of putting some spine into him.

"What is the delay here?" a cultured voice called fruitily.

"A short rest, sir," Alan called back. "We've done three trips so far and the hands are fagged out and thirsty."

"There's no time for that," the owner of that plumby voice dictated. "It's near midnight and there are thousands of troops still waiting to get across. Here, corporal, begin loading these two boats."

Several infantrymen began approaching Alan's boat laden with an assortment of boxes and bags. Alan could hear the clink of metal and glass from them.

"Military stores, sir?" Alan queried with a lazy sneer.

"Of course, they are, sir."

Alan stopped one of the soldiers and took a heavy canvas bag off him. He undid the knot at the top and pulled it apart to reach down into the burden and see for himself what was in it. He smiled in the dark.

"Silver candlesticks might make good langride if cut up, I suppose, sir," Alan drawled archly. "They're a bit too expensive to be melted down in a bullet mold, and I doubt anyone would appreciate them."

"Now look here . . ."

"No, sir. I am taking troops only. No personal baggage."

"Do you know who I am, sir?" the fruity-voiced officer snapped.

"A suddenly much poorer man, sir," Alan shot back. "Other than that, I could not give a fart who you are. Take your loot somewhere else, sir."

Thwarted, the officer railed for a few minutes longer, then made off up the beach for the piers to try other boats, pressed by the urgency of escape before dawn.

"That's enough rest," Alan called out. "Fletcher, Coe, fetch your men back to the boats."

"Aye, sir," Coe replied. "'Ere, lads, back ta work, now."

"Jus'a minute more, Mister Lewrie?" Fletcher whined, as usual. "We bin 'ard at it, sir, an' it's 'at tahred we are."

"Come here, Fletcher," Alan commanded with a good imitation of a quarterdeck rasp. The man approached, close enough for Lewrie to smell the scent of rum on his breath. He took him by the front of the shirt and drew him closer. "You will assemble your boat crew and get back to work right this instant, and you will work chearly for Mister Carey or I swear to God above, I shall see you laid open like a Yarmouth bloater for drunkenness and insubordination, if I have to chase you down in hell!"

"Aye, Mister Lewrie, sir. Aye, aye, sir!" Fletcher bobbled, agog at being seized and shaken so roughly. His perennial game of baiting, of walking the fine edge of insolence had never gotten a response such as that.

"Very well, carry on, Fletcher."

"Aye, aye, sir."

"How many boats here?" someone asked from the dark.

"Two."

"Three!" another voice said. "That you, Mister Lewrie?"

"Aye, that you, Mister Feather?"

"Aye, sir." The quartermaster's mate replied, beaching his boat.

"Three, then," Alan said as an officer approached him.

"Lieutenant, bring your people down here. There are three boats for you." The officer was calling out to a pack of men further up the beach.

"How many men in this unit, sir?" Alan asked. "I can normally take thirty in each boat, but the tide is slack and the current is getting stronger. And I don't care for the wind, sir."

The wind had indeed been rising in the last few minutes, stirring the boats to grinding on the shingle and making tiny whitecaps appear on the dark water, reflected in the glow of fires and shellbursts inland. There were also some flashes in the sky to the west that were not man-made, a display of lightning every few seconds that portended very nasty weather before morning.

"Some sixty all told, I believe," the officer said, coming up within visible distance. He was a major from Cornwallis's staff, one Alan had seen briefly the time he and Railsford had gone ashore together.

"Perhaps twenty men per boat would be best, sir, considering."

"Very well. Ah, here you are."

"Hello to you, sailor, how do you keep?" Lieutenant Chiswick cried, reaching out his hand to shake with Alan.

"Lieutenant Chiswick, sir, how good to see you!" Alan replied. "Is Burgess well?"

"Aye, just behind me a bit. Von Muecke and some of his Jagers, too. Do you have room for us all?"

"Only twenty men to a boat this trip, sir, sorry. But I believe there are more boats up toward the piers should we run short of room."

"Good. Mollow, eighteen men and yourself in this boat," the Loyalist officer said, pointing to Alan's boat. "I shall take passage with you, if you have no objections, Mister Lewrie."

"None at all," Alan told him, genuinely glad to see the Chiswicks once more, even if they and their unit did appear even scruffier than they had in past acquaintance.

"Burgess, it's Lewrie, come to ferry us cross the Styx," Governour told his brother. "Do you take eighteen men and the corporal with you in this next boat. Sar'n't, there's a boat to the left for you and your men."

"For me, bitte?" Von Muecke asked.

"Up near the piers, Mister von Mook-ah," Alan instructed.

"Fon Mehr-keh, gottverdammt!" the man complained, and Alan was sure he was wetting down that famous mustache once more in the dark.

Alan noticed that in most cases the North Carolina troops were each carrying an extra Ferguson rifle as they boarded the boat and settled down amidships. "Dead men's weapons, too valuable to leave," Governour informed him. "We'll be needed back home and there's no way to get more rifles. Else the new troops we raise will have to do with Brown Besses."

"You'll be marching the wrong way for the Carolinas."

"If any troops are going to get all the way to New York, it will be us," Governour assured him. "I cannot speak with any hope for the rest of this army."

Alan shrugged, unwilling to face the thought of total defeat and surrender of the last army England would raise, or could raise, for the war in the Colonies. What the Chiswicks would face in an America with Rebel forces victorious did not bear thinking about, so partisan was the prevailing mood on both sides.

"Loaded, Mister Lewrie," Feather told him. Carey admitted the same. There was nothing for it but to shove off for another trip across the York.

"Your crew is rested, Feather?"

"Aye, Mister Lewrie, on t'other side. I 'ave a boat compass."

"You lead off, then, and we shall steer in your wake. Shove off!"

The boats were man-handled off the beach and the men sprang back aboard, wet to the waists as the current plucked the barges right from the start and began to swirl them about like wood chips. The oars were shipped into the row ports quickly, and they had to stroke hard just to regain the distance they had lost.

Once out from behind the shadow of the northernmost spit of land and into deeper water, Lewrie realized they were out on a new and more dangerous river. The current was building up, possibly the result of a heavy rain inland from all that lightning and thunder that had not been distinguishable over the sound of the cannonading. Whitecaps were more prominent now, and the barges made a lot more leeway than they had on the last crossing. Alan took hold of the tiller bar with a firmer grip in fear of the water and the tendency of the ungainly barge to want to tip to leeward, steering more westerly to keep them from being blown out into the wider reaches of the river below Gloucester Point.

"You soldiers, shift your weight to larboard!" he shouted.

"Up 'ere, you silly buggers!" Coe directed. "Up ta the 'igh side."

There was a flash of lightning that lit up the entire river, and Alan could see that he was already to leeward of Feather's barge. He added a bit more lee helm to the tiller, pinching up the bows more toward the wind, which was also rising and beginning to moan across the water.

"Put your backs into it!" Alan ordered his oarsmen. "Pick up the stroke, Coe!"

"Aye, sir," Coe grunted.

They had barely gotten a quarter of the way across the narrows, and then the thunderstorm burst on them for real. Lightning crackled across the sky with greater and greater frequency, and the claps of thunder that followed seemed shockingly loud and close behind the flashes. The wind got up even more, strong enough to strip hats from people's heads, strong enough to hinder free breathing. And the wind smelled ominously wet, pregnant with rain to come.

Oh, Jesus, I am going to drown out here! Alan thought for the first of many times that night, his face as white as his waistcoat in his rising terror. He could easily see Feather's boat now in all the rivulets of lightning that split the darkness, pointing almost fully upriver to try for an eventual landfall on the distant point. They had the point on their right abeam, but were not making much headway, he realized, hard as the hands might strain at the oars. Governour Chiswick sat in the middle of the sternmost thwart before Lewrie, and even he was looking a bit worried.

"Should we put back in?" he shouted.

"Best to keep bows on to this," Alan shouted back. "We're committed now!"

He took off his cocked hat before he lost it overboard and stowed it under the stern thwart, just as the first truly fat drops of rain began to pelt at them with some force. Lewrie looked astern to Carey's boat and saw that he was close up still, with another boat behind him bearing what looked like a party of Jagers. The lightning was so continuous that he now had no trouble seeing in any direction.

"Goddamn!" Alan cried as the rain began in earnest. It came down in buckets; rather, it did not come down, but slanted in from the west at such an acute angle that he was almost blinded, and he envied the oarsmen who had their backs to it. His clothing was soaked right through in seconds as though he had just plunged into the river. Lightning or not, he was blinded by the force and volume of the rain and had to mop his face with a sodden sleeve. The wind picked up velocity and began to whine, and the boat began to pitch most alarmingly as it butted into the wind-driven waves rolling downstream. There was no way of seeing the face of his watch, but he judged it about midnight, and the tide was at the peak of the flood. Slack water from seaward could not even begin to counteract this sudden spate. He tasted once again over the side; it was fresh.

He looked up with alarm, squinting in panic, having as much trouble seeing in the teeming rain as he would opening his eyes in the middle of a stinging wave of seawater. He could not find Feather's boat ahead of him. All he could see was a tumbling field of whitecaps and small rollers. He was in the middle of the channel, he thought, right where it narrowed down and the rushing river gained speed from being confined by the bluffs and the shallows beneath them.

"Boat compass," Alan shouted to Governour, pointing at the mahogany box between his feet. "Hold it up for me to see!"

The soldier did as he was told after Alan had shouted himself hoarse three times. Alan leaned over it closely, mopping his face with a free forearm. He took hold of the box and swung it about to establish north.

Goddamme, I'm headed due west! he thought, unable to establish his position or direction now that the rain acted like a curtain beyond the reach of the oar looms. I shall have to bear off, maybe two points, no more, or we'll broach. Oh, what a goddamned cow this barge is. She is going to kill all of us.

He sat back and put a bit of larboard helm on, and the effect was immediate and terrifying. With the slightest small increase in the bow's freeboard exposed to the wind, she slopped crazily and began to broach to starboard, bringing cries of alarm from all concerned. He steered back to starboard to bring her bows back into the wind—it was all the direction the poor excuse for a boat would stand.

"Stroke!" Alan wailed. "Coe, drive 'em hard!"

For that brief near-broach, the men had lost the stroke, and it took precious seconds to disentangle the confused men, to get the oars back into the water again or retrieve them when they had been snatched out of the rower's hand by the rush of the current. It took too much time to get the men coordinated once more, stroking together to bring the most efficient force to bear against the elements.

Alan motioned for the boat compass again and peered into the box. They were back to a westerly heading, which was all they could manage.

"Chiswick, keep an eye on it," he ordered. "Tell me when I am *not* heading west."

"Right!"

For the most part, he could discern that the storm was coming out of the west, and if he kept the boat right on the eye of the wind and the worst rain, he was heading aright. He was enough of a sailor by then to feel the difference in pressure on each cheek by rotating his head back and forth, and correct his steering by that until Chiswick would shout at him with an additional correction.

"Stroke, damn you! Stroke like the devil!"

They were flagging, even if failing did mean their lives. Too many trips had sapped their strength, and too much was being demanded of them now. With the best will in the world, the men were slowing down and no longer able to pull with their full force. Alan could feel how the barge was beginning to wander to either side between strokes, only kept head-to-weather when the oars were dug in.

"Coe, make some of these soldiers to double up on the oars!"

It didn't help much. The soldiers were not experienced with boats or the heavy labor of a seaman's life. Their effort didn't crab anyone.

But that was about all that could be said of them.

The lightning still crashed down without pause, pulsing great pale blue glows in the curtains of rain, and the rain still came down heavy enough to sting the skin even through a broadcloth coat.

"Makin' water, Mister Lewrie!" Coe gaped, pointing at the bottom of the boat. There was about three inches of water sloshing about in the bottom that had not been there before. "A little salty, I thinks!" Coe concluded after lapping at a handful.

Sufferin' Jesus, what else tonight? Alan shuddered. It was not bad enough they were in the middle of a storm the like of which he had not seen even in the middle of the ocean, but the quickly slapped together barge was now working her seams and beginning to leak.

"Bail!" Alan commanded. "Use hats, anything!"

That took the soldiers off rowing duties so they could fill their wide-brimmed hats to scoop up water and fling it overboard, but it put all the onerous and aching burden of rowing back on the crew's exhausted hands.

Oh, shit, Alan thought as the boat began to yaw once more after a particularly laggard stroke. "More way, starboard!"

There was finally no holding her. The barge rose up over a roller and sloughed off to starboard with a trembling that ran right through her. Then they were broaching to, no matter what anyone could do at oars or the tiller. She tipped wildly, almost going onto her beam ends before putting her bow downwind and throwing everyone into a pile of thrashing bodies and screaming throats. Without thought, Alan put the tiller over up to windward to ride her through and succeeded in keeping her from spinning about like a leaf in a millrace. She came back to an even keel.

"We're headed . . . east-southeast!" Governour told him.

"Thort we wuz goners fer sure!" Coe panted, his eyes wide in his fear. "God a-mighty, praise God!"

There was enough way on the barge that Alan could steer easily as she was driven by wind and current. He experimented back and forth, peering over the compass box, then sat back on the sodden stern thwart.

"We'll be pooped if we keep on like this, won't we?"

"Don't know why the stern hain't been driven under arready, sir." Coe shuddered. "If we could get bows on, I'd put out a sea anchor."

"Make one up now, then," Alan ordered. "Give me six hands keeping a hard stroke to keep us faster than the current until you're ready with the drogue. Let the others have a rest."

Coe's sea anchor was three oars lashed together into a complicated cross, with a wooden bailing bucket lashed to the point of intersection so it would sink once over the side and provide more of a drag through the water. There was plenty of line from the light boat anchor up forward to use for lashings. As Coe and another man worked, and the six unfortunate oarsmen stroked away to outrun the creaming river waves that threatened to swamp the stern of the barge, everyone else sagged down in abject misery, keeping their faces out of the wind and driving rain, which was still coming down thick and hard enough to choke the unwary who looked up to see where they might be. In the quick flashes of lightning, Alan could see only with difficulty without drowning in the open air, but he was alarmed to note that landmarks or groves of trees were sliding astern at a fair clip. Not that he recognized a damned thing, but the scenery was continually changing as they raced the river current for survival.

Finally it was done.

"Ahoy, there!" Alan yelled. "We're going to be coming about. Coe is going to put over a drogue, and then we are going to have to turn her into the wind. Easy all for now, but stand by!"

"I'll trail the line from the starboard side, sir," Coe told him. "We'll need everythin' from larboard!"

"Stand by to give way, larboard! Stand by to back water, starboard!"

"Over she goes!"

The contraption hit the water and began to drift away out of sight behind them as the bucket filled with water and the barge continued on, too big and exposed to the wind and moving much faster downriver. Coe eyed the remaining line as it ran out. "Ready!"

"Helm's alee!" Alan cried. "Give way, larboard! Back water, starboard! Pull, men, pull!"

Just as the drogue began to exert pressure on the tow line, the boat swung about, drawn by the effort of her crew, and finally by the drag through the water of the drogue. She slewed about and ended up with her head into the wind once more.

"Easy all!"

They had to wait to see if the drogue would be effective. Alan could feel the tiller kicking from side to side like a live thing. With a stern-way on her, they could lose the rudder if they were not careful; the pintles and gudgeons were never made to steer a boat going backwards for very long.

"What now?" Governour Chiswick asked finally.

"We fuck about out here until the wind dies," Alan told him,

getting some of his courage (and his color) back after the barge had
steadied and no longer threatened to go arse over tit. "And don't ask
me where we are, because I ain't got a clue. Best I can say is out in a
boat on the water."

"Wish we'd liquored our boots before this journey," Governour
said with a sudden grin. "Do much of this?"

"First time for everything," Alan confessed.

"Scared me so badly I would not have trusted mine arse with a
fart," Governour said. "I am not a good swimmer."

"You're doing better than I. I can't swim a stroke. Most sailors
can't," Alan replied. Unconsciously his hand crept into his shirt to
feel the small leather sack hung around his neck. On Antigua, Lucy
Beauman had given it to him after one of her more trusted older
slaves, Old Isaac, had made it for him. It was reputedly a sure protection against drowning or other dangers of the sea. He had been
leery of it, since it smelled somewhat of chicken guts and other
cast-off organics when first presented to him, but for her sake he had
tied it about his neck and had forgotten its presence until then.
Whatever it contained, it was dessicated and only rustled now and
again when jostled heavily. Not that he was exactly eager to inspect
the sack's contents. Some things were best left unknown.

"Coe, can we get the hands back on the oars for a while? Just to
keep from being blown out to sea?" Alan shouted over the howl of
the wind.

"Aye, sir. Mebbe four at a time'd be best."

"Do so, then. I don't like making sternway this fast."

"Four men ta the oars, smartly now. You four."

There was no sign that the storm was going to cease, though. It
blew as hard as a hurricane, and the rain sheeted out of the sky as
though it had been flung by a hateful god. Even when the lightning
zigzagged on either hand, they could not see far enough to find anything familiar. The barge might as well have been driving up the
Loire River in France for all they knew.

"Wossat?" One hand at the bows called, waving off into the
night in the general direction to larboard.

"Where?"

"Two points offen th' larboard bow!"

As Alan peered hard into the driving rain, he saw a shadow

appear, a shadow that looked taller and wider and thicker as it approached.

"Coe, out oars now!" Alan screamed when he determined what the strange object was. "Row for your lives!"

It was a ship, perhaps blown free of her anchors upstream in the anchorage and running wild for the sea under the press of wind. And it was headed directly for them. If they did not get out of the way, their barge would be trampled under her forefoot and snapped in two.

"Row, damn you, row! Ahoy, the ship! Ahoy, there! Have you no eyes, you stupid bastard? Anyone have dry priming? Fire into her!"

No one did; all the firearms in the boat were soaked. All they could do was scream and thrash with the oars. The barge was under the jibboom and bowsprit. An oar was shattered on the hull of the strange ship. The stern bumped into her hull just below the larboard forechains, and a white face appeared over the ship's rail, staring down in surprise. Then they were seized by her creaming bow and quarter wave.

The barge thumped her stern heavily on the ship once more before being swirled out of reach, shoved aside like a piece of floating trash, and the ship proceeded on. In a flash of lightning, Alan could see that she was not running free, but was under way, with a foretops'l rigged loose, the yard resting on the cap of the foretop and the sail billowing and straining against a crow-footed "quick saver" to keep the sail from blowing out too far to the horizontal.

"Ahoy, you duck-fucker!" Coe shouted from leather lungs.

"Ahoy!" came the answering cry through a speaking trumpet.

"Give us a line!" Alan called, but before anyone aboard that ship could respond, she was almost out of reach. There was one more flash of lightning that illuminated her stern. And there, in proud gilt letters below the transom windows of her captain's cabin, was the name "Desperate."

"You planned it this way, you sonofabitch!" Alan roared, quite beside himself. His ship was getting away, and he was not in her! They had been given permission to try, and the storm would be a great opportunity to blow past the guarding frigates if they were even able to remain on station in such a gale. There would be a spate of water over the shoals and the tide had peaked and was now ebbing out into the bay. The night was black as a boot, and it would take an especially vigilant Frog lookout to even see her until she was close aboard. And she had most of her artillery to crush anyone who crossed her hawse as she flew on by invulnerable to any answering broadside. "Forrester, you bastard, you're aboard, I know it! Why not us? Why?"

"Easy, Mister Lewrie, sir. Le's just 'ope she makes it."

Yes, he thought. They'll think I'm a raving lunatic if I keep on. But how calm do I have to be now? We're left in the quag up to our hats and we'll end up in chains for the rest of the war.

"Ease your stroke, Coe," Alan ordered after taking a few deep breaths. "No sense in killing ourselves now."

"Er, Lewrie," Governour Chiswick said, raising one foot out of the water sloshing in the boat, "it's getting a bit deep."

"Christ!" Alan exclaimed. "We must have been stove in. Coe, we are leaking aft, I think."

"'Ere, sir," Coe said after kneeling down to feel the side timbers. "They's a plank busted."

"Take a soldier's blanket and staunch it. You soldiers, start bailing again."

And thank you very much, Captain Treghues, for kicking me up the arse in passing, Alan thought miserably. Christ, how much worse can this get, I wonder?

The wind finally began to drop in intensity, and the rain turned into a steady downpour. The lightning and thunder drifted off into the east toward the Atlantic, and the night became generally black once more. Alan peered into the face of his watch and could barely discern by the last lightning to the east that it was after four in the morning. The water was no longer set in rollers, but was beginning to flatten out under the press of rain, and the rudder no longer kicked like a mule.

"Coe, wake 'em up," Alan ordered, reaching over to shake his senior man awake. "I think we can begin to row in this."

Coe woke up, sniffed the wind and dug a hand over the side to take a taste of the water. He spat it out quickly. "Real salty, Mister Lewrie."

"We must be far down the river, almost in the bay," Alan said. "More reason to get going quick as we can."

There was a ration box of ship's biscuits in the barge, along with the barrico of water, and they all had a small breakfast and a sip of the water to wake them and give them a little strength for their labors. The soldiers had small flasks of corn whiskey to pass around generously, and that woke the hands up right enough.

They rowed up to their drogue and pulled it in. The salvaged oars were most welcome, since three had been shattered by their collision with Desperate as she had blown past them. As they got a way on once more, the rain began to ease off to an irritating drizzle. The river was still in spate, though, from all the rain that had been dumped into it from the swollen streams inland, plus the tidal out-flow, and they made painfully slow progress. There was just the first hint of grayness to the night when Alan next looked at his watch; half past five in the morning and dawn was expected at quarter past six.

"We shall have to hurry, or we shall be spotted by the French batteries on the right, where Mister Railsford said the marines were," he urged, though what the point of their efforts was, he did not know. Yorktown would be abandoned by then, and the Rebels and French would be ready to probe the silent redoubts and ramparts. The troops ferried to the Gloucester side during the night would probably be breaking out now.

They would miss the boat; the army would charge into the few Rebels and French on the north side and would be well away by the time Alan and his crippled barge could make it, and they would land in a hornet's nest of aroused soldiery who had been robbed of final victory. Their reception did not bear thinking about. Neither did the fact that he was in a boat slowly sinking from under him, possessing only what he had on his back or in his pockets. He had left his valuables in his sea chest once he had gotten back aboard ship and had not come equipped for a long stay. Alan had thought there would be time to get back to Desperate to be part of her attempt to break out. Soon, someone unworthy would be rifling his possessions, looting his gold and thinking him dead or captured while they sailed away, showing the French a clean pair of heels.

False dawn came, a gradual relieving of the gloom, and Alan took a good look around to try and discover where the hell they were. He had to admit that nothing looked familiar.

"Land, sir, ta larboard," Coe said.

"Yes, but damned if I can remember anything like that," Alan said under his breath. "Here, Mister Chiswick, you have a spyglass with you?"

"Yes," Governour replied, rousing from a half-sleep to offer it.

"Coe, take the tiller. Mister Chiswick, do hold me upright for a piece, if you would."

Alan took a good look at the land to the south. It was below Yorktown, that was for sure. Further east, his wandering eye espied some islands, and he began to get a queasy feeling. He turned his body to peer south and southwest.

"That is Toe's Point," he told them, sitting down on a thwart.

"Is that not near the mouth of the river?" Governour asked.

"Truly," Alan replied. "And to starboard, that is Jenkins Neck, an arm of Guinea Neck between the York and the Severn. We were blown all the way out into the bay. We're at least five miles from Yorktown and the narrows. One, perhaps two hours at the rate we're moving."

"The army has gone without us, then." Governour sighed. "They are to attack at first light, and we shall never catch up with them."

"Don't soun' like it, sirs," Coe stuck in, cupping an ear to hear sounds from the west. "They's still at it, 'ot an' 'eavy."

The faint sound of cannon fire could barely be heard, but it was still going on, over one hundred guns pounding away like a far-off storm.

"Jaysus!" One of the further forward oarsmen spat. "We's makin' warter up 'ere, too, Mister Lewrie."

"Stuff another blanket into it and hope for the best."

"We're makin' pretty fast, now, Mister Lewrie," Coe whispered to him as they sat together by the tiller bar. "Th' 'ole damn wale musta been smashed. Might not make five mile. An' even agin easy current, th' 'ands is 'bout played out."

"Might consider putting in and resting first?"

"Could be, Mister Lewrie," Coe agreed.

"Sail ho!" one of the oarsmen shouted, pointing aft. Alan turned to see a tops'l above the horizon. That would be a French frigate beating back to station in the mouth of the York, he decided. They might have an hour to get under cover before even a boat so low in the water could be seen.

The French and Rebels are around York, and the Frog ships are to the south and east. We'd best go into Jenkins Neck. Only foragers there.

"We shall put in on Jenkins Neck," Alan announced to his weary crew. "We have to make repairs before heading back for York-town. While ashore, we can dry out and get some rest. It will be dark before it is safe to be seen this far down the river, so you may all get some sleep."

Alan put the tiller over and urged his men to ply their oars for one more effort. They were shivering cold and resembled a pack of drowned rats worn down to the bone by all that had been asked of them during the night, and by their fears. But they were seamen, which meant that they were resilient, and if allowed time to rest up and get some warm food down, could do it all over again the next night.

They steered in for a small, marshy island at the tip of the tiny peninsula known as Jenkins Neck. Alan kept trying to picture the chart that Mister Monk had shown them the night before. They had concentrated on the region of the narrows and the Gloucester Point area, but it had been fully open on the desk, and Alan had glanced at it. The east end of the Gloucester peninsula was all salt marshes and low sandspits, threaded with creeks and rills like a river delta. There was a low island, known as Hog Island ahead of them. A little further upriver was a tiny spit of hard sand known as Sandy Point, a tiny cay connected by a tidal flat to Jenkins Neck; and to the western end of the neck, there was a large creek or inlet—two actually, one being grandly named Perrin River merely because it was a broader inlet than the other. Alan remembered seeing some tumble-down wharves along the shore; tobacco loading docks for the many shallow costal traders who worked the Chesapeake during the grow-ing seasons. He knew there would be less than three feet of water along that shore, even at high tide. They would have to be careful not to ground their barge on the mud until they had found some place sheltered in which to hide the boat and lay up while it was being repaired. There would be scrub pine enough in the thickets to cover them, and further inshore there might be something they could use to caulk or plug the holes in the barge's side.

"Mister Chiswick, give me your studied military opinion about something," Alan requested of the weary infantryman, which brought Governour's head up from his bleak study. "We could land on this shore along the river, but there are wharves, as I remember, and we might not wish to draw much attention to ourselves. Or, we could head north about Hog Island here and land in the marshes or on the far side of Jenkins Neck. Which would you prefer?"

"Each wharf is connected to a plantation," Governour told him. "That means Rebels. It might be better to hide in the marshes, but then I doubt if you could find what you need to repair the boat in those. I'd try the marshes, though, if we can find some high ground that is dry. My powder is soaked, and we could not fight off a pack of children now."

"Very well, the marshes it is," Alan agreed. "There is sure to be an inlet that leads to dry ground somewhere. And it's out of sight from those Frog ships in the river."

Once more he turned the tiller to larboard to steer the boat into the gap between Hog Island and another sandspit whose name he could not remember. There would be immediate cover behind them, at least.

"Boat, sir!" the bowman croaked.

"Hellfire and damnation!"

"Looks like it's stuck in the mud, sir."

Lewrie rose to his feet to use Chiswick's telescope once more as the hands ceased rowing for a much needed respite.

"Looks like one of our barges," Alan said. "Canted over in the mud on yonder tidal flat, but there's no one about it."

"Spare plank, sir." Coe brightened. "Ready-cut an' shaped."

"Right you are, Coe." Alan laughed. "Men, we are about to take a prize. Doubt if an Admiralty Prize Court would give us tuppence for her, and no head money, but she's ours. Give way."

They rowed up close enough to the stern of the abandoned

barge so that a hand from up forward could splash into the water and wade over the mud flat to the barge. He clambered into her and poked around.

"One o' ours, she is!" he called back. "They's blood on her, sir."

"God save us," Coe muttered softly.

"Hoy!" a man called from the low sandspit beyond the abandoned boat, standing up from the sedge and sea oats and waving a musket. "Hoy!"

"That's a British sailor, by God!" Alan exclaimed. "Hoy yourself!"

"Mister Lewrie, sir?" the stranded seaman yelled back. "Mister Feather, tis one o' our boats come fer us!"

They turned about and stroked to shore on the sandspit, grounding the bow into the beach as more of the boat's party came down to the shore to greet them. Feather was there, his head now wrapped in a bandage, some North Carolina Volunteers half caked with sand and mud, and half a dozen sailors from *Desperate*. Alan was relieved to see Burgess Chiswick, too.

"What happened to you, Mister Feather?" Alan inquired after they had gotten their own boat firmly beached.

"When 'at gale blew up, I got lost, sir," Feather admitted.

"So did we. We were blown all the way out into the bay."

"We got ashore on Gloucester, but twas beyond the lines on the right, an' we tangled with them French marines. Nobody's firelocks wuz worth a shit, an' they like ta cut us ta pieces with bayonets an' such. We drove 'em off an' got away, but I lost 'alf a dozen men adoin' it, an' mebbe 'alf a these soljers. Only 'ad the five oars left, so we couldn't do nothin' 'bout gettin' back upriver, an' tried ta 'ide in 'ere, but we grounded when the tide started agoin' out," Feather reported.

Alan looked at his watch, then studied the set of the tide over the mud flats. It would be at least an hour, maybe two, before they could expect the tide to refloat Feather's barge, hours in which they would be exposed as naked and helpless as foundlings to the full view of the French blocking ships now working back to their stations in the York. "We'll have to man-haul her into deeper water, then head for those marshes over there." Alan sighed wearily. "I have nine oars left. We'll share them and the crews out and find some place to hide."

"That's where I was agoin, sir," Feather agreed, careful not to nod his head too energetically. "They's a deep inlet round that second point ta the left, an' ya kin see the forests. We lost our water and biscuit, so me lads ain't 'ad nothin' since last night. We wuz gonna see what we could scrounge up afore 'eadin' back."

"We have some, not much. Share it out with your men, but be sparing," Alan told him.

"Aye, thankee, sir."

"Seen anyone else?" Alan asked. "Ours or theirs?"

"Mebbe two er three o' our barges went by upriver just 'bout dawn, but too far out ta 'ail. Frog ships're back in the mouth o' the river, but no patrol boats yit, sir."

Good as it was to know that they were not alone in their isolation, their situation had not been improved by the addition to the party.

Alan looked about the beach as he sat down at the high tide line among the screening sea oats. There were eighteen sailors, plus Feather the quartermaster's mate and Coe as steady senior hands. There were not thirty soldiers, including officers. They had one barrico of water, which would not make more than a taste for each man, one box of biscuits, which could not sustain life for more than a day or two, two boat compasses and two leaky and unseaworthy barges. Their powder was soaked, so they could not hunt, and if they did get some game, they might not be able to light a fire to cook with. His sailors had come away with only jackknives and cutlasses for weapons. Lewrie had two pistols on him, both sure to misfire after all the rain, his midshipman's dirk and a cutlass. Not exactly daunting prospects if they ran across Rebel troops ashore on the neck. Alan cocked his head to listen to the sound of the far-off cannonade around Yorktown. Bad as it would be back within the lines, they would be better off there than out in the wilds on their own so poorly equipped.

"Morning, Alan," Burgess Chiswick said, plopping down next to him on the sand as though it were merely another morning back in the redoubt.

"Burgess," Alan replied, "glad to see you still among the living."

"Not for want of trying on the foe's part, I assure you. The very devil of a quandary we're in here, is it not?" Burgess said.

"Goddamn Admiral Graves." Alan sighed. "He'll never come now."

"Nor will General Clinton, so goddamn him, too. Have a sip on this," Burgess said, offering a flask of liquor; it was corn whiskey.

"We must really be in trouble," Alan quipped after sliding that liquid fire down his gullet. "I am even beginning to like this stuff."

After a brief rest, there was enough water over the tidal flat to try to drag Feather's barge off. They shared out the hands to give equal rowing strength to both boats and started heading up north again, close enough together to talk back and forth. Feather, now that he felt rescued, was talkative and full of lore about the Chesapeake.

"Over ta starboard, that's Guinea Marsh." He pointed. "An' that's Big Island beyond. Now, ta larboard, we'll turn west inta this 'ere inlet. Round t'other side o' 'Og Island, ya'll see solid land. I 'member they's a cove, runs back like a notch offa this inlet. Damn near cuts Jenkins Neck inta an island, an' marshes on either 'and afore we gets to woods an' 'ard ground. No reason nobody'd come down 'ere alookin' fer us, an' mebbe not a dozen farmers down 'ere anyways."

"Been here before, have you?" Alan asked, weary of the garrulous lecturer. He wished fervently that Feather would shut the hell up and let him be as miserable as he wanted to be.

"Did some tradin' 'ereabouts 'tween hitches, afore the Rebellion." Feather went on. "Sweet li'l barque outa Boston, an' we'd row in ta pick up baccy an' whatnot an' land trade goods. Mind ya, twern't strictly legal, Mister Lewrie, 'cause the King's Stamps wasn't on everythin', but . . ."

"Is this your cove off the inlet?" Alan demanded, pointing to the left at a narrow waterway that led back almost to the south.

"No, sir, that's a false cove. Good beach fer smugglin' at low tide at the back of it, but we got further ta go. Now like I said, we wuz . . ."

I wonder if anyone would mind if I shot him? Alan asked himself.

At nearly nine in the morning they discovered the cove that Feather went on (and on) about, a long and narrow tongue of open water between salt marshes and some higher ground with scrubby coastal forest on it, and Alan could tell Feather to shut his gob in case there were enemy lookouts about, which brought a blissful silence, broken only by the sound of the oars and the birds, and the continual barrage that was by then a natural background sound, much like a ship groaning as it worked across the sea while they slept. It was shallow, and the barges dragged on the bottom now and then and had to be poled across in places though from the detritus on the shore they could see that there must be at least three feet of water at high tide.

"Lots of trash washed up." Governour was pointing. "Once we put in we can cut some brush and cover the boats easily enough. You could not spot 'em until you stumbled across 'em."

"Thank God for that," Alan said.

They came to the end of the cove. To the west there was still salt marsh and some barren sand humps broken by stunted scrub growth. On the left hand, to the east, there was firmer beach and a long finger of green land to screen them from the sea. A small creek poured down into the back of the cove and meandered off to the south and west, too shallow to be navigated. All about were thick stands of trees.

"Put in to the east of the creek," Alan said softly. "Fill that barrico first thing, if it's fresh water."

"My men can fill their canteens, and then we must needs reconnoiter," Governour said. "Your sailors should wait near the boats, just in case, ready to shove off. Wait as long as you can, mind."

"I'll not abandon you here, whatever you run into," Alan swore.

"God bless you, then," Governour said, readying his arms.

Almost as soon as the barges stuck their bows into shore, the Loyalist soldiers were off and gone as silently as smoke going up a chimney, rifles on half cock and long sword-bayonets fixed in case their cartouches and primings were bad. They faded off into the woods and the underbrush and disappeared, scouting like savages in all directions.

"Coe, take a party to fetch water. Feather, stand ready to cast off in case they run back here and say it's not safe."

Feather was silent and yawning with nervous trepidation now that they were back ashore in hostile territory, which was a blessing for Alan. The men clutched their cutlasses, those ashore squatting down near the high tide mark, those in the boats flexing their muscles to leap out and push off at the first "View Halloo."

Alan sat down on the bow of his boat, feet resting on the sand and carefully scraped the caked powder from his pistols' priming pans. He shook some loose powder from his powder flask and rolled it between his fingers to determine how dry it was, and reprimed his weapons. The pine plugs were still in the barrels, so there was a good chance that the charges were still dry in the muzzles. Both ends of the plugs were dry to the touch.

Mollow came creeping back through the scrub, bringing a gasp of alarm from the tense sailors, who were so keyed up even the sight of a red coat could frighten them.

"Mister Governour says tis clear," Mollow reported to Lewrie with his usual lack of formality. "But they's a plantation over yonder."

"Anyone about?" Alan asked as calmly as he could, repocketing the pistols.

"Looks ta be. Some house slaves, not so many," Mollow muttered. "That means somebody there ta keep 'em in line. Nothin' stirrin', though. Nobody in the fields, an' that rain las' night wouldna done that tabacca no good. Not much o' hit been harvested. Shoulda been dryin' in barns weeks ago."

"Big place?" Alan wondered aloud.

"Bigger'n some," Mollow allowed with a shrug, then busied himself with his damp canteen. "Water's frayush, iffen ya go up the crick a ways."

Burgess came drifting back to the cove and waved Alan to him.

"Quiet as a country church." He grinned as he offered his full canteen to Lewrie. "Looks to be only one farm this far down the neck, and it's a big one. Twenty, thirty slave cabins t'other side of these woods. Lots of corn and beans, and a fair tobacco crop gone to rot if they don't get it in soon. Looks like they tried. Most of the slave cabins are empty."

"Run off?"

"Probably. There's smoke coming from the house and the kitchen shed, so somebody's to home. Only slaves I could see were dressed good."

"House servants, your man Mollow suspected."

"Aye, most like. Nice big house, too. And barns and sheds. Four wagons but no stock other than a saddle horse or two, maybe coach horses. Livestock enough."

"Lumber and tools." Alan brightened at the possibilities. "No one would come down here this far to forage, would they?"

"Hard to say exactly. But we could be gone in a day," Burgess told him. "The cove here almost cuts the neck in two. There's one poor road to guard, and we could see anyone coming across the fields from the edge of the woods. It's not three hundred paces to the far shore, and half of the distance is marshy. It'd be a killing ground for a dozen riflemen."

"By God, let's do it!" Alan said. "We can take the place and use whatever they have to repair the barges. There's meat on the hoof and a whole parish full of vegetables to eat, plus whatever else we may find for our use."

"Let us allow Governour to decide," Burgess cautioned. "He's senior to both of us, and more used to this sort of thing."

Governour Chiswick took another quarter of an hour to make his way back to the beach, his rifle cradled in one arm but no longer at cock. His walk was looser, less concerned with ducking at the first odd noise as he had been when he left.

"I went as far as the far shore," he began. "Do you notice anything?"

Alan wondered what he was talking about. He looked the same as he had when he had departed on his scout; filthy and unshaven, just like the rest of them, and stinking of tidal flats and wet wool.

"Listen," Governour said. "The bombardment has stopped."

Once it was pointed out, Alan could notice the sudden absence of the muffled drumming of artillery. It had been such a part of their lives for the last few days that he had quite forgotten what dead silence was.

"One can see Yorktown from the far shore, just barely," Chiswick said. "After the smoke blew away, it's fairly clear. Dead as a grave."

"Then the army's gone on without us," Burgess said, sagging in weariness and defeat.

"I did not say that." Governour frowned. "As far as I can see, the army is still there, but there is no more shelling. I thought I saw boats ferrying men back from Gloucester to the Yorktown side. Now what does that suggest to you?"

"They could not break out," Burgess surmised.

"I believe that Lord Cornwallis's plans were upset by that storm last night, and he may be evacuating Tarleton and Simcoe's men over with his to make a last stand where he at least has entrenchments enough for all of them."

"No point to that. It was break out or go under last night," Alan said bleakly. "Maybe the French and Rebels stopped shelling because there is nothing left to shell. Why shell beaten troops ready to . . ."

"Surrender," Governour agreed softly.

"Does that apply to us?" Alan felt a chill.

"It had better not," Governour said. "Oh, your Navy men would get decent treatment, but I have little hopes for Loyalists once the regulars march off and leave us in the care of militia or irregulars."

"Then we don't surrender." Burgess smartened up. "Alan, you're a sailor, you have boats. You can get us out to sea, can't you?"

"Of course, I can," Alan promised, wondering to himself just how he was going to accomplish that miracle. Still, they were at liberty, and no one knew where they were . . . yet.

CHAPTER 11

THEY took possession of the plantation in the middle of the afternoon, after watching it for hours to see if there would be any surprises in store. They crept up through the empty slave cabins to the back of the house, exploring the barns and sheds as they went. As one party under Burgess Chiswick guarded the road and open ground to the west, the rest of them burst onto the grounds suddenly like a fox in a hen coop, raising about as much commotion until the sight of their weapons silenced all resistance.

There were about thirty-odd slaves, all women and children or very old men worn down to nubbins by a generation of hard work in the fields. There were perhaps half a dozen finer dressed house slaves to do for their masters, including a cook, maids and manservants.

There was an overseer, an older man with white hair who had been snoring away under the influence of a stone jug of rum, with a lusty black wench in his tumbledown shack near the main house.

"It's almost like home," Alan observed after they had secured the place. The house was magnificent, a homey, pale brick construction with a split-pine shingle roof; it was two stories tall and as imposing as any prosperous farmstead back in England. There was a squarish central core, the original house, and two wings extending to either side so that it made an imposing sight facing the York River and the wharves. There was a brick-laid terrace in back that led to various storehouses and the stables. There were six matched horses there, sleek and glossy and tossing their manes as though they were ready for a brisk canter up the road to the west to see the sights. There were also a few saddle horses, as well as a pen of mules for field work. The coach house held an open carriage and a closed equipage, both as freshly painted and shiny as any duke's coach in London, obviously not locally made and imported at some expense.

Entering the house reminded him even more of home. The floors were tight-laid oak parquet, covered with fine Turkey carpets. Heavy satin and velvet drapes hung by the large windows, and the walls were papered with what looked like new China paper. The quality of the furnishings, the brass and crystal, the framed pictures and the bright painted woodwork was astonishingly good. The ceiling in the foyer had been painted into an imaginative scene replete with cherubs, clouds and birds in blue and gilt by an artist of some talent as well. He was lost in admiration of the foyer when the mistress of the house and her entourage came down the stairs to see who had disturbed her peace.

"Well?" she demanded primly, her chest heaving in anger. "To what do I owe this invasion of my property? Who are you... *banditti?*"

Alan suddenly felt dirtier and shabbier than he had felt moments before, after being soaked all night, muddied with silt and sand.

"Lieutenant Chiswick, ma'am, of the North Carolina Volunteers. And you might be?" Governour said, sweeping off his wide hat to make a decent congé to her.

"Mrs. Elihu Hayley," she replied. "And was it necessary to come bargin' into my land and my house at the point of a gun, sir?"

"I assure you, ma'am, were circumstances different we would have come calling decently. You have nothing to fear as long as we are forced to remain, which shall not be any longer than necessary. We shall attempt not to discomfort you and yours, as much as the situation will admit of."

"I have quartered soldiers before, sir," she said, warming to the situation but still a bit peeved. "My husband is a captain in the Virginia Militia, or should I say, he was. Had I known, or been asked..."

"Hmm." Governour colored. "I fear you do not quite grasp our identity, ma'am. We are a Loyalist unit. This is Midshipman Lewrie of His Brittanic Majesty's Navy."

"Your servant, ma'am," Alan said, making a leg to her as well.

"God save us!" She blanched at the news. "I thought . . ."

"Your pardon for any misunderstandings, ma'am," Governour said. "There is only you in the house, I take it?"

"There is my son and my sister—and the servants o' course." She stammered, her chest still heaving in alarm. Alan thought it quite a nice chest, better than he had seen lately, at least.

"Your pardon, ma'am, for casting any aspersions on a lady of quality, but I must assure myself as to the veracity of your statements." Governour said. "You shall not mind if my men search the house? Good. Corporal Knevet? Search the house, carefully, mind. Don't break anything."

"Raght, Mister Governour," the dour corporal drawled, fetching a pair of troopers to help him.

"Now look here!" the woman began, but she was carefully shouldered out of the way as the men went up the stairs and she had no choice but to descend to the foyer level and fume.

Governour went to a handsomely carved wine cabinet and opened it. He lifted out a decanter of port and sniffed at it, then poured himself a glass. "Alan?"

"Don't mind if I do, sir." Alan grinned.

"Don't stand on ceremony. It's Governour. Ma'am, do you have spirits in the house or sheds besides this cabinet?"

"Go to the devil!" Mistress Hayley shot back, her back up once more. "Do you think you can take whatever you want from us?"

"Yes, ma'am, I do," Governour replied sternly. "You are admittedly a Rebel household, wife of a man in arms against his rightful King. We shall not, however, loot you. My men are hungry and we need certain items to stay in the field. Other than our immediate needs, your property shall be safe. But I must know about the spirits."

"I'll not give you or your men the pleasure!" she hissed, eager to dash the glass from Governour's hand if she could.

"It is a question of your safety, ma'am, I assure you."

"I shall say no more. Excuse me," she said regally, turning to go.

"If my troops, or Mister Lewrie's seamen find drink, ma'am, I cannot guarantee what sort of discipline or courtesy you may expect." Governour warned. "Better I know where it is so it may be guarded by trusted men than should they get cup-shot and forget all decency."

That stopped her in her tracks, and she whirled about, lifting the bottom of her skirts so that Alan could glimpse some rather fine ankles as well. She was pretty enough for an older woman, late thirties at best, with piles of dark hair and snapping brown eyes. A bit of a dumpling, but that had never stopped him before.

"Very well," she snapped. "There's the cabinet. There's a butler's pantry by the kitchen and there's rum and brandy kegs in the cellar we dole out to the field hands. Nothing is kept outside the house lest the slaves get to it and run wild."

"Your slaves seem rather thin on the ground," Governour observed. "Your crop will be ruined if you don't get it in."

"I sent the men off to Gloucester for labor at the request of a militia officer. I hope to have 'em back soon when your army is beat."

"Then that may be awhile yet, ma'am." Governour smiled as though Cornwallis was winning.

Corporal Knevet came back down the stairs, escorting another woman, this one a little younger and prettier than Mrs. Hayley, along with a frightened colored maid and a boy of about fifteen dressed in a fine suit of dittoes—snuff-colored coat, waistcoat and breeches. If his mother had been termagant, then he was a spitfire from hell, unsure whether to yell, cower against his mother's skirts or try to kill someone all at the same time.

"Damn ya," he hissed. "Damn ya all ta hell! We got ya beat, and you're all gonna die. When the soldiers come, I wanna watch ya die!"

"Then I hope you do not mind waiting a few days for the sight," Governour said, raising his glass in toast to the boy's spirit.

"House is clean," Knevet informed them. "Huntin' guns is all in the parlor, an' I took all the pistols and such I could find."

"Check the cellars," Governour said. "You'll find some kegs of rum and brandy, most like the cheapest swill ever turned a black's toes up. Issue at the normal rate with supper, but post a reliable man to guard it, else. No one to enter or leave the house but us."

Mrs. Hayley crossed to her son to shush him after his outburst, but he was having little of it. "Hush up, Rodney, or they'll kill us all this very instant!" she admonished.

"Dirty oppressor Tories, and press-gangers! Momma, what call they got ta trample on us? They're finished an' they know it!"

"Ma'am, your child is getting tiresome. Perhaps you might want to tuck him in for his nap?" Governour frowned.

"Come with me, Rodney," the sister said. "Sarah, I'll take him."

"I'll not!" Rodney spat.

"You will," his mother fumed.

"Governour," Alan muttered close. "I have some guineas on me. Perhaps we slipped them some chink, they wouldn't make such a fuss."

"You do? Sounds like it might work. Why don't you try?"

"Mrs. Hayley, we are not looters," Alan began. "There is no need for anyone to be put out by our brief stay, and I am empowered by my Sovereign to make recompense for anything we are forced to requisition."

"What good are promissory notes?" she complained.

"We have guineas, ma'am," Alan replied, digging the purse from his coat. He had at least one hundred guineas in it, and they gave off a pleasant jingle as he hefted them.

"Don't do it, mother," the boy named Rodney said.

"Go to your room, Rodney," she said to him. Prosperous as they all looked, there had been a shortage of specie in the Colonies since '76, and isolated as they were from the major smuggling cities or garrisons, they would be living on barter and the produce of the farm, with no outlet for the tobacco they had grown. She could at least be mollified by gold.

"I think it is an equitable offer," the sister said, and Alan saw that she was indeed very pretty, perhaps five or more years younger than her sister *la* Hayley. "Quite kind of you, considering."

"They killed my papa!" the boy cried. "They killed your Robert, and you'd take their filthy money?"

"Rodney, go to your room, now!" Mrs. Hayley said sharply, and the boy relented, sulking back up the stairs. "I shall consider your offer, sir. I may not accept, but I shall at least consider it. Come, Nancy. Sir, I shall require my servants to fix our supper and to do for us while you are here."

"If they remain in the house and the immediate grounds, there shall be no problem, ma'am," Governour told her cordially. "I shall keep your overseer separate, of course, if his presence is not needed."

Mrs. Hayley and her sister swept out of the room and up the stairs to their rooms. But the sister named Nancy did look back and give Alan a glance, lowering her lashes before turning to complete her ascent.

"Damme, what a pack of cats!" Alan chuckled once they were gone.

"Have some more port," Governour offered. "Damned interesting."

"What is?" Alan said, flinging himself down on a settee to take his ease. Governour poured him a healthy bumper.

"Here we have a framed portrait of a rather simple-looking man named Elihu Hayley, trimmed in black." Governour was observing a painting on the wall of the front parlor hanging in a prominent position. "And by the brass plaque we learn that he died in 1778, so she has been a widow for some time. The sister practically slavered when you mentioned gold and she got most missish over us. That long, flirtatious look from the top of the stairs. You did not notice?"

"Yes, I did," Alan said a little smugly.

"My black mammy once said that if times got hard, a rat'd eat red onions. There's not enough slave women or children to fill a quarter of those cabins, so the slaves did not go off suddenly, but were most likely sold a few at a time to raise money to keep all this style going," Chiswick said. "There's room in the stables for twenty horses, and that crop of tobacco is nothing like what this place could grow. Hardly any of it harvested to dry and the rest rotting. Not even been wormed or suckered."

"Whatever that means, Governour," Alan drawled lazily.

"Trust me. The drying barns are empty, and the storehouses do not have previous crops kegged up for shipment. I think your offer of gold mollified them into more positive sweetness than we could expect."

"Don't tell me we've stumbled into a knocking shop," Alan said.

"Hopefully, we won't be here long enough to know. Now, what may we do to guarantee our security here? Have any ideas, Alan?"

Alan leaned back and rested his head on the settee, his feet asprawl across the carpet as he thought on it.

"The overseer is no problem," he opined. "Keep him drunk and in with his black piece. Slaves aren't a worry, either, except for that butler and the manservant, but they'll stay locked in the house. And that boy ought to be chained to the wall. I'd watch him like a hawk."

"Very good. Go on."

"Anyone wanting to carry word of us would need a horse, so we keep them guarded. And perhaps we shouldn't let them see our numbers.

"There's Frog ships on the river we can see from here. Might want to post a lookout against anyone signaling them from the house with a light or something."

"Excellent!" Governour congratulated him. "You're nackier than I first thought. Let them see your people, I'll hide most of my troops. Now, about the boats. Is there enough here to repair them?"

"Have no idea." Alan sighed. He took a swig of his port and got to his feet. "Suppose I'd better go look before it gets dark. So we can get started on it in the morning."

"I won't make any demands of your sailors, then. Keep half of them on guard by the boats. Burgess and I shall bivouac half our people in the woods to stand guard while you get on with your repairs."

Alan finished his wine and went out through the back to the kitchen shed. He found a ham on the sideboard and carved himself off a healthy hunk, cut a wedge of cornbread from a skillet that had been set out to cool and headed for the barns, munching happily on his impromptu meal. Suddenly it hit him. Governour had almost shooed him out the door. He had not issued an order or made a suggestion, but it was his conversation that had gotten him moving when he would have much preferred to sit and drink and fall asleep on the settee. Damn you for a nacky one yourself, Governour! I'll have to study on how you did that.

Several of his sailors were trying to talk to the black women in the back gardens and stable area, and the slave women were responding shyly. The hands would consider them ripe for the plucking, much on par with the for-hire doxies they had grown familiar with on the islands, but the men had little or no money. It could get ugly if controls were not placed on them soon.

"Coe," Alan called, summoning his senior hand.

"Sir."

"There's rum and Frog spirits in the cellar of the house. We'll have an issue with supper," Alan said. Then he laid down strict instructions regarding dealings with the women. Any man who laid hands on one who did not cooperate willingly would be flogged half to death, as would anyone who looted or got drunk. They settled on several of the nearest slave cabins as quarters for the men so they could be watched and supervised more easily. Tired as the hands were, they were put to work cleaning them and making them more civilized. Storehouses would be searched by Coe personally for victuals, and abandoned cooking pots would be given out so the men could cook their dinners, appointing their own cooks if they could not cajole some of the idle women to do for them.

Sensing that he had given his men enough to do for the moment, Lewrie went on to speak with Feather, who was at the door of the larger barn with another older sailor.

Feather made an attempt to knuckle his injured brow as Lewrie joined him. He was chewing slowly on a plug of tobacco he had cut from an opened keg, a huge straight-sided barrel full of twisted leaves.

"Found anything to repair the boats, Feather?" Alan asked him.

"Rope, nails, barrel staves," Feather said, pausing to spit a juicy dollop of tobacco to the side. "A full carpenter's shop, sir."

"So we may begin in the morning at first light," Alan said.

"Aye, sir. Might take a look at mine, too, sir. Twas workin' more'n I liked. They's pitch an' tar out back, so's we kin pay all the seams while we're at it. But, beggin' yer pardon, sir, I don't know what we're adoin' with them boats oncet they's repaired. The 'ands is askin'."

"We're staying free, Feather," Alan said. "If that means getting out of the Chesapeake altogether past the French, then so be it."

Alan had not really considered a course of action. His only hope had been to get back on dry land without drowning in a leaking boat. Then perhaps they might go back to Yorktown, but Lieutenant Chiswick's observation upriver had made that moot; there was nothing to go back to, not if Cornwallis had not been able to break out. The French and the Rebels would never have stopped that killing barrage unless they thought the end was near.

"Outa the Chespeake, sir?" Feather wondered. "Doubt we'd make it in them barges. Why, it must be nigh on forty mile ta the other shore, an' the 'ands'd never be able ta row that far, not in one night, an' them old things'd be pure shit ta try sailin'. 'Sides, we ain't got no masts ner sailcloth ner nothin'. An' why leave the bay, when the army's not five mile upriver? The French patrols'd get us quick as ya could say Jack Ketch, sir."

"There's plenty of rope, you said," Alan pointed out. "Enough to rig them with a mast each, though two short ones would be better with the shallow draft they have. There's timber enough about for masts and spars, and enough sacking in this barn to sew sails from."

Alan did a quick survey of the barnyard. "Those wagon tongues are ready forked to fit around a mast—use 'em for booms. And look here." He knelt down in the dust and drew quick sketches with his dirk. "Sacrifice two oars for gaff booms, or if nothing else, sew up some lug sails instead of getting too complicated. There's block and tackle in the drying barns for hoisting. Rig 'em loose footed to the boom, maybe even loose to the mast if that's easier, like a Barbary Coast lugger."

"We could do it, I 'spect, Mister Lewrie, but them barges'd go ta loo'ard like a woodchip, an' unstable as the Devil," Feather carped.

"What would make them more stable?" Alan asked. "More ballast or a heavier keel, a deeper one?"

"Mebbe any keel at all, sir." Feather frowned, still unconvinced. "They's only 'bout six inches o' four by eight fer keel members now."

"Below the hull?"

"Aye, sir, below the 'ull. Mebbe could nail on some barn sidin'."

"You can tear this fucking barn down if you get some heavier timbers out of it," Alan said. "The barges are what, over forty feet long and nearly nine feet in beam—wider than normal river barges. What if you bolted some heavier timber onto the existing keels? Surely there are some finished beams about, squared off, maybe twelve feet long or better. Channel 'em in the center to fit over what protrudes below the hull, drill holes and fit pine dowels through the holes, or through-bolt 'em if we find iron."

"Wouldn't swim good." Feather shook his head. "'Ave ta fair 'em in with somethin' fore an' aft o' the added piece."

"We're not out to win a contract from the Board of Admiralty," Alan scoffed. "It doesn't have to be pretty. It doesn't even have to be all that fast, just as long as it will sail upright."

"'N then there's freeboard, Mister Lewrie. Might 'ave to add on ta the gunnels 'bout six more inches."

"Barn siding nailed into the existing gunwales."

"Mebbe. But they'd still make a lot o' leeway."

"Shallops, Mister Feather," the older seaman finally said through his own cheekful of tobacco twist. "Iver see 'em Dutchie coasters up in N'York? Got leeboards t'either beam. Swings 'em up outen th' warter on a 'ub."

"Well, I don't know nothin' 'bout that . . ." Feather stiffened at an unwanted suggestion from a common seaman. The hands were trained by society and by the harsh discipline of the Fleet to sit back and let the warrants and petty officers come up with the miracles, with an occasional flash of genius from the gentlemen officers that the middle ranks would translate into organized action. Talking without being given permission was, in some tautly run ships, an offense.

"Then I suggest you find out!" Alan barked, exasperated with the petty officer's intransigence. "We have two choices, Mister Feather. We repair these damned barges, make them seaworthy and get across to the other coast to escape, or we get taken by the French and the Rebels as prisoners of war, if they even give us a chance. We are on our own out here, so the sooner we get on our way, the better!"

Feather was used to taking orders, used to having an officer at hand to tell him what to do. He was not an imaginative man or a creative one. In the absence of authority, he had been floundering.

But with the midshipman making loud noises pretty much resembling those of a commissioned lieutenant, he fell into line readily. His former stubbornness dropped away like a veil, and when Alan left them, after delivering an order that they would begin boat construction at first light the next morning, Feather and the older seaman were busily drawing in the dust, walking about their plans and spitting tobacco in a juicy fit of naval architecture.

Once the slave cabins had been swept out and prepared for quarters, the men turned to washing up their few garments, scrubbing the worst dirt from their bodies and getting ready for the evening meal. Alan saw to the simmering pots that contained haunches of a fresh-slaughtered pair of sheep, inspecting the snap beans and ears of corn that would be the hands' suppers. Women were baking cornbread for them, and there were more smiles and flirtatious looks passing between his sailors and the slaves than before.

"Let them turn in after supper," Alan directed Coe. "We'll start on the boats in the morning. Just as long as there is no trouble."

"Won't be, Mister Lewrie." Coe smiled. "Once they eat their fill an' 'ave their grog, they'll be droppin' like tired puppies. Won't be no trouble from 'em tonight, I lay ya."

"I can believe that." Alan smiled back, realizing how bone-weary he was himself. His clothing itched and still smelled like dead fish—foul as a mud flat. He could feel grit every time he moved. "I shall be berthing in the house if you need me."

He entered the house through the back door and clumped to the parlor to pour himself a drink. There was a decanter of rhenish out on the sideboard already, and he filled up a large glass of it, slumping down on the settee once more in weariness. Someone had lit a fire in the parlor, and he stared at the tiny dancing flames as the hard wood began to take light from the pine shavings and kindling beneath it, almost mesmerized by exhaustion. Before his eyes could seal themselves shut with gritty sleep, Governour and Burgess came into the house by the front doors, forcing him to sit up and try to look alert.

"It's quite homey," Governour said happily, plopping down into a large wing chair nearer the fire and putting his legs up on a hassock.

"How are your men?" Burgess asked Lewrie. He poured himself a drink from the sideboard.

"Cleaned up, ready to eat and get their grog ration. Coe assures me they'll sleep like babies after last night."

"Mine, too," Burgess replied, coming to sit next to him on the settee. "Let some of them sleep the afternoon away so they'd be fresh on guard mount for the night. Lookouts are posted for anything, coming or going."

"Good," Alan said automatically, glad to leave their security in the capable hands of the North Carolina Volunteers.

"Now, what do we do to escape this muddle?" Governour asked from his chair, leaning back and almost lost behind the wings.

Alan outlined what they would do to make the barges seaworthy and where he hoped to go with them once they were ready to take the water.

"You are confident we can make it?" Governour said.

"We would have to leave at dusk, since there is no cover out in the inlets and marshes." Alan said slowly. "We'd be spotted if we left earlier. Only trouble is, the tide will be fully out and slack then, so we'll have to slave to get the barges poled out into deep water. Once we have depth enough, we may do a short row east through a pass called Monday Creek, north of Guinea Marsh and Big Island, if Feather has his geography right. Hoist sail there. It's forty miles or more to the eastern shore. With any decent wind at all, even against the incoming tide flow, we could . . ."

He paused to use his brain, and it was a painfully dull process.

"Yes?" Governour asked, thinking Alan asleep with his eyes wide open.

"Say . . . three knots over the ground at the least. We could make forty miles in twelve hours. Fetch the far shore around half past six the next morning, if we left here about half past four or so."

"Have to lay up for the day." Burgess said. "We don't know what the Rebels have for a coast watch on the other shore, if any."

"Yes," Alan agreed. "Then, another thirty miles or so the next night to get out to sea. There are islands off the coast we could lay up in until we spot a British ship. Or skulk from one to the other on our way north. There will be someone patrolling."

"But how do we get out past the French fleet?" Burgess asked.

"We stay close inshore round Cape Charles," Alan told him. "The main entrance they're guarding is south of the Middle Ground by Cape Henry. Nothing of any size may use the Cape Charles pass, and with our shallow draft we could negotiate the shoals close under the cape in the dark, where even an armed cutter could not pursue us."

"What about rations?" Burgess asked.

"Plenty here," Governour said. "Bake enough pone or waybread for all of us. Casks enough for storage. More water kegs. Meat would be a problem once it's cooked. Or we could slaughter and pack it in brine in small kegs, enough for two or three days at short commons."

"Too bad we could not jerk some meat, Governour," Burgess said. "I have no idea about domestic animals or the chance for fresh game on the eastern shore, or whether it would be safe to hunt."

"Johnny cake and jerky." Governour laughed softly. "Catch crabs and fish for a stew. Alan," he called out, bringing Lewrie back into their conversation, "how long to repair the boats?"

"Oh . . ." Lewrie pondered, having trouble lifting the glass to his lips. He concentrated on it hard. "Two days. Three at the outside. You would be amazed by what a British sailor can do."

"That long?" Governour said, obviously disappointed.

"Might take less. I don't know," Alan confessed.

"Two days, then." Burgess calculated. "Time enough to dry out all our powder. We're as helpless as kittens right now."

"There is that," Governour agreed. "We have the one box of cartouches that stayed dry, but that wouldn't make three decent volleys. Lot of smoke for all the labor we shall be doing. I hope it does not attract any curiosity from further up the neck."

Their voices droned on, putting Alan to sleep once more. His head slumped down on his chest and his grip on the wine glass loosened until a small trickle into his crotch woke him up with a start.

"Better get to bed," Governour said, rising to his feet. "You must be done to a frazzle by now."

"No, not yet," Alan countered stubbornly, forcing himself to stand as well. He slurped down the rest of the wine and headed out for the hall to go out back and find a spot where he could take a quick wash. He met the family of the house as they came down the last flight of stairs on the way to their supper in the dining room.

"Evening, ma'am." Alan smiled at their unwilling hostess.

"Sir," Mrs. Hayley said, nodding primly. Rodney glared daggers at him.

"Pardon me delaying your supper, ma'am, but would you have some washing facilities?" Alan asked her.

"Ask of the kitchen staff, sir," she replied stiffly.

"Thank you, ma'am."

"You shall not dine with us?" the younger sister Nancy asked.

"No!" Mrs. Hayley decided quickly, echoed by the son, and earning the woman a withering glance to even suggest such a traitorous thing.

"I thank you for your kind hospitality, ma'am," Alan said, addressing himself to the sister. "But as Lieutenant Chiswick said, we shall not intrude on your privacy. I expect our supper shall be later. Duties, you know."

"I have instructed the cook to set up a table in the parlor for you, sir." Mrs. Hayley softened slightly. "I shall not sit down to table with Tories or oppressors who usurp my property."

"Then I shall not delay you further, ma'am," Alan said, stung by the hostility and confused by how it waxed and waned by circumstances.

There was a laundry shed out behind the kitchens, and a black maid to stoke up a fire and set some hot water to steeping. Alan discovered a large tub as big as a fresh-water cask aboard ship that had been cut in half for use as a bathing tub. The servants filled it with well water, poured in the buckets of steaming hot water and provided soap and towels and a lantern, the youngest woman giggling unashamedly as Alan peeled off his coat and waistcoat until he shooed her out and finished undressing.

He stepped over the side and sank down into the hot water, giving off a moan of pleasure as he settled down chest-deep. All the salt sores and boils a seaman could expect to gather began to yelp painfully to his weary brain. He lathered up the soap with a rag, enjoying the sting of the lye and the pleasant scent of Hungary Water that had been added to the mixture when it was made. He stood and scrubbed every inch of his skin with soap, undid his queue and washed his hair, then found the buckets of fresh water with which to rinse, lifting them high and pouring them over his head.

"God, that did wonders!" He chuckled as he toweled down. The water had gone grayish brown from all the dirt he had accumulated. There was a knock on the door, the latch lifted and the young slave girl came back in with a bundle of fresh clothes. Alan yelped in alarm and held the towel close around him.

"Miz Nancy say I fetch ya some frayush linen, suh," the girl tittered, cocking one hip at him like a weapon. "They's planny ta th' house an' no mens aroun' ta wahr 'em."

"Uh, thank you," Alan replied.

"I take yer duhty thangs an' warsh 'em fer ya, suh."

He had to cross to his clothing and empty his pockets while the maid slunk closer, humming to herself and grinning lasciviously.

"Ah kin sponge this hyar coat down, suh. Have ta warsh evathin' aylse. Miz Nancy give ya britches an' clean stockin's ta wayur."

"That was most kind of her," Alan said, trying to keep the towel up with one hand and search his pockets with the other.

"You a real purty mans, suh," the girl crooned softly. "They calls me Sookie, they does. Laws, ah 'speck ah ain't seen sich a purty mans 'bout the place in a coon's age."

"Is that a long time?" Alan huffed. Fuck it, she's only a slave, to hell with modesty, he thought, letting the towel care for itself while he finished emptying his pockets. "What about your overseer, or the boy?"

"Hmmp, Missa Dan'l, he got his fav'rite." Sookie sulked. "An' Missa Rodney, his momma keep a leash on him. An' Miz Sarah, she done sol' mos'a the purty slaves. Not much come down the road no mo', 'cept them Franch mens an sich."

"What French men?" Alan asked, "How do you know they're French?"

"Why, Lordy, they's awavin' they han's an' bowin' an' kissin' so ovah Miz Sarah an' Miz Nancy, ah nevuh seen sich goin's on! Ize Miz Nancy's gal, suh. Ah seen me lo'sa mens ack the fool ovuh the ladies, but ah ain't seen nuffin' lak dat! All blue an' yaller unifo'ms, an' thezh hyar big tall caps look lak sewin' thimbles."

"Hussars?" Alan wondered at the girl's description of a shako. "So they come down the road a lot, do they? When were they last here?"

"Ah . . . ah, don't recolleck, suh." She paused, having said too much.

"Tell me, damn you!" Alan insisted, taking her arm.

"Two, three days back." Sookie finally told him: "They come down hyar ta sniff 'round the white wimmens. Took off the las'a the field bucks las' time. You ain't gonna hu't me none, is ya, suh, fer tellin' ya 'bout 'em? Miz Sarah'd have me whupped iffen she knew ah tol' ya."

"I won't tell on you, Sookie," he said, releasing her.

"Ah allus git me a spell wif a sargen' when they come. His name be Al-Bear, an' he allus gimme a whole shillin' ta let him top me. Ah cain' tell what he sayin' half the time, but he's some kinda buck, my, my! Ah'd do it wif you fer a shillin', iffen you was a mind ta."

At that moment, had Sookie been a perfumed and powdered Queen of Sheba in his private harem (secretly one of Alan's favorite fantasies) he could not have mounted her to save his life. Damme, the Frogs and the Rebels have been here, and they might come back before we can sail!

"I'd normally be honored, Sookie," he told her quickly. "But I've my men to look after, and can't do anything they can't."

"Ya warnt Miz Nancy, don'tcha?" Sookie said, put out by his reticence and misunderstanding his reasons.

"Well . . ."

"She would'n say no ta a purty mans lak yerself, suh."

"She wouldn't?" Alan asked, stopping his activities.

"Them Franch's an' sich what comes down hyar stays the night mos' times. Ah knows what goes on in them rooms upstairs." Sookie grinned. "Takes los'a money ta keep this place agoin', it sho do, suh."

"She does it for money?"

"Nossuh, but iffen one o' huh *lovers* warnta give huh somepin', she don' say no. Miz Sarah now'n agin, too, even she is a dried up thang."

"Hard times would indeed make a rat eat red onions," Alan said, remembering Governour's comment.

"Sho nuff, suh!" Sookie snickered with him. "You sho you don' warna take a poke at me?"

"Perhaps tomorrow night, Sookie, I am rather tired."

"Ah tells Miz Nancy, then, you warn huh?" the consumate little businesswoman asked, picking up the dirty clothing once more.

"Aye, that would be interesting." Alan smiled, almost shoving the maid out the door. He dressed quickly into fresh stockings, a pair of buff breeches that were too loose on him, a clean linen shirt and neckcloth, and a faded white waistcoat also much too large, idly wondering who they had belonged to before he got them.

His supper was waiting in the parlor before the fire. Two lanterns were lit on the mantel above the fireplace, and the fire was now a cheery blaze that threw off enough heat to take away the autumn chill of the house. The kitchen servant had laid out boiled mutton, a cold ham, boiled corn and beans, more bread and a crock of fresh butter.

"You look a lot more elegant than when you left," Burgess teased as he sat down. "And the aroma is better as well."

"I have learned something," Alan whispered, raising a hand to shush them. "Our hostesses received French soldiers, not two or three days ago. One's a whore on the side, the older is a schemer who accepts favors in trade to keep this plantation alive and in style."

Alan described what the maid Sookie had told him and then sat back to let the soldiers make up their own minds.

"Blue and yellow uniforms, and hussar fur turbans," Governour said, chewing. "Lauzun's Legion. Cavalry, foot and light artillery. They're Poles, Germans and renegade Irish, maybe some Scots as well who followed Charles over the water. Used for foreign service such as Senegal. Tough as nails, I'm told. They were up north in Newport with de Barras last year."

"Well, they are here now," Alan reminded him. "And their officers think this the most entertaining spot in two counties. We had better get to work and get out of here soon as dammit before they get the urge to come visiting the widows again."

"And prepare some positions should they come in strength," Burgess added. "Hell, cavalry! They'd ride right over us!"

"Keep your voice down, dear brother," Governour said. "We do not want our hostesses to know we are worried about anything. One show of fear and they'd find a way to get word to the other end of the peninsula and do for us. We shall have to maintain a bold front. How much gold do you have, Alan?"

"About one hundred guineas," Alan admitted, which brought a look of consternation to each Chiswick brother at his wealth.

"Stap me, we could buy the whole damned county for twenty!" Burgess exclaimed. "Think the ladies'd be more amenable to our presence if we flat out bribed 'em?"

"We cannot admit that weakness," Governour countered. "But if we seem to be a source of money, for victuals and such, they might wait for a while before trying to send out an alarm. Even so, we shall have to close down traffic up the peninsula so tightly a mouse could not get by."

"And lay some preparations to receive their cavalry."

"Yes, Burgess," Governour said. "If all else fails, we shall have to fight them—and defeat them."

"What, the whole of Lauzun's Legion?" Alan wondered aloud.

"Not at first, perhaps a troop at a time. Alan, this girl Sookie, she is a good source of information? Could you get any more out of her?"

"Not really." Allan frowned. "She'd reveal anything for a crown, but she knows nothing. It's her mistress that would know more, but there's no way to make her talk."

"You said she was a coquette, taking favors," Governour said.

"Well, yes."

"As I remember, you gain a lot of information from the whores," the younger Chiswick grinned. "Like you did in Charleston."

"You must reveal nothing to her of our plans, but you must learn more about those French troops who visit here, how many come at any time, how they're armed," Governour said. "Your man Feather and that sailor, Coe, can keep the work on the boats going, but we must have information. You work on that while Burgess and I build up some defenses at the narrows and in the woods."

"Well, if that is what's needed," Alan said. He shrugged. Damme, I've put the leg over lots of times for pleasure, but this is the first time I've ever been ordered to do it in the line of duty!

CHAPTER 12

FTER being awakened from a drugged sleep on a straw pallet in the front parlor at four in the morning, Lewrie put his seamen to work on the boats. They dragged them ashore onto X-shaped cradles so they could get to the keels, screened them with brush from sight should any patrolling boats enter the narrow inlet and began to repair them.

Alan's barge was in the most obvious need of fixing; most of the morning was spent ripping out her broken strakes, stiffening her broken ribs and nailing pieces of long tobacco-barrel staves into the gaps, while other hands began the work of shaping heavier timbers for the keels. The household was awakened by the sound of one of their outbuildings being demolished for timbers, yielding two twelve-foot-long beams eight inches on a side. The beams were adzed down on either end to improve their shape for traveling through a liquid medium, tapering to blunt points much like the beginning of very long and narrow log canoes. A start was made on a center trough in each beam with augers drilled down to a depth that would accept the shallow wooden barge keels, to be routed out later with small axes and chisels.

Other seamen chopped down four decent pine trees for masts and began to strip them of limbs and bark. Round holes were cut into the thwarts that Feather and his older seaman considered the best for holding a mast erect in the most advantageous position for boat trim and efficiency of sail pressure, and pieces were shaped as mast steps for the keelsons.

All in all, it was a profitable morning's work. The lower parts of the extemporized masts would have to be filed down to a smaller diameter, the steps would have to be nailed in, the scavenged barn siding—one-by-six board for the splash guards on the gunwales— still had to be sized and fitted (and were soaking in seawater to soften for bending to match the gunwales), but they had made a good start.

A large pot of pine tar was simmering over a fire, which they would use to pay over the repairs and the entire bottoms of both boats after dinner so that they would not leak any longer; or at least not as badly as they had before.

Alan went back to the house in a much happier frame of mind for his midday meal, thinking that a day and a half would see them off that cruel coast and across the bay, where they could expect to be rescued by a passing British ship. The maid Sookie met him, still flirting heavily even though he had rejected her. But she had his uniform for him.

Once changed, he sat down to a good lunch on the front terrace, where the cook had moved their dining table, it being a lovely fall day, too pretty to spend inside. Governour and Burgess joined him, removing their red tunics before sitting down at table.

"Our hostesses do not dine with us, I see," Governour said ironically. "They were on the back patio. Probably don't want to breathe the same air with us in the house."

"Mrs. Hayley was exercised about our tearing down that shed," the younger Chiswick said. "Alan, she said that if we were to tear her house down around her ears, some of that gold should be forthcoming."

"What do you think a shed is worth, Burgess?"

"Oh, one guinea, at least." Burgess shrugged and poured them all wine. "And perhaps one guinea a day for victuals and such. I cannot really blame them. They won't have a chicken left by the time we get through with them."

"You're being awfully free with my guineas," Alan complained.

"For which we shall gladly reimburse you as soon as we catch up with our paymasters," Governour promised grandly. "We were in arears before leaving Wilmington, so they owe us a good round sum by now."

"How are the boats coming?" Burgess asked.

"Less said around the house, the better," Governour cautioned. "After dinner we may take a stroll down to the woods where we may talk freely. Alan, have you had a chance to discover any information from Miss Nancy?"

"Not yet." Alan sighed. "I was busy this morning. It may be tonight before I can begin my campaign with her."

"Don't leave it too long," Governour pressed, then shut up as a black serving wench brought out a heaping platter of fried chicken.

It didn't take as long as Alan had thought. Once he had taken a cup of suspiciously good, strongly brewed coffee, he went back toward the northern end of the plantation to rejoin his workers on the boats. But suddenly, there was Miss Nancy, strolling idly in the same direction, shielding her fashionably pale complexion from the autumn sunshine with a parasol. She was turned out in a dark green dress and had obviously spent some time at her morning toilet to make herself more attractive. She was making a great production of swaying her hips, stopping to see each late-flowering bush or meander about as though she was waiting for him to catch up with her, which he did. The sight of him, when she finally turned to face him, was full of sudden alarm.

"Lah, Mister Lewrie, ya gave me *such* a fright!" she gasped, as though totally unaware of his presence until that moment. Alan tried not to smile; she was about as subtle as an unruly mob of drunks. He had run into her sort before and the artifice of courtship or the mechanics of the trade with high-classed prostitutes was no mystery.

"I did not intend to startle you, ma'am," Alan said, approaching her more closely. "Though I must own to appreciation of the color that my fright brought to your cheeks. And I am flattered that you would remember my name. I did not recall our having enough time to be formally introduced."

"Oh, my yes, sister mentioned your name ta me, sir," she said, making motions as though she would have appreciated having her fan with her so she could flutter it before her face for more air.

"And you are Miss Nancy." Alan grinned. "I wish to thank you for the loan of the clothes last night, and Sookie's tending to my uniform. From the greeting we received, I did not think any charity would be given to a King's officer."

"I am so glad ya found my actions charitable, sir," she simpered. "Tory or not, British or not, you are a young man far from home and not a personal emeny. How could I do any less for a fellow Christian?"

"It was most welcome, Miss Nancy."

"Oh, please, Mister Lewrie, do not be sa formal! I am Nancy Jane Ledbetter. But why don't ya just call me Nancy?"

"I would not presume any gross informality, Miss Nancy," he said, playing the gallant buck and enjoying the game. "While I may have your leave, I doubt if your sister would appreciate it, or her son."

"Oh, pooh!" she pouted. "Sarah's such a prune since Elihu died. Not that they were that loving a couple when he was alive. Since he was killed, she's been vindictive ta everyone. What do your friends call you, Mister Lewrie?"

Little bastard, he thought wryly, but said, "Tis Alan."

"And where ya from, Alan?" she asked, beginning to stroll once more, spinning her parasol coquettishly.

When he told her London, she went into paroxyms of delight and begged to be told all about it, having always wanted to go there. Alan filled her in about St. James Parish and the Strand, the restaurants and the gaming houses, the theatre and what had been new and entertaining when he was last there, what the fashions were and all the gossip that a still-youngish woman would delight in had she the chance to see it.

He was careful, however, during his discourse to steer her away from the woods at the back of the plantation and the creek where they were working on the barges. If she was disappointed, she gave no sign of it, allowing herself to be led more easterly on their stroll, toward another woodlot on the back of the property that overlooked the marsh.

"What a commotion ya'll started this morning, Alan!" she cried. "We were all roused from our beds thinking the Apocalypse had come. Sister was beside herself when she saw what ya'll had done ta her shed. But I suppose ya had good reason."

"Yes, we did," Alan said.

"Ya building a boat or something?" she teased.

Damme if the jade ain't trying to interrogate me instead, he realized with a start. Think of something, laddie. You're a clever liar if needs be.

"A sheltered wharf to land supplies," he said. "We've pounded the Frogs and the Rebels into ruin up at Yorktown and broken the siege. You notice there is no more cannon fire? We expect more troops from New York soon, and then we'll round up what they have here."

Her eyes widened even though she fought it, a moment's consternation, and then a calculating squint as she weighed this news.

"There had been foraging parties down our way," she admitted. "I was under the impression that it was the other way 'round."

"Well, what you hear from militia troops is always suspect until you see for yourself, don't ya know?" Alan said casually. "And if you'd run across some gasconading Frenchman, you'd think they won the war by themselves a year ago, when they haven't done much at all."

"Oh, poor Sarah, I swear!" Nancy sniffed, digging into her bosom for a handkerchief to dab at her eyes as she quickly changed the topic. "She had *such* hopes that all this would finally be over. How can I tell her? She cannot bear it. And Rodney shall be so crushed that he lost his daddy, and I my Robert, in vain."

"You were married?" Alan asked, waiting out the histrionics.

"Only in agreement about our future together, nothin' so formal as the banns," Nancy said from behind her handkerchief. "And Rodney admired him so!"

"My condolences to you and your sister, then," Alan said kindly. "I have lost good friends in this war as well. I am sure that you and your sister did have hopes the war would pass you by. I have heard many in the Colonies only want to stay out of danger, not favoring either side."

"That other officer is so hard, ta blame us for our menfolk's politics," Nancy cried. "Surely he must know women have no opinions."

"Rest assured you shall be safe and this property shall not be ravaged. We shall pay for what we use," Alan told her, wanting to get back to the main subject of his exercise with her. "Unlike the others."

"That was sa kind of ya ta offer gold, Alan," Nancy said. "The Continentals have but scrip, and no guarantee of that ever being honored. We could paper the walls with it and get more comfort. As ta that, I wish I could give sister some assurances about the money. The shed and the stock that's been slaughtered sa far, and all that."

"A little gold goes a long way, Nancy, especially in these times. We could settle up later. Have your sister present a list of what she thinks are fair prices to us."

"I shall," Nancy replied.

"It must have been hard on her, trying to run this farm and all those slaves by herself." Alan expanded on his theme. "Now most of 'em have been sold off, haven't they? And I believe the rest went over to Gloucester at the request of the Rebels?"

"Y . . . yes," Nancy replied, turning away and trying to remember how much Sarah had said at their first encounter the day before.

"Nothing in the storehouses, no hope of this year's crop and no way to get anything out past the blockade," Alan went on softly. "And the herds much reduced. This war must have pinched you terribly."

"We have managed," Nancy said, plying her handkerchief again for a self-pitying weep. "Though it has been damned hard, never knowing where the funds would come from, or if there would be enough ta eat, even."

"Yet you still set a fine table and have a good selection of wine. And that coffee at dinner!" Alan said. "I have not had the like aboard my ship in months. However did you get it?"

"We have, now and then, had ta depend on the kindness of our good neighbors," Nancy announced with a straight face. "Things do get through your blockade, and there are kind gentlemen who think of us in our need."

Alan laughed to himself. *I wager there are!*

Nancy turned away once more and began to stroll along the edge of the woodlot, heading for the environs of the main house, this time at a slow pace and without the flirtation she had shown before.

"Times will be better," Alan said to bridge the sullen silence that had sprung up between them. "Once we have reclaimed Virginia for the Crown, you will be alright. Think of the new goods coming in."

"Yes, that will be good," she said, "but it would be even nicer ta think of all the goods going out. We haven't sold even a barrel of our crops since '77."

"Yet they are not here." Alan wondered, considering whether he should have observed that or not to her. Damme, this spying and prying is harder work than getting her interested in bed.

"Sent off inland for safety, up near Williamsburg," Miss Nancy said quickly. "All the planters hereabouts do it."

Was she lying, or did they have some ship captain who would take their tobacco to the Caribbean for transshipment to Europe? There was too much in the way of luxuries about the plantation that could not be easily explained away, but at the same time not enough luxuries to mark them as smugglers or profiteers; else why should they have to sell off the slaves? Alan did not mention the news that Governour and Burgess had given him about those huge warehouses full of tobacco further inland that Arnold and Phillips had burned during their rampage through Virginia back in the spring. Surely, she would have known about it—it would have represented a total loss for them. He decided to switch the conversation to more venal topics.

"But, when you can sell your stored crops, there will be a flood of money again, and your house shall once more ring with laughter." Alan beamed at her. "And Miss Nancy shall charm all the county with her beauty and her grace, as I am sure she did before these hard times."

"Why, Alan Lewrie, how ya *do* go on!" She flushed happily.

"The fiddlers shall come to play at your balls, and everyone shall want to dance with you." He went on. "As a matter of fact, I wouldn't mind doing so myself." He could see that he was coaxing her into a better mood. She really was a pretty little thing, much nicer looking than her older sister. And there was no one around at the moment to see him take liberties with her, and a whole forest to explore her in.

"Were all the gentlemen as gallant as Alan Lewrie, I'd admire ta dance the night away, so I would!" She cooed, swaying her hips in wider arcs and spinning her parasol once more.

"Did we have a fiddler, I would admire to dance with you this very minute," Alan said, stepping closer to her, close enough to feel the heat of her body. "Would you join me in a country dance?"

"What would the darkies think, us capering about out here in the woods?" she complained, but made no move away from him.

He slipped a hand to her waist and brought her idle stroll to a halt. She turned to him, raising her face up to look at him directly. She leaned back a bit from his embrace, but she was smiling still.

"Ya seem a lot older than ya look, I swan," she said softly as he drew her closer. "One'd take ya for a boy at first reckoning."

"One ages a lot faster in a war," Alan told her as their loins touched. The scent of her was maddeningly fresh and feminine, and he had not held a woman since Charleston, nearly two months in the past.

"You're becoming more familiar with me than decency admits of, good sir," she protested, still wearing that enigmatic smile and looking him directly in the face. "And a moment ago, I called you *gallant.*"

He drew her to him even closer, put a hand on her back and brought her face close to his, brushing his lips on hers. She turned her head back and forth to avoid his kisses, but her lashes lowered invitingly, more teasing than in a genuine attempt to break away or deny him her pleasures. He kissed her cheeks in lieu of her mouth, her chin, her neck below her ears, and proceeded on to her bare and inviting shoulders when she made no greater objections.

"Mister Lewrie, how dare you use me so ill!" she whispered as she finally raised one hand to push his shoulder away from her. "This is not done! Slaves are always spying on their masters, and a lady and a gentleman do *not* give them grist for their amusement. I am not some goose girl ta tumble by the creek such as you did at home."

Just like home, anyway, Alan decided with a leer. Take your pleasures in private and keep the servants in the dark about 'em like you have the reputation of your class to uphold.

"There's no one about," he told her, resuming his exploration of her upper body with his lips.

"You don't know about living with slaves. There's always someone about," she objected. But she did not object when Alan broke away and took her by the hand to lead her into the low trees of the coastal scrub forest. Deep in the underbrush and low limbs and out of sight from the tilled fields and outbuildings, he drew her to him once more. She made futile squirmings to get away from him, but in her turnings and twistings their lips met, and he bore down on her. The hands that were weakly holding him away slowly slid up over his shoulders and caressed his hair, then her arms went about his neck as she returned his kisses. Given enough privacy in which to do so, Miss Nancy was as passionate as *any* goose girl allowing liberties to a squire's son. When she squirmed this time, it was with desire to draw her length against his.

They knelt down on the forest floor, on the hard sandy soil, and she made all the maddening noises of an aroused woman as he played with her breasts, slid a hand under her voluminous skirts to caress the silky feather softness of her thighs, raising her skirts out of the way so he could press the crotch of his breeches against her bare belly.

"No, no, there is no privacy here, Alan, dear," she protested, and broke away from him, getting to her feet and stepping back to lean on a tree, fanning her face with one hand. "La, what would you have of me?"

Goddamn the bitch! Alan raged silently as he knelt on the ground and wondered if his breeches buttons would burst with the painfully tumescent erection he had. "I would have you right now," he said huskily.

"Not here, dear," she cooed. He rose to grapple with her again, but there was no convincing her. "Can ya not wait until this evening?" she finally said. "Would I have any authority left with the Samboes after the event, I would pleasure ya here, Alan love, but please consider my reputation. It has been so long for me without the feel of a man that I shall not deny ya anything tonight. Only wait a few hours, I beg ya!"

"Tonight, then," Alan grumped, his humors still aflame.

"Ya sleep in the front parlor?" she asked, scheming even as they embraced at the edge of mindless lust. "Do ya get up the stairs, the back stairs off the butler's pantry. Left at the top of the stairs, and my chambers are at the end of the wing in front over the porch. But for my sake, don't attempt it before midnight, I pray you! Sarah's boy Rodney's a light sleeper, even if he is in the other wing of the house. He does not understand worldly matters so well, and . . ."

She bit her lip fetchingly to cease babbling things that were best left unsaid. Alan smiled with amusement at the thought of that spoiled and sullen little shit-sack having to watch his mother and aunt entertain the gentlemen that called. If Nancy wanted to play an innocent role, he would let her, as long as he got what he wanted from her, and information into the bargain.

"I must go back ta the house, love," she told him, and began to dust her skirts down to remove the pine needles and sand from them. He helped her, not without taking some more liberties with her body, which she no longer opposed; they stopped to kiss now and then, teasing themselves into more heat, then shying back until midnight could arrive.

"By the way, Alan dear," she said suddenly, "I must have a good excuse to explain why I was conversing with ya so long. May I say that I was negotiating with ya about payment for what ya've taken from the farm so far? If ya could, some gold would be convincing, and I know she would be much less hostile ta yer presence here if she had some in hand."

Alan sighed and dug into his waistcoat. He took out his purse and let her appreciate the sight and sound of it as he dug down and drew out five guineas, bright shining "yellowboys" that glittered in the sun about as brightly as her eyes at the sight of them. He pressed them into her soft palm and she flung herself on him with as much abandon as any sixpenny whore who had just been handed a shilling and told to keep the change. She trailed her fingertips over the bulge in his crotch, making him hiss with desire. But before he could do anything more, she broke away once more and began to head for the open fields.

"Until midnight, Alan my own," she said softly as she gave him one more lingering, possessing embrace, and then she was gone, calling over her shoulder to mind her instructions and not be overfamiliar with her should they meet at supper. She tripped her way out of sight, still adjusting her gown and pushing at her hair, her parasol bobbing over her shoulder and twirling with satisfaction at their dealings.

"Damme if I ain't one hell of a rake!" Alan crowed softly once she was out of sight and hearing. "Five guineas back home could have paid for a whole bagnio full of mutton, but I swear I think she's going to be worth it. And just wait'll I tell Governour and Burgess about this."

It was only after he was back with his seamen at the creekside boat yard that he realized that, in terms of information, he had gotten practically nothing from her. He had confirmed that she was a whore and that gentlemen visited them with gifts, but he had already known that. But, he assured himself smugly, he was only beginning to hit his stride with her, and bed talk would be more revealing after a tumble or two.

By late afternoon, both barges had been sealed and repaired well enough to keep them from leaking once they were back in the water. The gunwales had been increased in height to improve their freeboard in any sort of sea, and the keel beams had been tried for fit against the bottoms, which would improve their stability and ballast. Fastening them on, though, would take another half-day's work to drill holes through beams and existing keel members to accept either wooden dowels or iron bolts. The masts were fitted into the pierced thwarts, stepped to the keelsons, rigged by scavenged rope for shrouds, and the wagon-tongue booms and rope parrels ready and in place, though the blocks, halyards and sheets were not yet mounted, but that would not be a half-morning's labor.

Once he had been goaded into action, Feather had turned out a good amount of work, quite ingeniously, Lewrie thought, and he told him so to mollify the man's feelings from the night before.

"Got an ideer on them leeboards, Mister Lewrie," Feather said with a twinkle as the elder sailor nodded at his side. "Took a pair o' them wagon wheels an' axles offen the fronts. 'Thout the tongues, they ain't goin' nowheres, any'ow. Make 'em inta windlasses, see?"

"So you may hoist or lower the leeboards by a line wound round the windlass or axle?" Alan tried to picture it. The project was going much faster than he had thought, and their moment of escape was drawing closer all the time.

"Uh, nussir, we nail them leeboards ta the wheels, sir," the older sailor countered. "Lays 'em up close-aboard til ya needs 'em, then ya turns the wheel ta lower one inta the warter, sir. Keep tension til ya warnt one on a belayin' pin. Free the line an' down she goes, sir. Nail the axle ta the thwarts an' gunnels, wif the wheels outboard."

"That should be alright," Alan said. "But do they fit as they are, or do you need to cut longer axles?"

"New axles, sir," Feather said. "But they's plenny o' them eight-inch beams 'bout. Tried ta make frames fer the wheels, but it was . . ."

"Too complicated and heavy?" Alan finished for him as he searched for a break-teeth word, and both men nodded their heads vigorously.

"T'only thin', sir, we needs summat 'eavy'n solid fer the lee-boards, an' we can't make 'em outen pine bits," Feather said. "Bout four foot long'n mebbe two, three foot wide, ready planed. We kin taper 'em like a rudder piece, but I don't know what ta use."

"Take a look around the place carefully before it's dark," Alan ordered. "Is there any more we can accomplish tonight?"

"Nah, sir, be dark soon," Feather said. "But we'll have them new keels on by noon tamorrer. Could leave tamorrer night iffen we kin find what we need fer the leeboards."

"Very good, Feather!" Alan exclaimed, patting him on the shoulder in congratulations once more. "Give the hands an extra tot with supper for their good work."

"Aye, sir!" The men near the discussion perked up at that. There was little a British sailor could not do, and there was little a British sailor *would* not do if it could get him some extra drink.

"If we are leaving tomorrow night, then, best put a few men with Coe to start gathering up food and water to stow in the boats, then."

Alan made his way back up toward the house to pass on his good news to the Chiswick brothers, who had been out in the woods to the west all day since dinner, working on their own plans. He would have a wash, clean linen, a good supper and then a few hours with Nancy in her bedroom, though there was little point in trying to gain more information from her now if they would be departing the next evening.

He was in the bricked back terrace, ready to enter the house by the back door when a runner came panting in from the fields, calling for Leiutenant Chiswick, and everything went for nought.

"Riders acomin'!" he heard the runner gasp out.

Goddamn, the Rebels have found us! he thought in sudden fear. He dashed into the house to fetch his pistols and his cutlass and found both Chiswick brothers priming their officers' model Ferguson rifles and a squad of soldiers running into the front hall.

"What is it?" Alan demanded as he checked his own primings.

"Half a dozen riders coming, goddammit!" Burgess spat. "For your life, go and tell your men to keep out of sight. Do you have any arms with your men?"

"No, just a sentry or two along the creek."

"Move, Lewrie!" Governour ordered harshly.

Alan ran into Coe and passed the order, then went back into the house. North Carolina Volunteers by then were hiding by the windows, and another party was sprinting into the hedges to the east of the front yard. Governour shoved a Ferguson into Alan's hands.

"Here, load up. It's their lives or ours now."

Alan screwed the breech plug open, ripped a dry cartouche with his teeth and fumbled the ball into the breech, pouring in the powder behind it. His hands were trembling slightly and his insides were by turns hot and cold at the thought of discovery and battle.

"Mollow, Knevet, do you get to the upper windows. Take two men with you to keep the civilians from giving us away," Governour snapped to his noncoms, and his best marksmen.

Alan stood well back from the window as he primed the pan of the rifle with a metal flask. From the front parlor he could see six riders coming up the sand-and-shell drive to the big house, men in blue and yellow, the peculiar horizon blue of Lauzun's Legion that Governour had described to him at supper the night before, a couple of men in outlandish fringed hunting shirts of an almost purple color, waving their tricornes or their muskets over their heads and shouting as though they were after a fox.

They clattered up into the carriage drive that circled a large

flower garden before the front terrace. "Hello the house! Come out
and hear the wondrous news! Cornwallis is taken with his whole
army! They surrender tomorrow! Let's celebrate!"

"Let 'em dismount," Governour whispered. "Fire on my order
only."

But they did not dismount, continuing to curvet and wheel
about the drive, spilling over into the flower beds as their mounts
collided and pranced with their rider's excitement.

"Here, Mistress Hayley, Miss Ledbetter, come out and hear our
news," a rakish Legion officer called, sheathing the heavy cavalry
saber he had been flashing over his head.

"Maybe they've gone off," a militia officer said, frowning.

"Goddamn them." Governour spat. "Fire!"

He leveled his rifle and took aim. Burgess and two riflemen
went to the double doors and flung them open. Alan joined another
rifleman at his window, jabbing their muzzles through the glass panes
with a horrendous noise. Then came the sharp crack of rifle fire, and
men began to spill from their saddles. Horses neighed and screamed
as their riders screamed in sudden terror. The rakish Legion officer
was punched in the stomach with a rifle ball of .65 caliber and blood
spewed onto his saddle and his horse, though he kept his seat and
tried to make off. He did not get very far before a second ball
smashed his horse down, and they both tumbled into the flower beds
to thrash out their lives. The militia officer's horse reared back and
flung him. Even as he rolled to his feet Burgess shot him down. One
trooper tried to draw a musketoon from his saddle but was riddled by
two rounds from the upper windows. The rest were going down before they could get off a shot, except for one man on a roan who
thought discretion was the better part of valor and tried to ride off
back up the road for help or safety.

It had all happened so quickly that Alan had not had time to
even cock his rifle. He rushed out onto the front terrace with the
others in time to see two riflemen to the west stand up from cover
and blast the fleeing rider and his mount to the ground. There was
one final shriek as the man flipped out of his saddle and fell heavily.

A .65 caliber rifle ball fired from close range did hideous damage to a man. Alan walked out into the flower beds through all the

carnage and gore to a horse that had been gut-shot and was down and screaming. He cocked the rifle and laid the muzzle within an inch of the ear and put it out of its misery, sick to his stomach at the suddenness of the skirmish.

He had fought at sea often enough to see death and pain, but at least there a man was given warning and a chance to defend himself. The art of skirmish and ambush as practiced by the army left him shaken and weak, though it did not seem to affect the North Carolina Volunteers. They came trooping back into the yard, laughing and joking and commenting on their accuracy, flipping bodies over to see what damage they had done.

"Here, this one's still alive," Alan said, kneeling down by one young man dressed in the Legion's blue and yellow who had been shot in his lungs.

"Oh, God, I'm killed!" the man managed, rolling his head back and forth in pain and biting his lips. "Damn ye ta hell fer all eternity, ye baystards!"

"He won't last long," Governour said after looking at the hole in the man's chest through which blood pumped at every tortured breath. "Listen here, man. Who were you?"

"Hanrahan." The foe gasped. "Seamus Hanrahan."

"An Irish turncoat fighting against the Crown." Governour nodded. "What's this about Cornwallis?"

"He give up yesterday and surrenders his army in the mornin', ye Tory shit-sack," the dying man said, trying to smile. "Ye may ha' killed me, but you'll all be dead tamorra and joinin' me in hell!"

"Visiting the ladies to celebrate, were you?" Alan prodded. "A bit premature of you. How long before you're missed?"

"I'll not be givin' ye that," the man whispered as the effort to talk sapped his last strength. His skin was paling quickly and his lips were turning blue as his lungs filled with blood. He coughed once, a bright scarlet bloom of life burst from his lips and then he died.

Governour got to his feet and began to reload his rifle as if nothing untoward had happened. "Any more of 'em still have life in 'em?"

There were none.

"With luck, these will not be missed until tomorrow morning,"

Governour said as his troopers began to drag the dead away. "Here, they have some weapons we need. Strip 'em of their guns and powder."

Governour bent down to a dead horse and fetched off from the saddle a handsome pair of long-barreled dragoon pistols, which he presented to Lewrie. "You'll find these shoot straighter than your own pistols, and you'll need some extra weapons. That man will have powder, patches and ball on his corpse. The caliber will probably not fit your own."

They recovered a round dozen saddle pistols, two pair of shorter pocket pistols, four French model 1777 cavalry musketoons and a pair of .69 caliber St. Etienne muskets from the militia officer and his dead orderly, along with a welcome supply of dry powder, ball and flints. They had dried some of their own powder and cartouches, but more was always welcome since half the prepared rounds carried by each soldier had been soaked and rendered useless.

"What if they *are* missed, Governour?" Alan asked after he had found a pocket for all the iron he was collecting. "Wouldn't they be due back with their units in the morning?"

"Three very junior officers and their orderlies wouldn't be all that very important," Governour told him. "They may peeve their commanders by not being present for the surrender parade, but no one would think to search for them until it's all over. They're off celebrating victory in their own style with complaisant ladies! They might send a lone rider with a message, but it's a long way back to their positions at Gloucester, six miles, maybe further, because the road swings north to clear the swamps and marshes and goes above the shore of this Perrin River, and there's no bridges or ferries. Might take a rider four hours on bad roads to come and go."

"So if they had to be back by ten tomorrow morning," Burgess said. "Seems a reasonable hour . . . no one would comment on their continued absence until two or three in the afternoon, if they sent a messenger for them right away. That would be the earliest he and they could return to Gloucester. And we could be gone by then."

"What if we worked all night on the boats?" Governour asked Lewrie. "We could depart even sooner, could we not?"

"The tide would serve to get us out of the inlet," Alan replied. "Besides, if the messenger and these poor souls don't return by three or four, what would they do? Send another messenger? A troop of cavalry? More luck to them, 'cause we'll be out in the marshes by five, and by the time they get here around six, we'll be under sail."

"But once they arrive at the house and speak to the Hayleys, our goose is cooked," Governour said. "They could signal the French ships to send boats to cut us off. I'd really feel better leaving here tonight. Matter of fact, the more I think on it, it seems best."

"But the leeboards aren't ready," Alan said.

"Hang your bloody leeboards," Governour snapped.

"You cannot," Alan said, over his unease at the slaughter, and in a position of authority and knowledge for once with the land officers. "Oh, we could pole out right now, but with provisions and all, we'd be over-set within five miles. There's the keels still to be fitted, and without them, we're unstable as a cup-shot cow. And without the leeboards, we'll make as much leeway as we do forward. How do we know how calm the bay will be, or what strength the wind? We have to finish the boats—it's that or drown out there. And if you think the river was rough, just wait til we get out past Cape Charles and onto the ocean."

Governour puffed up as though he was about to burst.

"Believe me, I want to be away from this shitten place as badly as any of you, but there's simply no way," Alan assured him.

"Work at night, then," Governour demanded, adamant.

"By torch and firelight?" Alan asked.

"No, that would be even worse," Governour said finally. "We would be sure to draw attention from the French ships then. Forgive me my impatience, Lewrie."

"Governour, I know what impatience is," Alan laughed without much humor. "I've been impatient since I first saw Yorktown."

They went back into the house for a welcome drink from the wine cabinet and sideboard. Mrs. Hayley, her son and sister were at that moment being escorted back downstairs from whatever room they had been confined to during the brief action, their tears flowing copiously. Nancy could not look him in the eyes, but the other two were livid with rage and the shock of seeing men killed in their presence.

"Murtherers!" Mrs. Hayley shrilled as soon as she saw them. "You did not give them one Christian chance! Just shot 'em down like dogs! They were all our friends! One of 'em was a neighbor up the neck."

"There is little that is Christian in war, ma'am." Governour told the woman, knowing it would not penetrate but making the effort anyway.

"Is that how my daddy died?" Rodney hissed. "Shot from ambush by a cowardly, sneaking hound? Damn you all, I say!"

"Corp'rl Knevet?" Governour barked.

"Aye, Governour?" The non-com replied from the stairs.

"Mistress and her charges shall be confined to the upper floors tonight, and for all tomorrow until we are gone. Their meals to be brought to them. Keep a watch on their windows. No lanterns in their rooms, and make sure they have only what they need for decency's sake."

"Right, Governour."

"And shall we be shot as well, sir?" Mrs. Hayley objected. "Have Tories and King's men no honor toward innocent civilians? Where is that gentle treatment which you promised when first you came here?"

"I could care less what happens to Rebels and their broods." Governour snapped coldly. "Be thankful you shall have your lives and your property when the fighting is over, ma'am."

Once the women were hustled back upstairs, Alan opened the sideboard doors and found a stone jug of corn-whiskey. At that moment, he preferred it to other, weaker, spirits. He took a deep swig, rattled it about in his mouth, and gulped it down, holding.his breath until the fire had passed.

"Whew, what a mort she is!" He said.

"Can't blame her, really." Governour relented, unslinging his rifle and unloading his pockets of weapons. "Pour me a goodly measure of that while you're there, would you? Women know nothing of war, thank God, nor should they, so they have only the vaguest notions of how it is really conducted, or how bestial the average soldier becomes after he faces battle and death more than once. They will never have the slightest idea how rudely they and their property could be treated if we were not honorable gentlemen at heart."

"So leaving them more gold would not help any longer." Alan said. He was still jealous about having to part with his guineas, and if they did not have to do so, would be glad to keep them.

"No, we promised to pay for what we despoil." Governour sighed, flopping down into the wing chair and putting his feet up on a narrow padded bench before the cold fireplace. "Perhaps twenty pounds would do. And they'll be the only ones to profit by this campaign of ours."

"I already gave five, and got little for it."

"Did you learn anything, though it is moot now?"

"Not much. It was all I could do to keep her from spying on *us*." Alan admitted. "We were to tryst upstairs tonight. Perhaps I could still."

"Then I hope the lady is worth the socket-fee." Governour laughed.

"I have bargained for worse," Alan told him with a sheepish grin.

"We shall work through the night, anyway," Governour Chiswick said as Burgess joined them from cleaning up the last signs of the ambush. "We can at least slaughter and embrine meat, bake johnny cake and dry more powder in the tobacco barns. Anyone familiar with growing tobacco would expect to see drying fires on a plantation at night."

"I could put my men to work on the leeboards in the wagon sheds as well," Alan said. "We could burn torches in there to see by. Though we don't know what to use for the boards themselves."

"What sort of boards would they have to be?" Burgess asked, taking a glass of corn whiskey himself.

"Two or three feet wide, four feet long, ready planed from heavy wood, Feather told me. I suppose we can nail or peg something together that would suit."

"Heavy wood, you say." Burgess chuckled, going to the double doors to the front parlor. He rapped one of them significantly. "How would you prefer oiled mahogany. Inch and a half thick, over eight feet long and over three feet wide, both of them."

"Two sets of leeboards!" Alan exclaimed. "Burgess, you're a paragon! I was looking right at them and never gave 'em a thought!"

"I was ready to take 'em myself for our fortifications," Burgess said. "Damn the place, I'd strip it down to the raw bricks rather than be captured for the want of a nail."

"What fortifications?"

"Oh, brother and I have been busy in the woods," Burgess said. "Preparing a reception for anyone coming up the road. Our visitors tonight never even spotted 'em. We put up some rail fences and laid some surprises, too. See here, Alan, you said you were a hunter back in England, didn't you?"

"Yes, some."

"Ever see a fence you didn't want to put your horse to?"

"Never," Alan bragged, loosened up by the whiskey.

"Nor did I ever know a cavalryman that wouldn't either. There's *chevaux-de-frise* behind those new fences in the trees, not out front, mind, but in back, where you don't see 'em til you're in mid-leap, and if they had sent cavalry against us, they'd end up on the spikes." Burgess snickered with anticipation at the sight. "With our Fergusons, we could have had an edge, too, 'cause we could lay down to fire and load just as fast as standing. There's rifle pits in the woods, too, so we could have had several fall-back positions to snipe from while any infantry would have come at us standing up."

"Had they been necessary, we could have given anyone a hot reception," Governour boasted. "We even provided for you. Up by the creek it's too marshy for cavalry or infantry, but south of the woods, they could come across the fields. We put up some log ramparts for you and your sailors, covered with leaves and dead-fall to look like a pile of junk wood. Would have made a neat little redan to guard the boats while we covered things south of you."

"You were that confident?" Alan wondered aloud.

"If they had sent troops down here, and if they followed usual practice, we could have cut them to pieces. If they didn't send too many, that is. And after besting them we'd be gone before they could summon a larger force."

"It would have mattered how many they would have sent, though, would it not?" Alan asked, throwing a damper on their celebrations.

"Well, if a battalion had come, the best we could have hoped for was to fall back through the woods to you by the boats, while you held out," Governour said, since it was now moot speculation. "Your men and Mollow with a half-dozen riflemen could have slowed them up. After that . . ."

"After that, we would have swum for our lives to the boats and hoped they wouldn't have murdered us out in the open water," Alan said.

"We would have put up a damned hard fight they'd have re-membered for the rest of their lives," Governour said tautly. "Now, how much can you accomplish tonight if we work in the barns?"

"The leeboards," Alan said, shaking off the gruesome image of their entire force laid out defeated and dead, just like the revellers in the front yard. "The keels shall have to wait til morning, unless we want to show torches down by the boats."

"No. Get as much done as you can."

"Governour," Alan said, getting a premonitory chill once more, "we'll be days along the eastern shore, and God knows what we'll run into. Would it be possible if you or Burgess or Knevet worked with some of my free hands and drilled them on those spare Fergusons?"

"A damned sensible idea, Alan," Burgess said. "Best to be pre-pared for any eventuality."

"My thoughts exactly."

Using as few torches as possible in the barns to shield the lights from prying eyes, they had worked until nearly midnight. The ma-hogany door panels were taken down and drilled to accept the axles of the small wagon front wheels, nailed to the naves and ready for installation in the morning at first light on the barges through exist-ing rowports. Alan finally let his men get some rest and went back to the house to take his own. He entered the front parlor where Gov-ernour was already snoring on his pallet before the fire, sleeping rough on the carpet. Burgess was ensconced on a settee on his side. Even in repose, the Chiswick brothers were a ruthless looking crew, Alan thought as he studied them by firelight. They were taller than he was, which gave them authority in spite of their low ranks, slim and almost angular. Even if he had not seen them in action, he would walk warily about them if he met them on the street back home. They had an air about them of habitual command, the sense of being obeyed. Perhaps it came from owning slaves and bossing them about, Alan decided, but they were impressive creatures, per-

haps what that Frog Rousseau meant by natural nobility. Daunting
personalities, magnificent physical specimens, and pretty enough to
turn heads on the Strand or in the parks back in England, should
they ever live to get there. Burgess had told him they still had relations in Surrey somewhere, and with the Rebels in possession of
everything they had built up in the Carolinas, they were hoping to
return to England and make a new start. Such an enterprise was dear
to his own heart as well; he wished them joy of it.

He sat down in a chair by the sideboard and discovered a bottle
of rhenish that had been opened but barely touched. Being careful
not to wake his compatriots, he poured himself a glass and sat back
to ease his weary body. The house was silent as a tomb, except for
the Chiswicks and their snoring. The sentry at the foot of the stairs
was drowzing as well.

Don't I have an assignation waiting for me? Alan asked himself.
He checked his watch and discovered that it was a few minutes past
the appointed hour of midnight. 'No, after this afternoon, she'll hate
the very sight of me. Still, she's a whore, ain't she? What's another
guinea or two now?'

He stripped off his coat and waistcoat, undid his neckcloth and
tossed them onto the chair next to him. He lit a candle with a stick
of kindling that had fallen from the low-burning fire and made his
way out into the hallway with a bottle of wine and two glasses in one
hand, and the candle-stand in the other. There was no sentry on the
back stairs from the butler's pantry, though there was one at the back
steps wrapped in a blanket against the chill of the night, and very
much awake. Alan made his way up the dark stairs to the rear passage of the upper story. There was a door and a mean little narrow
corridor that gave entrance to the rooms above through the back, so
that night-soil and other unsavory removals could be done without
staining the main hallways. He went all the way to the end and
found a final doorway. He blew out the candle and opened the door
furtively, inch at a time to avoid creaking hinges. It opened noise-
lessly, though, obviously well-oiled to avoid disturbing anyone who
was using the chamber.

There was a sliver of moon coming through the windows, just
enough to see that he was in a large and well-furnished suite at the
end of the house. Surely, it had to be Nancy's; she had said her

bed-chambers were at the end of the house, overlooking the front yard and porches. He was in her sitting room. Groping like a blind man, he snaked his way on past all the furniture to the far doors, which stood open. Once his eyes were used to the gloom, he could espy a tall bed and several chests and wardrobes, a dressing table and a mirror that glinted moonlight.

With a smile, he crossed to the bed and found a small table by the headboard on which he could deposit his unlit candle-stand and his wine and glasses, though not without a tell-tale clink of glass on glass.

"Who's there?" A tremulously fearful small voice exclaimed.

"Tis Alan, Nancy love." He whispered back, removing his shoes.

"Oh God, after what happened today, ya still come to me and expect me to welcome ya?" She hissed, sitting up in bed with the sheets drawn up around her neck as a thin defense. "Leave my chambers at once, or I'll yell the house down."

"There'll be no more guineas if I do." He warned her, unbuttoning his shirt. "Your visitors this afternoon brought wine and tasty delicacies, but no gold for you."

"Wh . . . what do ya take me for!" She complained in the dark.

"Sookie told me about you. So why make such a show of outrage?"

"Oh, you smug bastard!" She cried. "If I ever gave my favors ta a man, it was not for coin, sir! What sort of vile creature are you, ta think all women are whores for your pleasure? Just 'cause you've bought some women in the past doesn't mean we're all for sale for ya!"

"So your lovers just *happen* to leave you something worthwhile on their way out the door." Alan scoffed.

"Goddamn ya, get out before I scream!" She said louder. "Ya shot down people I knew today, officers that'd been welcome here before, and now ya come creeping into my chambers with blood on your hands and think a guinea makes it alright? Get out, I mean it!"

To make her point, she picked something up from the nightstand and threw it at him. Whatever it was struck him on the shoulder and he flinched away from her anger. The object clanked to the floor noisily.

"Go, before I kill ya!" She warned.

"Very well." Alan fumed, heading for the door, bumping into the tables and chairs and making even more of a racket than she would have, trying to salvage his pride.

Once down-stairs, and into another bottle of wine to replace the one she had thrown at him as a parting gesture, he had to realize that he could not exactly blame her. One or more of the men who had been shot down in ambush had most likely been in her bed once before. What really made him mad was the way she had gulled him out of those guineas.

He was also unhappy that he had gained no useful information from her in spite of being at his most charming, as much as he would have been charming with a courtesan, and he had a nagging feeling that she had gotten more from him than he hoped to learn from her.

'Good thing we're leaving here tomorrow.' He thought grumpily as he poured himself another glass of wine. 'Before she found a way to get down the stairs some night and cut my nutmegs off for spite.'

CHAPTER 13

HE woke up feeling like the wrath of God had descended on his skull, having sat up and finished half the bottle on top of all his exertions the day before. A clock had chimed three before he had been calm enough to sleep, and he had been roused at five to head down to the boats to oversee the last construction.

While he was standing around trying to look commanding (and awake), Burgess Chiswick joined him, looking a lot fresher than Alan felt. He did, however, bring a large mug of coffee with him, which Alan appreciated.

"Well, this looks promising, I suppose." Burgess said. "Though I know little about the construction of boats. What are your men doing to those beams?"

"Drilling holes." Alan said. "We're ready, except for the keel pieces to add weight and stability. See the bore holes through the existing keels? We shall bolt these on."

"With what?"

"Pine dowels, slightly oversized and hammered into the boreholes. Like the bung in a beer barrel. Should hold for long enough to get us over to the eastern shore and round the capes." Alan said.

"Metal would be better, would it not?" Burgess asked.

"We found some flat angle-iron forged with holes in it for various uses, and some bolts, but nothing long enough to go all the way from side to side. They'd have to be nine or ten inches long."

"Thought I heard a disturbance upstairs last night. Did the fair Miss Nancy treat you well?" Burgess leered.

"No, she threw me out, along with a shower of glassware and stuff." Alan admitted ruefully. "Twas a bad idea after the ambush."

"Ah, well."

"Shit." Feather spat as the dowel he had shaped splintered as he tried to drive it into the first hole in a beam before lifting it up to fit against the keel member. "This 'ere pine's too light, sir. Even do we get it tamped down wi'out breakin', I wouldn't trust 'em in a seaway."

"What about a musket barrel?" Burgess suggested, kneeling down to look at one of the beams. "There's hunting guns and those French muskets to use. With a vise and a file, we could cut down some lengths to fit into the holes. And then, if some of those bolts are large enough, we could force-thread them down into the barrel bores. That would hold your angle-iron plates on to spread the load if they flex."

"An' iffen the bolts and plates fall off, sir, the musket barrel'd still be snug enough inside ta 'old." Feather smiled, revealing what few teeth he still possessed.

"Well, this isn't going to work." Alan frowned, angry at the delay. "We shall have to give them a try."

Using a piece of string, Feather measured the extreme width of a beam, knotted it carefully, and headed for the barn and carpenter shop to measure off lengths of musket barrel to file off. Queener left off the work with an auger and went with him. He was back in moments with one of the French muskets, trying it in the bore holes already made. With a piece of chalk, he scribed circles inside the marks already made on the shaped beams to show the size of the bore necessary, and dug into the wooden tool box to find an auger with a smaller bit, and to try various bolts until he found some that could be wound down the barrels.

The musket barrels worked well. They were driven down into the holes with mallets until they were flush, and the angle-iron plates were fitted on. Then the bolts were cranked down into the barrels, cutting their own threads in much the same fashion that a weapon was rifled by a worm-borer. After four hours of filing and sawing, drilling and turning, the barges were ready to be put back on the water. They were now as seaworthy as they could be made without starting from scratch in their construction. Borrowing a few soldiers for muscle power, they shoved them back off the X-shaped bow cradles onto the sand and mud, then hauled them into the still waters of the inlet.

"Hurrah, it floats!" Alan exulted as his crew cheered.

Coe and a small crew scrambled into the nearest barge and got to work to pole her out into deeper water where she would truly be floating instead of resting with her lowermost quickwork on the mud.

"Try sailing her while you're out there," Alan ordered. "There's a high tide, and enough water in the cove to see how she handles."

"Aye, sir."

"Thank you for your timely suggestion, Burgess," Alan said to the soldier. "For better or worse, we can do no more. Best start fetching food and whatever down from the barns so we may be ready to sail as soon as it's dark."

"I have never heard a better thing in my life," Burgess said, and trotted back toward the house. Alan turned back to the water and sat on a stump to watch how Coe was doing. The boat had a slight way on her from their last bit of poling as they raised the pair of lug sails. They were cut short but full so as not to overset the boat with too much pressure too high above the deck and her center of gravity. The barge paid off the wind for a while, then began to make her way forward. She heeled over more than Alan liked to see by the light wind in the inlet, but she was sailing. A few more hands to weather should counteract her tendency to heel, he thought, and heavier cargo of provisions and passengers would help.

The boat made a lot of leeway, but as soon as Coe and his men put the leeboards down and they bit into the water, she began to hold her own, no longer sloughing downwind at such an alarming rate.

"Damme if they don't work," he told Feather, who was standing by him. "I shall put you and your man in my report when we rejoin the fleet."

"Queener, sir. Name's Nat Queener," the old man stuck in, taking a pause in his tobacco chewing to nod and speak for himself.

"Well, it was handily done and damned clever work," Alan said.

"Thankee, sir, thankee right kindly." Queener bobbed, tugging at his forelock, or what was left of it, and Alan was struck once more by how little he had known about most of the men—not Coe or this Queener or Cony, wherever the devil he was at this moment, even after all those months on *Desperate*. Queener was too old and frail to play pulley-hauley at fores'ls or halyards, or take a strain on a tackle, too spavined by a hard life at sea to go aloft any longer, but he was a good member of the carpenter's crew and knew two lifetime's worth about boats. The Navy was full of such oldsters, and Alan vowed that he would not overlook their talents or their contributions again if given a chance.

Coe tacked the barge about and came back up the inlet at a goodly clip, the once ungainly barge now behaving like a well-found cutter. He bore up to the prevailing winds to try her close-hauled, but there was not enough width to the inlet, or wind, to judge her behavior. The best that could be said was that the boat was tractable. She would not win an impromptu race from anchorage to stores dock, but she could be sailed safely and would perform like a tired dray horse to get them off the Guinea Neck and out to sea, which was all they asked of her.

Coe finally brought her up to the shallows at the mouth of the creek, handed the sails and raised the leeboards, and let her drive onto the mud and sand in the shallows gently with the last of her forward motion. He and his crew waded ashore wearing smiles like landed conquerors.

"Them sodjers is acomin', Mister Lewrie," Feather said, directing his attention inland to a file of riflemen bearing the first boxes and small kegs of water, cornmeal travel bread, boiled and jerked meat, and the dried powder and ball cartouches.

"Feather, see to loading the boats and then make sure the hands have their dinner," Alan instructed. "We plan to leave on the falling tide around half past four or so while there's still enough water in the inlet to float 'em out easy."

"Aye, aye, sir."

Governour Chiswick was there with the advance party, his face set in what Alan recognized by enforced association as bleak anger. He waved for Alan to join him and stalked a way up the brambled bank of the creek for privacy.

"We have trouble," Chiswick whispered. "That damned Hayley brat is missing. Little bastard took off sometime in the night. So you know where he headed."

"Jesus," Alan said, "how did he get past your guards? I thought you had the neck watched so a mouse couldn't escape?"

"Keep your voice down, damn you," Governour warned. "We don't need to panic your sailors, or my people. And yes, he shouldn't have been able to get through, but he stole a rifleman's tunic and the sentries didn't remark on him strolling right past them. We shall have to get out of here now, before he can bring troops down here from Gloucester Point."

"We could pole out into the marshes by Big Island, but we'd be naked as dammit until the sun went down. There's not cover enough out there for a snake. Night is the best time."

"*Now* is the best time, Alan," Governour insisted. "Unless you want to be killed or captured. After yesterday's ambush, I doubt if anyone is going to offer quarter to us, not if they belong to the same unit as those men we shot down."

"What time did he go, do you think?" Alan said, thinking.

"We think around five this morning, just before first light," Governour explained, impatient to even bother. "One of the sentries on the perimeter thinks he saw someone heading off west, but he thought it was one of our men going to relieve himself. And the sentry who lost his tunic was guarding the house. He got off at four, and took an hour with that Sookie, and when he turned out his coat was gone, so it had to be between four and five."

"Sookie!" Alan gasped. "I'll bet her mistress put her up to that. They must have planned it."

"Of *course* they planned it," Governour fumed.

"He went on foot?" Alan asked.

"Yes. No horses are missing."

"It is two hours up the peninsula, the roads are so bad," Alan speculated. "Say he left at five, so he could not get there before eight in the morning on foot, even if he knew the country. Take an hour to get someone to act and get a party on the roads. If they sent cavalry, they could have gotten here by eleven to start scouting us. Hell, even infantry could have been here by now!"

"Hmm, there is that," Governour said, puffing out his cheeks as he studied his watch. "Tis just gone one in the afternoon."

"There is the possibility he could have come across a snake, or no one believed him," Alan said.

"No, they'd believe him if he got there. I would."

"So where are they, then?" Alan asked.

"Cornwallis is supposed to be surrendering this morning, as are Tarleton and Simcoe on this side of the river. Perhaps they are waiting until the formalities are over before gathering up our little band of stragglers. We hid our true numbers from the brat, damn his blood, so they may not think eighteen or twenty survivors are all that important. A stupid reason, I grant you, but stupider things have happened in war."

"Take this whole damned campaign as a case in point," Alan said. "But, they wouldn't be coming to collect survivors, they'd be coming with blood in their eyes, Governour. We killed six of them yesterday, did we not? Why aren't they here already, howling for revenge?"

"I don't know," Governour admitted, a hard thing for him to do. "We've seen no boats going downriver, so no one has raised the hue and cry yet. Nothing stirring on those French ships blockading the river to the east. Look, once we get the boats loaded, what are the chances of getting out of here?"

"Just like I said last night. Horrible," Alan said. "There's no cover out there in the marshes. Big Island isn't high enough to hide a small dog. We put our bows outside Monday Creek and those French will blow us out of the water with artillery. With this out-flowing tide, we could gain two knots, and the wind is fair enough, but it's also fair for a frigate to run us down north of the Guinea Neck shoals before we could get ten miles."

"We should have left last night," Governour said petulantly.

"In boats that would have capsized without the leeboards and decent keels." Alan sniffed, wondering just how thick in the skull one had to be to wear a red coat and go for a soldier.

"I grow weary of your attitude, you stubborn jack-ass," Governour said. "A couple of years in the navy doesn't make you a genius at nautical matters."

"But it beats what you know of boats by a long chalk." Alan shot right back. "I'm not King Canute, and neither are you, we can't change things to suit. We cannot get away until dark, we've already discussed that. Now, what do we do until then? You tell me, *you're* the bloody soldier! But don't come raw with me."

Oh, shit, he thought. This brute's going to kill me for that, see if he doesn't. But he'll not blame this on me. God, are we fucked for fair. The Rebels an' Frogs are going to come down here and knacker us like sheep. What's the bloody difference, him or them; now or later?

Governour did indeed appear as if murder was on his mind, his face turning purple with anger, and his hands twitching out of control. But after a long minute in which they locked stares and would be damned if either would be the first to look away, Governour spun on his heels and stalked off on his long legs, hands jabbed together in the small of his back, and Alan let out a soft breath of relief that he was still alive.

His relief was short, however, for Governour Chiswick turned just as suddenly and stalked back toward him, and it was all Alan could do to stand his ground without fleeing into the woods.

"You're a know-it-all Captain Sharp, Lewrie," Governour said in a rasp, not a sword's length away from him. "Damn your blood, sir. And damn you for being right. My apologies for rowing at you."

A hand was extended, from which Alan almost flinched until he realized it didn't hold a weapon. They shook hands.

"Sorry I lost my temper as well, Governour," Alan said warmly, his legs almost turning to jelly with surprise.

"Well, until dusk, there's nothing to do but do what soldiers do best," Governour said, smiling as much as he could while still grinding his teeth. "Wait. Take positions in the woods by our preparations and hope for the best."

"And have everything ready for a quick getaway," Alan added.

"If they come, Alan, we shall have no chance of retreat, and damned little of surrender, either, you know?" Governour softened. "I believe we can prevail, but until we see how many troops come, we won't know. I wish to God I could have gotten Burgess away, for my family's sake. The rest of our regiment, what's left of it, is going into Rebel hands this day. I have to save what I can. They're my neighbors, my friends, they trust me . . . oh, damme for a weak puling . . ."

"I have a crew to worry about as well, Governour, men from my own ship," Alan told him. "They're depending on me, too."

"You understand. Good," Governour said. "Good lad."

Maybe not as well as you'd like, Alan thought. I'd like to get the hell out of here with a whole skin, and damn the ones who run too slow. But you can't say that aloud, can you, can't even think it, but have to go all noble and talk of Duty and the King and Honor and be the last arse-hole into the boat. God help me, but He *must* know I'm such a canting hypocrite! If you're dead-serious in what you say, Governour, then you're a hell of a lot better than I'll ever be.

They finished loading the boats and drew them out nearly fifty yards off the mouth of the creek, where there was water deep enough to float them. The North Carolina Volunteers filtered off into the woods with their rifles and cartridge pouches to stand guard, and Alan put his own men on watch as well, drilling them once more on loading and firing the Ferguson rifle, just in case. They ate a late dinner of cold boiled meat and dry cornbread, while over by York-town, the shattered remnants of a once-proud army marched into captivity with their flags cased, dressed in the last finery the quarter-masters had issued instead of letting it be captured still in the crates. They marched drunk and surly, as though by infusions of rum and hot sneers they could belittle the victors. By battalion and regiments, they tramped through a gauntlet of Rebel and French troops to lay down their colors and honor-draped drums, pile their muskets and accoutrements and march away naked and helpless. Lord Corn-wallis pleaded illness and sent his second-in-command to represent him. That officer surrendered his sword to Washington's second-in-command, while a British band of fifers played gay music to lessen the shame.

Alan thought of going back up to the house and giving the Hayley sisters some guineas for what they had taken, but after their deception he could not find the generosity in heart to do so, and was sure that if he did go up to the house, he would most likely be tempted to torch the damned place. Had they just sat there, we'd be away with no one hurt by dusk, but they could not leave well enough alone, and that damned imp, he thought furiously, probably thinks he's a fucking hero!

As the afternoon drew on, he began to feel a lot calmer. There was no sign of the enemy, no movement from any of the ships out in the river to put a landing party ashore or come closer for a peek. He started to think they could get away Scot-free after all.

But then, a little after three, an outlying picket that had been watching the ford onto the neck came drifting back from tree to tree to carry word that there was an enemy force on the Gloucester road.

"How many men?" Governour asked his scout as they held a quick conference in the trees at the eastern end of the tobacco fields near the muddy lane.

"'Bout a dozen hoss, Governour," the thatch-haired private named Hatmaker told him. "Dragoons, some mounted officers. Mebbe forty, fifty foot ahind 'em, all Frenchies, look like. Blue an' yeller, an bearskin shakoes, dressed purty much like the troopers."

"Lauzun's Legion." Governour nodded. "Odd they sent so few. No one behind them?"

"I waited til they wuz past couple minutes afore I cut across country, Governour. Didn't see nobody else."

"We may have a chance after all," Governour smiled wolfishly. "We shall stand and fight. Mark you this, though. We're going to have to kill every last mother-son of them, or word gets out and we'll never have a chance to escape. Mollow, take six riflemen with Mister Lewrie to stiffen his defenses up by the creek. Lewrie, you must cover everything north of the road and around the boats and the creek. Burge, you and Knevet take twelve men and guard behind the *chevaux-de-frise* in the woods a little north of the road and put some snipers along the lane. Don't expose yourself until they charge right on top of you."

"Right, brother," Burgess said, a trifle breathless.

"I shall make a demonstration there, south of the road, and draw them onto me. I shall hold my ground until over-run, but I think I may blunt them and force them to seek a flank to turn to my right, along the road and north of it," Governour said, drawing in the dirt with the tip of his sword-bayonet. "Burge, you'll be my first surprise for them. Lewrie, you shall be my last surprise."

"Aye?" he replied, feeling a trifle dubious a surprise.

"Hold your log redan up there until they pass you, and then fall on *their* flank. Do it from ambush, don't risk your sailors in the open. They're not used to our practice. Hold your ground and don't be drawn unless I send a runner to tell you to advance south toward the road. If you don't hear from me direct, hold your ground and keep the boats safe."

"Let 'em get stuck into you and then kick 'em up the arse?" He said through dry lips. "I can do that."

"Don't fire too soon, or they get away. And if there are more of them behind this bunch, they may come your way to flank us even wider. Trust Mollow, he's a veteran at this. If I have to break, we shall fall back on you. Wait for us as long as you can, then get your people out of it."

"Aye, Governour," Alan agreed.

"In any case, wait no more than ten minutes after we have opened fire, and it should be over one way or another," Governour concluded.

"The hell with that," Alan told him, shaky but determined. "We're in this together. If we fall back on the boats, we'll just be grand targets splashing through the shallows. Might as well stand or fall on land, dammit to hell."

"Well said, sailor," Governour said, taking his hand and giving him a farewell shake. "Now let's take our positions before they see us."

Alan did not know what to expect once he got back to his hastily made positions up by the creek. Would the enemy come with drums and fifes like the Rebels that had marched into the parallels facing the Yorktown entrenchments, or would they come filtering through the woods like so many painted savages? He could see no sign of them as yet, and was dying of curiosity. He told his men they would have to stand their ground just like guarding their bulwarks against boarders, gave them a short pep talk, which he did not much believe even as he said it, and knelt down by Mollow and another rifleman to wait out of sight.

About fifteen minutes later, a lone horseman came out of the trees on the far side of the tobacco fields on the road, about four hundred yards away, a fine figure in horizon blue and yellow on a splendid mount. He sat and studied the ground before him for a long moment, before three other riders cantered up to hold a short conference with him. Even at that distance, Alan could see that two were also Lauzun's Legion officers in their hussar shakoes and the third wore blue and white with a tricorne.

The riders stiffened in their saddles and pointed across the brown fields of neglected tobacco plants as Governour's men stepped out of cover south of Alan's vantage.

"Are they deranged to expose themselves like that?" Alan asked.

"Dem'stration," the private next to him said, spitting a dollop of tobacco juice on the rotting log in front of him and wiping his lips. "Same's bait, they is. Hey, here's yer Frogs."

A body of cavalry appeared on the road, cantered past the officers and formed a single line abreast on either side of the muddy road, while one officer joined them. A second Legion officer walked his mount over to take position with a company of infantry that appeared behind the cavalry, these men in horizon blue tunics with yellow facings, white breeches and gaiters and tall bearskin shakoes. They were four abreast as they wheeled south, halted once in the middle of the tobacco field, faced east and formed two ranks facing the North Carolina riflemen. To their flank, the cavalrymen drew their heavy sabers and flourished them in the late afternoon sun with appallingly good precision.

"Heh, Governour's a puttin' on a show fer 'em." The private chuckled.

"Hatmaker, get yer fuckin' haid down," Mollow told him.

Governour had twelve men in a single rank, impossible odds even if they were riflemen, perhaps two hundred yards away from the waiting enemy ranks. As Alan watched, they went through a drill that Alan did not think such informal troops knew, while Governour stood to one end and called orders that wafted to his ears.

"Poise firelocks!"

"Like musket men." Alan understood.

"Half cock firelocks! Handle cartridge!" Governour called, while a corporal beat the time with what seemed a half spontoon. "Prime pans!"

"They'll think they're reg'lars," Mollow snickered. "Fooled more'n a few that way. Stupid bastards."

"Shut pans! Charge with cartridge!"

The dozen men were pretending at that long range to load from the muzzle with cartridge, though their rifles were already loaded and ready to fire. At the word of command, they seemed to ply rammers, which were really their cleaning rods, and tamp down cartouches, returning the rammers and coming to attention once more at the command "shoulder firelocks," ordering arms and affixing bayonets, the long sword-bayonets which should have given the game away. But the foe still stood and watched as though mesmerized.

"Why don't they just charge them?" Alan whispered.

"*Honor.*" Mollow spat, as though it was a dirty word.

Only when they had finished their evolutions did the senior Legion officer ride out from his lines to converse with Governour. They saluted each other punctiliously, their words unheard from a distance but obviously couched in tortured and convoluted syntax of two gentlemen expressing the highest respect and admiration for each other, no matter what they really thought of each other. The Frog was removing his shako and bowing from the waist, making a beckoning gesture as though he were granting permission to fire first to Governour, and Governour gave his own back, removing his wide-brimmed campaign hat and sweeping it across his chest, making a gesture to the waiting French troops in turn.

The Frenchman finally spurred his horse about and rode back to his men. He called out once more in a loud voice, and Alan could understand the last offer to surrender peaceably, which Governour spurned.

"Poise firelocks!" Governour called, unshouldering his own piece. "Take aim!"

The French troops at a word of command began to advance slowly, their muskets held out before them with the butts by their thighs and the muzzles up, with the bayonets glinting sharp silver. They were getting into decent musket range, for by firing at one hundred yards one could fire at the moon and achieve just as much good.

"Fire!" Governor shouted, bringing his arm down in an arc.

The rifles cracked, and ten men in the front rank of the French troops were punched backwards into their fellows by the weight of .65 caliber balls. Their own volley came a moment later as they halted and brought their weapons up to fire, but Alan was delighted to see that the Volunteers had knelt down to reload, no longer playing the stiff regular musketeer, and the volley mostly went over their heads.

The cavalry, though, as though spurred into motion by the first noise of battle, lurched forward, their mounts hunkering their hindquarters down and the sabers sweeping off the shoulders to point at the Volunteers, blades held upside down and point slightly down at the charge.

Governour gave the infantry one more volley from a kneeling position, and then faded away back into the pines behind the zigzag fences as the spent powder smoke from his firing formed almost a solid wall through which his men went invisible. But the cavalry was almost upon them, out to one side and swinging in to jump those fences. The cavalrymen whooped and screamed, eager to put sword to the foe and show the dazed infantry who was the better fighter. In a torrent of Gaelic, Polish, German or French, they came on like a tidal wave.

"Should we . . ." Alan began.

"Nah, Burgess'll be makin' his move 'bout now." Mollow laughed.

"But . . ." The infantry had fired the second rank volley into nothing, and then they came on at the charge themselves, now that they had an enemy on the run, wanting to be in at the kill before the cavalry earned all the honors. The mounted officer with them loped alongside them, waving his sword over his head and urging them on.

"Looky thar!" Hatmaker, the private soldier, called out over the sound of battle. "More o' the shits."

"Thort they wuzn't ta come down hyar 'thout they brung a whole passel of 'em," Mollow said, pointing out the second company of troops that was emerging on the road, led by the third officer in blue and white with the tricorne hat. "Virginia Militia, looks like."

They were an outlandish looking bunch of soldiers, some dressed in purplish long-fringed hunting shirts, some in castoff blue and white tunics over a variety of civilian breeches and waistcoats, some in gray or tan tunics without facings. They formed well enough, though, and came on at a trot, four columns abreast with ten men in each file, jogging forward to the north of the road through the tobacco plants as though they meant to flank the fighting and skirmish through the woods, swinging wide of the cavalry.

The change in sound from the south got Alan's attention and he turned his head to see the first cavalrymen spur their horses and soar up and over those fences. The roars of challenge changed to shrill and womanish screams as they came down on the double row of *chevaux-de-frise* that had been hidden in the shadows. Mounts neighed in pain and terror as they skewered themselves on the sharp wood spikes. Those cavalry that had been balked and were milling about in front of the fence suddenly came under fire from Burgess and his men, and gaudily dressed troopers were spilled from their saddles, their useless sabers spinning in the air.

There was time for Governour to get off a volley as well, directly in the face of the charging infantry, punching their officer off his horse before they faded back into the woods for the first of their lines of rifle pits, bringing the French charge to a sudden halt as half a dozen more of their men were smashed down. They stopped to reload, and the quicker-loading and quicker-firing snipers in the woods knocked down more of them before they could raise their weapons to return fire.

"Should we stand ready for this bunch?" Alan asked as the militia seemed to trot forward on a beeline for their own low dead-fall log ramparts.

"Lie down an' keep quiet, now, but do ya be ready ta rise up an' give 'em a volley when I give ya the word," Corporal Knevet ordered, calm as a man in church.

"Steady, men," Alan seconded him, crawling along his line of sailors, who clutched their borrowed rifles with white-knuckled hands. "You can get off two volleys to their one if you're steady. They can't face that. We're going to give it to them point-blank and run their ragged arses all the way back to Gloucester Point."

And I wouldn't believe me for a second, he thought fearfully.

"On, boys, we got the bastards skinned!" the militia officer was encouraging his panting soldiers. He was off his horse, having left it in the rear, a heavyset, sweating man in a too-small uniform wrapped with a large red sash of command, with a gaudy bullion epaulette on each shoulder like a general, far above his true rank. Alan peered out from a gap between two of the mossy dead-fall logs as they came on, swishing through the weeds and the dried leaves of tobacco, their accoutrements jangling and thumping on their bodies, musket butts knocking against each other as they jogged shoulder to shoulder for comradely support.

"Now?" Alan asked Mollow.

"Not yit, be quiet, young'un," Mollow cautioned. "They's swingin' off ta our left. Let 'em get in real close fuhst."

"Ware them logs thar!" someone yelled to their front.

"Shit," Corporal Knevet groaned, realizing they had been spotted. "Stand to! Take aim . . . fire!"

They stood up from behind their barriers, to find the militia company not thirty yards away, turned slightly oblique to them and stumbling to a halt at the sight of their weapons. The volley was a blow to the heart, right in their astonished faces, a ragged crackling of shots that took the front rank and the nearest column of files down, so close Alan could see the blood fly from the nearest men struck.

"Load!" Alan cried, not knowing where his first shot had gone. His hands seemed to have plans of their own as he cranked the breech of the Ferguson open, flipped up the pan cover and dug into the pouch at his side for a fresh cartridge to rip open with his teeth.

"Face left!" The officer was screaming, waving a huge straight sword and shoving numb survivors of that fatal volley off to his left to lead out the unharmed files. "Form two ranks!"

Mollow, Knevet, Hatmaker and the other soldiers got off another volley as they shambled into order, quickly followed by Alan and his men, who were less familiar and comfortable with the rifles. Alan saw some of his sailors grounding their rifles to begin the process of loading from the muzzle, as they had been trained on the Brown Bess muskets aboard the ship, before coming to their senses, or being swatted by a senior hand.

More enemy soldiers were being laid out on the ground, groaning and crying in terror as they were hit.

"Front rank, kneel! Take aim . . . fire!" the militia officer yelled.

They got off a volley, and at that close range it was deadly, no matter that half the militiamen had not even bothered to do more than stick their muzzles in the right direction. Volunteers and sailors shrieked in agony as they were smacked down behind the log barrier, which suddenly seemed to be about knee high instead of waist deep.

"Charge 'em!" the officer screamed.

"Fire when ready!" Alan screamed back, trying to be heard over all the noise. Rifles cracked, his own slamming back into his shoulder and the white-bearded older man who had been running at him was struck on the breastbone and was slammed backwards as though jerked on a rope to drop to the ground with his heels flying in the air.

"Better fall back ta the boats," Knevet suggested.

"Once my boys run, there's no stoppin' 'em," Alan shouted right into his face. The enemy charge was coming forward, bayonets pointing for them big as plough shares and shining wickedly.

The men were fumbling at the loading and firing of their Fergusons, hands trembling like fresh killed cocks at the sight of the enemy at the charge. If they waited to get off a last volley, they would be all over them, and he was still outnumbered.

"Boarders!" Alan howled, drawing his pair of dragoon pistols and dropping the Ferguson. "Away boarders! Take 'em, Desperates!"

Alan brought up the first pistol in his right hand, aimed and lit off the charge as his men began to surge forward over the barrier to meet the militiamen. He did not hear the explosion, but a ragged man with a half spontoon leveled like a pike spouted a scarlet bloom below his chin.

Alan dropped the spent pistol and transferred the other to his right hand. He fired, and a soldier in dirty blue and white almost up to the barrier gave a great silent scream and his waistcoat turned red over one lung.

Then Alan was over the barrier himself, cutlass in his right hand and one of his own pistols in his left. A bayonet lunged for him, and he nicked his blade into the wood of the forestock, shoving it out of the way, then slashed back to his right, inside the soldier's guard. He sank his cutlass into flesh and bone on the man's right arm, knocking him down to the dust and the weeds, chopped downward again and laid his opponent's face open. Another man was close, and Alan brought up his pistol and fired. There was a soft pop, but that man's face writhed in terror and he dropped away, clutching at his stomach and droppping the musket that had been near to taking Alan in the chest.

There was a lot of screaming going on, but he heard little of it, for he moved in an unreal fog, a swirling, shifting kaleidoscope of colors through which he waded. Grays and blues and tans, flesh and blood, dark wood and bright metal. He discharged his last pistol somewhere along the way and had no idea where the ball went, found his dirk in one hand and the cutlass in the other as he slipped in under someone's guard and took the man in the abdomen. He was in among the trampled and broken dry tobacco plants, slashing about as though he was cutting a path through them to get at the enemy.

He came face to face with the sweaty, obese enemy officer with the glittering epaulettes, his hat gone and his eyes huge with fear and shock. The man brought up that heavy straight sword, big as a Scottish claymore, but Alan smashed it aside as easily as a feather and the man opened his mouth to scream before he turned to flee, dropping his sword in fright.

Alan seemed to float forward like some vengeful Greek god masquerading as a man in the *Iliad* under the walls of Troy; he brought down that heavy cutlass blade and cut the officer's back open, tumbling him into the dirt and mud of the field between the tobacco rows, brought it down again and almost severed the head from the shoulders, hacked on the body until he began to hear things beside the ringing in his ears.

"Load up!" someone was ordering. "Load 'an face the road!"

Mollow was at his side, fending off his bloody cutlass with his rifle stock as Alan thought him another foe to deal with. "Hold on, thar, boy! Git yerself a rifle, an' we're gonna do some hawg-killin'!"

The closest weapons Alan could find were militia muskets, and he did not have the right caliber ball for them. He searched back and forth across the fields until he came across the soldier Hatmaker, who had been shot in the chest and would no longer need his rifle.

"Form ranks, form two ranks!" Knevet was shouting, manhandling stunned sailors and surviving riflemen into some sort of order. There seemed too few to be credited. "Spread out, ten foot apart! Load up an' stand by ta fire!"

Alan loaded Hatmaker's rifle, wiping the blood from the breech and stock as he did so. He looked up to see French soldiers from Lauzun's Legion stumble from the woods south of the road, along with a few men from the militia company who had run off from the fighting and had gotten mixed in with them. Cavalrymen in shakoes, sabers abandoned and bearing short musketoons and dragoon pistols, infantry in bearskin headresses with muskets, a wounded officer with a sword in hand being helped along by his orderly. There seemed too damned few of them to be credited, either. As he watched they turned to fire back into the woods from which they came, then spun about to continue running.

"First rank . . . fire!" Knevet called, and six or seven rifles made a harsh sound, spewing out a thick cloud of powder. "Reload! Second rank . . . fire!"

This time, Alan aimed and fired, his hands so weak that he could have just as easily hit either the ground at his feet or the bay beyond. A third volley sounded from the woods by the zigzag fences as Governour, Burgess and their survivors came into sight, and they had the French and Rebels caught in an L-shaped killing ground, just about one hundred yards away, too far for accurate musket fire even for steady men, but as Governour had predicted, close enough to do terrible practice with Fergusons. The enemy melted away, spun off their feet to fall like limp rags.

"Kill 'em! Kill 'em all, goddammit!" someone ordered.

"Close 'em!" Knevet said, and the two ragged ranks began to walk forward, angling right to keep up with the fleeing foe as they finally broke and fled. There were not a dozen left on their feet, then eight; another volley and there were three, a few scattered shots and there were none left standing, only the writhing wounded crying out for quarter as the soldiers walked among them with their bayonet blades prodding at the dead.

Wanting no part of such a gruesome activity, Alan sank to his knees and concentrated on drawing breath into his lungs. He felt as though he had run a mile, and every limb of his body ached as though he had carried something heavy as he had done so.

"Ye hurt?" Mollow asked him, kneeling down by him.

"No, I don't think so," Alan panted. "You?"

"Cut're two, nothin' much." Mollow grimaced. He swung his

canteen around from his hip and took a swallow, then offered it to Alan, who half drained it before handing it back reluctantly.

"Bastards worn't ready fer this kinda fightin'," Mollow commented. "Bet them Lauzun boys thort they'd tangled with red Injuns back in them woods. Them Virginia Militia put up a good fight fer a minute thar, though."

Alan got to his feet and looked back to the north. He could follow the trail of the fighting through the tobacco fields where plants had been knocked flat by struggling, falling men, like a swath left by a reaper. And the swath was littered with bodies all the way back to the log barrier, bodies spilled on the ground like bundles of clothing empty of the men who had worn them, looking sunk into the ground in ungainly postures, a few squirming back and forth in pain still.

"God Almighty in Heaven," Alan muttered in shock.

"Purty bad, wuhst iver I seen, an' I seen me some fightin'." Mollow went on as they walked stiff legged back toward the north. "You an' yer Navy boys stand killin' better'n most, I'll 'low ya that. Whoo, all them cutlasses aswangin' an' them sailors ayellin' and stampin' fit ta bust, like ta curdled my jizzum!"

"Is fighting on land always like this?" Alan gaped in awe.

"Naw, mos' times hit's almost civilized."

There was Hatmaker, curled up like a singed worm, his yellow hair muddied and his eyes staring at a beetle that crawled under his nose. A sailor was next, struck in the belly, flat on his back with his shirt up to reveal the huge purple bruise and bullet hole that he had clutched before he bled to death through the exit wound in his back. Nearer the logs there was Feather, the stubborn quartermaster's mate, sprawled across the body of a Virginia militiaman, a musket bayonet still in his chest and the musket sagged to the ground like a fallen mast.

And there was old Nat Queener that Coe was trying to help, shot through the body and feebly fluttering his hands over his slashed belly, life draining from him as Alan watched. He knelt down next to him and the old man turned his face to him. "We done good, didn't we, Mister Lewrie?"

"Aye, we did, Mister Queener," Alan told him, tears coming to his eyes at the sight of him. He wasn't long for the world with a wound like that. "Anyone you want to know about you being hurt?"

"Ain't nobody back home, I outlived 'em all, Mister Lewrie. Mebbe 'Chips' an' a few o' me mates in *Desperate,* iffen they made it."

"I'm so damned sorry, Queener." Alan shuddered.

"Don' ya take on so, sir. Hands'll be lookin' ta ya. Aw, I'd admire me somethin' wet afore I go, Coe. Got anythin'?"

Coe lifted up a small leather bottle of rum and Queener gulped at it greedily.

Alan got to his feet, hearing Queener give a groan and the last breath rattling in his throat.

"'E's gone, sir," Coe said. "'E were a good shipmate."

"Aye, he was. How many dead and wounded from our people?"

"Dunno, sir."

"Find out and give me a list, Coe. You're senior hand, now."

"Aye, aye, sir."

Alan wandered off to pick his way across the field, to retrieve his dropped pistols, the dragoon pistols, and to gather up the Ferguson he had discarded at the barrier. He ran across Governour, limping from a sword cut on his leg that was already bound up.

"Hard fight," Governour said matter-of-factly. "But we got 'em all. No one to tell the tale back up at Gloucester Point, so we should be able to get away. It's after four. Once we make the worst wounded comfortable, we should think of being on our way."

"What about the dead?" Alan demanded, suddenly angry that the officer was so callous.

"Have to leave 'em where they lay." Governour shrugged. "We'll put the worst hurt up at the house where the Hayleys and their slaves can care for 'em. They'll send for surgeons. We can't care for them."

"Goddamn you!" Alan shouted, whirling on him.

"Would you rather that was us?" Governour said with a sad smile, pointing to the nearest mutilated dead. "Grow up, for God's sake, Lewrie. Get the names of the dead to leave with the Hayley family. Maybe they'll put something up over their graves, I don't know, but that's all you can do after something like this. You're a Navy officer, or the nearest thing we have to one right now. Act like one."

They laid out their own dead with as much dignity as they

could. Of the thirty soldiers and officers from the Volunteers, there were eighteen dead or so badly wounded they would have to be left behind. Of the eighteen sailors and petty officers, only nine would be leaving on the boats. Of the French and Rebel militia, there were not twenty men left alive from the nearly hundred who had come to take them.

Alan copied out his list of dead and badly wounded, then went up to the house, where Mrs. Hayley and her sister Nancy waited on the porch by the back terrace, aghast at the carnage, tears flowing down their faces at the horror that had come to their peaceful farm.

"Mrs. Hayley, Miss Ledbetter," Alan said, doffing his hat to them. "We are leaving soon. I have here a list of the people we left behind in your care, and the names of the dead. I trust in your Christian generosity to tend to them as gently as possible."

"Yes, yes we shall," Mrs. Hayley managed, stunned.

"I was going to give you some guineas, to pay for what we had to requisition, but I would admire if you used it instead to pay the surgeon who comes and perhaps to put up a small marker for our dead, along with the militiamen and French who died here today."

"That is good of you, sir," Mrs. Hayley whispered. "I . . ."

"This was a pointless, useless battle that no one'll remember in a year, most like," Alan went on coldly. "Had we gotten clean away, none of these poor men would have died. It solved nothing, it meant nothing."

"I'm sorry!" Mrs. Hayley wailed, no longer able to bear his words of reproach, knowing full well that she had given her son her consent to carry word down the Neck, scheming happily to get him away unseen so he could play a hero's part and she could be a patriot as well, never having seen the cost of patriotism firsthand.

"What happened to Rodney?" Nancy asked, her face ashen.

"I have no idea, nor do I particularly care," Alan said. "He may be safe up the Neck, or he may lie dead out in the fields or woods. Tis all one to me. He brought it on himself if he was hurt or killed."

"You're a brutal young man, sir." Nancy wept, clutching the small bag of coins he offered her along with the paper. "How can you go through life so uncaring about others?"

"Think on this, Mistress Ledbetter," Alan said. "You and your scheming and spying killed nigh on an hundred men, maybe killed your own nephew, too. How brutal were you, my dear? Would you have wept a tear on my corpse? I doubt it. You'd have bedded me if you thought there was anything more to gain by it, all to bring this about. How can you live with yourself, I ask you, instead? Good-bye, Mistress Ledbetter."

He turned to go, but she clutched at his sleeve. "Forgive us!" she pleaded. "We did not know. . ."

"Take it up with God. He's better at forgiveness than I am."

So saying, Alan made his way down to the boat landing, stopping to give what cheer he could to the wounded sailors and those soldiers he recognized in one of the slave huts where they had been installed to heal or die as God willed.

He got down to the boats, where the small party waited to board for the escape across the bay. The tide was running out rapidly now, and the sun was almost gone. The barges twitched at the end of their painters as the inlet emptied with the outrush to the sea. They floated high instead of canting over with their keels in the tidal flats.

"Coe, take charge of the first boat." He ordered his senior hand. "Corporal Knevet, better get your party aboard with Coe, here."

"Yes, sir," Knevet replied, wading out to the boat with the sailors.

Sir, Alan thought. The bastard actually called me "sir"!

There was a sharp pop up the creek, which had everyone diving for their rifles and a spot of cover from which to fire, but after a moment Governour and Burgess came out of the gloomy thickets to join them, the heavy dragoon pistol in Governour's hand still smoking.

"What was that?" Alan asked.

"Nothing much," Governour replied. "We ready to depart?"

"Aye. Burgess?"

Burgess wore a bandage about his head and one arm was in a sling, but he shouldered past Alan to splash out into the shallows without one word, tears running down his face.

"Let's go, then," Governour said.

There was no need to pole or row out of the inlet, for the wind was out of the southeast, so once past the mouth of the narrow inlet, with the lug sails set, they could wear up on the wind to beat through the pass at Monday Creek and get out into the bay far above the watching frigates in the mouth of the York. With the leeboards down in deep water, they were making a goodly clip, lost in the first of the night, dark sails and tarred hulls indistinguishable from the almost moonless waters.

"We want to keep a heading east nor'east, Burgess," Alan told the soldier, who was seated in his boat. "Keep an eye on the compass for me."

"Yes, I will," Burgess snuffled.

"What happened back there?" Alan asked, leaning close.

"God save us, it was George all over again," Burgess said with a catch in his voice as he tried to mutter too soft to be overheard.

"George? Oh, your younger brother? What was?"

"We caught that Hayley brat," Burgess told him. "Governour said he owed him a debt of blood, and he shot him in the belly, so he'd take days dying. We left him out there in the brambles, out of sight."

Alan waited for a sense of shock, but his nerves were about out of the ability to be shocked by much of anything after all he had seen or done. He pondered how he felt about this revelation.

"Oh? Good," Alan finally said, "serves the little bugger right."

"God, Alan!" Burgess shuddered. "That makes us no better than the bastard who killed George. What does it matter, anyway? We've lost the army, mayhap lost the whole damned war here in the Chesapeake. All we had left was our honor, and now that's gone, too. What's a gentleman without his honor?"

"Alive," Alan told him evenly. "And, if he's not caught with his breeches down or the weapon in his hand, he is still a gentleman to everyone else. I'd have shot the little shit-sack myself if I'd run across him first. Now you and Governour have these men to look after, and your family down in Wilmington to worry about. Forget it."

"I'll never."

"Hard times'd make a rat eat red onions," Alan quoted back to him. "You do what you have to. This war has all cost us most of our decency, and it's not through with us yet. Like our sailing master says, the more you cry, the less you'll piss. Buck up and swear you'll never do it again, but it's done, and it wasn't your hand done it. Governour's still your brother. Worry about how he's dealing with it."

"You're trying to make me feel *good* about it?" Burgess marveled.

"Let me know when you do." Alan grinned in the dark. "Now keep an eye on that compass. There's just enough moon to steer by. What's our heading?"

"Um . . . just a touch north of east."

Alan looked to the eastern horizon above them and found a star to steer by, swung the tiller slightly until he was on a close reach to the southeast breeze and leaned back, blanking his mind to what Burgess had just told him, blanking his mind to everything except getting across the bay before sunrise.

CHAPTER 14

"**S**O you made it out past Cape Charles on the night of the twenty-first, sheltered on Curtis Island, coasted to Chingoteag the next night and were finally picked up by the brig *Dandelion* on the twenty-fourth," Admiral Hood's flag captain said after reading the report before him.

"Aye, sir," Alan replied.

The flag captain looked up from the written account that Alan had penned once ferried over to the *Barfleur*. It was an amazing document of raw courage, unbelievable bravery and clever extemporizing to make the river barges seaworthy. Had there not been corroborating reports from the Loyalist Volunteer officers and the surviving seamen's testimony, the captain would have dismissed it as the work of a fabulist, much on a par with the adventures of a Munchausen.

He studied the young man that stood before his desk, swaying easy to the motion of the flagship. The flag captain was of the common opinion that the finest intelligence, the best character and the most courage were usually found in the most attractive physical specimens, and he found nothing to dissuade this opinion in Midshipman Lewrie. The uniform was stained and faded, but that did not signify; the lad's hair was neat and clean, shorter than the usual mode and not roached back into such a severe style, the queue short and tied with a black silk ribbon, a pleasant light brown touched blonde where the sun reached it from long service in tropic sun-

321

shine. The face was not too horsey and long, regular in appearance, the jaw not too prominent, but it was a firm jaw. The skin was tanned by sea service, and in the dim cabins, with only swaying lamps for illumination, the face was relaxed from the permanent squint sailors developed, showing the whitish chalk marks of frown lines and wrinkles to-be in later years, held so squinted the sun could not stain them as it did the rest of the skin. And the eyes, which at first the captain believed to be aristocratic gray, now seemed more pale blue, of a most penetrating and arresting nature, windows to the restless soul within.

Had he not been in King's uniform, he would have dismissed him as one of those pretty lads more given to the theatres and low amusements of the city, almost too pretty, except for that pale scar on the cheek. As for the rest of him, the shoulders were broad without being common, and he was slim, well knit and wiry; the waist and hips were narrow, showing a good leg in breeches and stockings, instead of being beef to the heel like a gunner's mate or a representative of the lower orders. Could have been a courtier, but he gave off the redolence of a tarpaulin man.

"Hate to say so, but this report shall have to be redone," the captain said with a rueful grin that was not unkindly. "It's one thing to state the facts, but all these... adjectives and adverbs and what you may call 'ems, my word. And one does not make recommendations as to rewards for army officers, or suggestions on adopting Ferguson rifles for the Sea Service and all, you see?"

"I do, sir," Alan replied evenly, showing no fatigue or disappointment at this news. It was all one to him, tired as he was.

"The main thing is to be professional in tone, no emotions at all. Wouldn't want your contemporaries to think you were glory hunting. And none of this 'it is my sad and inconsolable duty to report' that so and so passed over', d'ya see? Tone it down and list the dead and wounded later, preceded by the phrase, 'as per margin.'"

"I list them in the margin, sir?" Alan wondered.

"No, but that is the form most preferred by Mr. Phillip Stephens, the First Secretary to the Admiralty. But you cannot address it to him, as you did, but to your captain or commanding officer."

"Forgive me my ignorance, sir, but I have never had cause to write a report on anything before, even when in temporary command of a prize."

"Well, such a report as yours shall cause a good stir back home, and in the *Chronicle*, I am sure, soon after, so one must adhere to the forms. I'll lend you my secretary to aid you in couching it in the proper manner, but it must be redone before I may pass it on to the admiral or post it to London."

"Aye, sir."

Admiral Hood entered the cabins at that moment, on his way aft to his own quarters under *Barfleur's* poop. Alan recognized him from Antigua and felt such a surge of loathing arise after witnessing the inexplicable behavior of a man with a reputation as a fighting admiral that he felt he had to bite his tongue to control his features.

"See me soon as you're through with your miscreant, sir," Hood told his flag captain.

"Not a miscreant, sir, this is Lewrie, the one in charge of those barges we picked up today."

"Ah," Hood said, peering down at him over that beaky nose from his superior height. Alan was five and three-quarter feet tall, and he was having trouble finding headroom between the beams, even here in flag country, and Hood had to stoop to even walk, yet he gave the impression of great height in spite of the nearness of the overhead. "Met you once, I think."

"At Admiral Sir Onsley Matthews' farewell ball on Antigua, sir."

"Oh, that's it. This your report?"

"Needs rewriting, sir, as I was telling him."

"Hmm," Hood said, rubbing his nose as he leaned closer to one of the swaying lamps to peruse the document. "Yes, I dare say it does need a large dose of Navalese. Still, quite an adventure."

"Aye, sir," Alan replied, too upset to worry about toadying for once. He wanted to blurt out a question of why Hood had hung back at the Battle of the Chesapeake, wanted to demand why they had not come to rescue the army, which had resulted in so much misery.

"Welcome back to the Fleet, Lewrie," Hood said, tossing the draft of the report down and walking off aft.

"Well, do your best with this," the flag captain said.

"Aye, sir. Er, excuse me, sir, but would you happen to know if the *Desperate* frigate made it out as well, or what happened to her?"

"Oh, yes, she was your ship." The captain frowned. "Off to New York for a quick refit, but she made it."

"I would wish to get back aboard as soon as I could, sir."

"Yes, quite understandable." The captain frowned again, as though there were something wrong. "Well, that's all for now, Lewrie. Have that report back to me before the forenoon watch tomorrow."

"Aye, aye, sir."

"I'm free now, sir," the flag captain told Hood in the admiral's day cabin after tidying up the last of the paperwork necessary for the proper nautical administration of fourteen sail of the line and all their artillery, men and officers, their provisioning and discipline.

"Good," Hood said, seated at ease behind his desk. "Before I forget, make a note regarding that young man, what was his name?"

"Lewrie, sir?"

"Yes. Seems a promising sort, did he not strike you so?" Hood asked.

"A most promising young man, sir, indeed," the flag captain said with a pleased expression, gratified that he was such a discerning judge of his fellow man that even Admiral Samuel Hood agreed with his opinion.

Near the end of the month Alan reported back aboard *Desperate*.

He was free of the Chiswicks, free of the land once more, back in the dubious bosom of the Navy for good and all, reporting back aboard his own ship to a sea of familiar faces. Railsford was there to welcome him, pumping his paw heartily. Peck, the marine officer, Mister Monk the sailing master, Coke the bosun and his mates Weems and Toliver, Knatchbull and Sitwell and Hogan 1 from the fo'c'sle guns, Hogan 2 from the loblolly boys, Tuckett and Cony laughing and waving at him, Dr. Dorne and the purser Mister Cheatham making shines over his reappearance. Even David Avery was there once he had gotten below, to clasp him to him as though he had arisen from the dead.

"Lord, what a pack of iron!" David laughed, offering him a glass of Black Strap as Alan unpacked his canvas seabag of the pair of dragoon pistols, his own smaller pistols, cutlass and all the tools that went along with the weapons, including bullet molds for the odd calibers.

"And all of it damned useful at one time or another," Alan told his friend. "How the hell did you escape Yorktown?"

"When the storm blew up, I was washed downriver and thumped into the ship just before she cut her cables. They threw down a line and we got towed out into the bay," David related. "Spent the night bouncing on the waves and the wake like a chariot being drawn by Poseidon's horses. Did you see anything of Carey?"

"Only at the boat landing before my last trip." Alan sighed. "I suppose he's a prisoner by now, if he lived."

"Yes, the sloop *Bonetta* came in bringing word from Cornwallis and a list of those taken. Him and Forrester, both. The captain was mighty upset about that. I saw Forrester. He was part of the *Bonetta's* crew."

"Paroled?" Alan asked.

"On his word of honor to return to the Chesapeake. He came for his chest, and Carey's, so at least we know the little chub's alive. It was odd, but hate him as much as I did, I felt sorry for Francis at the end."

"He'll be exchanged soon enough, if he gave parole. And he'll be home sooner than us," Alan said. Giving one's parole allowed one to be swapped for an officer or supernumary of equal rank from the other side's prison hulks, but one had to swear to no longer bear arms in the current conflict, which would remove one from service until some sort of peace treaty was signed. With rumors flying that England could not get together another decent regiment to fight in the Colonies, much less one more army of the strength of Cornwallis's force, a peace was expected to be negotiated. There were also rumors flying that the Lord North government would soon be voted out, and a more accommodating prime minister installed intent on ending the war.

"Where's McGregor?" Alan asked, seeing that both master's mates' dog boxes were standing empty.

"Left behind. Where's Feather?" David said.

"Dead," Alan told him. He stripped off his filthy uniform and called for Freeling, who appeared after an insolently long time. "Get me a bucket of seawater to scrub up with, Freeling."

"Goona make ha mess, zur, an' them decks jus' scrubbed thees mornin', they wuz," Freeling said dolefully.

"Freeling, you'll do what I tell you soon as dammit, or I'll have a new steward down here and you'll be hauling on the halyards with the other idlers and waisters. That's after you've been up for punishment and gotten two dozen for insubordination, so move your stubborn arse and do it!" Alan said in a rush. Freeling took a look at him, felt the subtle difference in their prodigal midshipman and stumbled away to perform his lowly duty without another word, knowing his game of truculent behavior was over.

"Damme, how did you do that?" Avery gawped.

"Life's too short to put up with his insolence," Alan snapped, opening his chest. He dug out fresh linen, a clean uniform, and took the time to reach down and feel the bundle of gold to reassure himself it was still there.

"What happened to you?" Avery asked, intent on this miracle. "By God, I thought you were turning hard before you got left behind, but now you seem . . . I don't know, even more so."

"I feel I've spent the last few days in hell, David," Alan confessed. As he scrubbed up and dressed in a fresh uniform, he related his recent experiences to an open-mouthed David Avery, who found it hard to credit that anyone could live through them and still have any shred of sanity or decency left to him.

"Much as I thought I despised the Navy, David, it's a walk in a sunny park compared to land service. By God, I'll be glad to leave war behind me forever, should I live to be paid off, even as a two-a-penny midshipman with no prospects. I'll find something to do. I am just so glad to be back aboard *Desperate*, where my friends are."

"Don't be too glad," David warned him. "There's talk about her."

"What talk?"

"About being the only ship to escape before the surrender."

"Talk from who, these canting whip-jacks, these imitation tars, who found an hundred excuses to stay in New York instead of sailing to fight de Grasse one more time?" Alan sneered. "By God, it was one hell of a piece of ship-handling to get her downriver and through the shoals and the blockade in that storm, even if she did almost drown me. What did this pack of poltroons do, I ask you? Wrung their hands and said it was too bad. Let's wait for Digby and his three ships of the line. Let's throw dinners and balls and parades for His Royal Highness Prince William Henry. Hey, wasn't Virginia to be his personal royal colony? Let's not sail until all the powder's been replaced, everything Bristol Fashion from keelson to truck! God, I'm sick of the lot of 'em!"

Alan had knocked back his third glass of Black Strap, and the lack of sleep and adequate rations were playing hob with his senses. He was on his way to a good argumentative drunk.

"Even though Captain Treghues had written permission from Captain Symonds to try to break out, the impression is that we ran out on everyone back there," David said, feeling little pain, either. "There's nothing official."

"Aye, back-biting never is," Alan agreed vehemently. "Bastards!"

"Passing the word for Mister Lewrie!" a marine called.

"Stap me, if that's Treghues, he'll jump down my throat with both boots on, the state I'm in," Alan said, setting aside his fourth glass of wine untouched. "Do I look sober enough to see him if that's what it is?"

"No one ever is, but you may pass inspection. Here."

David offered him a precious lime from the Indies, a green and semishriveled fruit brought aboard God knew how long before, but Alan bit into it and sucked as much of the juice into his mouth that he could stand, to kill the odor of wine on his breath. For safety, he tucked a piece of rind into his cheek to chew on, and went on deck.

"God bless you for that, David, you're a true Christian."

"Aye, I'm up to the Apocrypha now." David smiled.

It was indeed a summons from the great cabins aft to see their captain. Alan removed his cocked hat and entered as the marine stamped his musket and bawled an announcement of his arrival.

Treghues had aged. He was sprouting the first hints of gray in his hair at the temples, and his face was thin and drawn as though there was still some lingering effect of that blow to the head back in August—that, or Dr. Dorne's "slight trephination." Perhaps it was, Alan thought, the ill repute which *Desperate* had gathered after her daring escape from the Chesapeake Bay. For the son of a lord of the realm, the slightest hint of incompetence or cowardice that could only be answered by requesting an inquiry, would be galling in the extreme. Even a physically fit man would have trouble dealing with it and sleeping sound at night, and Treghues did not look as though he had been sleeping well.

"Mister Lewrie," Treghues said, sitting prim behind his glossy mahogany desk, with his hands folded as though kneeling at a prayer rail.

"Sir."

"Admiral Hood's flag secretary sent me a fair copy of your report regarding your activities ashore. He also sent a short note of commendation with it. I . . . I find this extremely difficult to say, Lewrie, after our recent contretemps, but he stated, Admiral Hood, that is, stated, that I should be very proud of you. And I am."

"He did?" Alan beamed with sudden pleasure. "Thank you, sir, thankee very kindly, indeed."

"Perhaps this will go a long way to removing the *odor* which this poor vessel has acquired of late. You are aware to which I allude, sir?"

"Avery discovered it to me, sir."

"A bitter sort of poetic justice," Treghues mused, taking up a clay churchwarden pipe and cramming tobacco into the bowl, an activity he had not been known for before. "I was a bit too hasty to judge you for what you had been before joining the Navy, allowed prejudice to cloud my judgments. And now, I am hoist by my own petard, as the Bard would have said, from the clouded judgments of others."

Captains ain't supposed to be like this, Alan thought. They don't have to explain shit. Why is he cosseting me suddenly? I ain't changed that much at all, maybe for the worse if anything.

"Jealousy and backstabbing I can understand, but I cannot abide what our escape has done to my ship, Lewrie," Treghues said sharply, with a hint of that old rigidity and moral rectitude. "Better we had gone into captivity after burning her to the waterline than endure the sneers from . . . from these dominee do-littles."

"You went out with flags flying, sir," Alan said, only half pissing down Treghues's back, half expressing his own outrage at the unfairness of any recriminations against *Desperate* and her people. "That's more than any of these scoundrels attempted. Had they stirred their arses up properly, there'd still be a base on the York, and we'd have been covered in glory."

Damme, you've let the wine speak! Alan thought. He's going to have me flogged raw. And he's got his memory back. I'm fucked.

"Bless you, that was bravely said, sir!" Treghues barked with a smile that was most disconcerting to see. "And never a truer word spoken."

"She's my ship, too, sir. Too many good men died making her what she is, too many died ashore doing everything they could for the army."

"Aye, you love her, too," Treghues responded as he lit his pipe with a taper dipped into an overhead lantern. It was hard to tell if the smoke, or the emotion, misted his eyes. "I had not expected this from you, Mister Lewrie. I was under the impression you hated the Sea Service."

"I've done some growing up, sir. And there's no law says I can't change my mind about some things." Alan replied, feeling the wine pricking at the back of his eyes. Damme, he thought, is it the wine speaking, or do I really feel . . . comfortable in the navy now? Must be the wine. Bastards like me have no noble emotions.

"By Heaven above, I love this ship," Treghues said, the smoke wreathing about his head, and Alan thought it possibly the oddest smelling tobacco he had ever come across, almost herbal and acrid, not like Virginia leaf or Turkey. "We're shorthanded once more, short four guns aft, but we'll make something brave of her yet. Have you really had a sea change, Mister Lewrie? Are you prepared to do your utmost to restore her honor and reputation?"

"Aye, sir." What other answer was there to a question like that?

"We may receive some older brass nines from the army ashore, short nines, but better than nothing," Treghues continued. "And I must make up the lack of leadership and competence. With Admiral Hood's commendation and his conjurement to do something for you as suitable reward, I am appointing you an acting master's mate, effective immediately. See Mister Railsford to change your watch and quarter bills, and then apprise the sailing master of your promotion. There is a salary with it, and though there is the chance you may not be confirmed once back in the Indies and shall be liable for stoppages, I doubt that should occur, if you make a good showing during a probationary phase."

"I . . . I don't know how to thank you, sir," Alan said, overcome at the honor paid him. Approval from the flag was a mere formality in such cases, and the Admiralty in faraway London paid no attention to such mundane matters, not like making someone a commissioned officer or giving a young boy command of a ship. If he did not do something completely stupid during the trial period, he would be made a full master's mate within two months or so. And from that very instant, he was a junior watch stander, a deck officer in a short-handed ship, with better quarters than a hammock, the right to wear a sword instead of a boy's dirk and two pounds, two shillings a month of real pay (or certificates attesting to it in lieu of coin) instead of being allowed money from his annuity. His rations would be the same, the air belowdecks would be the same and the dangers of the sea would be the same for all, but everyone below David in rank would now have to call him "sir" or Mister Lewrie.

"Miscreant or not, you have earned it," Treghues said, turning prim once more, as though he had said too much and had let down that rigid guard a captain must keep over his emotions, or had failed to maintain the separation from the ship's people that made his authority absolute. "That will be all, sir."

"Aye, aye, sir," Alan replied crisply. Damme, maybe I can make a commission out of this after all, he told himself once he was on deck and sniffing at the coolness of the air.

"Seen the captain, have you?" Railsford asked, as though he knew what the news was already.

"Aye, sir. He has appointed me master's mate, acting for a time," Alan related proudly. "Who would have thought it?"

"Well, if you do not wish to accept the promotion . . ."

"No, sir, I'll accept gladly," Alan hastened to assure him.

"Congratulations, then. Now get you below and sort yourself out into your new quarters. Take one of the mates' dog boxes,"

Railsford said kindly. "But if you fuck off or let this go to your head, I'll kick your arse for you, see if I don't."

"I'll not let you down, sir," Alan replied.

"*Or* the captain," Railsford whispered, stepping close to him. "He needs us badly now. No matter how he slurred you in the past, the poor man needs our help. Captains cannot ask, and they cannot be seen to be in need of anything. Were you my younger brother, and you let him down, I'd break you and send you forrard in pusser's slops. It's not just obedience you owe him or the loyalty which is his due, but true loyalty. May I count on you for that, Mister Lewrie? Have you that devotion?"

"Aye, sir," Alan said. "I believe I do."

"No more of your moonshines, no more boyish pranks and japes," Railsford went on. "You're in an important job now, and too many people depend on you. I know you fairly well, and I trust you with the well-being of this ship when you have charge of the deck, as you will, shorthanded as we are. The captain has put his utmost trust in you as well. That's something new for you, being trusted, I know."

"Aye, it is, sir," Alan had to admit, feeling a surge of pride that people were beginning to put power in his hands and delegate authority to his judgment, something that would never have happened in his former life as a rake-hell back in London. "Very sobering."

"Odd choice of words with the reek of the wine-table on your breath." Railsford grinned suddenly. "Enough said for now, then. Get."

Alan went below to the lower deck, then aft to the midshipmen's mess and took hold of his chest to drag it into a vacant dog-box cabin, to Avery's consternation. He had Freeling make up his narrow berth and hung up some spare clothes from the pegs. Like the tiny quarters aboard the schooner *Parrot* that had been meant for privateer prize masters, the dog box was made up of thin deal partitions and a canvas door that enclosed a space just large enough for the bed, his chest, a tiny book rack, a mirror and wash stand and the line of pegs that would be his wardrobe; but it was his, all his, and he could shut the door like a commissioned officer and turn off the sounds of the ship when he was off watch, could even have a lie-down instead of waiting for the evening pipe to call the hands to reclaim their hammocks. There was a small pewter lamp gimbaled on a swinging mount over the headboard of the bed, which he could burn later than others to read in bed, if he felt like it until nine at night.

He doubted, though, if he would be using that berth much, not if he wished to shine at his new duties and not let Railsford down after the serious nature of the warning he had given him. He did not know if he really felt that devotion to Treghues that Railsford had asked for; Treghues was too alien to his sybaritic nature, too cold and puritanical, too swept up in morality (which was damned rare in these times), but the gunner, Mister Gwynn, had said once before that Treghues would take a great affection for someone for the oddest reasons and dote on them before turning on them again for reasons unknown. The wheel had come half circle, and he was no longer a Godless sinner in the captain's eyes. He was now in favor, and he did not intend to let anything put a blot on that new reputation, not if he could help it.

He could, however, show true devotion to Railsford, and to Monk and the other senior warrants who had held a good opinion of him even in the worst days of Treghues's displeasure. He could feel a warm stirring in his soul when he thought of *Desperate* tarred with a dirty brush, and that could sustain him. By devoting himself to earning his advancement he could fulfill everyone's expectations, and backhandedly give Treghues his share in the proceess.

"It's going to be hard work," he whispered to himself in the privacy of his little cabin. "But I've learned enough to handle hard work. I can do this. But damme if I can see how I can have much fun in the next few months."

Was it unspoken displeasure at *Desperate*? It was hard to figure out, but, with the passing of the equinox, the Leeward Islands Squadron had to go back to the West Indies, or winter on the American coast, so they sailed. *Desperate*, however, was left behind, to replace artillery at first, refit and restock provisions and then be sent off with some lighter ships for Wilmington, North Carolina. Lord Cornwallis had taken most of the good troops in the south up to Yorktown, and they were lost forever. Charleston was still strongly garrisoned but had no men to spare for the minor ports. Wilmington would be evacuated, and *Desperate* would take part in the evacuation flotilla, the strongest ship in their little gathering. With Monk, Alan spent hours off watch poring over the Cape Fear charts, for it was the very devil of a place to enter safely.

South of Onslow Bay and a former pirate's lair known as Topsail Island, there was a long peninsula that hooked south like a saber blade, narrowing at the tip to a malarial spit of sand which held Fort Johnston to guard the entrance inlet to the Cape Fear River. There were dozens of low islands and seas of marsh and salt grass gathered around the mouth of the river, and only one safe, deep pass. The lower reaches of the river were pretty desolate, except around Brunswick, a town gradually losing out to Wilmington sixteen miles further upriver, and now almost taken back by the weeds and scrub pine. Wilmington was on the east, or seaward, bank of Cape Fear, hard to get to but a safe harbor in storms and a bustling trading center. For a time it had been Cornwallis's headquarters before he had marched off to disaster in Virginia. Now the garrison that had been left behind, the troops and guns at Fort Johnston were to be evacuated. Along with them would come the hundreds of Loyalists from the southeastern portion of the colony who had already fled the wrath of their cousins up-country.

Alan's prophecy about using his cabin so seldom had come true on the way down from New York. If he was not on the orlop deck supervising the proper stowage of provisions and munitions, then he was standing night watches, fully in command of *Desperate* as her real officers slept. He kept log entries, saw that the glass was turned on the half hour and the bells were struck; that the course was steered as laid down and that the quartermasters on the wheel stayed awake. He toured belowdecks when he could to see that all lights were out and the hands were behaving, that the lookouts were attentive, that the night signal book was close at hand and signal fusees ready for emergencies. He saw that the fire buckets were full, that the bosun of the watch and his hands were trimming the sails for best efficiency, that there was no navigational hazard in their path and no ship on a course for an imminent collision, that the knot log was cast to determine their speed at regular intervals and that in soundings along the coast the leadsmen regularly plumbed the ocean depths.

He also had to keep a weather eye out for privateers or some part of the French fleet, which had not been reported leaving the American coast yet and could still be somewhere near.

It was such a quantum leap in duties and responsibility that he almost (but not quite) swore off strong drink, and there was no rest, not for a moment on deck. At first he was too embarrassed to have to summon Railsford, Monk or the captain at the slightest hint of doubt, and got cobbed for waiting too late. On the other hand, when he summoned them too often, he got cobbed for that, too, and developed a slightly haunted look after one week of his new duties.

There was some reward, even so; to stand on deck when everything was running smoothly, hands behind his back and rocking on the balls of his feet, feeling *Desperate* surge along with a tremble and hum of wind and sea on her rigging and hull, totally under his control. Four hundred and fifty tons of warship worth more than twelve thousand pounds; aboard were twenty pieces of artillery, over 150 lives, and it was, for intervals, all his to command.

Another joy was to simply finish the middle watch, see the first hint of dawn, pipe up hands from below, sign the log and turn things over to Railsford without incident. There might be a single grunt of satisfaction that he had done what was required without killing anyone, or sinking the ship in the process, or tearing the masts right out of her. Usually, there would be a quick conference aft as the hands knelt to scrub decks forward, and Railsford or Treghues would give him a critique on the night's work—what he had done right and what he had done wrong. And so far, there had been enough right things to counterbalance the few wrong.

Another change was in the way he was remonstrated; no more being bent over a gun for a dozen strokes of a stiffened rope starter, no more tongue lashings. The cobbings were short, to the point and were couched as admonitions from a senior officer to a junior officer, done out of hearing from the hands so his authority with the crew would not suffer.

When he began, he thought he had been prepared for standing watch by his stint in the schooner *Parrot*, but he realized that that period had been all play and schoolwork. Lieutenant Kenyon, *Parrot*'s master and commmander, had assigned Lewrie and the late Thad Purnell together to do the work of a single adult, with senior bosun's mates or quartermasters to act as a safety net should they run into trouble, someone to prompt them into the right answer, keep them out of real difficulty, and keep their playfulness in check.

Desperate was not schoolwork, and there was no one to turn to as tutor in the night watches; he was the lone man with no one to backstop him. If he failed at this, he would never get another chance, so he took a round turn and two half hitches, as one said in naval parlance, and tried to begin to act like the sea officer they expected him to be, and the sea officer he aspired to be.

They sweated blood to make it in past Cape Fear (it was not named Fear for nought, after all) and into the river between the true coast and the long peninsula. If anything, it looked even more desolate than most stretches of the southern American coast, low barrier islands with only sea oats and dune grass, low forests of wind-sculpted pines on the banks, and the salt-grass marshes stretching off to either hand, with only swamp behind. *Desperate* could, by staying to the middle of the channel, just barely make it upriver, and that took real skill. With a tide running in, they could ride the flood, but would have no control over the helm. They had reefed tops'ls, jibs and spanker set, with a light wind off the great curve of Onslow Bay that gave them just enough forward momentum to give the rudder a bite, but not so much speed that they could run into trouble before dropping a kedge anchor from the stern if they took the ground on the mud and sand shoals.

"Point ta starboard, quartermaster, put your helm ta looard, handsomely, now," Monk cautioned.

"Five fathom, five fathom to starboard!" the bosun's mate in the foremast chains chanted.

"Sonofa..." Monk growled, wanting to stand on, but worried about shoaling. Off to larboard, there was an eddy that swirled as though the tidal flood was caressing something substantial, which he had just altered course to avoid.

"That's a back eddy, Mister Monk," Alan said, remembering how the current would spin about in the Cape Fear River from his earlier voyages in *Parrot*. "Lieutenant Kenyon said there was no harm in it, and we stood in quite close to it."

"Aye, but what'd ya draw in yer schooner?" Monk asked, working on a quid of tobacco so vigorously it made Alan's jaws ache to watch him.

"A foot shy of two fathom, sir. But the main channel was far off to the larboard, ran right up alongside Eagle Island."

"Aye, if yer a coaster," Monk said. "The Thoroughfare, they calls it, but it's too shallow fer the likes o' us."

"And a half four."

"Helm aweather half a point," Monk said compromising.

"Six fathom, six fathom on this line," the larboard man called.

"Aye," Monk went on, puffing with relief to find deep water. "I s'pose ya know the main channel's on the west side, 'least til ya get ta Old Town Creek an' the Dram Tree?"

He pointed out a huge bearded cypress on the right bank farther upriver. "Bad shoal at Old Town Creek. Mosta the big ships don't go no further than Campbell Island an' the Dram Tree. Sailors take a dram afore hoistin' sail fer a long voyage from the Cape Fear. What's Campbell Island bear now?"

"Two points to larboard, sir."

"Captain, my respects, an' once past Campbell Island, I suggest we do anchor."

"Very well, Mister Monk," Treghues said lazily. "We'll round up into the wind, let go the best bower and back the mizzen tops'l to let the wind and tide end her up bows downriver. Mister Coke?"

"Aye, sir?" the bosun said.

"I'll not let her fall back too far from the bower, mind. Hang the kedge in the cutter and row her out to drop. Veer out half a cable aft and a half cable forrard. Take Mister Avery with one of your mates."

"Aye, sir."

Lewrie cast a glance at David Avery standing by the quarterdeck nettings overlooking the waist. Much like the change in attitude when Keith Ashburn had been made an acting lieutenant into *Glatton*, the squadron flagship when Alan's first ship *Ariadne* was condemned, it seemed as if a friendship was being tested once more. In the past, it had been Keith Ashburn who had placed the distance between them to protect the authority of his new commission. Here,

it was Avery who was distancing himself from Lewrie, finding it difficult to say "Alan" instead of "Mr. Lewrie" or "sir," even in the mess.
There did not seem to be any animosity, even though Avery had
been in the Navy over four years and was still a midshipman while
Alan had risen like a comet to an acting mate in a little less than
two. He was still friendly, but no longer close, and Alan regretted it.
And there was little he could do about it without stepping out of role
and playing favorites. Railsford had warned him of that one night
when he had come on deck to catch a breeze. Best do it now, he had
said, before new midshipmen come aboard, and you have no bad
habits to break.

When they did receive new midshipmen, Alan and the new
master's mate who would be appointed into *Desperate* would have to
rule the mess, supervise the newlies and keep order without playing
favorites. It was sad, all the same, just another slice of naval life
Alan detested.

"Mister Railsford, round her up into the wind, if you would be
so kind, and bring her to," Treghues finally ordered. *Desperate* swung
about in a tight turn, her helm hard over until her bows were
pointed for the sea she had left. At a sharp arm gesture, the bower
dropped into the water with a great splash and she began to pay off
upriver, driven by tide and sea breeze on her backed mizzen tops'l,
while everything else was handed or taken in by the topmen and
fo'c'slemen. They spent half an hour rowing out the kedge anchor
from the stern, letting her go and winching the ship forward onto
her bower; they lashed the heavy cable to the mooring bitts and
hauled in on the kedge cable until they had her firmly moored in the
river fore and aft. The shallow coasters they had escorted in had to
take what moorings they could, since *Desperate*, as leading ship up
channel, had taken the best mooring for herself, and devil take the
hindmost.

"Mister Railsford, now we've the cutter free, my compliments to
you, and would you depute for me ashore with Major Craig concerning his plans for evacuation. There are orders from General Leslie in
Charleston to convey, as well," Treghues drawled.

"I should be delighted, sir."

"Um, excuse me, sir," Alan said.

"Aye, Mister Lewrie?" Treghues asked, turning to face him.

"If you would not mind, sir, I should like to go ashore with the first lieutenant," Alan said.

"Not ten days into your new rating, and you think you have earned a right to caterwaul through the streets of this unfortunate town?" The captain frowned. "You disappoint me, Mister Lewrie. I had thought you had learned your lesson about debauchery."

"Not debauchery, sir." Alan gaped in a fair approximation of shock, or what he hoped would pass for it. "It is the Chiswick family, sir. You mind them, the officers that came off Jenkins Neck with me? Their family is here in Wilmington at last report, and I have tidings and money from their sons to help their passage. I promised Lieutenant Chiswick I would look them up, if possible, sir."

"Hmm," Treghues murmured, cradling his jaw to study him. "On your sacred honor, this is true, sir?"

"'Pon my sacred honor, sir," Alan swore. "I gave them my word, sir."

"Very well, then, but if you come back aboard the worse for wear, as you did in Charleston, I'll not merely disrate you from master's mate, I'll put you forward as an ordinary seaman."

"I understand, sir," Alan said. And God, please don't let me run across anything tempting this time! he pleaded silently.

They landed at the foot of Market and Third Street, just below St. James church and the white house that Cornwallis had used as his headquarters. The church was in terrible shape compared to the last time Alan had seen it, but it was his destination, operating on the theory that Loyalists would be Church of England if they had any pretensions at all to gentility, and the parish vicar would know where the Chiswicks resided, if they were members.

He knocked on the door to the manse, and a wizened fellow came to open it, more a hedge-priest than anything else, dressed in black breeches and waistcoat gone rusty with age and abuse, and his linen and ample neck-stock a bit rusty as well, as though he had to wash and iron himself.

"Yes, what do you want, sir?" the man asked him, wiping his hands on a blue apron, and Alan wondered if the man was a curate or a publican doing double duty if the parish was not living enough.

"I am seeking information about a family named Chiswick, sir," he said. "I thought perhaps they might be temporary members of your parish. Is the vicar in?"

"The *rector* is out, sir." The man sniffed, eyeing the King's uniform up and down as though it were a distasteful sight to him. "And I know no one by the name of Chiswick, not in our regular parish."

"They came down from around Campbelltown," Alan prompted. "New arrivals to Wilmington."

"Oh." The man frowned. "And their reason for leaving that country?"

"I believe they were burned out," Alan said, getting a little put out with the man's effrontery.

"Loyalists, then." The man nodded, stiffening up and glowering.

"Here, this is Church of England still, is it not?"

"It is not, sir." The man huffed up his small frame as though insulted. "More to the point, Episcopal, but not Church of *England*. Had we been else, Tarleton and his troopers would not have used our nave for a stable, sir!"

"Then who ministers to the Tories?" Alan demanded.

"We do, when called, sir. We are Christians, you know."

"Couldn't tell it by me. Who would know, then?"

"Try across the street at the Burgwin House, if you can come away with your soul from Major Craig's torture cellars! Ask of your own kind! Good day to you, sir!" The little man said with satisfaction as he backed into the manse and closed the door.

God, what a lunatick country! he grumbled to himself as he went to the house that had been Cornwallis's residence. "Half the Regulators and Piedmont still against the Tidewater, the rest just Rebels, half of 'em still Tory, Scots who hated George the Second fighting for George the Third. The Tidewater mostly Rebel no matter what the Piedmonters think and at each other's throats anyway. And you can't even find an Anglican that'll answer to the name anymore. They're welcome to this asylum and good riddance."

The Burgwin House was headquarters for the notorious Major Craig and his 'witch-finder', that anti-Rebel David Fanning, who was rumored to be so eaten with the scrofula, the King's Evil, that he hated all of mankind. For such a nice house, it did have a bad air about it, due Alan thought to the smells arising from the cellars, which had been used as prisons for some time. Was it his imagination, fed by the choler of that . . . whatever he had been . . . at the manse, that he thought he heard the moans of tortured bodies from below?

He did find a harried staff officer who knew most of the refugees and steered Alan in the right direction down to Dock Street and then inland five blocks, up over the crest of the hill and down into the flats to a tumble-down mansion that had seen better days. It was a daunting sight; the yard was full of crates and junk, the stableyard full of carriages and wagons crammed in any-old-how. Laundry hung from every window and railing, and the place swarmed with men, women and children in faded finery, with the occasional black face still in livery. People came and went on errands continually. He noticed it was shunned by most residents of the town—he would have shunned it himself if given a choice; it looked like a debtor's prison.

The Chiswick family residence was a single downstairs room. Alan knocked on the doors and heard a stirring within. He tugged down his waistcoat, fiddled with his neckcloth and adjusted his lovely silver-fitted sword at his side, waiting for admittance.

The rooms had once been a sort of smaller back dining room, for the doors slid back into pockets. The girl who opened the doors regarded him with a cool regality, a cautious nose-in-the-air aloofness at his presence.

"Have I found the Chiswick family?" Alan asked, taking off his cocked hat preparatory to a formal introductory bow.

"It is, sir," she replied, a hitch in her voice. One hand flew to her lips, as if in fear that a man in uniform seeking them could only mean dire news about Governour, Burgess or both.

"Allow me to introduce myself, miss. I am Alan Lewrie, Royal Navy. I bring you tidings from Lieutenant Governour Chiswick and Ensign Burgess Chiswick," he said, making congé to her in the hall to the amusement of several small children who had followed him in from the front porches.

"Oh, my God!" she gasped, almost biting a knuckle.

"Glad tidings, I assure you," Alan went on, rising from his bow.

"Come in, come in, good sir!" she gushed. "Are they well, were they hurt? We heard the army had surrendered and feared..."

"They are in New York at present, both well," Alan said.

Her face broke from seriousness or fear into the widest, most wondrous smile, and she flung herself on him and bounced up and down in glee, giving a little shriek of delight.

"Say you truly, sir? They are alive and well?" She beamed.

"Truly, miss," Alan said, shaken by her emotion and how her slim body had felt against him as she jounced on her toes in relief and glee.

"Momma, Daddy, there's a Navy officer here, he's seen Gov and Burge, and they're safe and well!" she called into the room. Taking him by the hand, she almost dragged him into the room. There had been some attempts made to provide privacy by hanging figured quilts and blankets from light rope strung from one picture rail to another, but the rooms were cramped by furniture; a large bed for the parents could be espied through a part in the curtains, another impromptu bedchamber further back—most likely for the enthusiastic girl—and a small cot sharing the space for a large black woman, obviously an old family retainer, who came trundling out clapping her hands and weeping for joy at the news.

The parents had been seated in the middle of the rooms, fenced off into a tiny parlor of quilts by the hearth. A small fire tried to relieve the late-fall chill without much success. The man looked to be in his fifties, his hair already white and lank, and he had difficulty rising to greet his guest without support from a cane, and the daughter at his elbow. The mother was sprier, slim and straight-backed, her hair also almost white, and her face lined with care and years. Tears flowed freely as he was introduced to Mr. Sewallis Chiswick and his wife Charlotte. When they got around to it, the black woman was referred to as "Mammy," and the tall slim girl who had opened the door turned out to be the sister Caroline that Burgess had mentioned.

"Give ye joy, Mister Lewrie!" the mother said once everyone had had a good weep and a snuffle. "And did you meet my boys in New York?"

"No ma'am, I was at Yorktown with them, from the very first," he said, taking his ease as best he could in an old-fashioned dining chair that threatened to go to flinders if he shifted too much or leaned back too far. "Our ship was trapped in the York River with the army and I had to go ashore with artillery. I met them there."

"Then they *were* with the army," Caroline said. "However did then ya'll escape the fate of the others?"

There was nothing Alan liked better than a receptive audience, so he regaled them for an exceedingly pleasing few minutes, telling them all about the thwarted evacuation, the storm and their adventure on Jenkins Neck, glossing over the battle and their eventual escape to sea.

"Stap me, what a grand adventure," the father said, thumping his cane on the floor in pleasure and upsetting the teacup which had been balanced on his knee. There was an uncomfortable silence for a second, but the girl leapt to kneel and begin picking up the pieces while the mother shifted uneasily and gave a loud sniff. Alan thought the old fool had broken one of her priceless wedding china. The black woman puffed into action, trying to do the job instead.

"Sit back, girl, an' let Mammy at it. Lord knows ah kin do fer the mister, ain't nothin' new ta me, my, my. Res' easy, Miz Chalotte."

"I have letters from Governour and Burgess," Alan said to break the embarrassing scene, realizing he had monopolized their time too long.

"Have ye now?" The man beamed, the incident of the cup forgotten. "Carry, where's my spectacles? I want ta read 'em. May I have 'em, sir?"

"Daddy, you know they're lost these two weeks past," Caroline told him firmly, getting back to her feet. "But I have young eyes, I'll read them to us all, would you like that, Daddy? Momma, you shift your chair over here so you can read over my shoulder. I know you want to see 'em just as bad as Daddy." She went on like a governess cajoling children.

"Perhaps I should intrude on your joy no longer," Alan said, beginning to realize that Mr. Sewallis Chiswick was adrift in his dotage and was an embarrassment to the mother and daughter. The man spent a full minute patting himself down searching for the lost spectacles, and then called Mammy to fetch them. The daughter got a sad look and shared it with the black woman.

"Lawsy, Missa S'wallis, yo speck-ticles ain't nowheres ta be foun' an us all lookin' fer 'em all las' week, we has," she chided.

"Let me be your eyes, Daddy," Caroline said soothingly. She sat down by his side on the shabby settee and patted him on the shoulder until he calmed down.

"Yes, you read that letter, Carry. And you stay, young man, and hear about my boys up in Virginia. Mose, get this lad a glass of something, will you? Where is that lazy black squint-a-pipes, anyway?"

Caroline looked up at him, as though daring Alan to even think a single bad thought about her family, and he was forced back into the rickety chair as though driven. The mother was busy shifting her chair, insisting that Mammy assist her. Alan rose instead and did it for her, and the chair was as light as a feather, something even a child would have no trouble shifting. As he resumed his chair, Mammy fetched out a silver service and poured tea for them, carefully rationing the sugar. The tea was not much better than hot water, so she must have been rationing the tea leaves as well. There were, however, some fresh ginger cookies, and Alan chewed on one while the daughter broke the seal on the letter to reveal large folio sheets of vellum. She smoothed them free of travel wrinkles, (she cannily saved the wax wafer seal for later use) and began to read.

God, I wish I was anywhere but here, Alan thought as he let the first part of the letter wash over him without impression. *If I hadn't promised the brothers, I'd have just dropped this off and been on my merry way.*

He let his attention wander about the place to take some sort of inventory of their furnishings and possessions, to see if they were as rich as Burgess had stated, and it was hard to judge. There was good silver and china alongside cracked glasses. There were gilt-framed paintings of nature scenes and relations leaning against some of the most hideous, scratched furniture he had ever laid eyes on. Having found nothing of interest in the room, he let his eyes wander over to the people; the mother sitting rigid as a grenadier guard with a handkerchief screwed into her bony little fists, awaiting bad news; the old man, almost drowsing with a faint smile on his face as he listened to the family chatter from his sons; and the daughter.

She struck him as gawky, God help her. Taking her measure

from how she had hugged him with so much abandon at the door, he thought her barely an inch or two less than his five feet nine, much too tall for beauty. Most men, Alan included, liked their girls a lot smaller, more petite, and more roundly feminine. This one was long and lanky, almost skinny. He tried to remember how old Burgess had said she was—eighteen? Maybe she would fill out, but she could also shoot up like a cornstalk and become even less desirable.

Probably going to be a spinster for life, poor girl, Alan thought. Be lucky if she can take service with some monied family, and that'll be a comedown, though you can't get much further down than this shabbiness now. Maybe a poor tradesman or curate would have her. Hell, even a peer's daughter would have problems getting a husband, being that tall. Don't know though, if she gave up heeled shoes, had any sort of decent portion, she might be worth troubling with. She is pretty, in a way.

The more he studied her, the prettier she looked, but Alan put that down to his lack of mutton for comparison lately, except for the Hayley sisters back in Virginia, and they had not been raving beauties fit enough to light up a London season.

Her forehead was high, her brows arched naturally. Her face was a long oval, but not horsey long; her chin firm but small; her mouth was wide and expressive, one minute pensive, the next curving up and dimpling her lower face, stretching lines from chin to near her nicely rounded cheeks. She wore no powder or artifice, but her skin was clear and smooth, with just the hint of the lightest down. At one moment her eyes would be wide with happiness, hazel eyes like her brothers, the next minute they squinted in concern or concentration. Her hair was long and straight and very dark blonde, fine and a little flyaway. Had she the same ash-blonde hair of Governour or Burgess, she would have been too severe, but she gave off more warmth by her very appearance than ever either of those worthies did.

She read well, with a pleasant voice, and Alan did not mind her provincial accent, for it was soft and lyrical. Of course, after listening to sailors for nearly two weeks, creaking iron doors could have seemed lyrical. More than that, she did not falter over words, nor did she read slowly in a monotone, but was expressive enough to give life to the letter, and Alan could imagine Governour reading it aloud. Someone had spent some time educating her along with her brothers, he decided, even if it ended up being wasted on novels and housewifely guides like most of the women back in England, who had so little to do.

Rather cute nose, he decided also, after thinking on it.

She was slim, though; tall and slim, almost skinny. Alan thought she would not gross between 7 and 8 stone even soaking wet. Her bosom was small and neat. Though she does have a nice neck, Alan thought.

He shifted in his precarious chair with an ominous squeaking of weak joins, and crossed his legs. She looked up at him, pausing at the end of one page, and gave him a smile that raised another squeak from the chair as he sat up straighter and smiled back.

"And so we arrived in safety in New York, and expect to sail to Charleston once the elements shall admit safe passage. Father, I enclose a list of those of our men from the Royal North Carolina Regiment of Volunteer Rifles we know for certain have fallen, or have suffered wounds for their rightful King." She read on, frowning sadly as she did so. "Some of the most grievous hurt we were forced to leave behind in the care of the enemy, praying to Providence that they shall have decent treatment. Alan Lewrie generously gave twenty guineas to our hostesses for the better victualing and physicking of our men. All others who escaped with us, I also detail, so their families may know they are well and whole."

"That was good of you, young man," the mother wept, plying at her eyes with a fresh handkerchief.

"It was the least I could do, ma'am," Alan said modestly, feeling truly modest for once in that emotion-tinged room. "There were several of my sailors left behind as well, too hurt to be moved without causing them more suffering."

"We must confess," Caroline began again, "that the fight to save our boats was a spirited engagement of the most desperate neck-or-nothing nature, and only by the utmost bravery and pluck did we prevail, though whatever joy we had in a final victory over the Levellers and their allies, the slaves of a Catholic King, could not assuage the grief of losing so many fine men and neighbors. The bearer of this particular copy of our letter, Alan Lewrie, we recommend to you, and trust that you shall show him what you can of Carolinian hospitality and gratitude."

Alan made much of his teacup and looked down at the carpet as his pride began to scratch at him; false modesty be damned, he thought he had been pretty good back there during their adventures.

"As a comrade in our distress, we have not, in a Cause replete with leaders and fighters suitable for commendation and emulation, seen the like in our mutual experience," Caroline read. She looked up at him with such a smile and such a fetching rise of her bosom that Alan could look nowhere else but directly at her. "To him, we owe our very lives. Were it not for his sublime courage, even in the times when things looked blackest, his canny knowledge of the sea and its navigation, we would now be prisoners of war, or worse. He knew no exhaustion, no sense of gloom, no defeatism and brought us out of bondage like Moses fetched his Israelites. He . . ."

She had to stop and take a deep breath or two, and lift a handkerchief to her own eyes before continuing. "He is the finest comrade in arms we have ever had the privilege to know, and can only conjure you to share your gratitude at our good fortune with him."

Damme, that's a pretty high praise for a toadying little shit like me, Alan marveled. Now when was I canny and optimistic? I can't remember anything like that. Still, have to remember, this letter was penned by one of the coldest murthering black-hearted rogues I've ever seen.

"God bless you, Mister Lewrie," the mother bawled, rising to give him a hearty hug, some slobbery kisses on the cheeks and pats on the back that stung right through his wool uniform and waistcoat. He had to help her back to her chair before she swooned, then got pawed by the old man as well, who could not rise, and Alan had to bend down to receive the elder Chiswick's benison. The black mammy had at him next, and it felt as if he was trying to wrestle his way out of a bear-baiting pit. Caroline hugged him and wept on his shoulder, swearing he was the finest Christian in the world, and he got a chance to take a circumspect survey of her charms, which seemed a lot nicer than his first impressions.

"I cannot pretend to understand military or nautical matters,"

Caroline said, stepping back from him but keeping her slim hands tight on his sleeves, "but you kept my brothers alive and got them out safely, and I shall forever be indebted to you."

"And we shall regard you as fondly as any member of our family," Mrs. Chiswick said in a high, fruity voice, to which her husband lent his vociferous agreement with so many "hear hears" he sounded like the Vicar of Bray in a Parliament backbench.

"We have something, finally, for which we give thanks," Chiswick senior roared heartily. "There's a tom turkey much too fat for his own good strutting the yard. We should roast the gentleman before he's one hour older. Mother, where are our manners? There's two dozen of claret in the pantry, is there not? Tell Old Mose to fetch a couple out! I want to take a glad bumper or two with this young fellow."

Once again, Alan got the impression that something was wrong, for the happy mood dissolved in an instant, the mother going for her handkerchief again, the black maid piping her eyes and Caroline had to go to her father and cosset him into a calmer mood. Alan looked about the room. There was no pantry, no sign of a crate bearing even a bottle or two and most definitely there was no black male servant named Old Mose, or he would have been in the room to hear the news with Mammy. Alan got the impression that Sewallis Chiswick was living in some dreamland in the past, before they had been burned out by their own cousins and run to Wilmington with what little he saw in their rented lodgings, and those were damned poor, at that.

"But I want to take a glass with the lad, Caroline," Mr. Chiswick whined in a pet, and Caroline gave Alan a stern look, touching her lips with a finger and shaking her head slightly.

"Mr. Chiswick, under any other circumstances, I would be delighted to accept your hospitality. I have not had a good roast tom since I left London nearly two years ago, and normally I'd not say no to a glass," Alan replied, rising, "but, my captain only allowed me a few minutes ashore to see you, and I must not allow even the most charming surroundings, and company"—he bowed slightly to the mother, which made her chirp with some remembered coquetry, and to Caroline, who was nodding as though he was a good pupil to say his lesson so well—"to detain me from my duties. Perhaps in future, before the town is evacuated, we could visit again, if you would be so gracious as to receive me."

"Of course we shall!" Mr. Chiswick laughed. "Damme to hell if we shan't, young sir, or my name ain't Chiswick. We may not have been the biggest nabobs in the county, but no one could say that we did not set a fine and merry table. You come back and see us again, soon. You can see George. He'd like you. Wants to be a dragoon or a hussar, but . . ."

"I would enjoy that immensely, Mister Chiswick, sir," Alan said, feeling his clothing crawl with embarrassment for them.

"He's out riding now," Mr. Chiswick said proudly. "Damme, what a seat that boy has, and such a way with a horse. I've told him the Navy would be surer, but what can you do, eh? Perhaps you could speak to him."

"I would admire that, sir," Alan replied, backing for the door. Jesus, get me out of here before we all die of mortification. The old fart's gone barking mad, he thought to himself.

He said his good-byes and got out into the hall as quickly as decent politeness would allow. He then had to plow through the herd of snotty children who had gathered to watch his departure and who ran shrieking for the porch as he emerged from the lodgings.

"Mister Lewrie," Caroline said, coming out of the rooms and shutting the doors on that pathetic scene. Her eyes were wet with tears. "I must apologize to you. He has been getting better, but the excitement was too much for him, I fear."

"You don't have to apologize to me, Mistress Chiswick," Alan offered. "Burgess told me what happened to your plantation and to your brother George. I am heartily sorry. Better men have broken under the hurt and the strain. My own captain recently went through a debilitating experience himself."

"Thank you for humoring him, though I don't know if that is the best course in the long run." She shuddered, dabbing at her eyes. With a single deep breath that took all her concentration to inhale and hold she calmed herself and gave him a quick, sad smile.

"I clean forgot this," Alan said, digging for a small purse.

"I could not accept that, Mister Lewrie," she said as he hefted it.

"'Tis not from me, Mistress Chiswick," he told her truthfully.

"Burgess and Governour finally got paid what was due since they marched from Wilmington, and they sent this in my care once they knew I would be putting in here for certain. It will help you to set yourselves up in Charleston once you get there."

"Charleston?" she asked, taking the purse from him finally. "I do not understand."

"Wilmington is going to be evacuated. The naval stores will be loaded up and taken off, and the garrison goes south to Charleston. After Yorktown, there aren't troops enough to protect the place. All loyal subjects who wish to go shall find shipping, before a Rebel force marches against Wilmington."

"How soon?" she asked, perplexed.

"We begin tomorrow," Alan said. "We hope to empty the town in ten days. If you need any help with packing or arranging transport to the wharves, send me a note to the *Desperate* frigate and I can provide some hands and a boat for you and your household."

"Oh, God, this is so cruel." She sagged in defeat against the doorjamb. "When the Rebels take everything and set up their wretched republic where shall we light? What shall be left for us?"

"They haven't won it yet," Alan said, as if trying to boast.

"Have they not?" She laughed without glee. "If Cornwallis and all his troops are taken and Wilmington is evacuated, then how long before a Rebel force descends on Charleston as well? Then where do we go?"

"For someone who does not pretend to understand military matters, that is an astute observation," he said, trying to piss down her back, and also expressing a real admiration for her perspicacity. Damme, she's not half intelligent! he thought in wonder. That won't get her a husband, either, poor tit.

"One can only listen to the menfolks and glean what one can from their discourse, though half of it goes right past me, I fear," she said, backpedaling into the traditional woman's role.

"I recollect Burgess saying you had family in Surrey," Alan said. "If things really turn that sour, you could go home to England. Surrey is a pretty place, gentle and peaceful, full of sheep now, but wonderful farm country still. Lots of fine houses, where a young lady such as yourself would make the very devil of an impression."

"*This* is our home, Mister Lewrie," she told him directly, standing back erect from her slump. "My grandparents sleep in Carolina. And every step we take forces us further away from our land and our heritage. Forgive me, but this is hard on us."

"I shall do everything in my power to help you make the process easier, Mistress Chiswick." Alan told her. "Governour and Burgess saved my bacon a couple of times as well, and I could do no less for them and theirs."

"God bless you, Mister Lewrie," she said, perking up a bit. "I truly believe that the Lord above has sent you to aid us in our time of troubles."

If He has, He's a devilish sense of humor to pick me for your deliverer, Alan thought to himself, but he shrugged modestly in answer.

"Please do come again, Mister Lewrie," Caroline said, putting on a smile which lit up her face, making Alan notice for the first time that she had the funniest little underlining folds of skin below her eyes, a fault that made her eyes seem incredibly merry. "Daddy isn't always lost in the past, and we do so want to repay you with whatever little we still have to offer, if only to feel part of a family for a short while after so much time at sea, away from your own."

"I would appreciate that more than you know, Mistress Chiswick," Alan told her. He took her hand and held it for a moment, but she leaned forward and bestowed a sisterly kiss on his cheek, gave his fingers one slight squeeze and went back inside.

Alan regained the street and shambled back down Dock Street over the brow of the hill and stood looking down the road towards St. James and the handsome houses that reached almost to the wharves. He waited to digest what he had seen and heard at the Chiswicks. They had opened their home, such as it was, to him, and he felt an odd longing to go back and take advantage of their hospitality, painful as it would be to see the old man maundering through an evening, waiting for him to open his mouth and say something inane.

"I've never been part of a family," he muttered. "So what's the point now? Probably be bored shitless in an hour. If Governour or Burgess were there, 'twould be a different kettle of fish. The old man's gone Tom O'Bedlam and his wife ain't far behind him, even on her best days. The girl's the only attraction, and she's so . . ."

He was going to say "pitifully gawky," but the word "handsome" swam to the fore instead, which thought made him shake himself all over.

One thing for certain, he needed a drink after all that familial bumf, so he betook himself down to Market Street and entered an ordinary. He considered a brandy, but didn't think that was the thing to have on his breath when returning to the ship, so he settled on an ale. He stretched his legs out by the fire to warm himself from the damp winds that chilled the street, noting how the locals shied away from him and stopped conversing so loudly as long as a man in King's uniform was in sight. The ordinary was attached to a chandler's next door, and after finishing his beer, he wandered in. Foraged over as the countryside had to be, there was a goodly selection of foodstuffs present, a sure sign that the prices would be high, bespeaking Rebel connections inland.

"Need anythin', sir?" the publican asked, clad in the universal blue apron that seemed so homey in this alien and hostile land.

"Do you mind the refugee house on Dock Street, across the hill?"

"Aye, I knows it well, sir. Send a lot o' trade up here."

"I'd like to send something to one of the families."

"Ah, the Henrys, I expect."

"No, the Chiswicks."

"Across the hall from the Henrys. Good customers in past, afore the troubles," the man said, seeming almost kindly compared to the rest of the citizenry toward Tories, as they called them.

"I'd like to send a dinner up to them. Have you turkeys?"

"Aye, sir, I'm turkey poor at this moment," the man smiled. "I kin cook up anythin' ya want an' deliver it."

"I want a truly magnificent bird, with all the trimmings you can think of. What you'd put on your own table had you the mind for it."

"I'd be layin' in a couple bottles o' wine, too, with mine, sir," the publican said. "Dinner fer. . . ."

"Four, including the old black servant woman," Alan told him.

"Got a bird that'll feed 'em all fer nigh on a week, an' all the trimmin's, with a couple bottles . . . say, ten shillings fer all, sir."

"So be it." Alan winced at the price. A dinner like that back in

London from even a Piccadilly or Strand ordinary-kitchen would not go over a crown, and the bird not a penny a pound of it. "Let me send a note with it."

"Be a ha' penny fer paper, sir, an' a ha' penny fer the King's stamp," the man said slyly. "God knows, tax stamps got us in this mess, so we got ta obey the King's laws, ain't we now, sir?"

"I take it the ink's free," Alan said wryly.

"Scribble away, sir, scribble away!"

Allan left the shop and headed for the boat landing on Market Street, feeling... good about himself, savoring the emotion of having done a kind act for the Chiswicks and wondering just how big a fool he was for doing it, and if the man even intended to deliver the dinner.

Yorktown must have deranged me, he thought. Here I am worrying over a family I never clapped eyes on before, acting serious as a sober parson for the first time in my life and going back aboard without even a try for some mutton. And I can't even share that dinner, much as I'd like to look at the girl some more, even if she is poor as mud. Maybe they really will bury me a bishop.

CHAPTER 15

IT was only after most of the civilians had been put aboard the shallow coastal ships in the river that they began to extricate the army from the garrison. Patrols had found no organized Rebel activity beyond the town, so it was thought possible to finish up the evacuation.

Alan had gotten a nice "thank you" note from the Chiswicks and an invitation to dinner, but he was worked much too hard to be able to accept for days. He did not know how much their sons had sent them, so he did not wish to intrude on their penury if they had to lay out money only to entertain him. The food in *Desperate* was good enough now they were in harbor, and the chandlers and purveyors could get in their last good selling season on the fleeing Loyalists and ships' crews. He ate his fill of some very good dinners that Freeling did not mangle or burn.

Toward the last week of November, though, as the weather turned rainy and cold, he was surprised to get a note from Caroline Chiswick, asking for that promised aid in packing and moving. After showing the note to Treghues, he was allowed ashore once more on a private errand.

He took Cony and several sturdy hands to do the fetching and carrying and to row the cutter through the blustery morning wind and rain. Sopping wet even through a tarpaulin watch coat, he reached their lodgings to find absolute disorganisation.

"Mister Lewrie, thank you for coming." Caroline smiled in relief

as he entered the frowsty warm room. "I did not wish to throw ourselves on you, or be a burden to you, but . . ."

"If you need help, then there's nothing for it but to get some,
Mistress Chiswick." He was smiling back, feeling glad to be in her
presence once more. "Now, what may I do? I'd have thought you
would have been on one of the ships long since, so I must own to
some surprise to receive your note this morning."

"Daddy hasn't been feeling well." She sighed, her hands knit
together as though she was at the end of her own tether. "He . . ."

She led him to one corner where they could converse without
the rest of the family—or his curious seamen—overhearing them.

"He became more lucid in the last few days, less involved in his
memories, but then he began to weep over all we've lost, and nothing could console him. I sent for a physician, but there was little he
could do but put him to bed and told us to cosset him and wait it
out. Otherwise we would have taken passage with the Henrys, who
had lodgings across the hall. But they could not wait, and they had
so much to pack . . ."

"How is he doing today, then?" Alan asked, stripping off the
tarpaulin garment. "Pardon my familiarity in presuming to pry."

"He thinks he is home," she whispered in a small voice, the
pain making her shake so that she had to place a hand on his
shoulder to steady herself, something Alan was only too glad to
allow. "He doesn't understand why we have to pack up and leave,
and Momma doesn't want to upset him. I've tried packing what I
could, but as soon as he sees me gathering things up, he . . . oh,
dammit!" she finally burst out, catching herself almost at once and
apologizing for losing control. "I have tried, the good Lord shall
witness I have tried, but I'm only a weak woman."

"I don't think you weak at all, Mistress Chiswick," Alan told
her, his heart going out to her in her travail of trying to nurse a
loony and cajole a stubborn but weak mother at the same time. "Is
he rational enough to listen to reason?"

"No, I fear not."

"Then lie to him," Alan said bluntly. "If he doesn't know where
he is, then you may tell him you're already in Charleston, ready to
go home, or going to Charleston to see his sons, who are already
there. You must go there now and again."

"Only once in our lives," she confessed. "Wilmington is the biggest town we've seen, except for that. But, he always did love going. I could try. Oh, thank you, Mister Lewrie, you're inspiring."

"Sneaky, but inspiring." He grinned.

"The Lord shall forgive us a small lie, in a good cause," she said with a firmness he was glad to see.

"You go work on him, and I shall have my men gather up your belongings and get them into your wagon. Which one is yours?"

"We have none," she said. "We had to sell the wagon and the carriage and all the horses just to pay for lodging and food once our coin ran out. No one extends credit, and everything is dear."

"No problem." Alan grinned. "Cony?"

"Aye, sir?"

"Go out and hire us a wagon. Handle the drays yourself and we'll save tuppence or two. Hold on, how much is to go?"

Alan saw all the heavy furniture, the beds and the chairs, the tables and paintings, the carpets on the floor, even if they were far past the times when Axminster or Wilton would have claimed them as their work. Caroline must not have been able to pack up much, he surmised.

"The mattresses and pillows, the crates that Mammy and I have already packed, and the trunks."

"The rest?" Alan wondered.

"It came with the lodgings, or was found from other unfortunates such as we for a few pence," Caroline said, trying to put a brave face on it. "I have one large trunk for the last of our clothes, and one for all the quilts and such still hanging. The rest is packed."

"One 'orse dray, sir," Cony said, looking at the meager pile of possessions that represented three generations of work and life.

"Go get one then," Alan told him grimly.

Caroline ducked through a quilt barrier to her parents' bedroom and began to speak to her father. Alan could hear her telling him that he was there to take them to Charleston to see Gov and Burge, see all the sights and buy new horses and a slave or two, some "fancies."

The old man was having little of it, however, and insisted that there were good reasons to stay where they were snug in their own beds at home on their own lands. Alan didn't want to hear all of that, so he got busy ordering the hands to shift everything out to the front of the lodging house, letting Mammy point out what was to go and what was to stay while she had herself a short weep between loads.

They finally got the room picked clean of all the Chiswick belongings, and the landlord came in to see that nothing of his would be going.

"They owe fer the last two days, sir," he said, leaning on the doorjamb as though he would not move until he got his money.

"How much?" Alan asked.

"A crown," the man said smiling hopefully.

"Bugger me!" Alan gawped. "I wouldn't pay that much to sleep in St. James' Place!"

"They ain't leavin' til I get my money." The man blustered.

Alan crooked a finger at one of his hands, a fo'c'sle man named Fields, who easily stood taller than Alan and weighed fifteen stone, the sort who could seize a headsail sheet and almost walk away with it himself in a full gale.

"Now, sir," Alan crooned softly, dragging the little man into the hallway. "There's a lot of furniture been added to this room to make it livable, some of it rather good and bought for a penny on the pound, unless I miss my guess. Why don't you take that in trade? If you do, then I won't have to have Fields here tear off your legs and cram 'em up your fundament."

"You wouldn't dare, sir!"

"Take him out back and dismember him, Fields."

"Aye, sir," Fields said, lumbering within reach. "Hain't never tried ta rip a man's legs h'off afore. Might be a treat."

"Alright, go, just go!" the landlord cried, ducking out of range.

Finally, Mr. Chiswick was bundled up into winter clothing and was carried out to the dray, protesting all the while that he could walk, and his wife stumbled alongside him while two seamen linked arms to make a chair for his frail body. Caroline came out of the house in a dark red velvet traveling cloak with the hood up over her fair hair, and a muff over her hands, and the sailors winked and leered at Lewrie, thinking him quite the fellow to have become friends with such a pretty girl.

"Do we have everything?" Alan asked, getting back into his watch coat and going to her side on the porch.

"Aye, I made a last check." She sighed, finally looking weak and helpless for a change instead of so rigid and self-controlled. They made their way down to the boat, loaded all the possessions into it and rowed out to the small schooner which Caroline had booked for passage. But the master bluntly informed them that he was full up, since they had not paid to reserve their space and others had come aboard since.

They had to pick their way through the anchored shipping, searching for a ship that would take them.

"Like Joseph and Mary looking for lodging," Caroline said, trying to smile and regard it as an adventure.

"I'm cold," Mr. Chiswick complained.

"We'll find the right boat soon, Daddy," she told him.

They tried a brigantine, a ship lying near *Desperate*, but once more they were rebuffed. A passenger came to the rail and gave the Chiswicks a hearty hello, but had no joy for them.

"Mister Henry, sir, surely our few belongings would take no room at all," Caroline bargained, and Alan could see that though she was trying to stay friendly, her teeth were set on edge with frustration. "We could sleep four to a pallet in the corner of a cabin, or hang our quilts for privacy."

"But my dear girl, that would crowd my family so, and the others aboard this poor ship," Henry shouted back smarmily. He was a richly dressed man, and his wife looked as fashionable as a London belle on her way to a ball. Alan was sure they had as much room as a post-captain.

"They's a tiny bit o' room, young miss," the master called down. "But I'm overloaded now, an' the risk o' takin' more weight . . . if there be the four o' ya an' all that dunnage, I couldn't do it fer less'n twenty pounds."

Caroline considered this, though Alan was sure it was most of their money. She shut her eyes and took a deep breath, a strange smile still on her features.

"The hell you shall," Alan said. "Cox'n, get a way on her and steer for *Desperate*."

"Aye, aye, sir!" the man replied. "Give way tagither!"

Minutes later, he clambered to the deck through the entry port, sought out an audience with Commander Treghues and explained the situation, stressing that no one would show a decent, God-fearing family the slightest Christian charity. He knew how Treghues thought by then.

"They have no money for passage?" Treghues asked.

"They do, sir, but so little that the tariff would break them, and all they have is what their sons sent them from New York. Mr. Sewallis Chiswick was a prominent Loyalist, helped to outfit local military units, and they'd hang him sure as fate if he doesn't get away," Alan said.

"And how pretty is the girl, Mister Lewrie?" Treghues asked with a twinkle in his eyes.

"Sir?" Alan gaped. Damme, he's having a good day, I didn't know he was that sharp anymore, Alan thought.

"I know you, Mister Lewrie," Treghues warned, still smiling that lazy, superior smile. "Since Yorktown you seem a changed person, for the better, I might add, but as Horace tells us, men may change their latitudes but not their character, or something like that. I'll not ensconce an innocent and impressionable young girl aboard to liven your social life."

"If you would but see them, sir. They wouldn't take up much room, they have so little left of their possessions. They could do quite well in the chart space, all four of them. They'd sleep in hammocks if that was all we had to offer."

"Very well, I shall take a look at your refugees," Treghues said, rising from his desk and shrugging on a grogram watch coat over his uniform.

Once Treghues looked down over the rail at the bedraggled family seated in the cutter among their treasured possessions, dripping wet and freezing, he lurched into action. Stay tackle went over the side, and the dunnage went soaring aloft in parbuckles. Bosun's chairs were rigged to hoist the old man and his womenfolk into the air and deposit them on deck. Judkin, the captain's steward, and a wardroom steward were there in minutes with hot rum toddies. Treghues offered up the use of his day cabin aft for their comfort, while he would berth in the chart space. The carpenter began sawing and hammering to create new bed boxes, and the duty bosun's mate rushed aft with rope and tackle to rig them from the deckhead so the heel of the ship would not disturb their rest. The old man and his wife were tucked into the first beds finished, with warming pans and hot bricks wrapped in sailcloth to thaw them out from their sojourn on the chilly river.

"However do you do it, Mister Lewrie?" Railsford asked him mildly as Alan thawed his hands around a pewter mug of rum toddy on the quarterdeck once the cutter had been tied up alongside and its crew dispersed.

"Do what, sir?" Alan shivered, savoring the fumes rising from the mug.

"Go skylarking ashore and discover the most ravishing creatures, time after time, so I hear. That Miss Lucy Beauman on Antigua, for one, and now Miss Chiswick for another."

"One does what one can for the young women of this world, sir," Alan replied feeling just a little smug at Railsford's attitude and from the crew's reaction. They had taken the unfortunate Chiswicks into their care as gently as if they had been their own aged parents.

"You sly-boots!" Railsford went on. "Still, it was a decent act. So unlike the old Lewrie, I'd wager there was a different person masquerading as a master's mate."

"I promised the Chiswicks I would look out for them, sir," Alan said. "Even a rake-hell may have a heart now and then."

"Still, our rake-hell would not have had a heart if the girl was not so lovely."

"Do you find her so, sir?" Alan grinned tightly, cocking a brow.

"A bit too tall for fashion, but that don't always signify."

"Mister Lewrie?" Treghues called from the larboard quarterdeck ladder.

"Aye, sir."

"That was a charitable thing you did, sir, bringing that family out here to *Desperate*. I'm told most of the shipping is filling up and I have word from ashore that there are more people who wish to depart."

"Aye, sir, people who could not rub shoulders with the rich and fashionable, who need their *space*." Alan sneered. "Or merchant captains who want five pounds a head for a two-day journey at best.

They'd gouge the dead for a shovelful of dirt on their coffins."

"And that," Treghues stated primly, "is why a gentleman, or one who has any pretensions to gentility, should never consider a career in Trade. It's all buying and selling and usury and following the dictates of Mammon to the exclusion of any decent sentiments. Easier a camel may pass through the eye of a needle than a rich man, or one who has traded in the misery of his fellow man, enter the kingdom of heaven."

But prize money's just devilish fine, Alan thought cynically.

"I want you to go ashore again, Mister Lewrie."

"Aye, sir?"

"Give my compliments to Major Craig and his staff. There are but the ships reserved for the troops and their equipment. If there are more loyal subjects who wish to embark, I shall find room for them in those merchantmen, if I have to do it with Peck and the marines to enforce it. And, since you have started the procedure, we shall take on as many who wish to go. Look especially for those poor and with few possessions who will not crowd us overly much. We may double up the wardroom and senior warrant berths. It has not been so long that you slept in a hammock, and as you say, it is only for the two days."

"Aye, sir," Alan said, trying to keep from screaming. Damme, I believe I have fucked up again. There won't be room belowdecks to swing a cat without getting fur in one's mouth at this rate.

On November 30th, only two days behind schedule, the flotilla of ships and coasters hoisted anchor and made their way slowly and carefully down the Cape Fear River on the very first of the ebb tide. To the chants of the leadsmen, they braved the shoals and eddies. Their passengers, and there were a lot of them by that time, crowded the decks to take their last looks at Wilmington. When Alan had a chance he took a look at the place, too. He had had fun there, and the next time he saw it there would most likely be a new flag flying over it, lost forever to the egalitarian notions of a jackass stubborn pack of rogues who had defied their King and had muddled their way to victory over one of the most powerful nations and the most powerful navy in the world. That most of their victories had been the result of even more incredible muddling on the part of the King's forces was hard to bear. What debt they would owe the French and Spanish, and what form of payment their insincere allies would demand would possibly shatter the existing world order, placing both of the Indies in jeopardy. Until some damned Whig majority was voted in and brought the whole shameful thing to an end in a wave of weariness and self-abasement (but call it what it was, abject surrender), the war would probably stagger on, mostly to prevent the Frogs and Dagos from grabbing everything in sight, and if the Whigs cried penury for the huge debt run up by the war, they could walk off with everything England had, and leave her as helpless as the Danes, with few overseas possessions, little trade and a Navy more suitable for a child's daydreams on a duck pond. Would the French be so encouraged by this that de Grasse would go home and put together the invasion force that succeeded in crossing the channel and recreating the Norman Conquest, Alan wondered?

"Ten fathom, ten fathom with this line!"

Alan drew his attention back to the ship and took a bearing on one of the tiny sandspits in midchannel. They would pass it safely to larboard, in a channel marked from their earlier ascension as better than fifteen fathoms. No danger.

The Chiswicks were on the taffrail, looking sternward at the land they would never see again either. The father was propped up on the flag lockers, his wife to one side and Mammy to the other to support him. Caroline wore her dark red traveling cloak with the hood thrown back, gripping the ornately carved taffrail with hands that looked kid-glove white even at that distance. Alan had suffered in silence aboard *Desperate* before and had found solace aft out of everyone's way, gripping the rail in that way, so he could sympathize with her at that moment.

Once Wilmington had fallen out of sight astern and nothing was left but the barren narrow cape and the bleak salt-grass meadow shore, she came forward to about the larboard mizzen chains, more intent on the working of the ship than in pining away for the shoreline.

"Mister Lewrie, do ya see them marsh grasses yonder?" Monk asked.

"Aye, sir. Swirling," Alan said. "Wind's heading us a point.

Hands to the lee braces, prepare to harden up! Quartermaster, stand
by to give us a point free."

"Clear ta starboard, iffen we do," Monk grumped, staring with a
telescope at the shore to their right. "Half a mile afore we gets inta
trouble over there."

"Here it comes," Railsford said, gripping the hammock nettings.

The wind ruffled cat's paws on the choppy waters, and *Desperate*
leaned heavily as the gust hit them.

"Give us a point free!" Railsford called.

"Bosun, tail on the lee braces!"

"Don't forget the tops'l set," Railsford cautioned.

"Tops'l braces, off belays and haul away!" Alan cried. "How's
her helm, quartermaster?"

"Worn't 'nuff fer a good bite at first, sir, but she's fine now," the
quartermaster said, as he and his mate spun the wheel gingerly a few
spokes at a time to demonstrate better control with more flow on the
rudder.

"We get headed like that again and we'll have to bear up sharp
and tack her on a short board to larboard before we can come back
onto the safe pass," Alan griped.

"Somebody whistlin' on deck?" Monk asked, peering about to
see if someone was violating one of the cardinal superstitions of a
seafarer's life. Whistling on deck *always* brought the wind, usually
from a direction and in such strength that would put lives at hazard
to reef down aloft. Even marines and idlers knew better.

"Wimmen on a ship, Mister Monk," the quartermaster whispered. "I'd take a whistler any day."

Alan didn't mind women aboard ship, especially the particular
woman who had come to observe him in action, and he was pleased
that he was showing well, being all nautical and tarry-handed, conversing as an equal with the first officer and the sailing master.

"Taut enough, sir?" Alan asked Railsford.

"Aye, Bosun, belay every inch of that!"

Alan turned as though to peer at the cape peninsula with one of
the telescopes, and in so doing took a look at Caroline Chiswick.
Her color was high, whether from emotion at being driven from
Wilmington as a refugee or from the sea breeze, he could not say, but
she was smiling, which was more than she had done in the last few

days after being ensconced aft, and when he glanced at her, she gave him a wider smile, which he could feel all the way down to his toes. Pauper or not, she was an attractive diversion until he could get back to the West Indies.

The wind shifted once more, this time backing almost a point and a half, giving them a perfect breeze to make it out to sea past the last low islands. The first rollers in the open bay struck her and set her pitching her bows up and rolling to starboard.

"Hands make sail, Mister Railsford," Treghues ordered. "Plain sail, with two reefs in the tops'ls for now and two reefs in the courses. And I'll have the main topmast staysail run aloft to steady her helm."

"Full an' bye'll get us our offin', sir," Monk said, studying the long, whipping commissioning pendant aloft as a rough wind indication.

"Make sail and then we'll harden up and lay her close hauled." Treghues said. "Mister Coke, better get some more buckets on deck. Our live lumber will be casting their accounts into the Atlantic soon."

"Aye, sir." Coke glowered, thinking of the ruin of his pristine decks as their passengers began to spew.

Half an hour later, with *Desperate* in the lead to windward, the evacuation fleet stood out to sea headed roughly sou'west to make an offing from that treacherous shore where the soundings were always wrong and they had enough sea room off a lee shore should the wind turn foul. The passengers were indeed having a rough time of it, losing their breakfasts over the side, or hugging the buckets. All the Chiswicks but Caroline went below to get out of the raw wind. Now free of duties until the day watch, Alan went to the windward rail to join her.

"This is quite exciting, Mister Lewrie," she said, her face glowing in the breeze and her hair ready to escape from her pins. "I never knew there was so much involved in sailing. All those men going aloft and walking on air, it seemed, to work on the sails! Do you do that?"

"I did, until my promotion," Alan said.

"You have had a promotion," she said. "How wonderful for you."

"I was a midshipman, have been for almost the last two years. In a way, I still am, but I was made acting master's mate the first week of November. Until then I spent half my life aloft."

They chattered on until Treghues came back on deck, and Alan took her hand. "If you wish to stay on this side of the deck our captain will oblige you, but I must go to loo'ard."

"Why?"

"It's tradition. The windward side of the quarterdeck is for the captain alone, and the rest of the watch standers must go down to leeward."

She accepted his hand and he led her down the slanting deck along the nettings at the front of the quarterdeck.

"You call it loo'ard once and leeward the next," she said. "I believe you are speaking a foreign language."

The next half hour, until Treghues retired aft, they spent laughing as he explained a sailor's life, some of the pranks they played on each other, and the seeming nonsense of the seaman's vocabulary, until Alan noticed she was shivering in the wind, which had turned quite cold.

"You'll catch your death up here. You should go below and get warm. They'll be piping dinner soon, anyway," he told her.

"Forgive me, Mister Lewrie, but I could not bear to do so. I have monopolized you, I fear, for purely selfish purposes, but I could not face another moment in the cabin. Getting away for a while has been most refreshing."

"I'm sorry there is only you to . . . bear up under this burden on your family," he said.

"I was raised to be self-reliant," she said, her face growing pensive as she stared back toward the distant shore. "All of us were. But lately, there has been so *much* duty, and no one to help me cope."

"I know what that is." Alan grinned. "This promotion has piled a load on me, too."

"The morning you came in answer to my note, I was ready to give way to despair. Without your timely assistance, we would still be looking for a ship. Thank you for taking charge as you did, Mister

Lewrie. I appreciated that more than you could ever know."

"I was glad to be of any help to you," he said, turning gallant. "Someone as young and pretty as you, Mistress Chiswick, should not have to bear such a heavy burden. There are gayer things to consider."

"Why, thank you, Mister Lewrie." She colored prettily. "But surely such amusements as you suggest are only folly and frivolity. Perhaps in better times, but for now, we do what we must, and I would be an ungrateful daughter to even think of such things while my momma and daddy need me. Just as you must suspend your own amusements until the ship is tied up in some harbor, is that not so?"

"Yes, I suppose so." He shrugged.

"Our journey began long ago, upriver," she said, trying to be light about it but not able to hide the sadness in her. "Now we're only on one stage of it and where we'll have to go from Charleston I don't know. Maybe back to England with our relatives in Surrey, as you suggested. Maybe the Indies, or Florida or Canada, or the Moon."

"Then will you consider frivolous things?" he prompted, to get her out of her sad mood.

"I promise you I shall be nothing but frivolous," she told him, smiling once more. But the shore was almost under the horizon, and the refugee fleet aft of them was in the way, so the smile didn't linger.

"If you would like to be alone with your feelings for a while, I could walk you aft," Alan suggested, wondering why he was trying to cajole her when she seemed ready for a good cry.

"No, that's the last thing I need right now, I pray you," she said quickly. "Things come, things go, and you can't change that. But I will miss this country. A few more years and... do you remember seeing that very fine house on the way downriver, on the right? This side of the ship?"

"Just before we picked up the ships at Fort Johnston, yes."

"The Orton house. We were ready to expand our house to copy it, just before all the troubles began." Caroline smiled in fond memory. "I don't think we could have ever really afforded it, but Momma was set on it after seeing an oil of it, and Daddy usually let her have her way in most things. It would have been a sign that we belonged here for good. Now I'm glad we didn't build on, it would have been too much to lose."

"You lost a lot, so Burgess told me," Alan said, trying to find a way to continue talking to her that didn't set off her bitter memories.

"Aye, we did, but not as much as others, more than some. If we had not declared for the Crown, in spite of how bad they tried to run the colony and how venal their appointed men were . . . well, it would have been a Tarleton or a Fanning that burned us out, anyway. Maybe God wants the Chiswicks back in England. Just the way that perhaps God wanted you to be a sailor."

In spite of his best efforts, Alan had to break out into a fit of guffaws, which prompted Caroline to forget her musings and try to cozen the reason for his humor from him, which, naturally, improved her own.

"Do you mock the Good Lord, sir?" she said, pretending to frown.

"No, and I don't mock you, either, but the idea of me being meant for a sailor set me off. Sorry. I'll tell you about it someday, but it wasn't my first choice for a career."

"Ah, second sons get no choice, do they?" She smiled, thinking she understood. "What would you have been otherwise?"

"A man who sleeps late and dines well," Alan told her.

"And a less somber one, I think." She grinned as though they had shared a great secret. "You really must *smile* more, Mister Lewrie."

"Me?" He laughed gently. "But I'm a merry sort almost all the time. Too much so for some. Ask anyone."

"So serious for . . . twenty?"

"Almost nineteen, in January. And you," he said, taking liberties with her good humor, "are such a sober thing for eighteen."

"Burgess told you of me?" she asked, cocking an eyebrow and turning her mouth up in a wry expression, as though she was trying to gnaw on her cheek. "He would. What did he say?"

"That you were the prettiest girl in two counties, but too serious by half, and that's an opinion with which I heartily agree."

Caroline made no answer to this, but turned away to savor the compliment from her brother, and the corroboration from a handsome young man at her side, trying to hide her pleased expression.

The bosun's mate of the watch, Weems, took a squint at the half-hour glass by the belfry and put his whistle to his lips. He blew the welcome call "Clear decks and up spirits" while the purser and an acting quartermaster's mate brought up a keg of rum. The hands began to queue up for their predinner rum ration.

"That means the men shall get their rum and water," Alan said. "They can get a little rowdy, and dinner shall be served aft in half an hour. Best you get below, much as I hate to send you."

"Much as I hate to go," she replied. "Shall you be here after we have dined?"

"Yes, but I shall be in the watch today, and I am sure the other officers think I have monopolized you enough." He chuckled. "Though you might wish to come on deck when four bells chime in the late afternoon. We stand to the guns for evening quarters then, and it is interesting to watch."

"They just rang seven."

"One for every half-hour turn of the glass, eight bells for a four-hour watch," he explained, walking her aft to the upper entrance to the great cabins to avoid the milling crowd of seamen on the gun deck. "After dinner there will be eight bells at four in the afternoon, then when you hear four bells again, that will be halfway through the first dogwatch, five in the afternoon."

"Every half hour?" she teased. "I believe you are making this up to make sport with me. More of your nautical cant and humbug."

"That's exactly what I called it for a long time." He laughed. "Enjoy your dinner, and my best regards to your mother and father."

She gave him one last smile and departed the deck for her cabins, leaving Alan shivering on the deck, though warmed by a glow inside at her evident fondness. He had enjoyed talking with her and laughing with her, for she had a merry disposition in her nature that she had to hide most of the time in her dealings with the world. And as the most rational member of her family present, she had her sobering responsibilities to consider first and foremost. But when free of them, she could be a charming and waggish companion, more so than any other female Alan had come across. Others did not pretend to so much wit and shunned repartee that would unsex them and make them a conversational equal to their men.

Alan thought that the Colonies did not regard mental feeble-
ness as a desirable trait in their women, or spent more time and
effort educating their daughters and allowing them free participation
in discourse, much like what only a peer's daughter could expect.
Still, she was not as free with her tongue and wit as a Frenchwoman
at a *levée*, conversing on just any topic at hand in *le haute monde*
salon society he had heard mentioned as the vogue in Paris.

He was looking forward to seeing her in late afternoon, but
when she emerged on deck, it was Treghues who escorted her and
her mother, and Alan had to stand down to leeward from them and
attend to his duties on the watch. Alan felt a pang of . . . annoyance
. . . (he would not dare to call it jealousy) at that development.

His captain was another new and different man with the Chiswicks, slightly raffish without crudity, jolly and charming, and was
even heard to laugh lightly now and then, an event that made hands
stop in their tracks and goggle at this unheard of novelty from a
naval captain.

The humorless fart's wooing her! Alan glowered inwardly. I
swear, there's a pretty picture. Trust the son of a lord to get what he
wants, every time. And she's eating it up like plum duff, damme if
she ain't! Just like a woman to sniff out the boss cock with the most
chink and start spoonin' him up. And I thought she was better than
that. Now I've got the proper reckoning of her. Let her lick his boots
if that's her game. I've had better, anyway. Gawky bitch.

Alan contented himself with the thought that Treghues would
not have any ulterior designs on her, at least, thinking his captain
too holy a hedge-priest to do more than hold hands and gawp, even
if he felt the urge, which Alan doubted as well. Treghues was too
moral to even admit to the desires of the flesh. And he had to admit
that if the Chiswick family was gone smash and reduced to impover-
ished misery, then Treghues at least had the blessings of future title,
rents, land and all that prize money to offer them in exchange for
what few lusty demands (if any, Alan thought smugly) he would
make on their daughter. He even had to smile at the thought of
somber and pious Treghues wed to the get of a bankrupt colonial too
tall and skinny for fashion, and how his aristocratic friends would
make sport of them behind their backs every time they took the air
or attended some "tasteful and acceptable" entertainment.

Hope you like praying a lot, my dear, he sneered. If you ally yourself with such a one as him, you'll be doing a lot of it.

"Watcher luff, quartermaster," Monk warned coming to the wheel. "Mister Lewrie, attend yer mind ta duties, would ya please, sir?"

"Aye, Mister Monk," Alan piped, torn from watching the couple as they took the air on the windward rail.

"Han'some piece, she is." Monk grinned as he studied the pair. "Though slimmer'n an eel, an' not a spare ounce o' nothin' to grab hold of. I likes my women bouncier."

"So do most, Mister Monk," Alan said, gazing up at the set of the sails, all duty again. "So do I."

"Still, she's got the captain laughin', damme if she ain't. Now there's a thing. Be good fer him. He's not had much joy these last few months. I never heard tell o' him messin' with the ladies much, nor even goin' ashore fer pleasure o' any sort. Holds himself taut as a forestay, he does."

"How much of that is Treghues, and how much of that is demanded of a captain, Mister Monk?" Alan inquired innocently.

"I've had captains'd take a girl to sea right in their cabins." Monk grinned. "Mind ya Augustus Hervey? When he was a young post-captain in the Mediterranean back in the sixties, he musta made sport with over two hundred women in one commission. Duchesses, servin' girls an' two nuns ta top it off. Twas a wonder his weddin' tackle didn't drop off."

"Nuns, Mister Monk?" Alan asked.

"Ya know them breast-beatin' priests an' popes is the randiest pack o' rogues goin', no matter what anyone says. They don't wear them cassocks fer nothin'. Finest garments in the world fer fornicatin' when the humor's strong on ya. Ya think ya seen somethin' when the bum-boats come 'round the fleet when we hit port, ya ain't seen nothing 'til ya put foot ashore in a Catholic land. 'Course, ya could keep Mother Phillips at the Green Canister in silver from all the condoms ya'd wear out, an' come home ta find Half Moon Street richer'n St. James' Place."

The humor was on Alan strongly after this short talk, and he felt an unbearable urge to readjust his privates, but could not, not as long as the Chiswicks were on deck. She suddenly looked a whole lot more desirable to him, however, after Monk's dissertation.

Dusk grew on the sea as the short early winter day began to end, and the hands were piped to quarters. Treghues's fifers and drummers came on deck in their livery and began to rattle and toot bravely while the marines turned up in their scarlet finery, and the seamen cast off the gun tackle and stood swaying by their pieces. Aft, in Treghues's quarters, the missing artillery had been replaced by short nines, older bronze guns not as reliable or as long as the newer long nines made of iron that were *Desperate*'s original equipment.

For half an hour, until almost full dark, they stood waiting for the appearance of an enemy ship, while Treghues prated on from the nettings overlooking the waist about the ship and what would happen should battle present itself, to which the Chiswick women nodded often.

Finally, the hands were released from quarters, the guns bowsed down once more and the men gathered up their hammocks from the nets to take them below. The overhead lookouts were stood down, and the men of the duty watch took up vantage points on the gangways and upper decks.

Treghues led the women aft toward the entrance to their cabins, and Alan was in their way. He looked at Caroline and tried to smile politely, but could not find it in him to be that charitable; he doffed his hat in a civil gesture, then turned away to his duties once more and missed the sudden frown that knit Caroline's brows together, hearing only Treghues inviting them to dine with him and share a captain's largesse.

There was a full moon that night that rode through a cold and clear sky. The stars stood out like candle flames, and the sea shone a lambent silver in the moon trough, each wavetop to either side to moonward flecked with sparkling glints. At the cast of the log, Alan found that *Desperate* was sailing at a fair five and a half knots even with three reefs in courses and tops'ls so that the slower and shorter merchantmen could keep up with her. He was aft, using the night glass to study their charges and count them when he heard footsteps approaching. He turned to see Caroline Chiswick pacing the deck, and he stiffened as much as if Commander Treghues had caught him napping. He could see in the faint light of the taffrail lanterns that she wore her hooded traveling cloak and muff.

"Good evening, Mister Lewrie," she said, hesitant about approaching him.

"Good evening, Mistress Chiswick," he replied civilly.

"I could not sleep," she said. "All the creaking and groaning the ship makes. And footsteps overhead constantly."

"I shall order the quarterdeck people to walk softer," Alan said.

Two bells had already pealed from the fo'c'sle belfry, so it was after one in the morning, he knew. An odd hour for a girl to be up and about, especially without her momma or servant as chaperone. The lack of supervision intrigued him.

"Do not do anything on my account, sir," Caroline said, stepping to the rail for a secure hold on the canted deck. "You must not make any changes in routine for our sakes, I pray."

"Do your parents rest well, miss?" Alan asked.

"They sleep soundly, thank you for asking, Mister Lewrie," she replied. "Um, this afternoon, Mister Lewrie, did I do something to disturb you?"

"I cannot think of anything, Mistress Chiswick." Alan frowned as though sifting his memory.

"When we went below, you answered my smile with such a look of complete . . . disinterest . . . that I feared I had inadvertently angered you in some way," she said with a haste that was out of character for the studied girl Alan had learned she was in their short acquaintance.

"I was on watch, after all." Alan shrugged in dismissal. "Our sailing master had already cautioned me to be attentive to my duties, and Captain Treghues was present as well. He's the one made me an acting mate, and I am still on sufferance to keep the rating."

"I see," she said, a slight line still creasing her forehead. "And you can do nothing to hurt your career in the Navy. You must love it, then, in spite of what you said before dinner."

"Actually, I detest it like the Plague," Alan confessed, screwing his mouth into a wry grin. "It was not my idea to enter the Navy, but I have become competent at this life, and it's most likely the only career I shall have."

"I had not gained that impression," she said. "Not the competent part, I assure you. You seemed most competent, in all things, when we sailed today. And competent at organizing our entrance into this ship, in everything. Surely, it's not that awful for you, is it?"

"I have come to accept it," Alan replied stiffly.

"I am sorry, I did not know that they could press-gang people as midshipmen," she said, attempting a smile as wry as his. "I had heard the food was bad and all, but... well, I'll not pry into a private concern of yours if it is bothersome of you to speak of it."

"I suppose you could call it press-ganged," Alan told her. "My family... look, I'm a second son, not in line to inherit, and there wasn't much to go around even then, not enough to keep me as a gentleman at home in London. And I was only an adopted son at that, without the blessing of the family name."

That sounds innocent enough, he decided. If she knew my real background, she'd go screaming for the ladders.

"And what did your father do?"

"Not much of anything." Alan grimaced. "He was knighted for something in the last war on Gibraltar—Sir Hugo St. George Willoughby. We lived in St. James, at the mercy of his creditors, most of the time. Had land and rents in Kent, nothing big, though, far as I know."

"But the Navy is a respectable career for a gentleman," she pressed, shifting a half step towards him. "Your captain was kindly disposed to you when we asked of you at supper. He said you were, how did he say it... shaping quite well as an officer-to-be."

"He did?" Alan marveled. Which only goes to prove that he's as barking mad as a pack of wolves, he thought.

"Oh, yes, he did. Though I am afraid he seemed a little put out that you were such a prominent topic," she whispered hesitantly.

"Oh?" Alan marveled some more, quite happy to hear that Treghues had been put out, and that he had been talked of.

"He said you came aboard after you had fought a duel for a girl's honor, the daughter of an admiral?" Her voice had a shiver of dread.

"The admiral's niece," Alan said, preening a little. "He has not seemed enamored of me, for that and a few other reasons."

"Did you hurt your foe?"

"I killed him," Alan informed her. "That's where I got this," he went on, lightly touching his left cheek which still bore the faint horizontal scar that Lieutenant Wyndham of the Twelfth Foot had administered.

"Because he ruined your beauty?" Caroline chuckled waggishly.

"No, that was a by-blow," Alan said, unable to credit a woman who could jape about something like that. "Excuse me, but I must return to the helmsmen. I have spent too long aft."

"Have I angered you again?" she asked.

"No, you haven't," Alan said. "And if you can stand the wind, I would be delighted to converse with your further, but I cannot skylark back here. I've the ship to run, and don't want the captain to catch me."

"Then I would be delighted to join you," she said, slipping her arm between his for support as they walked forward. "Your captain is a bit stiff, isn't he?"

"Absolutely rigid," Alan snickered softly, leaning his head near her so the hands would not hear him make complaint of a captain.

"Dining with him was like having a traveling evangel making free with your hospitality when he's out riding the circuit in the backcountry," Caroline whispered. "I was quite relieved when we retired."

"I am sorry you had such a poor time."

"Are you?" she wondered aloud, one eyebrow lifted.

"Yes, for your sake," Alan rejoined.

"Ah, now I see why you treated me so coldly," she said, dragging him to a stop before they reached the wheel.

"Nothing of the kind," he assured her, damning himself for looking so obvious. "It was fear of seeming slack on watch."

"From someone my brothers said fears nothing?" she teased. "From what little I know of you, Mister Lewrie, I could not imagine there is anything in this life you fear."

"I hide it damn well, just like everyone else does."

"Such language in the presence of an impressionable young lady!" she gasped in mock distress. "Where will it all end? Tsk, tsk."

"My ar..." he began to say, but stopped himself before he could utter his favorite expression. Even joshing with a girl had its limits, especially if he truly nettled her and it was reported.

"My arse on a bandbox?" she blushed, as though she had stepped over her own line and was abashed at her own daring. "Remember, Mister Lewrie, I have two rowdy brothers and have lived in the country around ordinary yeomen farmers all of my life. Could I have been allowed to speak freely when vexed, I might use the phrase myself, instead of just thinking it. I hope I have not shocked you, instead."

"Not a bit of it," Alan replied, grinning widely. "Let there be perfect freedom between us, Mistress Chiswick."

"Then please call me Caroline."

"Caroline, I shall. Could you wait here for a moment, though? I really must see to the helm and the ship for a moment."

"Show me what you must see, I pray."

At her injunction he led her down the deck from the weather rail to the binnacle box before the wheel to speak to the quartermaster.

"Evening, Tate."

"Ev'nin', sir. Ev'nin,' miss," the helmsman said, almost swallowing his quid of tobacco at the miraculous appearance of a pretty young lady on the deck. His assisting quartermaster's mate, Weems is a bosun of the watch, and one of the ship's boys drifted closer to ogle her, the boy gazing up in snot-nosed wonder, earning a smoothing of his unruly hair from her gloved hand that turned him into an adoring worshiper.

"How's her head?" Alan inquired.

"Sou'sou'west, 'alf south, sir," Tate answered.

Three bells chimed from up forward.

"Mister Weems, I'd admire another cast of the log," Alan ordered. "Turn the glass, boy."

"Aye, zur," the boy replied, fumbling with the half-hour glass on the binnacle, never tearing his eyes away from the pretty lady in the faint light from the compass box lanterns.

"How's the helm, Tate? Any problem with those bronze guns aft, or do we need to shift some stores to lighten the bows?"

"Ah, seems harright, Mister Lewrie." Tate turned to spit into the kid, and flushed with embarrassment. "Sorry, miss."

"We grew tobacco in the Carolinas, Mister Tate." She smiled. "In the backcountry where I was a girl, even the women wouldn't turn their nose up to a chew now and then. My granny smoked a pipe."

"An' me own, too, miss." Tate, marveling at himself for daring to even open his mouth in the presence of an officer of the watch, grinned foolishly.

Alan looked up to check the set of the sails that shone like pale blue ghosts in the moonlight. There was nothing to complain of in their angle to the winds, and the commissioning pendant stood out in a lazy whip like a black worm on the sky, pointing perfectly abeam towards shore. The yard braces seemed taut enough to leave alone as well.

"So this is how you steer the ship," Caroline said.

"Yes, with this wheel. Though it's not always this easy. Sometimes it takes four or more men to manage the wheel when the sea and the wind kick up. When you want to go left, you put the helm to starboard."

"That sounds backwards," she said, shaking her head in confusion.

"Turning the wheel left turns the rudder so that it's leading edge faces right, so it is backwards, in a way. You'd say helm alee to make her head up more into the wind."

"You sailors are a contrary lot." She laughed gently. "And you have to keep adjusting it as Tate is doing?"

"Yuss, miss," Tate said, playing a spoke or two to either side as he spoke. "Back an' forth, hever sa gentle like."

"A wave will push her bows off course," Alan explained. "You watch the compass bowl, the wind pendants, and the luff of the sails and the way the wind strikes them, the way the sea is coming at you and, on a clear night such as this, a star or constellation as well."

"It seems so complicated."

"Try it," Alan urged. Before she could demur she was behind the wheel to the weather side, hands on two spokes, with Tate off to the lee side to lend his strength just in case and Alan at her side with his hands atop hers.

"It is harder to turn than I thought," she said after a few minutes of effort, as Alan bubbled happily on about what a proper luff looked like. They let her steer by herself, letting her get the feel of it. A bow wave thudded gently and creamed down their larboard side, and the helm fell off, but she corrected, almost grunting with the effort to add a spoke or two to windward. She gave Alan a puff and a smile, but her hazel eyes were gleaming like golden nuggets in the binnacle lights.

"Gentlemen, I thank you for sparing the time for such a weakling to learn a thing or two, but you'd best take your ship back before I run it on the rocks or something," she finally said, and suffered to be led away from the wheel to the nettings over the waist up forward.

"Did you enjoy that?" Alan asked, standing by her.

"Aye, I did, thank you." She smiled. "Much more than the lecture I received today from Captain Treghues. What a strange man your captain is, so enamored of his own voice at one moment and so somber the next."

"He has his moods," Alan replied cryptically, noting that was perhaps the five hundredth time he had heard that said in *Desperate*.

"After months of this at a stretch, I can imagine that it could grow wearisome, but being at sea can be fun, too, can't it, Alan?" she enthused, leaning forward over the waist and the gun deck. "The ocean is beautiful tonight with the moon on it. Like a blanket made of jewels."

"Yes, it is pretty tonight," Alan admitted as he half froze next to her. "There are many pretty days, and it can be exciting and fun, sometimes. But the sea's a chimera. She can seem peaceful one minute and try to kill you the next. You always have to be on your guard."

"The sea sounds much like life itself in that regard."

"Such sagacity from one so young," he chided her. "And such a cynical outlook. Chary as a burned child. Where will it end, tsk tsk?"

"Had I grown up in London with nothing more distressing in my life than balls and the theatre, it might seem so," she replied, stiffening. He turned to study her face in the moonlight, and saw that the serious mien was upon her once more.

"I am sorry to have raised such a frown from you in the middle of your enjoyment, Caroline," he said. "I've spoiled it for you; if I have I regret it."

"You've spoiled nothing, Alan," she said, patting the back of his hand that rested on the railing. "You gave me back my brothers, got us aboard a ship and away from retribution of our Rebels, brought joy to my parents and have provided me with a few precious moments of diversion. God knows I have needed some. You are pleasant company."

"And so are you, Caroline. Very easy to be with," he told her, realizing that it was so. There was no formality with her, as there was with many young women, no call for stilted triteness that passed for decent conversation. "I shall be sorry to reach Charleston tomorrow."

"And you shall go back to the Indies from there?" she said in a softer voice.

"Yes. This Admiral de Grasse still has a French fleet of nearly thirty sail. He'll not rest on his laurels until we've met him once more and beaten him."

"I shall pray God for your safety every moment," she promised. "But I expect there are more than a few young ladies who are already doing the same thing, eh?"

"Your prayers for me would be most welcome, Caroline," Alan said, looking at her and seeing the hesitant nature of her smile. *That's not teasing, that's fishing for information, by God,* he thought.

"This seafaring life leaves little room for young ladies, much to my regret," he added quickly. "There is no one back in England. Even if there had been, I've not been back in nearly two years."

"But there is the admiral's relation, is there not? Surely, she is kindly disposed towards you, and you her, or you would not have fought to defend her honor." She almost stammered this out, trying to appear nonchalant and only slightly interested.

"No one in her family could ever be enthused about the prospects of a two-a-penny midshipman." He shrugged. "I believe she is in Jamaica now, back with her family. We exchange letters now and then, but . . ."

"I only ask because of the sisterly affection I feel towards you, and the gratitude for saving Gov and Burge at Yorktown," she insisted, also shrugging most eloquently. "You'll be off across the ocean soon, and we shall never see each other again. Is that not the way of life, that people meet and part so quickly? I and my family shall always hold you in our memories, but . . ."

"It doesn't have to be that way," Alan said, placing his hand over hers, and he was excited to feel her fingers spread to take hold of his. "Should you still feel the need of diverting moments, we could correspond. If you are willing, I shall ask your parents for permission to write you, and you may keep me informed as to Governour and Burgess, and how your father and mother keep. Why let aimless life dictate to us?"

"'Scuse me, Mister Lewrie, but the last cast o' the log shows no change. Still adoin' five an' a half knots."

"Thank you, Mister Weems." Alan almost barked at him.

"If ya'd be wantin' anything else, sir?" Weems went on. "Almost time to check the lookouts, an' tour belowdecks with the master-at-arms."

"Thank you, Weems, but that will be all for now. I shall join you shortly!" Alan said, biting his cheek to keep from screaming for the idiot to drop straight to hell.

"Aye, sir."

Alan turned back to Caroline and was amazed to see that she was gazing straight ahead at the bows, one side of her mouth turned up in an attempt to keep from laughing out loud. Once Weems was aft by the wheel, she let go and began to shake with silent glee, and their eyes met in a shared amusement, but she did not let go of his hand; in fact, returned squeeze for squeeze.

"Did I sound half as ridiculous as I thought I did?" he whispered.

"Yes," she said frankly. "Pretty ridiculous." But there was no harm in her critique, or at least Alan felt none. "People who can laugh at themselves are rare, Alan. You're very refreshing."

"Well, some people have more to laugh at than others," he admitted easily. "Seriously, do you think your parents would mind if we wrote?"

"I think they would feel honored. As would I. If they did not approve, then I am the final judge, after all. I would hope we could always be friends and correspondents."

"That sounds delightful to me," Alan replied warmly. "Dammit, you are so easy to talk to. So easy to know."

"I was just about to say the very same thing about you, Alan." They stood there, hand in hand for long moments, staring at each other and smiling foolishly until she lowered her eyes and grew shy.

"Well, it must be getting late," she said sadly.

As if in confirmation, four bells chimed from the belfry.

"And you must be freezing up here on deck. You should be snug in your bed," Alan murmured, feeling the urge to tuck the both of them into the same narrow hanging cot and pull the blankets up to their necks.

"I must own to sleepiness, at last."

"Nothing like being bored to make you sleep well."

"Not bored at all!" she replied, her breath coming a bit quicker.

"Lots to do in the morning, packing up and getting ready to leave the ship. We'll cross the bar just before noon, if the wind holds. Let me walk you aft and see you safely into the cabins."

"I would appreciate that," she said.

He led her arm in arm past the helm and the crew, who all took a sudden interest in the rigging, the rails or the horizon as they passed—all but the ship's boy, who snuffled and wiped his nose with the back of his sleeve, getting his last look at the awfully beautiful young lady who had touched him so gently, as no one else in his miserable short life, as though she was a waking fantasy.

They stopped at the top of the ladder that led through the upper hatch to the cabins, stood holding hands for a moment longer, and leaned close together as the ship rolled on a slight surge. Of one mind, they stumbled together, and she raised those great eyes to meet his.

He bent forward and their lips brushed shyly, not too far forward, for she raised her face higher and met him. Her arms took his sleeves, and he put an arm about her waist with as much trepidation as if she were made of porcelain and would shatter at his touch. One of her gloved hands went to the back of his neck, then stroked his cheek, while the other kept a death grip on his arm. They shuffled forward a little more, pressing their lips together, cold lips and hot breath at first, then icy skin and warm lips, then breaking away; she because of the power of the feeling she felt, and Alan because he did not want her to feel ravished.

"Good night, Caroline," he muttered huskily. "Sleep soundly."

"Good night, Alan," she whispered back, sliding her hand down to his for one last firm squeeze, then she was gone below into the dark.

Something to be said for gawky women, Alan thought, his head in a spin from the warmth and the intense passion that had come on him of a sudden. Her faint scent was still in his nostrils, so fresh and clean and light, his bare hand was still warm from her grip, and he savored the feel of her long body drawn so close to his, wanted to go back and crush her to him and take her true measure. He had not felt like that in a long time, had never felt that overpowering rush to the brain that went with the rush to the groin he was used to. He could not put a name to it, for it was not in his experience, but it was something more than dumb lust.

Did I feel like that with Lucy Beauman? he wondered. I think I did, but that was months ago, and she's not here, nor will I see her anytime soon. God, don't tell me I'm swooning for the mort! She's not got two shillings to rub together, and most like never shall. No future for me with a girl with no prospects. Still, she's so sweet!

He shuddered with more than winter chill as he thought of how shy he had behaved with her, knowing it was not part of his nature to be so backward with women. Even allowing for the fact that he could not take her below and bed her, could not have at her on deck where there was no privacy, could still feel Governour's sharp eyes on the back of his neck, could picture being caught in mid-ravish by Captain Treghues and had not the slightest intention of ever being in the same hemisphere with her after leaving Charleston, he could not explain it.

Next afternoon, the evacuation fleet reached Charleston, and there was a long bustle to clear all the passengers off the ship. The Chiswicks were among the last to debark, with Mr. Chiswick seeming sprier than in past, as though eager to get ashore and see his sons, or take his pleasures in the larger city. Treghues was hovering around them, but Alan did get to say his good-byes before they were hoisted over the side and into a waiting boat with their belongings. Caroline was fetching in a blue velvet gown, her hair tied back loosely and her eyes shining.

"Mistress Chiswick, allow me to say how delighted I was that I could enjoy your company aboard the *Desperate* these two days past," Treghues said, doffing his hat to her. He had turned out in his best coat, had shaved closely and was immaculate from head to toe, fit to appear at the Admiralty or the palace. "All my best wishes go with you and your parents for better fortune in future."

"Thank you, Captain Treghues," Caroline replied.

"I would appreciate your informing me of your progress," Treghues went on, almost squirming with unfamiliar embarrassment as his crew bustled about to assist her into the bosun's chair. "As I told you and your father at supper last night, there may be much I could do to alleviate your distress, perhaps aid in finding your brothers suitable commissions in the regular forces. Governour, pardon my familiarity at using his Christian name, ha-ha, your elder brother sounds like a proper Tartar, the sort we need in a good regiment. And your second brother, Burgess, if he has, as you said, any interest in the Sea Service, there is always the possibility of a berth as a marine lieutenant."

"We would appreciate any interest you could take in us, Captain," Caroline replied. "I cannot speak for my brothers. After Yorktown, I do not know how enamored they are of a continued military career. And truthfully, we do not know where we shall light if the rebellion has any more successes."

"I could write and keep in touch," Treghues suggested. "And, in the meantime, allow me to present you with this, a token only, you know, but every little bit helps, ha-ha."

Treghues was trying to press a small purse of money on her, and Caroline was blushing with embarrassment as well.

"I could not accept such a gift, sir," she said directly, though not eager to pass up free guineas, not in their straitened financial condition. "I wish you had made offer to my father. He is head of our house still, sir. And as to writing to us, that is also his decision, and I am governed by my father's will."

"As a God-fearing girl should be, in faith," Treghues agreed, booming too loud and firm. "I commend your spirit, Mistress Chiswick, but please believe that I lay no conditions on the acceptance of such a paltry gift, but only do it from a heart . . . a sense of admiration of your plucky . . . er, spirit in the face of adversity."

God, I almost feel sorry for the artless bugger, Alan thought grinning in silent amusement. It's a wonder there's a Treghues alive if that's the way they court their women. He couldn't get fucked in a buttock shop!

"What conditions could you lay, sir?" Caroline asked archly, getting a little vexed and anxious to be in the boat with her father, who could be heard grumbling about something already.

"A thousand pardons, Mistress Chiswick, if I offend by generosity, but it is a sin of excess only in the sense that..." Treghues blundered on, not knowing how to stop or get himself out of the hole he had dug with his tongue. "You would do me a great honor if I knew you and yours were secure for a time. What else could a fellow Christian mean to another?"

"Then I shall accept, sir, though it is not my place to do so," she finally said, as long as there were no strings attached to that purse. "And I shall consider it a loan made in fellowship and human kindness, as all mercy should be."

"Just as long as you do not consider me a *total* Samaritan, I beg of you, Mistress Chiswick," Treghues said, sounding almost humble.

"I shall not, sir. And I thank you kindly for all your ministrations to us in our time of need and salvation," she said.

"I shall keep you and your family close in my thoughts and in my prayers, Mistress Chiswick," Treghues said, taking her hand.

"And we you, sir. Ah, Mister Lewrie."

"Mistress Chiswick," he said formally, though their eyes danced at the sight of each other as he doffed his cocked hat.

"Bless you for everything you have done for us, Mister Lewrie." She spoke warmly, though she tried to hide her emotions as the captain was still standing there like a catch-fart waiting for an errand. "We shall never forget you."

"My regards to Gov and Burge when next you meet. Tell them to write to me and let me know how they're faring. And all my thanks to your parents for showing me true hospitality and what it is like to be in the bosom of a family once more," Alan said, stepping close to her as she sat swaying in the bosun's chair before the hands tailed away on the stay tackle to lift her out of his life.

"Hoist away, bosun," Treghues snapped.

Caroline looked annoyed as she began to reach for Alan but she was hoisted out of his grasp before their fingers could even begin to touch. He waved to her and she to him as she went up and over the side.

He stepped to the bulwark to watch her into the boat, and she looked up at him, pantomiming speech, saying "Write to me, please," and much in that warm vein, while he returned her sentiments as well.

"As the Spaniards say, *Vaya Con Dios.* Go with God," he shouted down to the Chiswicks, then mouthed silently "Caroline."

He watched the civilians begin to row the loaded boat towards the shore, feeling suddenly deprived of her presence. Damme, I wish we'd had longer together, he suddenly thought. There goes the only girl I've ever met who was interesting to talk to for more than half an hour. Easy to talk to, comfortable like. And smart, smart as paint, and don't make no bones about it. A good, sweet nature. Maybe a little artless compared to most I've known, like a country girl. Holds herself so stiff, but I'll wager there's a passionate side hidden deep. Might be amusing to be the one to bring it out. Ah well, that'll be never. If only her daddy had some chink, she might be worth keeping up with.

He waved once more and she waved back, and then their boat swept round the stern of an anchored brig out of sight, so Alan turned back inboard to meet Treghues, who was regarding him with an annoyed look of his own. The captain turned away and stalked off.

Oh shit, Alan thought. The silly clown's jealous. He'll make my life a living hell. He wanted her himself, though for what I can't imagine. Might take him a year to aspire to holding her hand.

Alan felt a cold chill in his innards as he further realized that Treghues *had* to have heard her pass his jury-rigged cabin during the night to go on deck, and could have peeked from the door to see them embrace as he said good night to her.

There was nothing new, however, in Treghues making his life a living hell; he had had months of it already, so he shrugged philosophically and headed aft. Neither of them could have her, and by the time the war was over, both could be either dead or out of contention, while she followed her own mind thousands of miles away. It had been, Alan assured himself once more, merely an idle flirtation, a passing dalliance just because she was there and grateful to him, nothing more meaningful than what passed in society at any drum or rout among the fashionable in London. He vowed to put her out of his mind. He had duties to fulfill, a ship to run and an irked captain to mollify, if he wanted to keep his new rating.

CHAPTER 16

ENGLISH Harbor at Antigua was like an old shoe, familiar and comfortable. Storm season was over and the island was beginning to green up after all the rain. After the chill of the American coast, the lush warmth felt good, and the sun baked the decks daily, not as hot as it had been when they had departed for the Chesapeake back in August, but warm enough to thaw out the tired blood.

Desperate was for many days almost the only ship in harbor, for Admiral Hood had taken the Leeward Islands Squadron down to Barbados. The ship lolled in almost idleness as they took on a draft of replacements newly arrived from home in the first transports that would brave the mid-Atlantic Trades before the hurricanes truly left the region for another year.

There were three new midshipmen in the once empty and echoing mess. Two were mere boys of twelve or thirteen, fresh-caught newlies still gawking in wonder at the height of the masts. There was an older boy of some years' service named Burney, about sixteen and so handsome looking that one was tempted to throw a shoe at him on first sight. He and Avery had hit it off and were busy enforcing their superiority on the newlies with all the old pranks that midshipmen played on each other, and Alan found the two younger ones so abysmally stupid that he had no pity for them and let them make fools of themselves quite easily. The new master's mate was an American from Maryland, a painfully thin and awkward thatch-haired man of twenty or so named Micah Sedge, another victim of the Rebels, almost burning with zeal for bloody revenge.

Almost as soon as they had reached port, Alan had been confirmed by Commodore Sir George Sinclair in his position of master's mate, followed shortly thereafter by Hood's approval as well, so he was no longer "acting," and his two pounds, two shillings a lunar month was safe. He still walked small about Treghues, but there had been no sign as of yet that that worthy was contemplating anything frightful because he had not gained Caroline Chiswick's immediate affections.

Sinclair's approbation concerning his new rating had come as a surprise to Alan; he had thought the man nursed a grudge against him because of who Alan's father was and the circumstances in which Sinclair's flag captain, Captain Bevan, had snatched him from London under threat of arrest by the watch for the alleged rape of his half sister Belinda. Alan wondered if Sinclair really cared one way or another, or if he had been poisoned by his nephew Francis Forrester, now languishing in some Rebel or French prison after his capture at Yorktown. If Sinclair had any animosity at all, it was toward *Desperate* as a whole for her "lucky" escape, or towards Treghues for losing the Commodore his nephew. They were dead last on the list for provision, powder or shot or rigging, a sure sign of a senior officer's displeasure.

"Mail coom h'aboard, zurs," Freeling said mournfully as he dumped a sack on the mess table. The midshipmen dived for it, but Alan had but to bark "Still!" to freeze their grubby paws in midpounce.

"You young gentlemen should know, even from your limited experience, that Mister Sedge and I get first crack," Alan informed them lazily, seating himself at the table to open the sack. "Not so, Mister Sedge?"

"Indeed so, Mister Lewrie," Sedge replied. He was still stiff and uncomfortable in his new berth, but willing to give Alan a grudging try. "And any packages from home get shared, and not hogged to yourselves."

"Ah, what do we have here?" Alan asked, laying out the contents. "A letter for you, I believe, Mister Sedge."

"Thankee kindly, Mister Lewrie. Huh, from me dad in Halifax."

Alan sorted out the mail, finding several of his own dating back for months, mostly from Lucy Beauman in Jamaica, a few from London from the Matthews, Lord and Lady Cantner, and one from his father's petti-fogging solicitor, Pilchard. He hoped it was his annuity; he was getting short.

"Another missive for you, Mister Sedge, in a fair round hand, from New York. Scented too, I swear."

"Gimme that," Sedge snapped, eager for the letter from some female admirer, and not a man to be trifled with at that moment. He gathered up his few communications from those dear to him and went into his cabin.

Alan decided to save Lucy's letters for later; they would take some deciphering, anyway, since the little mort had the world's worst skill at spelling. He would tackle Pilchard's letter first.

"You missed one, Mister Lewrie," David Avery said, digging into the sack. He held up a large and thick letter, almost a rival to the long, continued sea-letters that Alan wrote between spells of duty. David sniffed at it to the delight of the other midshipmen, who were pawing through their own correspondence. "Damme if this one ain't scented, too. From Charleston."

"Ah?" Alan said, unwilling to be drawn.

"And it's not from Lady Jane's." David grinned innocently.

"Gimme, then," Alan said eagerly, reaching for it, but David held it further away and aloft for a second. "Kick your backside if you don't, you ugly Cornish pirate."

"Very well, then," David said, making to hand it over once more but drawing it back at the last second. Alan grabbed his wrist and took it.

"While you tell our newlies of Lady Jane's, I shall read this," Alan said, smiling to let David know there were no hard feelings. "Boys, I recommend you listen attentively to Mister Avery's tale of sport. You could learn a good lesson from it."

He disappeared into his small dog-box cabin and shut the door, flung himself down on the thin mattress of his bunk and opened the seal of the Charleston letter first. Pilchard could go hang for awhile longer. It was from Caroline, informing him of their new address, of how her father was improving now that Governour and Burgess were on their way to Charleston to bring the survivors of their detatchment home to add to the garrison and try and raise a new force of riflemen. He was more excited than he would have expected to be reading her carefully formed words and seeing how sensibly she formed her thoughts and expressed herself; he saw nothing so formal and stilted as to make him twist his tongue trying to figure it out, but everything straightforward and plain, as though she were talking to him familiarly.

There was a lot of teasing, just shy of saying something fond but twisting the sentiment into japery, skirting about what she really might have wished to say to him. It raised a warm glow in him anyway, and he thought of her fondly, scratching at his crotch and grinning in delight.

It *had* been scented, with the same light, fresh and clean aroma that he remembered from their one embrace aboard ship, a citrus sort of Hungary Water overlaid with a redolence of some unidentifiable flower. He folded her letter up after reading it through three times, to save it for later. He opened Pilchard's. It was dated nearly nine months earlier.

"You bastard!" he shrieked, beside himself with sudden anger, nearly concussing himself on the low deck beam overhead his berth as he sat up quickly.

It was Pilchard's sad duty to inform him that his father had had second thoughts about the extravagant sum of one hundred guineas a year as his remittance and that Sir Hugo was suspending the annuity, effective January of 1782. That meant that he would not be getting any more money from home and would have to live on the twenty-five pounds, four shillings of a master's mate, less a pound a month for provisions and whatever he purchased from the purser's stores, which meant just about all of it. He already owed Cheatham near fifteen pounds already.

The Yorktown business had reduced his kit horribly, and he had pledged another part of the annuity to tailors ashore in English Harbor for new uniforms and shoes. He could always dig down into his secret money from the *Ephegenie*, but it was more the thought that counted.

Sir Hugo's excuse was that from what he had read in the *Chronicle*, Alan was prospering enough from all the prizes taken and no longer needed to be supported. In short, he was on his own bottom now, and must stand or fall as a man with no crutch from home. It was for his own good.

"Lying shit!" Alan swore. "It's for *your* own good! You've spent yourself into a hole and it's cut me off or debtor's prison for you! Damme, what did I do to get such a father?"

Still, the idea of his father, his half sister and his butt-fucking half brother Gerald turfed out into the street was cheering, if they had fallen afoul of creditors. Alan had no idea how much money the Willoughbys had; they weren't related to the Willoughbys who counted in the scheme of things. There had always seemed more than enough, but only Heaven knew where it came from, or where it went that he did not see.

There was a knock on his thin slat and canvas door, and he snatched it open to reveal the purser's assistant, the Jack in the Bread Room.

"Pusser wants ta see ya, sir. 'Is complamints, an' could ya join 'im in the spirit store, sir?"

"I shall be there directly, thank you," Alan said, shrugging off his foul mood. He dressed quickly in his new uniform and went out to the steep ladder that led to the orlop, then aft to the locked compartments in the stern that held the wine and brandy for the officers' mess and the captain's steward.

"Sit ye down, Mister Lewrie," Cheatham said, looking up from a stack of papers he held on a rough fold-down desk at which it appeared he had been doing inventory of Navy Victualing Board issue spirits; rum, Miss Taylor and Black Strap. "Have a cup of cheer, my boy."

"I'll take a cup, but there's damned little to cheer about," Alan groused, taking a seat on a wine keg. Cheatham poured from a bottle into a clean glass. "Um, this is quite good. Not for the hands, I take it."

"Something I found in port last week," Cheatham said, putting away his quill and ink pot. "Wardroom stuff. I have here some information about you, Mister Lewrie. From my brother at Coutts' Bank and your solicitor. Wondrous and strange things have been going on in London since your departure for Sea Service."

"I don't have a solicitor, sir," Alan said, mystified, but stirring in anticipation. "Perhaps I need one, though. My father has cut me off. Not a penny more for me. Without a mate's pay, I'd be begging rations."

"Where did you hear that?"

Alan explained the letter from Pilchard.

"And when was it dated?"

"March of last year."

"Ah ha, just about the time things got interesting, according to Jemmy." Cheatham smiled serenely. "Your father had to cut you off, for he no longer had a groat to send you. He is in considerable difficulties."

"He is!" Alan beamed in sudden and total joy. He took a deep breath or two, then let out a whoop of glee loud enough to echo off the hull, piercing enough to startle Red Indians. "The bastard got his comeuppance at last! How? When did it happen? Did he lose everything?"

"Slowly now, let me explain this at its own pace, for it's rather complicated a legal and personal matter," Cheatham said. "My brother Jemmy went to work discovering your background after I bade him do so, and he has found some wondrous interesting facts. First of all, as to your heritage, and the background of the Lewrie family. It seems that in the winter of 1762, your mother Elizabeth, then twenty-two years of age, was in London for exposure at a season, with close relatives, and met your father, at that time Captain Sir Hugo St. George Willoughby, just back from service on Gibraltar, where he had won his knighthood in service with a distinguished foot regiment, the Fourth, King's Own. Now, there are under English common law two separate and distinct parts to a marriage, as the law would say, *de futuro*, which are the spousals in which a couple pledge public affirmation of their mutual agreement to be wed, which can take form as the banns published in the parish or a short mutual statement in the presence of witnesses that they shall at a future time take the other as husband or wife. The witnesses may be summoned to a court of law, and the exchange of gifts and love letters may be used as proof of their intent. The second form, the nuptials, is termed *de praesenti*, and is usually celebrated by a certifiable churchman."

"You're losing me, Mister Cheatham," Alan said, his mind already in full yawn, wishing to skip over the legal mustifications and get to the existence of a Lewrie estate, and how much it could be.

"Patience, my boy, patience, and all shall be discovered to you in full measure," Cheatham cautioned. "In 1753, Hawkinge's Marriage Act was passed in Parliament to do away with such scandals as the Fleet St. wedding chapels to save young girls from being robbed by unscrupulous suitors, so that a marriage ceremony with an officiating clergyman is now recognized as necessary to settle all legal questions. Otherwise, two people could leap out of bed, swear themselves wed before witnesses, and it would assign the husband coverture over whatever estate the young lady possessed for the rest of their lives. The Ecclesiastical Courts had the very devil of a time with complaints before this law. But, and this is a very important but, a spousal *de futuro* is as legally binding on both of the parties who partake willingly in it as a nuptial *de praesenti* when it comes to settling parenthood of any children. Your parents announced the intention to wed before witnesses at a dinner party where officers of his regiment and friends of hers were present, so you are not a bastard as you have always assumed, but legally born of a legitimate couple."

"So I am really a Willoughby." Alan sighed.

"A lot more than Gerald and Belinda are." Cheatham grinned. "You see, you are the only living issue from your father's loins. That he may wish to claim, that is."

"I don't understand."

"Let me settle up the Lewrie part, and then I shall touch on the later events, in strict chronological order, so that it shall all be of a piece. Spousals being exchanged, love letters and gifts also being exchanged—'I give my love a packet of pins, and this is how our love begins,' remember that one?—your parents took up lodgings together as man and wife, and you were conceived shortly thereafter in 1762. But the Lewrie family, who reside in Wheddon Cross, Devon, just north of Exeter—"

"How terrible for them," Alan commented, never a fan of the rustic life.

"The father, a Mister Dudley Lewrie, Esquire, was, as the Lewrie family solicitor for many years, a Mister Kittredge, assures us, a most strict religionist and somewhat of a Tartar to deal with. He had hated his only living daughter going off to London for a season, but the mother had cozened him into it to assure Elizabeth a chance to meet a better sort of husband than she could locally, or be assured of bonafides better than the moonshine one hears at Bath or another resort, when a footman with the chink may appear as grand as his master, and the rules of society in a resort town allow perfect freedom between classes."

"Yes, yes, get on with it, I beg you, Mister Cheatham."

"Well, there's your father and mother cohabiting, she pregnant with you, and the parents descending on the town to snatch her back. The happy couple flee to Holland after having a quick marriage performed to make it legally binding. The only problem was that the officiant was not certified as a recognized cleric able to celebrate a nuptial, just some hedge-priest that one of Sir Hugo's fellow officers found for them at short notice, obviously not understanding the need for *real* clergy. So Sir Hugo never got true coverture over the Lewrie estate, or that share of it that Elizabeth Willoughby *née* Lewrie would have inherited. And Sir Hugo was not well-off at all, his own estate almost an empty shell by his profligate spending and the cost of his commission to remove him from some scandalous doings in fifty-eight. She was beautiful, and one of two heirs to a sizable estate, so the temptation must have been the very devil on him."

"I can understand that," Alan said wryly. "So far, sir."

"Well, Sir Hugo abandoned your mother in Holland, taking off with her cash and jewels, quite a valuable prize to purloin, I'm told."

"The sorry bastard!"

"Well, according to this Kittredge fellow, your grandfather Dudley washed his hands of his daughter Elizabeth after that, allowing her to lay in the bed she made for herself. I told you he was a Tartar. But your grandmother Barbara Lewrie was made of more charitable stuff. She had borne her husband ten children, but only two were living and the only son due to inherit was a sickly sort, a man in his twenties named Phillip who was at Oxford, and when he wasn't deathly ill with some disease, he was suffering from either the pox or barrel fever. Barbara Lewrie sent money to pay Elizabeth's way back from Holland, enough to set her up in decent lodgings in London once home, so that her only grandson would be amply provided for. Phillip was showing no signs of giving her grandchildren, or signs of living long enough to wed formally, so you were the only hope for the family name, you see."

Alan smiled greedily at that. It sounded suspiciously as if there would be some "yellow boys" in his future, but he put his questions in abeyance, letting Cheatham get on at his own slow pace.

"Your mother evidently took ill on passage, and never regained her health," Cheatham said somberly. "She passed on just before the turn of the year, in late 1763. Her last parish was St. Martin in the Fields, and with no one to claim you, you were consigned to the parish. There you languished, until 1766, when you were three. Dudley Lewrie died in 1766, and this rescue of you is more than a coincidence. There is record that your father, Sir Hugo, and his solicitor, Pilchard even then, claimed you under your mother's maiden name of Lewrie, and took you in as his son at that time."

"So there would be on record a male heir to the Lewrie estate, a legitimate one," Alan said, suddenly understanding. "If he'd claimed me as a Willoughby I would have been harder to prove. God, what a scheming hound he is. All this time, all these years he told me I was the son of a whore, a poor bastard of no account. I could kill him for that!"

"That was most likely his motive. But, Sir Hugo had landed on his feet. Once your mother died, he was free of marriage in the strict legal sense, and though your grandmother sued him for return of your mother's jewelry, he presented a letter from Elizabeth proving she had given him her paraphernalia. This was obviously forged, but the court could find no fault with it, since it was your mother's hand to the letter, so he got off Scot-free. He had remarried almost as soon as he set foot ashore in England. The jewelry must have been turned into cash, for he made a grand show the summer of sixty-four in Bath, where he legally wed one Agnes Cockspur, a widow of some means with two small children, one Gerald and a girl named Belinda."

"They weren't his!" Alan exclaimed.

"Only in the sense that to make sure that he would have control over their portion of the Cockspur estate, he adopted them as Willoughbys. The widow became pregnant, but was carried off by childbed fever, along with the issue of their marriage," Cheatham said, stopping to drain his glass and top both of them up. "This is dry work, and unsavory, too. In court, your father presented what surely must be another forgery, her conveyance of her entire estate to the care of her husband. You know that a husband only has coverture over the bride's portion of the wife's estate brought to marriage, and the management of her estate by coverture only for the life of the wife, unless she specifically signs it over to him so that after her death he retains possession. Pilchard figured into this again, so we may begin to discern his true skills other than the knowledge and practice of law. The other Cockspur sisters, who had lost a sizable fortune at this conveyance, had no legal recourse, and got farmed out with small annuities to husbands less than what they had expected. I mention this because of their present interest. But, now we come to the meat of the matter, what transpired after you were shipped off aboard *Ariadne*."

"For God's sake, yes, what happened?"

"Not a month after you were safely at sea, your father and this Pilchard creature went into court with a document you had signed, one giving Sir Hugo control over your estate."

"But what happened to all that stuff I signed about giving up all inheritance from either side?" Alan asked. "What about the agreement that made me leave England and enter the Fleet and never go home?"

"No mention of it," Cheatham said with a shrug. "You see, the grandfather had gone over to a higher reward in sixty-six, the son Phillip had died without issue in seventy-two, and at the last, Barbara Lewrie was reputed to be in ill health and of advanced years, and near her own deathbed in seventy-nine. Once again, we may see more than coincidence at work. You would be the only Lewrie still living in line to inherit, your father proved you as legitimate, could show his informal adoption of you as his son and had proof in your own hand that you wished him to administer your estate while you were in the Navy and overseas. There would be a good chance that if the grandmother passed on while you were away, and you were bound never to come home, he could have gotten it all and you none the wiser, fobbed off with one hundred guineas a year, while he got thousands. And should you die in naval service, a distinct possibility, he would be free to use it as his own."

"The scheming dog!" Alan roared, rising to pace the small space of the spirit room. "I'll see him in hell for this."

"It was a nacky plan, but there was only one bad part to it: he had to go to court to prove it, and the Lewrie family had to be informed that the long-lost male heir had resurfaced."

"How did I get lost, then? Wouldn't my grandmother have searched for me? And what did she do when I was revealed?"

"She did, on the sly with her pin money, but your mother's last official parish was St. Clement Dane, and she died in St. Martin's, so after a year or so of searching, you were as good as lost, and few children survive more than a year in a poorhouse or foster care, more's the pity, so you may understand why she abandoned hope for finding you. As to her reaction at your discovery, she immediately had this Kittredge claim you as the last male Lewrie heir. Your father had gotten what he wanted, and you were safely out of Barbara Lewrie's reach, so she could not help you or pass this knowledge on to you. She knew Sir Hugo from before, though, and felt that you would be cheated. There was little she could do when presented later with proof in your own signature that you had given up hope of inheritance and had been banished for the alleged rape of your sister. This was not in the courts, the last part, but part of a personal confrontation with her and Sir Hugo, so she never tried to write to you."

"I sound most awesomely poor from all this, Mister Cheatham."

"You might have been, but for one thing, the deviousness of women." Cheatham laughed, clapping him on the shoulder and bidding him sit once more. "Your grandmother did not die, in fact, at last report some six months ago is still, surprisingly, with us. She rallied, sir! If I may paraphrase the noted lexicographer Dr. Johnson, one's impending death concentrates the mind most wonderfully. She not only rallied and left her deathbed, but she immediately was wed to an old friend of hers, a Mr. Thomas Nuttbush, Esquire, of the same parish in Devon."

"But my father still has the estate," Alan said miserably.

"One, not until she passes over, and two, not if the Lewrie estate is signed over to a husband by legal conveyance awarding him coverture after her death. To make matters even worse for Sir Hugo,

Thomas Nuttbush is possessed of three fine, healthy sons, so if there is no Lewrie estate but a Nuttbush estate, you are no longer the eldest male issue of either side in line to inherit. He has guardianship over nothing, and when you reach your majority, there is nothing for him to steal from you at that time, or at the death of your grandmother. The legal paper which Kittredge saw informally at the meeting with Sir Hugo lists you as giving up inheritance in both Willoughby and Lewrie estates, assigning everything to your father. But it says nothing about the Nuttbush estate."

"Holy God, am I part of it?" Alan yelled, hoping against hope.

"You are, sir. A codicil to the conveyance assigning Mr. Nuttbush lifetime coverture provides you an inheritance," Cheatham told him with great glee. "Oh, your grandmother's a sly-boots, Lewrie, and I see which side of the family you get your own nackiness from. Your grandmother's paraphernalia does not come under coverture of a husband, so that is what shall be your portion upon your grandmother's passing. My brother Jemmy has been in touch with Mr. Kittredge, and he assures me that there is jewelry and plate to the value of four thousand pounds at present, and your grandmother has purchased more lately, all to be held at Coutts' Bank under her new name in the vault, so your father can never touch it or place lien on it in your name. And, Mr. Kittredge has dealt with the bank to make sure that you shall receive the sum of two hundred pounds in annuity for life."

"Holy shit on a biscuit," Alan said, having trouble breathing for a moment. "I'm rich. I'm as rich as Croesus. Goddamme, but I'm rich!"

"Well, perhaps not strictly wealthy, but as well-off as a squire's son back home. With your prize certificates, your new naval pay and the annuity, you shall get by more than comfortably, better than a post-captain, really," Cheatham said. "There will be money enough to set yourself up in fashionable lodgings in London once the war is over. And still enough left to provide a house and some land when you find the perfect girl to make your wife, with enough money to assure you a comfortable existence, as long as your taste does not aspire to emulate a peer's son, or you let your pleasures rule your purse. It's more than a middling income, though. And should you marry well—and all this allows you entrance to a better sort of selection in young women—you could do very well indeed."

"My God, it's a sight more than what I had half an hour ago." Alan laughed in relief and joy. "To my lights, I'm rich."

"Aye," Cheatham agreed heartily.

"I'm legitimate. I'm not the sorry bastard I was always told."

"True again," Cheatham rejoined.

"And if this letter from Pilchard is correct, if my father doesn't honor his half of the agreement about my banishment, then I no longer have to honor mine," Alan speculated. "By God, I'm free of the old fart. I *can* go home when the war ends."

"Once again, true," Cheatham said. "In fact, that is what your solicitor is suing your father for. Pay the annuity or you come home."

"I'm suing my father?" Alan gaped, breaking into laughter once he saw the irony of it. "My God, this is lovely. I love it, I truly do!"

"Kittredge could not represent you, since you would be a plaintiff when your grandmother passes over, but he is paying your legal expenses. He found you a younger solicitor, a Matthew Mountjoy, to represent you. He has made presentation that you signed away all hopes to the Willoughby and Lewrie estates and cannot be considered a source of money for Sir Hugo's creditors to fall back on if he does not have enough to clear his debts."

"Sir Hugo's in trouble with creditors?"

"More and more. Evidently, the Cockspur estates are as empty as his own by now, and he's sold off most of the country property to keep going in proper style, and your Gerald and Belinda must be expensive little darlings, too, quite a drain on his resources. It seems Gerald and Belinda are also suing your father for wasting and mismanaging their share of the Cockspur estates."

Alan whooped and kicked his heels against the keg on which he sat, utterly floored by this turn of events. "Serves the bastard right!" he crowed in a joy that almost transported him to ecstasy. "Confusion to his cause, and may he get what's due him at long last. He could go to prison, couldn't he? Debtor's prison at the least, and real confinement as a felon if there is a just God in Heaven! I love it! I love it!"

"To victory," Cheatham proposed, raising his glass to Alan's.

"And revenge, Mister Cheatham. Don't forget sweet revenge!"

"And revenge on your foes," Cheatham said. "Now, I hope you

do not mind, but you are now a depositor with Coutts' Bank in London. It seemed a good way to help repay my brother Jemmy for all his research and investigative work. Coutts' is a solid bank, near as good as the Bank of England, even if it is privately held. Your annuity shall be remitted you within the month, less fifty pounds which Jemmy had to spend for postage, travel expenses and hiring some hungry young lawyers to do the discovery of all the background material. I hope you do not mind."

"Mister Cheatham, that's better than what my father would have sent me. So as far as I'm concerned, I'm fifty pounds to the good. I can't thank you enough, you and your brother James, for doing all this for me. You went to so much trouble to determine my heritage, and got what was due me. You believed in a scoundrel, and I'll find a way to repay you for your kindnesses."

"Well, before you do that, you should reflect on the fact that the Lewrie estate was worth fifty thousand pounds in freehold and copyhold lands, and between the home-farm, the rents and returns on investments, provided over three thousand pounds a year income. You'll not share in that." The purser told him with a shrug of comiseration.

"Hang the money, I'm still delighted," Alan vowed. Hold on, did I just say that? I must be deranged to think something like that. But, I'm due double what I would have gotten from Sir Hugo, and there might be eight or ten thousand waiting for me when my grandmother dies. And I still have my two thousand from *Ephegenie*, he rapidly calculated.

"Remember what I told you about having friends in this world, in the Navy, who care about you with genuine affection," Cheatham said, his eyes moist with emotion. "You could not have earned that affection unless we thought you worthy of it, no matter what you thought of yourself. Oh, Mister Lewrie—Alan—when you expressed your disgust with yourself months ago, pronounced yourself so unworthy of any love or real friendship in this world, my heart went right out to you. Treated so badly by your father, with the word "bastard" branded into your soul as a cruel lie all these years, no wonder you thought yourself base and unworthy. Now you know the truth about yourself. You're legitimate, with a fine name that anyone in England could be proud of. Forced to naval life or no, you've done well at it, whether you loved it or not, and have the beginnings of a fine career in the Sea Service, and that's a gentlemanly calling a thousand lads would sell their souls to have. Do not let what you thought of yourself in the past color the rest of your life. Reflect on what you have gained and how a truly just God has brought the wheel of righteous retribution full circle until you may come into your own. Not just the money, but this new beginning, this clean slate upon which you may . . . oh, devil take it, I . . ." Cheatham wept.

"I shall, Mister Cheatham. I promise you I shall," Alan said in all seriousness. He set down his wine glass and the men embraced and thumped each other on the back.

"Well," Cheatham said, stepping back to fetch out his handkerchief and blow his nose and wipe his eyes. "There is a power of correspondence for you in this packet from Jemmy. Legal bumf explaining all the particulars, word from your solicitor Mr. Mountjoy with reports of the progress of your suit and a letter from your grandmother, too, I believe. You will most likely wish to avail yourself of it, and I have work to do, God knows. My reward in all this is in seeing the salvation of a fine young man from eventual ruin by his own disgust at himself, and your retribution in society, in being restored to the bosom of your rightful family. And the restoration of your birthright."

"Words cannot express my undying gratitude to you, Mister Cheatham. Yes, I'm sort of like Cain restored, I suppose."

"Hmm, those sessions with the captain and the Good Book have done little for your biblical knowledge, I fear." Cheatham smiled. "I was thinking more like an Esau restored his birthright, with the curse falling on Rebekah, where it belongs. Rebekah being Sir Hugo, in this instance."

Alan shook hands with Cheatham and took all the papers back to his mess, to shut himself into the stifling cabin and read, shaking his head over and over at the intricate schemes, either confirmed or implied, that Sir Hugo his father and the solicitor Pilchard had perpetrated over the years against all his children. No wonder he never had a kind moment for any of us, Alan thought. We were just sources of income to him all that time. He never loved anyone but himself.

"By God, no matter how big a sinner I have been," Alan whispered in the privacy of his cabin, "I would never have been such a heartless, evil rogue as to do that to anyone."

Well, perhaps I might have, if pushed to it, he thought sadly. That's the way I was raised in his house, and without two hundred pounds per annum, or one hundred, I would have been up against it devilish hard. Who knows what I might have done to fill my needs? No! He's not that much a part of me, and I'm not the base bastard he told me I was, by God! I'm an English gentleman, a damned rich one, at that. I've my honor and my good name, and no one'll ever put a blot on that again. I've a name to be proud of now, and can hold up my head anywhere.

Even with Lucy Beauman, he realized. Her father had been chary of him even writing to her, safely removed from his presence as she was back on Jamaica. He had had no people he could boast about, no lands, no rents, no hopes of inheritance, and only the Navy as a future, but it was all different now. With his annuity and promised estate, he could support any wife as well as the next man. Lucy, he figured, would be worth at least four thousand pounds as a bride's portion, plus land and slaves in the Indies, or an estate back home. He was suddenly a suitable prospect to come calling on her, as good as even the pickiest daddy could ask for.

With that happy thought in mind, Alan opened the packet of letters from the lovely Lucy and began to read them, which activity took more of his patience as he stumbled over the words she had misspelled so badly that he could not discover what she had meant. There had been almost a letter a week in August and early September, full of "bawls" and "tee's" and a "sworay," whatever the hell that was, many carriage rides, many dances, an accounting of some Gothick novel so gruesome she had not slept in three nights for fear of something coming for her from the night, her screed about a new harpsichord to replace the old one that had been eaten by termites so badly she could no longer play it in public and her undying shame at her father's frugality in not immediately replacing it that very week, a sea voyage from England to import the new one be damned.

The letters became more plaintive in mid-September, shorter and cooler in tone, with much sighing over his silence, much heart-break that he no longer wished to write her and more descriptions of the gallants who had "skwyred" her to some party or other. Even though they had been most forthright in their presentations of affection, she still held her heart for Her Sailor.

"Damn the mort, what does she expect, penny post from Yorktown?" he grumbled. He had written to her immediately he had gotten to New York and rejoined his ship, but there was no answer as yet to that one. "I'm dealing with the feeblest woman on God's earth."

But, he could vividly remember how beautiful she had looked when last they had been together, that final ball on Antigua, and how stunning a beauty she really was, how fine her figure, how lustrous her eyes and how every male that hadn't been docked or had the slightest pretension to manhood had panted to be near her. She was short, petite, ripely feminine—and unfortunately, as ignorant as sheep.

"No matter, she's rich as hell, and she'll be mine one day," he vowed. His last letter had been full of derring-do, a flattering account of Yorktown and his escape, just the sort of thing to bring a girl like her to heel once more and excuse his silence. And in so doing, make her feel the worst sort of colly-wobbles when she reflected on how ill she had used him while he was off risking life and limb for King and Country.

The rest of his mail was interesting; Sir Onsley and Lady Maude back in London were full of chattiness about the Admiralty and the London season, noting how the scandal about his father had been an eight-day wonder and how much sympathy the populace (the better sort, anyway) felt for Midshipman Lewrie. Sir Onsley hinted that there might be a change of command in the Indies and that he would drop a word in the new admiral's ear regarding his favorites.

The Cantners wrote to say that with the impending end of the Lord North government they were retiring to the country for a space, but he would be welcome to call whenever he returned home. They also made much over the scandal, providing clippings from the more aristocratic West End papers. There was also a veiled promise that even in the Opposition, Lord Cantner could still do him good, once Parliament reconvened.

The letter from his grandmother he saved til last, and it was a poignant tale of how she had been torn between wanting to rescue him from his father's house, but not wanting to give Sir Hugo a penny by recognizing him as heir, and her eternal grief that she had left it so late, and that he would not get the full estate. Barbara Nuttbush (*née* Lewrie) had evidently not known the full circumstances of his joining the Navy, for she declared him to be a true patriot and a fine English lad to volunteer for Sea Service. Bad as her health was, she lived only to see him once before she passed over, if he should come home when the war ended, and to her poor mind, that seemed soon, the way people were talking. There had even been a motion made in Parliament, voted down of course, that anyone who recommended or supported the continuation of the war should be tried for sedition. There was talk of a peace conference, talk of an envoy from the Crown to be sent to treat with this Continental Congress in Philadelphia or Boston.

There was also a postscript full of pride at the honor he had done the Lewrie name by his daring escape from Yorktown, so the report to the Admiralty from Hood, Graves and the new man Digby must have already been released at home.

> *I can but shew only the most heart-felt Relief and lift up my prayers to the Almighty that you escaped the Clutches of that despicable Monster, and have shewn such Courage and Honour as to be an ever-lasting Credit to the memory of your poor Mother. If it is your Wish to remain a Sea-Officer, then uphold the Lewrie name with Boldness and Pride and pass the name on to your own Sons and Daughters once more untarnished.*

Poor old girl doesn't know me at all, does she? Alan thought. Maybe it's best she doesn't. I'd let her down sooner or later.

Still, there was a good name to uphold now. With all the favorable comment in London and in the Fleet once the news got about, he would be remembered, remarked upon, not just for his past deeds, but for Yorktown as well, and for coming out of the scandal with clean hands. Let them say anything about me, as long as they say something, he thought, remembering a piece of advice he had read or heard in conversation. There might be a new admiral in the West Indies soon, to take over from Hood, and he would have gotten a tip in the right direction from Sir Onsley, perhaps even from Lord and

Lady Cantner, would have heard the name Alan Lewrie in the papers before he left England, and would know him at least by reputation, which was thankfully good. He had made master's mate — could a commission be that far away? Would he have to wait four more years to strictly fulfill the qualifications Samuel Pepys laid down so many years before? Or could he count on a promotion by the will of a local admiral, whose decisions on promotions were almost never questioned by higher authorities as long as they made the slightest bit of sense?

Alan got a pot of ink and a new quill from his chest, laid out some fresh stationery and went out to the mess table where the light was better to write letters. His grandmother first; then his solicitor and then Cheatham's brother at Coutts'; then Sir Onsley and Lady Maude; then the Cantners.

His hand was cramping by the time he got around to writing to Lucy Beauman with the delightful news of his new fortune, but for some reason the first words he scrawled on a fresh sheet of paper were:

Aboard the Desperate *frigate, English Harbor, Antigua*
January 5th, 1782
Dear Mistress Caroline,

Now why the devil did I do that? he wondered, ready to cross it out. But that would waste a sheet of vellum, and Lucy would go barking mad if she received a letter headed by another girl's name, even crossed out, and he was not so rich that he could take that liberty with her.

I am rich enough for even a girl who could bring nothing as her portion but her bedding and linens, he thought. No, best put her out of your mind, laddy. Just 'cause I dallied with her is no reason to even consider such a thing. She's an artless country wench and I'd be bored silly raising pigs — don't know the first thing about farming and bringing in the sheaves and all that. It's London and Lucy Beauman for me, and if I ever rise before ten in the morning, it'll be the Second Coming that wakes me. Only livestock I want to see'll be stuffed removes.

Still, he did not want to waste the paper — it was dear in the islands. He continued the letter, relating his good news about his inheritance, glossing over the reason he had to go to sea, as though he had been cheated in his properly patriotic absence. He was teasingly charming, striking serious notes when asking as to the health of her dad and mother, inquiring about her brothers. He put tongue in cheek and could not resist making the subtlest allusions to their night on deck, and when he read it back, he thought it clever and only mildly romantic, just the very thing to liven the poor gawk's days.

Only then did he put himself in the proper frame of mind and begin a letter to Lucy Beauman, a short one that could go off in the next packet boat.

Desperate loafed along, conducting a slow cruising patrol on her passage for Barbados to join with the Leeward Islands Squadron, and the Inshore squadron of smaller sloops and brigs and cruizers now with Hood.

South of Antigua, there were many French-controlled islands, the main one being their base on Martinique, home to de Grasse's fleet and a host of privateers. There was a possibility that *Desperate* could snatch a prize or two, take a privateer or enter combat with a French naval vessel, as long as she was not of overpowering might. That had been the plan, anyway, but so far it had not come to fruition, for the sea looked as empty as on the dawn of the second day of Creation, when there was but ocean and light and land had been only a project.

Alan didn't mind particularly; he had had enough excitement in the last few months, and if the war wound down quietly, then that was fine to his way of thinking. The Trades were blowing fresh and cool out of the east-northeast and the ship rolled along gently on a beam reach, a soldier's wind. He was off-watch and skylarking on the weather bulwarks, watching the gun crews go through the motions of loading and firing, jumping from one battery to another as the excess crew took care of reloading while the others competed to be the first run out on the other beam. At his most energetic, he conversed with the yeoman of the sheets on the larboard gangway as that gentleman and some of the topmen rerove fresh rope for sheets and braces where they had begun to chafe, or took a splice aloft to remove the chafed portions but save the ropes.

"Sail ho!" the mainmast lookout called down. "Dead astern!"

Alan wandered back to the quarterdeck while Lieutenant Railsford studied the sea over the taffrails.

"See her yet, sir?"

"Yes," Railsford said, trying to suppress his excitement. "Full-rigged, flying everything but her laundry and coming on fast. Top-gallants, royals and stuns'ls, too. Can't tell what she is yet, though."

"French, perhaps?" Alan speculated.

"We'll know in about an hour, the rate she's coming."

"Where away, Mister Railsford?" Treghues demanded, emerging on deck from a nap below. His eyes were rheumy with sleep, his pupils mere dots, which Alan put down to more of Dr. Dorne's medicaments. While the first lieutenant passed on what little intelligence he had about their stranger, the captain took the telescope and went up the mizzen rigging to at least the beginning of the futtock shrouds to get a better look. He came down minutes later and handed Railsford the telescope again.

"Looks like one of ours, I think," Treghues said. "Still, let's not be taken by surprise. Suspend the gun drill and get sail on her, all plain sail for now."

"Aye, sir. Bosun, pipe 'all hands.'"

Treghues went below while the hands lashed their guns down and began to hoist the yards, go aloft and free the courses and the reefs in the tops'ls, undo the brails on the topgallants and draw them down so they filled with air. *Desperate* ceased loafing and came alive, leaning her starboard side into the sea, creating a creamy white furrow of foam in her wake. The faster she went, the stronger the wind felt and the more the yards had to be angled to take apparent wind at a more efficient angle. When Treghues came back on deck he had scrubbed his face, put on clean uniform and stood four-square in cocked hat, new neckcloth and sword.

"Eight knots, sir!" Alan reported, coming from the taffrail where they had done a cast of the log and he had gotten soaked in spray.

"Still coming on strong, sir," Railsford said after another peek at their strange pursuer. "If she's French, she's eager to close with us. Do you wish us to hoist the royals, sir?"

"No, we shall let her," Treghues said. He took out his silver pocket watch and studied it. "Please be so good as to pipe the rum issue early and have the cooks serve as soon as everything's hot. We may be throwing the galley fires overboard, and can't wait for the proper hour for dinner."

"Aye, sir."

Alan thought it odd to let the enemy, if enemy she was, get up close. *Desperate* could go like a Cambridge coach if turned up onto the wind, or could run like a frightened cat to leeward if called upon to do so with stuns'ls and stays'ls. He studied Treghues as he paced the deck, wondering if his eagerness for battle had anything to do with the way the ship had been treated after escaping Yorktown. Did his captain have something to prove, some blot on their name that could only be erased by a victory, a *geste* of such derring-do that no one could comment on her any longer with a sneer? He had been acting odd enough ever since they had taken *Ephegenie* back in the Virgins, and Alan would no longer discount anything. A cautious captain would assume the other ship was an enemy and try to outrun her. A rash captain would put about and charge down offering battle. Only a timid and indecisive captain would allow the stranger to close them in this manner, and Treghues had never shown himself to be a timid or indecisive man. Certifiably eccentric, perhaps, but not that.

"Mister Lewrie," Treghues said, coming to his side in his pacing.

"Aye, sir?" he responded brightly.

"Walk with me."

"Aye, sir."

"Mister Cheatham informs me that you have had a stroke of good fortune come your way. And, he implies that you may soon be cleared that whiff of shame that followed you from England. For that I am grateful and pleased for you." Treghues spoke softly as they walked the weather rail, to the consternation of the other quarterdeck people. Treghues did not look much gratified, nor very pleased, but the words were kind enough, and Alan expressed his thanks.

"You should write your friends and patrons and let them know of it. I suppose you wasted no time informing the Beauman family. You are permitted to write the young lady, I remember?"

"Aye, sir, I already have."

"And your new friends the Chiswicks in Charleston," Treghues said. "Heard from them yet?"

Alan looked at him sidelong; his captain's face was almost red with shame, and Alan knew he must be crawling to have to solicit information of such a personal nature from an underling. Treghues had formed an instant affection for Caroline Chiswick, perhaps out of pity, or out of long-suppressed longings brought to the surface by his head injury and the dubious "cure" that had followed. Alan was his only link, his only source of intelligence as to their new address, and hard as it was for a proud man, a commissioned officer, a ship's captain, and a stiff-neck like Treghues to ask, he was asking for a crumb. The girl had not said yes to his proposal to write, after all his charm and pleasantness.

Dammit, captains don't do such things, Alan thought. Does he see the mail come aboard first, does he know I have a letter from her? If he did, he'd have seen the address, so he wouldn't be asking. Is it safe to lie? What the hell, I'll chance it. Caroline did put her name and address on the outside sheet.

"Not yet, sir, though I have hopes."

"I was quite taken with their plight. The father is not well, is he?"

"Not well at all, sir, mostly in his mind," Alan breathed out, not catching any sign of true awareness in Treghues's voice or expression. "And Mrs. Chiswick, well . . . she may be in good health, but she is not a person meant for adversity, if you get my meaning."

"That poor young girl," Treghues said, with such emotion that Alan thought him ready to shudder. "Forced to cope with all that, barely a penny to their names from all that land and property stolen from them by the Rebels, taking care of her parents so dutifully. . . ."

"It's a da . . . a terrible shame, sir, and a burden I marvel she could bear for long," Alan agreed. "Did you know that her brother Burgess told me the principal rogues who turfed them out were their own cousins?"

"Were they?" Treghues said, stopping their perambulations and seizing Alan's sleeve with an iron grip. "Were they, indeed, sir? God, I pity those who could not flee retribution of that pack of Rebels! What sort of country can they hope to have, built on the blood of their betters, allowing just any fool the right to vote, dictated to by the Mob and resorting to bloody revolution and civil strife at the merest trifles. We'll have to go back in and restore order some day when they find they cannot govern such a herd of malcontents. How shall they collect taxes, when they would not pay what they owed the Crown? How often shall they call out the militia or the troops sworn to this rebellious Congress to put down a new outbreak? You mark my words, within ten years they'll be cheering the sight of a scarlet coat to save them from their egregious folly. I only pray the Chiswicks get away safely to England and are spared the abuse and frightfulness of the Mob's fury."

"They have relatives in Surrey, sir. There was talk they may take passage if Charleston is threatened," Alan said, wondering if he should try to break loose, for Treghues was gripping him so hard he was fearful for his arm. "Though what they'll use for money, I don't know."

"Aye." Treghues almost sobbed, turning Alan loose and resuming their walk toward the taffrail. "I lent them one hundred pounds. I hope it is enough. My heart went out to her . . . and her family. Had I only the means to rescue every loyal Briton who escaped . . . Do you know the name of their relatives in Surrey?"

"No, sir, I'm sorry, I don't. Chiswick, I should think, though, sir, same as them," Alan replied, massaging his arm on the sly.

"Should you ever hear from them, I would be deeply obliged to you if you let me know their address, Mister Lewrie. There is much I could do for them if only I was allowed," Treghues ordered, then looked off into the middle distance. "I feel it my Christian duty as a God-fearing man, as a Briton, to help at least that family if I cannot do for all of the unfortunates torn loose from all they held dear by this terrible war."

"Oh, I shall, sir," Alan promised, lying like a butcher's dog. He tried to keep a straight and uninterested face as Treghues peered at him.

Alan found it hard, even so, to look Treghues in the eyes, but that was alright, for the captain also got a shifty look and could not face him, either.

"Thank you, Mister Lewrie. That shall be all. Again, my congratulations on your good news from home. Return to your duties, sir."

"Aye aye, sir." Poor shit, he thought. Mooning away over the girl and having to finagle her whereabouts from a rogue like me must have half killed his soul. He's getting devilish strange, even worse than before. And that funny tobacco he smokes now, whew! God knows where Dr. Dorne found it, but it has to be medicinal as hell, like smoking mildew and oakum. God, if there's a sane captain in the Navy, I've yet to meet him. Command must drive you loony!

Alan realized that sooner or later he would have to tell Treghues the Chiswick's address, if only to retain the captain's favor, but damned if he'd enjoy doing it. It was rather confusing, the feelings he had for Lucy Beauman, the most perfect beauty of the age he had seen, and Caroline Chiswick, who was pretty in her own quiet way. He still could not call it *jealousy*, but he was a lot closer to that opinion than he had been before.

"Hull up now, sir," Railsford said with a hint of concern.

Alan turned to look aft and could see all the sails of their pursuer, with the hint of a darker streak now and then above the waves that would be her hull. He took hold of the hilt of his sword and gave it a hitch to a more comfortable position. He might be using it in an hour.

"British, by God!" Monk spoke suddenly, as a distant patch of color appeared on the stranger's foremast top.

"Mister Monk, I weary of correcting your unfortunate habit of taking our Lord's name in vain so frequently," Treghues said for the thousandth time. "It may be a ruse."

"Signal, sir!" the lookout called, and David Avery was sent aloft with a glass and the signal book to spy it out.

"Recognition signal, sir!" he screamed down minutes later. "This month's! Tis *Roebuck*, sir, her private number!"

"Hands been fed, Mister Railsford?" Treghues asked.

"Aye, sir."

"Douse the galley fires and clear for action, just in case."

"Aye, sir."

But the stranger was indeed *Roebuck,* one of the ship-rigged sloops of war that had accompanied them on their raid on the Danish Virgins back in the late summer of 1781. She surged up close and her captain took up a brass speaking trumpet to speak *Desperate.*

"What lit a fire under you, captain?" Treghues shouted, with his leather lungs and cupped hands around his mouth in lieu of a trumpet.

"The French, Captain Treghues!" the other retorted. "Thirty sail of the line and a transport fleet have fallen on St. Kitts!"

"Jesus!" Alan muttered. St. Kitts was part of a pair of islands, Nevis and St. Kitts, that were not a day's sail from Antigua, and Antigua was the main base of the Leeward Islands. Admiral de Grasse was wasting no time in making use of his splendid fleet after returning to the Indies from the Chesapeake and Yorktown. Lewrie frowned in depression as he thought of his last few months; a failed opportunity at the Chesapeake battle, the loss of England's last field army at Yorktown, the evacuation of Wilmington and the rumors of a revitalized Rebel army under General Greene closing in on Charleston; now this disaster. If the French took St. Kitts, Nevis was barely five miles across a safe channel. Then what came next, English Harbor? They had already retaken St. Eustatius, Admiral Rodney's treasure trove. If Antigua went, there went the Indies.

"They struck two days ago, on the eleventh." *Roebuck's* captain was continuing to shout. "Anchored off Basse Terre and marched on Brimstone Hill. They're holding out so far. I am to carry word to Hood off Barbados."

"God speed you, then!" Treghues called back. "We shall follow as best we are able!"

He turned back to them with a hard expression on his face, "Well, gentlemen, we have been here before, have we not? It seems we must deal with this devil de Grasse one more time to rescue a British army as we attempted in the Chesapeake. This time they may have bitten off more than they can chew. Brimstone Hill is on a high cliff ten miles march from Basse Terre Roads, and the island is not big enough to support a large land force by foraging as the Virginias supported Rochambeau and Washington. Brimstone Hill is a proper stone fortress, well stocked with artillery and powder. Their fleet must wait for results ashore, and when Admiral Hood lights into them this time, there will be no timidity such as we saw from Admiral Graves. We shall see something wonderful then, and we'll square this Frog's yards for him for good and all this time! Questions?"

"May I get off here, sir?" Alan quipped, only half kidding, though everyone treated his comment as a jest only, laughing heartily and calling him the very devil of a merry wag and other such complimentary comments.

"To your stations. Stand the hands down from quarters, Mister Railsford, and send them aloft to make sail, all the sail *Desperate*'ll fly. Should *Roebuck* fall across the hawse of a French ship or fail in her mission, then we may also carry word to Admiral Hood."

Good Christ Almighty, Alan thought sadly. It's not as if I haven't done enough already, is it? There's only so many times I can put myself in the line of fire before I get knackered, and if it's only going to be half as bad as that muddle up in Virginia, then I'm a dead man this time. A very wealthy dead man, at that. Just when things were turning sweet for once. Just when I thought life was giving me a fair hand at last!

Realizing there was nothing for it but to go game, he went forward to Mister Monle's side by the wheel. At least, he could appear enthusiastic.

AFTERWORD

THE incident concerning the gruesome fate of the infant and mother really did happen during the Virginia campaign, though not at that time and place; Washington and Rochambeau's troops discovered the scene on their march down from Head Of Elk, Maryland. I ran across it in Barbara Tuchman's book, *The First Salute*, which provided me with much pertinent information about Yorktown.

The Revolution was not the clean, glorious endeavor so familiar from history books and post-office murals; it was a bloody civil war as bitter as any armed conflict between neighbors, though never approaching the cruelties of the French Revolution.

David Fanning, "Bloody Bill" Cunningham and the local commander of Wilmington's garrison, Major Craig, were real people on the Loyalist side during the Revolution, and their memories are still hateful for their depredations as irregular partisans and oppressive occupiers, held in as much contempt as Quantrill's raiders or the James boys during the Civil War.

While the sentiments of the time forbade harm to be inflicted by direct action upon non-combatants, harm was inflicted to civilians nonetheless on both sides, first by the less disciplined irregular militias and partisan rangers, then later by regular troops. And the fate of the Loyalists and their property after our Rebels had won is still a subject as closed as the fate of the Creek and Cherokee in the American version of history. I do not wish to give the impression,

since my events happened in the South, that this was solely a problem limited to the Carolinas; Northern Rebels and Loyalists suffered
just as much.

The British did indeed muddle their way to defeat time after
time, and one begins to wonder if they ever had mixed feelings about
fighting their blood-cousins in the first place. There were few examples of military genius on either side until the impartial French arrived.

The actions of Graves and Hood at the battle of The Chesapeake, and Graves' failure to relieve Cornwallis's army were the final
nails in the coffin for British hopes of victory. As one historian
wrote, Graves didn't really lose a single ship in the battle (although
HM *Terrible* had to be sunk later); he didn't lose the battle, so much
as call it a draw and broke it off; what he lost was America. Hood
went on to great success against de Grasse, and with Adm. Sir
George Bridges Rodney, won undying fame at the Saintes a year
later. His hanging back at the Chesapeake has never been satisfacto-
rily explained.

The contributions of Adm. Paul Comte de Grasse, the unseen
eminence in this novel, Gen. Rochambeau, Adm. de Barras (dila-
tory as he was up in Newport), Gen. St. Simon and his superb
artillery trains, and the regiments Touraine, Gatenois, Saintonge,
Royal Deux-Ponts and Soissons are also glossed over, and only Lafayette is given the honor due them all. But, had it not been for
direct French intervention in 1781, and material and monetary support in 1778, we would still be subjects of Great Britain.

Unlike the history taught about the Revolution, mostly written
by North-East educated historians, the war did not revolve around
New York and the upper colonies; most of it was fought in the
South, and there are many patriots who should be famous, who did
more to capture our freedom than Washington or his New York state
generals.

I wish to apologize to those who thought the Pennsylvania (or
Kentucky) rifle won the Revolution, but opposed to common myth,
the piece was a light hunting rifle, stripped down to the basics, slow
to load and fire due to the rifling in the barrel, which made ramming home a grease-patched ball difficult, and the militia and minute-
men who faced up to British regulars did not lay them out in

windrows, but usually got themselves tromped and skewered by more rapid smooth-bore musket fire and fixed bayonets, just as the Chiswick brothers described. The Continental Army and the various state militias became a force to be feared in the field equipped with French muskets and bayonets, captured British arms, or those few American-built copies of European muskets. Much money was spent and little was received from contractors who promised the moon, much like military budgets today.

My apologies to anyone whose ancestors really lived on Jenkins Neck, which only appears as described geographically and in the map; the Hayley plantation never existed except in my imagination.

I'd like to acknowledge a debt to Mrs. Diane Cobb Cashman and her lovely book, *Cape Fear Adventure, An Illustrated History of Wilmington*, about my favorite seaport town which figured in *The French Admiral*. Lastly, thanks to Jimmy Buffett for just about everything he ever wrote or recorded, which figured prominently in late-night sessions.

Dewey Lambdin
September 12, 1989
Percy Priest Lake
Nashville, Tennessee

6/90